WHITE MAN'S GRAVE

FARRAR, STRAUS AND GIROUX · NEW YORK

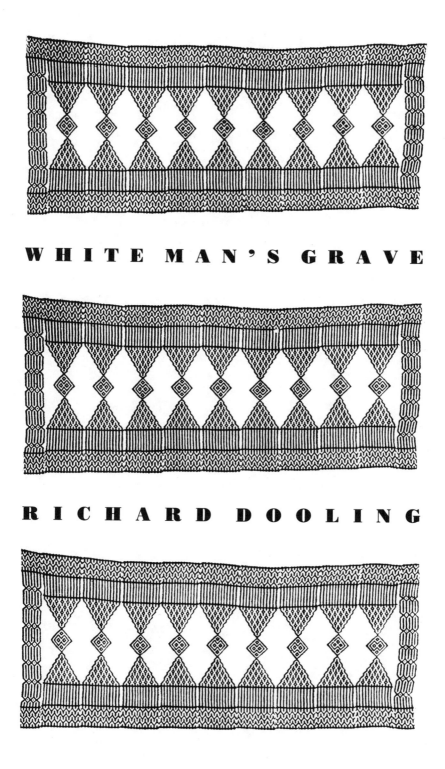

WHITE MAN'S GRAVE

RICHARD DOOLING

Library of Congress Cataloging-in-Publication Data
Dooling, Richard.
White man's grave / Richard Dooling. — 1st ed.
p.   cm.
1. Americans—Travel—Africa, West—Fiction.   2. Missing persons—
Africa, West—Fiction.   I. Title.
PS3554.O583W45   1994   813'.54—dc20   93-37427CIP

For my mom,

for my big brother, Lahai Hindowa,

and in memory of Pa Moussa Gbembo

The fiend in his own shape is

less hideous than when he rages

in the breast of man.

—NATHANIEL HAWTHORNE

Young Goodman Brown

WHITE MAN'S GRAVE

(1)

Randall Killigan was a senior partner in the biggest law firm in Indianapolis, chairman of its bankruptcy department, and commanding officer when his firm did battle in federal bankruptcy court. Being the best bankruptcy lawyer in Indianapolis kept him happy for a month or two, but then he wanted to be the best bankruptcy lawyer in the Seventh Circuit, which in the federal court system comprises the states of Indiana, Illinois, and Wisconsin. Illinois contained Chicago and the biggest obstacle to his fame, because it was swarming with excellent bankruptcy lawyers operating out of huge law offices that serviced national and international clients whose bankruptcies made the front page of *The Wall Street Journal.* It would be a few years before Randall could scorch the earth in enough Chicago bankruptcy courts to make his name synonymous with commercial savagery in the Seventh Circuit, but he was working on it. He was building a national bankruptcy practice from a home base in an unremarkable midwestern city, working out of Sterling & Sterling, a partnership and professional corporation consisting of only 240 lawyers, most of whom were beholden to Killigan for the work he sent them.

He had the thin but shapeless body of a middle-aged desk jockey and courtroom general who burned most of his calories exercising his adrenal glands. Randall learned early in life that the best-paying jobs were often the most stressful ones, so he taught himself not only to endure stress but to enjoy it. Before long, he developed a craving for it, the way other people craved caffeine or nicotine. But then (at least according to his wife) he went too far and became a stress junkie—living a life that was devoid of meaning or excitement unless he was mainlining stress, arguing on behalf of a client who had paid him and his firm millions in fees to confirm a Chapter 11 plan of reorganization.

Randall lived and breathed the Bankruptcy Code, and intimidated anybody who crossed him by quoting it chapter, section, and verse. The famous biologist James Watson lived and breathed the problem of DNA until the structure of the double helix was revealed to him in a dream. Descartes nodded off and discovered the order of all the sciences in a dream. The nineteenth-century chemist Friedrich August Kekulé von Stradonitz dreamed of a serpent swallowing its tail, and woke up to discover the closed carbon ring structure of the benzene molecule. When Randall Killigan slept, he dreamed sections of the U.S. Bankruptcy Code, and woke up to discover money—lots of it—eagerly paid by clients who had insatiable appetites for his special insights into the Code.

He tilted back in his leather recliner and spun around for a corner-office view of downtown Indianapolis, revealing a banner of computer paper Scotch-taped to the back of his chair, where emblazoned in four-inch bold type were the words KING OF THE BEASTS. Randall's protégé, the young Mack Saplinger, had hung the beast banner as a joke, after one of Randall's more notable victories; Randall had left it there. His desk and three enormous worktables were scattered with trophies from proceedings gone by: logos and tokens from companies he had reorganized under Chapter 11, gifts from especially grateful bank officers in the form of paperweights engraved with his name and maybe the date of a dispositive hearing.

Immediately to his right, the head of a huge stuffed black bear was mounted on the lid of a metal wastebasket. Randall had killed the bear in Alaska on a bankruptcy retreat with the boys and the lone female associate, Liza Spontoon. The bear's eyes stared up at the ceiling, the jaws were open, the white fangs gleamed, and, best of all, the thing ate paper.

Randall hated paper, which was why he glowered when Mack appeared and discreetly placed a hard copy of the lift-stay motion in the Beach Cove case somewhere on the back forty acres of Randall's partner-sized desk, so it would be handy if Randall needed it during his conference call.

"Get that out of here," Randall said, pointing first at the document, then at the computer screen, where the same document was already displayed in white letters on a blue field.

As a rule, paper contained either worthless information or valuable information that was effectively useless and unretrievable until it was stored on a computer's hard disk. His associates all knew that memos to Randall were sent by E-mail. Randall had an E-mail macro that, every hour on the hour, intercepted any memo to his terminal exceeding 6,000 bytes, or about the length of one single-spaced typewritten page. The macro automatically opened such memos, then time- and date-stamped them with the following message:

Your memo to this terminal was returned unread because it was excessively verbose. Save your prolixity for our opponents in federal district court. In the future, check your E-mail menu screen and be sure that your memo contains fewer than 6,000 bytes of information before sending it to this terminal.

RSK

Before the conference call, Randall was due to meet with the creditors in the WestCo Manufacturing case, who were waiting for him down the hall in one of the Sterling conference rooms.

"Do you want the memo on debtor-in-possession financing for the WestCo meeting?" asked Mack.

Randall shook his head in exasperation and pointed at his notebook computer. The kid was loyal and hardworking, he thought, but needed reminding.

"I'll fetch the battery packs, master," Mack said with a grin, and slipped back out.

Mack filled a place in Randall's solar system that belonged to his only son, Michael Killigan, who, instead of going to law school after college, ran off and joined the Peace Corps, and was now stationed in a country whose name Randall could never remember: Sierra Liberia, or Sierra Coast, some blighted range of snake-infested hills in West Africa, full of nothing but swamps and bush villages and naked Africans living in mud huts with no running water or electricity. For some reason, Michael Killigan chose to live there too. Trying to be his own man, Randall figured, rebelling in the shadow of a giant, looking around for footsteps that were closer together than the mighty strides of his old man. He let the kid go, hoping that a couple months of sweltering in a shack, together with the attentions of a few colonies of intestinal parasites, would have his son back at home and eager to take the law school admissions test before the year was out.

Eighteen months later, Michael had sent home a photograph of an African village girl in a headwrap, and the youthful insurrection threatened to become a permanent revolution. The camera shot was of her head and bare shoulders, with a piece of bone or horn or a large fang on a leather string around her neck, and a big toothy smile for the camera. When Michael had come home on medical leave with a case of meningitis, Randall reasoned with him, then begged, threatened, bribed, even ordered him to stay, all of which did nothing but afflict his son with the selective deafness so often seen in the offspring of desperate parents. Michael had returned to Africa as soon as he could walk.

Randall had dictated a long letter to his son. Choosing his words with a lawyer's caution, he warned him that, while two years in the Peace Corps could be viewed as a character-building experience, *three* years might cause résumé problems: a flag indicating a possible lack of ambition, the appearance of shirking responsibilities, a professional demeanor that might be rough around the edges because of lingering reverse culture shock, a concern that reentry may have been incomplete. When he read his words on paper, Randall concluded that mailing the letter would probably obliterate any chance that his son would screw his head on straight and come home; it was still in his correspondence drawer.

So, instead of having his son at his right hand, Randall made do with the eager young Saplinger, an associate who distinguished himself by sleeping on the floor of the document room for two weeks running during the plan confirmation hearings of the Marauder Corporation case.

Expecting Mack to appear with the computer battery packs he needed for the meeting, Randall was annoyed when, instead, one of the firm's messengers walked into his office bearing a package of some kind.

"What the fuck is that?" Randall asked, grabbing and tilting a cardboard box held together with frizzy twine and addressed in black marker to "Master Rondoll Killigan."

"UPS," the messenger said, unruffled and apparently accustomed to Randall's spontaneous profanity. The messenger read from the receipt, "Freetown, Sierra Leone. Some place in Africa."

Randall tore the twine off, opened the box, removed several wads of newspaper packing, and found a black bundle of tightly wrapped rags the size of a small football, with a two-inch hollow red tube made out of some kind of porous stone or mineral sticking out of the apex.

"What is this shit? An African fuck bump?" Randall looked up and found his office empty, and was quite annoyed that the messenger had left before he could give the box back to him or yell at him for bringing it into his office in the first place. No note. Nothing. Just a black bundle from Africa.

Randall had less and less time for nonbankruptcy irritations and intrusions into his professional life. His first thought was that he must have an employee somewhere to whom he could hand this object, with instructions to figure out what it was, where it came from, who sent it, and what he was supposed to do with it, but nobody came to mind.

Distinctly sinister, it looked like a dark, petrified egg, laid by some huge, extinct bird of prey. He fingered the blood-colored spout and found it was mounted or sewn securely into the parcel's interior. He dropped the thing into the box of wadded newspaper and dusted his fingers over it. A foul smell emanated from it, and he was afraid to unravel the rags, which were held together with some kind of pitch or glue. He uncrumpled one of the newspaper wads and found it was a page of the *Sierra Leone Sentinel*, published in Freetown.

He considered feeding the whole mess to his bear, then reconsidered, set it on the floor under his desk, and resolved to call his wife at the first opportunity to see if Michael had said anything about sending back any African artifacts. Maybe it was just another rattle or drum for his collection. But *Master Rondoll?* That did not fit.

Mack appeared with the batteries. Killigan grabbed his custom-made notebook computer and slipped a CD-ROM disk containing the entire annotated Bankruptcy Code into one slot, fed the battery into another slot, and headed out the door and down the hall.

The attorneys representing all the major creditors in the WestCo Manufacturing case had arrayed themselves around a conference table, with their associates sitting demurely behind them, notepads and pens at the ready. The table was studded with notebook computers, briefcases, pitchers of ice water, notepads, cellular phones, and glasses fogging in the sunlight pouring in from the bay windows. Randall took his place at the head of the table and prepared to divide the spoils of WestCo Manufacturing among the lawyers for the various classes of creditors.

In primitive societies, the dominant male of the tribe apportioned the kill according to the skill and valor of the members of the hunting party. As far as Killigan was concerned, nothing much had changed for twentieth-century man, except that the weapons had become rules—complex and abstract rules—and the warriors were now lawyers. The kill was relatively bloodless (except for the occasional unhinged, atavistic client who showed up now and again on the six o'clock news dragging a lawyer around in a noose of piano wire attached to a shotgun). In Randall's hands, the U.S. Bankruptcy Code was a weapon, anything from a blazing scimitar to a neutron bomb, depending upon how much destruction he was being paid to inflict on his client's adversaries. International corporate behemoths—like WestCo—were weakened strays bleeding money, suffocated by debt, and falling behind the pack, where they could be picked off, dropped in the crosshairs of Randall's scope rifle, and plundered like carcasses rotting in the sun.

But bankruptcy law went far beyond the hunt, for the kill was always followed by brutal, expensive combat among the contending classes of creditors. Sure, passions ran high at Troy when Agamemnon took Achilles' beautiful sex slave for himself, but a bondholder who's being asked to take out-of-the-money warrants instead of principal plus interest at 14 percent is something else. Blood and gore. Section 1129 of the Code coyly referred to it as "plan confirmation," but when things went awry every bankruptcy lawyer in the country called the process "cram down," and for a good reason. After months or years of acrimonious, adversarial proceedings, one supreme warrior eventually emerged with a plan of reorganization, which he crammed down the throats of the vanquished creditors, so the spoils could be distributed to the victorious.

As far as Randall was concerned, he might as well have stood at the head of the table smeared with the grime of warfare, reeking of smoke, streaked with blood, and blackened with powder burns. For months, he had stood in crowded courtrooms with other lawyers who were just waiting for him to look the other way so they could blindside him with a nightstick. If he dropped his guard for a moment, if he took one case too many, if he failed to take every precaution, mistakenly trusted an associate with a crucial issue that turned out all wrong, forgot to have an associate check the computer services for the newest controlling case, missed a filing deadline, made only one important mistake . . . he could look up from counsel's table just in time to catch a poleax in the solar plexus. Some ruthless mercenary who had been studying Randall's techniques for years would step on his throat and show him the face of victory—all fangs and war paint, screaming with laughter. If he stumbled once or twice, he could always recover and retake the high ground. But if he ever actually *fell* . . . Too terrible to think about. They would be on him like hyenas, ripping him apart and drinking his blood before he could draw another breath.

The meeting went well enough. Only the bondholders were in a position to make trouble for him, and they were represented by a lawyer in a toupee who was afraid of Randall. Randall made sure everyone agreed on the deal points, flashed his teeth at the attorney for the bondholders, then headed down the hallway and back to his office, pausing when his administrative assistant stuck her hand out of an inner office and fanned a stack of pink messages commemorating calls that had come in during his meeting. He paused and flipped through them, crumpled one and threw it in the wastebasket, and handed the rest back to the hand, which was still patiently supine.

"Did Bilksteen call for the Beach Cove conference call yet?"

"No," she said.

"Put him through when he does. And enter the rest of these in the to-do with a four-thirty time," he said.

"You've got Mr. Haley and the DropCo unsecured creditors calling at four-thirty," she said, scrolling through his afternoon on the screen.

"N-A-T," he said, walking away from her.

"That's tomorrow," she called after him. "The next available time is tomorrow."

"Fine," he said, drifting back into his office. "Call them all and tell them it will be tomorrow."

At his desk, he switched on his notebook computer, which had been custom-made to his specifications. He had a Pentium chip; the other lawyers had only 386s. He had a CD-ROM drive installed containing the entire, annotated Bankruptcy Code, as well as the Bankruptcy Rules and the Federal Rules of Civil Procedure; nobody else had a CD-ROM drive in their notebook computers, because there was no such animal on the market; Randall had paid a technician to build one for him. Battery life? Six hours plus. Let the other wanna-bes struggle with their extension cords and their extra battery packs. Hard disk, 340 megabytes, which his paralegal had loaded with every relevant document in each of his cases, including a complete set of the pleadings for each proceeding, which had been scanned by an optical character reader and stored in his computer. He had discovered early in his career that if he worked harder than everyone else and knew more about the Code, the facts, and the case law than anyone else in the courtroom, he would win. And each victory made him that much stronger, because he could then afford more staff and better equipment, state-of-the-art litigation support software, and MIS personnel who knew how to make it sing with evidence and case law when Killigan needed them.

Mack appeared.

"Beach Cove," said Randall, and they both laughed.

"Should we send Bilksteen to a taxidermist and get him stuffed?" asked Randall. "You could fix his head up as a cover for your wastebasket, like I did with old Benjy here."

Mack noted Randall's annoyed glance at his watch. "I'll tell Whitlow and Spontoon to get in here," he said, referring to the other two associates who were scheduled to participate in the eleven o'clock conference call from opposing counsel in the Beach Cove bankruptcy proceedings.

The speakerphone buzzed, his conference call was ready, and Mack appeared with the other two Sterling associates in tow.

"Go ahead, Tom," Randall said into his speakerphone, adjusting the volume so the other lawyers in attendance could hear, while Tom Bilksteen yammered over the speaker, his voice sounding like the Minotaur calling on a cellular phone from the bowels of the Cretan labyrinth.

"Wait a second!" barked Randall. "Who's in there with you?"

"What do you mean?" said Bilksteen. "Nobody's with me. I'm in my office alone and the door is shut."

"Then pick up, you piece of shit," yelled Randall, his belligerence belied by the grin he showed his associates. "You're not putting me on speaker just because you're too damn lazy to lift the receiver. Pick up, goddamnit!"

Mack sat in the preferred chair at Randall's right hand, wrote a message on his legal pad, and held it up, showing Randall a scrawl that said: "Should we tell him?"

Randall shook his head, slowly and definitely, another grin spreading the width of his face. He tore off the page and fed it to his bear.

"Touchy, touchy," said Bilksteen, picking up his phone, his voice surfacing from the nether regions.

One associate was never enough for any matter entrusted to Randall Killigan, and the two associates who took seats in the hard-back chairs in front of Randall's desk neatly personified his mixed feelings about female attorneys. Liza Spontoon was single, brilliant, and homely, all of which in Randall's book would earn her a ride on the bus, if she had the fare. But she was also a succinct and combative legal writer and turned in billable hours that made the firm accountants whistle softly into their computer screens. She was in Randall's office because she was the best legal draftsman in the firm and had authored a memorandum in support of a lift-stay motion that was going to end the career of the lawyer at the other end of the line.

The other female attorney was Marissa Whitlow Carbuncle—an initially appealing, highly intelligent redhead with a nervous, unhappy smile, whose good looks were promptly ruined for Randall when he learned she was a feminist. Her husband was a thoracic surgeon, and she had two small children, meaning she had taken three months of maternity leave at full pay, not once, but *twice.* She was in Randall's office because he had sent for her, so he could try once more to make her life so miserable she would quit the firm before she became eligible for partnership consideration.

In Randall's book, both women should be voted down for partner because neither one of them had ever brought in a single new piece of business. If Randall had his way, he would give Spontoon a 20 percent pay raise and make her a permanent associate, and he would send Whitlow home to raise her kids, or off to California, where she could join one of those politically correct, multicultural law firms with enlightened attitudes about working for a living. The people on the compensation and partnership committees annually and shrilly accused Killigan of chauvinism and sex discrimination.

"I'm not a chauvinist," he had objected. "All I want is for everyone to be treated equally. I'll stay home for three months and look after my family if you guys send me the same draw I make billing sixty hours a week down here."

Randall had struggled with his conscience. He wanted to understand. "Let me get this straight," he had pleaded with the management committee. "We are supposed to pay Whitlow good money for *not* working, right? You and I, we'll stay down here on Saturday afternoons billing time, and Whitlow will be home knitting booties, right? Three months at full salary for no work, is that it? Why stop there? Let's make her a fucking dairy farmer so we can pay her for not producing milk too!"

Randall made no secret of his opinion of Ms. Whitlow's chances for partnership and his avid search for the most mundane, time-consuming work he could possibly find to assign her, via E-mail, on Friday evenings at six o'clock. She in turn made no secret of her sudden interest in the law of sex discrimination and sexual harassment in the workplace, specifically a 1989 U.S. Supreme Court case called *Price Waterhouse* v. *Hopkins*, in which a female accountant sued and won after being denied partnership in an international accounting firm. Whitlow also told Randall that she believed his use of foul and obscene language in the workplace constituted a hostile environment within the meaning of Title VII. Randall marveled at the way she drew him a map, with diagrams and a big red arrow, and a legend that said: *This is my hot button. Push it if you want to make me absolutely miserable.*

Threatening Randall with litigation was like sending him two free tickets to a Chicago Bulls game at the Hoosier Dome, center court and six rows up. Just the rumor of a sex discrimination suit had Randall salivating and humming to himself: visions of Whitlow on the witness stand with a bloody nose; Whitlow thrown out on her ass by a directed verdict after her own evidence showed she had the lowest billable hours in the entire firm; Whitlow trying to explain how she had to stay home for three months and earn twenty thousand dollars plus benefits to a jury of slack-jawed minimum-wagers who could not believe they were listening to a woman who made eighty thousand dollars a year complain about hearing a bankruptcy lawyer use the F-word. *Please sue me*, Randall pleaded in his daydreams, *and don't forget, I like it hard and fast.*

All three associates were avidly taking notes of the attorney's voice coming over the speakerphone (all probably taking the same notes, Randall guessed), not that the voice was saying anything of consequence. Note taking was something Randall noticed most associates did, because they were being billed out at over $125 an hour and wanted to justify the expense by looking busy. In time, they would be nourished along their career paths and weaned of their legal pads, given Dictaphones and speakerphones, until they achieved the serene self-confidence of senior partners, who never touched writing utensils, and charged over $200 an hour just for *thinking* about legal problems.

The voice on the speakerphone—still yammering—belonged to Tom Bilksteen, the attorney for a limited partnership that owned a hundred-unit condominium complex called Beach Cove. Randall's client, Comco Banks, had lent the Beach Cove partners fifteen million dollars in secured loans to build a suburban paradise around a man-made lake, which was to be advertised as "only twenty-five minutes from downtown Indianapolis." Then the bond issue to build the spur connecting Beach Cove to Interstate 70 was voted down, leaving ninety empty Beach Cove condominium units and ten gullible souls who sat in traffic listening to drive-time talk shows, behind cars waiting to make left turns off of congested two-lane suburban thoroughfares, and then made it downtown in a little over an hour, on Sunday mornings.

The Beach Cove partners defaulted on their loan; Randall and Comco moved in to foreclose; and Bilksteen put Beach Cove into Chapter 11. Now Bilksteen was taunting Randall over the speakerphone, safe in the knowledge that the U.S. Bankruptcy Code explicitly provided for something called an "automatic stay" of all creditor attempts to collect from the debtor or seize the debtor's property, which meant that Randall and Comco could not foreclose on Beach Cove or get any of the bank's money back out of the project for at least a year, probably longer. Although Randall and his people had filed a motion to lift the automatic stay, Bilksteen and every other bankruptcy lawyer knew that lift-stay motions—though almost always filed—were almost always denied.

Bilksteen was savoring this minor triumph, jerking Randall's chain, telling him that Comco would be lucky to get ten cents on the dollar for the fifteen million it had lent to the Beach Cove partners and that if Randall did not cooperate with him, he would keep the property tied up in bankruptcy court for three years.

"Three years with all that money earning no interest," Bilksteen said. "I don't know, Randall. I'd be wanting to deal if I were Comco."

What Bilksteen did *not* know was that Randall's protégé, Mack, had played softball just last night with U.S. bankruptcy judge Richard Foote's law clerk, a classmate of Mack's at Northwestern. After a few cold frosties, the clerk had let slip that Judge Foote, Randall's favorite bankruptcy judge, was going to grant Randall's motion to lift the stay on the Beach Cove properties and allow Randall's client Comco to foreclose on the complex immediately. A lift-stay order from Judge Foote would mortally wound Beach Cove, would legally annihilate the Beach Cove partners, and would publicly humiliate Bilksteen, who would be the laughingstock of the bankruptcy bar as soon as the word got out that he could not even protect his clients by filing a simple single-asset bankruptcy.

By Randall's reckoning, Judge Foote would probably issue the lift-stay order after he got back from lunch, meaning that in another hour or so the court clerk would be calling Bilksteen with the news, and Bilksteen would be turning a bluish gray, rummaging through his desk drawers looking for his nitroglycerin tablets.

"You know, Killigan," said Bilksteen, "sooner or later you and the other creditors are going to have to come to the table and give the condo people a deal they can live with."

Randall decided it was time to use the mute button on the speakerphone. When pressed, the button cut off voice transmission from Killigan's end of the line without affecting reception, allowing those in attendance to both listen to the caller and carry on private conversations, while the party at the other end of the line remained oblivious that Killigan and his crew were doing anything but listening attentively.

Bilksteen blustered over the speakerphone about how Randall and Comco would be forced to accept an unfavorable plan of reorganization, how moths would eat the bound pleadings in the case before Comco saw a penny of its money. Killigan grinned at Whitlow, then fetched a Halloween broadsword he used for a letter opener and kept in a plastic scabbard at the console. He grasped the hilt dagger-style and stabbed the speakerphone, depressing the mute button with the plastic point of the toy sword.

"You pathetic village idiot," Killigan said over Bilksteen's legal patter. "You can use your goddamned plan of reorganization as insulation in your shithouse, boy. I am going to cut your fucking head off and mount it on a pike in the middle of your front lawn, understand?"

Mack smirked. Spontoon covered her mouth and giggled. Whitlow's face flushed and then drained, leaving a livid mask dotted with freckles. She thought about leaving, until Bilksteen said something about exchanging discovery, which was her responsibility, according to the E-mail message Randall had issued when he summoned her to his royal chambers.

Killigan released the mute button. "Sure," said Killigan, wagging slightly in his recliner and cleaning a thumbnail with the point of the broadsword. "Sure, Tom, we'll get you that discovery this afternoon, right after we get Judge Foote's order on the lift-stay motion." Killigan again poked the mute button with the toy sword. "And after I cut your head off, I'm going to pull your guts out and feed them to the family dog."

"Yeah," said Bilksteen. "I can't believe you guys bill your clients for those ridiculous lift-stay motions. I mean, when was the last time a bankruptcy judge granted one?"

Mack all but swallowed his tongue in stifling a belly laugh.

"Gee," Randall said without a wrinkle. "You know, you've got me there, Tom. It's been a while since Judge Foote granted a lift-stay motion in a case as big as this one. You know, I've always admired your horse sense about these things. You didn't go to Michigan like I did, and you're not sitting on top of the biggest firm in town like I am, but you are one smart lawyer, Mr. Bilksteen." The sword stabbed the mute button. "You pig's ass. Get yourself all hog-dressed and go waddle into Judge Foote's court, because you are going to come out a six-foot fucking sausage!"

"Shucks," Bilksteen said, "I just try and do my job."

Killigan released the mute button.

"You won't tell Comco how we've been wasting their money on a lift-stay motion, will you?" Randall asked, sliding Mack a look that said: *What do other people do for fun?*

"Your secret's safe with me," Bilksteen said with a benevolent chuckle. "Long as you give me a break on down the ways."

"You bet," Randall said, then stabbed the mute button. "Break your neck for you in an act of mercy maybe. At least I'll put your clients out of their misery."

"So you'll be sending somebody over with discovery this afternoon?"

"That's right," Randall said. "Right after we get the order from Judge Foote on the lift-stay motion. I'll talk at you then."

Randall was having the time of his life, but he had phone calls to make. And he saw a message from his stockbroker flash in white letters across the sea-blue screen of his desktop computer: "Merck up 4½ on big volume. You are a very wealthy man."

Let the mass of men lead lives of quiet desperation; Randall was busy leading one of riotous exaltation. Let timid, cowardly investors follow the prevailing wisdom of the balanced portfolio; Randall dumped all the money he could get his hands on into Merck, a year ago, when it was trading down around sixty bucks a share. These days it was bouncing up from a new floor of 160, while the rest of the market was comatose.

"OK, Whitlow," said Randall after he hung up the phone. "You heard the man. Mr. Bilksteen needs his discovery this afternoon."

"I thought Judge Foote was issuing a lift-stay order?" Whitlow said, glancing at her watch with a look that said lunch plans. "If we get a lift-stay order, the discovery on the condominium properties will be moot."

"Do we have a lift-stay order?" asked Randall.

"No," said Whitlow, "but . . ."

"Well? Until we do, we will comply with the rules of the court and prepare to provide our adversary with the discovery he has requested. If you have our responses to the interrogatories and the requests for production of documents as well as the documents themselves on my desk by two o'clock, I can look them over before my two-thirty conference call from New York."

He dismissed the associates with a backhanded flip of the broadsword and looked once more at the black egg in its nest of newspapers. *Maybe there's a shrunken head inside*, he thought. Maybe he should have someone call his wife and ask her if Michael had said anything about sending a package from West Africa. This would take time and might lead to a conversation with his wife, which would take even more time because her conversations typically wandered all over the map of pointless and irrelevant topics, none of them having a thing to do with bankruptcy or advancing his career.

She was one of those innocents who thought she could call one of the most powerful bankruptcy attorneys in the Seventh Circuit— who was billed out at over $300 an hour, a third higher than any other partner in the firm—and just kind of meander along in aimless conversation.

Other people do not live this way, he often realized. They could never handle the incessant pressure, the competition, the dizzying heights, the long way down if there was just one slipup. To the rabble, self-discipline meant trying to watch less TV or lose weight. They could never live in mortal combat for months on end, litigating eight hours a day, then going back to the office and spending another eight hours preparing for the next day's campaign. He could say it, couldn't he? They were his inferiors. What were all those postal employees and factory workers doing while he was in law school reading law books twelve hours a day? They were putting in their six-and-a-half-hour shifts with two fifteen-minute breaks and an hour for lunch. Then they went home and sat on the couch with a bag of chips, a liter of diet soda, and *The Brady Bunch*. And how did society reward *him*? By taxing him.

"What are you doing now?" Mack asked his boss, watching Randall rummage through a red jacket pouch from the DropCo case.

"What am I doing now?" Randall repeated, opening several spreadsheets, which described the assets of DropCo Steel Inc. "I'm sitting here hoping a Democrat gets elected President."

"But you're a Republican," Mack said.

"I am a Republican."

"Then why are you hoping for a Democratic President?"

"Because," said Randall, "if a Democrat gets elected they'll raise my taxes. I make five hundred thousand dollars a year, and right now I only pay two hundred thousand in taxes. The Democrats will be wanting to make me pay at least three hundred thousand dollars a year in taxes."

"You're hoping for that?"

"I'm hoping for instant retirement," Randall said, "which is what will happen as soon as some fucking politician raises my taxes. My father told me never, *never* work more than two days a week for the government. I'll quit first. And do you know what will happen then?"

"What?"

"Twenty lawyers, ten paralegals, fifteen secretaries, and five ancillary personnel will lose their jobs. Poof! Is it *jobs* these shopping-mall sheep are bleating about every day on the front page of the paper? I *create* jobs, but only if I'm working, and like I said, I ain't gonna work more than two days a week for the government. Go ahead," he hollered, brandishing the toy broadsword. "Tax me! Fifty employees and their families will lose their salary, their health, life, and dental insurance, their self-esteem, and the money they pay to their cable TV companies and the IRS. If you know any of those people who are thinking about voting for people who will raise my taxes, you might mention to them that it will cost them their jobs! Go ahead! Tax me just once more, and I'll show them exactly how it works! I'll put a full-page open letter in the fucking newspaper explaining why I shut down!"

His computer beeped, a purple window opened at the top, and white letters streamed onto the screen: "Wife. Line two. Urgent!!!!"

Randall waved Mack away with the broadsword and punched line two.

"Marjorie?"

"You'd better come home, Randy."

His wife's voice was calm, almost formal, which told him something was terribly wrong, and she didn't want to tell him on the phone, because she was afraid he would lean out of the clouds on Olympus and throw lightning bolts at her.

"You wrecked the car," he said, knowing it was worse than that, because in his twenty-five years of practice she had never called him at work and told him to come home.

"They can't find Michael, Randy. He's missing from his village," she said in the same strange controlled tone. "They just phoned me from Washington."

Randall's stomach tightened, and nausea crawled up the back of his throat, but he remained calm and organized his thinking—if nothing else, he had been trained to think clearly in the face of the worst possible tragedies.

"Is this by way of the State Department or the Peace Corps?" he asked.

"Both," she said.

"It's probably nothing," he said tersely, searching his memory for other instances in which the ineptitude of the United States government had manifested itself in a false alarm of this magnitude.

"No," she said. "It's *something*. He's been missing for almost two weeks. They can't *find* him!"

The furniture and equipment in his office were suddenly drained of mass and significance. The accustomed feel of his chair, the pale blood color of his carpeting, the prints hanging on his walls, all of them became the sensations and possessions of some other, formerly powerful bankruptcy attorney. His heart skipped one beat, then raced to catch up.

"Maybe he left early to go traveling with the Westfall kid," said Randall. "They were supposed to meet in Paris, weren't they?"

"Yes, they were supposed to meet in Paris," she said quietly. "But neither the Peace Corps nor the American Embassy has any record of Michael leaving Sierra Leone. There are forms and customs, immigration people he would have to see . . . He's just gone. And the Peace Corps Director says there's some kind of political unrest, a rebellion, going on over there."

"He's off on some lark in the bush," Randall said with a catch in his voice, as his eyes landed on the black bundle of rags and the red spout in the box on the floor.

"There are guerrillas crossing the borders from Liberia into Sierra Leone," she said. "It's even on the news."

Randall had trouble breathing, unwilling to grasp the dimensions of the anxiety that was descending on him like nightfall in a black-out: never knowing if his son was dying, already dead, held in a compound somewhere by fanatics or rebels with no respect for human life. *My only son!* he screamed inside. But he carefully controlled his voice, because he knew he had to be strong for his wife.

"I actually considered not telling you about it," she said, "because . . . Your heart . . . You won't be able to sleep. I know what this is going to do to you, Randy."

He let her go on whistling in the dark and pretending that she was the strong one. She had her strengths, but an appreciation of his intellectual prowess was not one of them. She failed to realize that his fits of anxiety and his intense physical complaints were just the idiosyncrasies of an exceptionally gifted attorney, a high-strung racehorse with special physical needs.

"Where's the Westfall kid?" he snapped. "Has anybody talked to him?"

"He's in Paris and can't be reached by phone. I'm sending him a letter by two-day air to the American Express office in Paris. His mother said he gets mail there every other day or so."

"Let me make some calls," he said, steadying his voice, "and I'll come right home, hear me?"

"I'll call your mother," she said quietly. "Please don't wreck the car again," she added.

This was typical. She would now indulge in absolutely useless behaviors which had nothing to do with the problem at hand. What possible good could come from calling his mom? And the car thing? Why bring that up at a time like this? It was typical of her total inability to prioritize problems.

As soon as she hung up, blood surged into Randall's face and he pushed a button on his intercom. "Cancel everything and don't let anybody in here," he said. He pushed a speed-dial button on his phone and gritted his teeth through four rings.

"Good afternoon. Senator Swanson's office. This is Amanda, may I help you?" a voice said.

"I need to talk to him *right away*," Randall said.

"May I ask who's calling?" the voice said diffidently.

"Yeah," Randall said. "Tell him it's Mr. PAC and it's extremely important."

"Mr. *Pac*," the woman repeated. "Forgive me, but could you spell that for me?"

"Political Action Committee," Randall shouted. "Dollar signs. Money. Checks. Big ones. Tell him it's Randall Killigan on the line with a problem that needs his attention right now!"

The Senator could not be reached on his car phone, so Randall was shunted to an administrative assistant, who was hiding under her desk by the time Randall finished screaming into the phone.

He hung up and paced the floor of his office, biting his thumb and feeling pretrial heart arrhythmias erupting in his chest.

After an eternity spanning less than twenty minutes, the intercom beeped, and his secretary announced: "Mr. Warren Holmes, State Department, calling at the request of Senator Swanson."

"Mr. Killigan, I spoke with your wife earlier today, and I got off the phone with Senator Swanson just a few minutes ago . . ."

"Are you in touch with people in Africa?" asked Randall. "Are these embassy people, or what? I want to know what's happened to my son."

"I have been on the phone all afternoon with Ambassador Walsh and his political officer in Freetown," said Holmes succinctly. "Let me tell you what we have. Liberia and Sierra Leone are both unstable at this time. In fact, almost all of West Africa is unstable. We have three reports, two of them anonymous, which confirm the fact that your son has disappeared. The particulars differ. Normally, I would not even pass these along, because they range from unreliable to simply reliable. Nothing confirmed, you understand. But Senator Swanson said this was VIP priority and that I should pass information straight on to you . . ."

"What are the reports?" interrupted Randall.

"The accounts from all three sources agree that there was an attack of some kind on your son's village, and after it was over, no one could find him. One witness claims she heard the attackers speaking Liberian Krio, which could mean that Michael has been abducted by Liberian rebels controlled by the infamous Charles Taylor, who essentially has started his own country in the middle of Liberia. Another villager swears the attackers spoke Sierra Leonean Krio, meaning Michael might still be in-country and held by Sierra Leonean rebels, loose allies of Taylor's men across the border."

"What was the third report?" said Randall.

"The third report is . . . ah . . . probably not reliable. It's from a boy, an adolescent, a villager. Very unreliable."

"Who said what?" Randall asked.

"I don't know how much you know about indigenous Africans, Mr. Killigan," said Holmes. "Let me just say that, once you get outside the capital cities, the belief in the supernatural is pretty well entrenched in the culture."

"What did he say?" Randall said.

"This was a Krio boy who apparently reported to one of the Red Cross stations in Pujehun. The boy said he was in Michael Killigan's village attending a funeral at the time of the raid. The Red Cross people say the boy's account of the conflict was so fraught with superstitious hallucinations that they couldn't get much hard information out of him. But they did ask him if Michael Killigan was safe."

"Are you a lawyer?" asked Randall. "I said, what the fuck did the kid say?" He kicked a button on the floor operating the electro-magnetic device that held his door open, and it swung quietly closed.

"He said . . ." Holmes paused to the sound of flipping pages. "I'll read it to you straight from the advisory: 'Michael Killigan now roams the paths at night in the shape of a bush devil hungry for the souls of the witchmen who killed him.' "

(2)

Three weeks before Randall received his bundle from Africa, Boone Westfall had left his home in Indianapolis, Indiana, with a backpack containing one change of winter clothes, one change of summer clothes, one extra T-shirt, a raincoat, a sleeping bag, toiletries, vitamins, and antimalarial medicine. Around his waist and inside his pants, he wore a nylon money belt into which he had zippered his passport and $5,000 in traveler's checks. He had a yellow International Certificate of Vaccinations, showing he had been vaccinated against cholera, typhoid, and yellow fever, and he had visas to India, China, Greece, and three African countries. He had no idea where in the world he would end up; he knew only that it would not be Indiana. Tired of life in the Land of the TV and the Home of the Airwaves, he was ready to try anything once—illness, rapture, misfortune, romance—as long as it was not in video. He was scheduled to meet his best friend, Michael Killigan, in Paris in three weeks; after that, life would be an open book with blank pages.

Graduation from Indiana University with a degree in fine arts had earned him a job sifting papers and making phone calls from a cubicle in his father's insurance office. He had rented a studio apartment and had acquired a bookful of car payment tickets. The single women whose apartments he had haunted all looked and sounded the same; only their majors, the names of their ex-boyfriends, and their hair colors varied. His work as an insurance claims adjuster had taught him what it must be like to wake up each day to a terminal illness: not yet unbearably painful, but insidiously debilitating. The cardinal virtues necessary for the job were punctuality, good grooming, and a mind-set that never looked beyond the task at hand.

In college, he had dedicated himself to art and literature. Then he graduated with everything he needed to be an artist, a painter, a sculptor, and a poet . . . but where to apply? His father, a prominent insurance executive, and his three older brothers (all of whom had gone straight into the family business) had started calling Boone the "artiste," hissing the *ee* invectively through clenched teeth. His father also asked him pointedly about the nature of his degree and where he was planning to live and work, now that he was a college graduate. As an undergraduate, Boone had always shunned business, accounting, finance, marketing, and all the other members of the barbiturate class of drugs, so he was unqualified for even entry-level corporate positions. He had managed to devour four years of liberal arts without learning a single useful skill, which seemed all right to him at the time, for he had no wish to be used. His thoughts turned to income, too late.

As nonchalantly as possible, Boone had moved his stuff out of the dorm and into the basement of his family's house, where he had planned to furnish a temporary studio and struggle with the great questions of twentieth-century postmodern visual forms. Within a year or two, he had hoped, he could perfect his technique and then play the major art galleries off against each other when they called, begging for permission to display his work.

His father had interrupted him during the construction of the basement studio.

"Have you ever heard of the saying 'You can't go home again'?" the old man had asked.

"As a matter of fact, I have," Boone had admitted. "It's a figurative expression, isn't it? Thomas Wolfe, right?"

"I wouldn't know," his dad had said. "I like literal expressions. Figurative expressions are too vague and abstract. You could stay up all night arguing about whether somebody can or cannot go home in a metaphorical sense. That's why I like the version I used on your older brothers better. Have you ever heard the expression 'You may not go home again'? It's much simpler and more concrete. If rent is a problem, you may apply for a job at the company."

"But I'm an artist," Boone had protested.

"I hate art," his dad had said, for the twentieth time in four years. "And even if you were Mike Angelo, my name ain't Lorenzo de'

Medici or Cosimo d'Arrivederci, or whatever his name was, and I'd rather patronize the National Rifle Association."

Shortly thereafter, Boone's big brother, Pete, oriented the artist to his new job as an insurance claims processor.

Pete escorted him into a huge room partitioned into dozens of work stations by four-foot-square interlocking beige panels, with one patch of fabric on the interior of each panel, where the employees could tack up snapshots of their families, or their own special wacky cartoons and slogans, something to really set their space off from the otherwise monotonous assemblage of beige cubicles, something like a heavily photocopied "You don't have to be crazy to work here but it helps" sign—very distinctive, probably found in less than 30 percent of the cubicles.

His brother paused at an empty cube and showed Boone into a nine-foot-square ergonomically designed work station with a phone, a computer terminal, and a keyboard.

"These are claims," his older brother explained, grabbing a stack of paper-clipped and clamped wads of papers and forms from a bin outside the cubicle marked IN. "Your job is to deny them."

"I see," Boone had said. "You mean, I sort through the claims and deny all the fraudulent ones, right?"

His brother implored heaven for patience with a roll of his eyes, then sighed a gust of wintry disgust. "The fraudulent claims were picked out downstairs by high school graduates and denied three months ago. Anybody can deny a fraudulent claim. You're a college graduate. Your job is to find a way to deny legitimate claims."

"But . . ."

"Look," said Pete, "I know how you feel about coming to work here. I used to be a Nietzsche scholar myself, and from there I was on my way to Wittgenstein. But you can't pay the rent with that kind of behavior."

"I'm familiar with your views," said Boone. "You once told me that my salary would be society's report card."

"I said that?" asked Pete. "I better start writing this stuff down." He handed Boone the wad of claims.

"As I said, these are claims. Claims are filed by greedy people who do not understand how the insurance business works. People who file claims believe that money will make them happy and will somehow compensate them for their losses. This idea—that money makes misfortune easier to bear—is an illusion that can only be enjoyed by those who have *not* suffered an actual loss. Is this making any sense?"

"Not yet," said Boone, "but keep talking."

"The most terrifying thing about life is knowing that, at any moment, a freak accident, violence, mayhem, a psychotic break, an addiction, a heart attack, a sexually transmitted disease, cancer, an earthquake, or some other act of God, or worse can take all of your happiness away from you in the time it takes you to pick up the phone and get the news. That's why people buy insurance, because they think it will protect them from catastrophes."

"OK," said Boone uncertainly.

"But we are in the insurance business," said Pete. "We *know* there is no protection from catastrophes. No matter what you do, there's always a chance that a catastrophe will come along, tear your heart out of your chest, and rub it in your face."

"Uh, uh," said Boone, still frowning.

"When you're crawling on the bathroom floor sick with grief," said Pete, "wondering why God failed to give you the courage to kill yourself, a big check from the insurance company looks like a swatch of wallpaper. You're in a place money can't reach."

"So . . . ," said Boone.

"So, insurance only works if catastrophe does *not* strike," he earnestly explained. "We don't sell protection. We sell peace of mind. For a premium, we agree to give the consumer the illusion that money will protect him from every possible foreseeable catastrophe. Once the premium is paid and before catastrophe strikes, the consumer is free to wallow in the illusion that if something terrible happens money will take the sting out of it. When a catastrophe actually occurs, the illusion is shattered and there's nothing to be done but drag yourself out of bed every morning and get on with your life."

"But if what you say is true," asked Boone, "then you are charging people thousands of dollars for . . . an illusion."

"Exactly," said Pete. "Peace of mind. The money is irrelevant. You probably subscribe to the notion that insurance is a way to pool risk and share liability. You think premiums should be based upon risk. Nothing could be more wrong. Premiums should be based upon line thirty-one of your federal tax return, adjusted gross income. Our objective is to charge the insured just enough to make it hurt. We are looking for the financial pain threshold, because only when it hurts does the insured really believe he is obtaining something of value, and, as I've shown, he is indeed obtaining peace of mind for nothing more than money."

"But . . ."

"So, the first order of business is for you to understand that paying claims is not what insurance is about. Insurance is about paying *premiums*. Premiums buy peace of mind. Do you realize that there are parts of the world—whole countries!—where you can't buy peace of mind? Only in America is this really possible."

"But what about *paying claims*?" Boone asked, holding the stack of papers out to his brother.

"Here," said Pete, "I'll help you get started."

His brother unbanded the bundles of claim forms and took the first wad. "OK, here's a claim for fire damage. Looks like the guy's house burned to the ground. OK, do we pay for fire damage?"

"Yes," said Boone. "We do, I think. Don't we?"

"That's right," said his brother. "We do, sometimes. Your job is to think about what we *don't* pay for. We don't pay for wear and tear, contamination, loss by animals, structural movement, escaping water, freezing water, surface water, groundwater, neglect, intentional acts, negligent planning, construction, maintenance, earthquake, earth movement, acts of war, or nuclear or radiation hazard."

"That's a lot of stuff we don't pay for," said Boone.

"Damn straight," said his brother, clapping him on the back. "Now, start off with something easy. For instance, do we have any evidence of neglect?"

"I don't know," said Boone. "Let me see the file."

"What do you need the file for?" his brother yelled. "Here's a guy who stood back and let his fucking house burn down, and you want to see the file before you can say whether he neglected it? Well-maintained homes don't burn down. And if this yahoo wants us to pay him any money, he's going to have to *prove* that his house was not neglected or negligently maintained. Issue him a notice advising him that the claim is denied pending submission of proof by the insured in the form of a home inspection that the dwelling was well maintained at the time of the property damage."

"Wait a second," Boone had protested. "You said the house *burned down*. There's nothing to inspect."

"Exactly," said his brother. "You'll move up fast, once you learn not to belabor the obvious. Look at this," he said, riffling a few pages of the same bundle in Boone's face. "We do not cover loss by animals, which means we do not cover any loss caused by birds, vermin, insects, rodents, or domestic animals. There's not a shred of evidence in this file showing that the house fire was not caused by rodents. What if a rodent chewed through a gas line, or knocked over a jar of paintbrushes that were soaking in turpentine over the gas water heater? Have you ever seen what happens if a rodent gets its teeth into a box of those strike-anywhere matches? Poof! This is one of the flimsiest claims I've ever seen."

"It is?" Boone had said.

"Next claim."

Boone selected a sheaf from the pile and perused the cover sheet. "Looks like some kind of health insurance claim, for medical costs."

"Medical?" Pete had said. "If it's reasonable, go ahead and pay it."

"Looks like it's a bone marrow transplant for a cancer victim."

"That's totally unreasonable. A hundred grand, easy. Hugely unreasonable. Deny it."

"Deny it?" Boone had swallowed hard. "How can you deny a cancer victim's medical claims after taking his premiums for ten years?!"

"Easy," his brother said. "It's either experimental treatment or treatment for a preexisting condition. I am so sick of these ridiculous medical claims we're always getting from dying people who try to tell me that their cancer and their heart disease were not preexisting conditions. *Everything* is a preexisting condition, except maybe injuries from automobile accidents. But don't take my word for it! Who said, 'We carry the seeds of our own destruction with us from birth'? Socrates, or somebody, I don't know. And who said, 'Everyone has within him, from the first moment of his life, the cause of his death'? Voltaire, that's who. But what do they know? OK, let's say the three-toed sloths who file these claims don't know Voltaire from Fred Astaire, and let's say they think Socrates is a free safety for the Seattle Seahawks. They've heard of genetic predisposition, haven't they? They've seen it talked about on TV, haven't they? Who are they kidding? Three out of four natural grandparents and both natural parents croak from cancer, and now the insured has the face to tell me that his cancer was not a preexisting condition? Try that bone on another dog! Get him out of here! Drag him out of town with a meat hook! Send him to hell and wake him up for meals! This is the nineties! Can these people read newspapers? The savings and loan crisis is a ripple on a farm pond compared to the tidal wave of the coming insurance crisis. What are we supposed to do, give away money and make it worse?"

"You actually deny cancer patients the money to pay their medical bills?" Boone had asked in shocked disbelief.

"Master the fundamentals," said his brother, "but don't dwell on them. Don't say things like 'Gee, you mean we get to keep whatever we don't pay out' to the other employees. People will think you're the mailman's son."

Boone had hated the job from day one, and told his father as much. Complaining had gotten him nowhere.

"Why do you think they call it *work*?" his father had fairly shouted. "I send you to college, and you come out thinking you're supposed to *enjoy* working for a living? But hey! Don't listen to your dear old dad. I guess work is for capitalist pigs like me, who want to slaughter cash cows and wallow in blood money. Work is for venal philistines and grasping boors who want to send their kids to college and put food on the table. I wouldn't want a refined sensibility like yours sullying its precious self with work. Don't squander your rare talents manning a galley oar in this corporate slave ship. I think you should just quit! Far nobler pursuits are waiting for the likes of you. Resign! See what it's like sleeping in a shipping crate on the streets and eating out of garbage cans. Maybe that'll suit your artistic temperament better than earning a living in the insurance business!"

Boone realized that if he did not drink excessively, did not overeat, lived in the right parts of town, used his salad fork at the proper time, committed no physical violence against others, refrained from stealing, moved his bowels only in private, and was a coward in money matters, he would eventually succeed. His peers and progenitors would clap him warmly on the back. *"Well done, Boone. You're making money at a point and a half above prime. You should be proud."* Life would pass at a measured pace, with moments of happiness scheduled to occur during hard-won vacations. Unforeseen tragedies could be accommodated by taking sick pay or funeral leaves.

He had seen it all coming. In bed one night, in an apartment complex named after the meadow that had been paved to provide its parking lots and tennis courts, he had suddenly realized he would make money, receive a promotion, get married, spend money, bear children, receive another promotion, make more money, get sick, spend more money, and die. He would never see the ruins at Luxor, Egypt. He would buy a new car every three years, laugh along with television audiences, wait in line, watch his weight, renew his driver's license every four years, and grow too old to travel to Nepal or the heights of Machu Picchu. Danger would mean running a yellow light, or maybe cheating on his taxes. Ecstasy would consist in knowing one was well insured, or maybe the thrill of a free oil change with a tune-up, or the euphoria of a fat-free frozen dessert that tasted just like ice cream, with only half the calories.

Instead of hanging around Indiana and waiting for his first coronary bypass operation, his second wife, his third child, his fourth incremental pay raise, and his fifth of single-malt scotch, he decided to do something drastic. Something Gauguin or Henry Miller might do, something impulsive and irrational, financially irresponsible, and dangerous. He knew where to find guidance in such matters: his best friend, Michael Killigan.

What makes a best friend? Horatio had no revenue except his good spirits, but his blood and judgment were so well commeddled that Hamlet wore him in his heart of hearts. The best friends of Greek legend, Damon and Pythias, loved each other so much that when the tyrant Dionysius condemned Pythias to death and would not allow him to go home and arrange his affairs unless someone agreed to take his place and be executed if Pythias failed to return, Damon bound himself over. When Pythias was delayed, Damon was led off to be put to death, but Pythias arrived just in time, ready to take his place, save his best friend, and be executed. Dionysius was so impressed he pardoned both of them. These would be nothing but sentimental poetry and purple yarns if Boone had not grown up with Michael Killigan and met a friend for whom he would bind himself over.

Like Boone, most of their college classmates had graduated and stepped into the harnesses of house payments, car payments, and insurance premiums. Not Killigan. He had no intention of growing a belly and settling into the couch for a life of channel surfing and television commercials, listening to the Orwellian hog calls of the advertisers rattling their sticks in swill buckets. He had wanted none of it. Killigan had joined up with the Peace Corps and had gone away to Sierra Leone, West Africa, to live in a village, where there were no televisions, no electricity, no running water, and no over-weight white people talking about their cholesterol. Then, Killigan sent Africa back to Boone in letters, sometimes three or four in a week.

In the beginning, the letters were effusive celebrations of African village life, precise descriptions of the ceremonies that attended birth, death, marriage, sharing a meal, and the other universals of human existence. They evidenced a mind enchanted by the people and customs of West Africa. Later came descriptions of magic, div-ination, the clairvoyance and cultic powers of twins, the men's and the women's secret societies and their elaborate initiation rites, cer-emonial dancing devils who wore masks carved by magician black-smiths. Still later, descriptions of witchmen, juju, the various protective charms and "medicines," potions or pouches containing scorpions, the heads of snakes, even the charred remains of powerful men; the mechanics of "putting" or "pulling" a swear or curse, the abilities of "shape-shifters," people who could transform themselves into snakes, bats, or predatory animals, and the even more secret Leopard and Baboon Societies, outlawed since the British tried and hanged Leopard Men and Baboon Men from the gallows at Freetown in 1905, for dressing themselves in animal skins and performing ritual cannibalism.

It must have been a beautiful place, for Killigan had extended his two-year stint to three, and then to four, and the letters veered from enchantment with Africa into disenchantment with America —called, as Killigan had pointed out in one of his letters, "that fat, adolescent, and delinquent millionaire" by the Nigerian novelist Chinua Achebe. Killigan came to believe that Africa's misery was not an accident, not caused by primitive ignorance or the harsh equatorial climate, or disease vectors, but was, instead, a direct consequence of America's comparative wealth and the cunning of white "big men." Boone never quite decided whether he was un-convinced or unconcerned.

When Killigan had come home on medical leave with meningitis, he was cynically antisocial and used his illness as an excuse not to receive friends and visitors long after the fevers and the headaches were gone. His six-foot frame went from an already thin 160 to a flesh-fallen 140. He wanted only rice topped with various pepper sauces to eat, and he would not take alcohol. He seemed happy enough to see his parents and to see Boone, whom he called "me American brothah with yella hair," but he talked about Americans as if they were foreigners, and not very pleasant ones.

Before Killigan went back to Africa, Boone told him of his restlessness, and they made a vow to meet one year later in Paris, with enough money for a year's travel on the cheap. After Paris, they would wander in the general direction of Greece, resisting itineraries, so they could accommodate the whims of beautiful women they would meet along the way. Before Killigan got on the plane to go back to Sierra Leone, he handed Boone an envelope. Inside was a folded piece of paper that said: Paris, November 1.

In addition to his claims adjusting, Boone took a job as a night radio dispatcher for a trucking company. Making money in two jobs kept him tired for a year, but he kept telling himself that he would sleep it off in a hammock on a beach in Sri Lanka. The year passed quickly in a blur of mindless menial labor, and before he knew it, he was shopping for gear.

"One backpack," Killigan had warned him in a letter. "Everything must fit into one backpack, including the sleeping bag." But Killigan had radical ideas picked up from his time abroad. "Underwear simply collects sweat instead of letting it run off the body," he had written in one of his letters. "Leave it at home."

August had found Boone restless and ready to bag both jobs and head out. As near as he could gather from Killigan's correspondence, Killigan could not leave Sierra Leone during the rainy season—which lasted from May through October—because the dirt roads leading from his village to the paved highways were impassable; thus the plan was to meet in Paris as soon as the West African climate would permit travel. Boone was to await word by mail to the Paris American Express office of Killigan's departure from Africa and of his arrival in Paris, on or after November 1.

Boone had hit the five-grand mark in late September, and could no longer stand being a cipher crushed between two occupations. He left for Paris in early October, hoping to find the room where Henry Miller squashed bedbugs on the wall, the loft where Picasso painted Gertrude Stein's portrait, the son of the garage mechanic who told Hemingway and his expatriate pals that they were all a lost generation, the bowels of the restaurant where George Orwell peeled onions and potatoes.

Boone was unable to find Alice B. Toklas and obtain an introduction at 27 rue de Fleurus; instead he made sleeping arrangements among the dead in Montmartre Cemetery, where his squirming blue sleeping bag looked like a huge nylon maggot—royal blue against gray headstones and bone-white crypts—burrowing into sleep and the wormwood earth.

•

October predawn. Montmartre Cemetery in Paris contained several thousand unremarkable decomposing bodies resting eternally, another fifty or so famous decomposing bodies, also resting eternally, and one slumbering American vagrant resting temporally in a sleeping bag, with a sweater rolled around a pair of sneakers for his pillow. An empty bottle of table wine rested against a headstone. A screech owl waited on a branch, mistrusting the stench of the sleeping carcass, wondering if the thing could smell that bad and still have fight left in it. The resident cats nervously patrolled their territories, crouching behind tombstones every time the thing snored, wondering why the body had been left out in the night air.

Boone Westfall felt a ghoul's graveclothes brush his cheek and woke with a start to find a black cat batting the laces of the sneakers into his face.

"Scat!" he snarled, backhanding the wicked thing into a somersault and onto the grave of Hector Berlioz, a famous decomposing French composer.

Boone stretched and reached under his head, making sure he still owned both sneakers, then felt for the nylon money belt at his waist, which contained his passport and $4,200 in traveler's checks. He yawned, pulled the shoes and sweater into a steeper prop, and watched moisture from his lungs condense in the October air.

Would he one day wake up in heaven, relieved at having escaped the dreamy life of an American vagrant in Paris, the same way he was now waking up in Paris, congratulating himself on escaping the tedium of the life he had left behind in suburban Indiana?

"Yes," the cat said with a grin, and walked off in a stiff-legged huff.

The faint purples and grays of morning seeped into the clouds above him. He scratched himself and yawned again. A wind came up, and it occurred to him that perhaps God had yawned also. Paris stirred in the distance, its engines and factories rumbling faintly in the earth beneath his shoulder blades. A car passed over the rue

Caulaincourt, which straddled the cemetery on iron bridgework that clanked under the weight of the passing vehicle. The blurred silhouettes of crypts, crosses, and burial vaults slowly emerged from the misty darkness, like shrouded mourners bearing crucifixes out of the skyless fog.

He hoped this was the end of his search for decent outdoor accommodations in Paris. He had passed a restful night in the cemetery, free of the prostitutes and transvestites who had plagued his dreams in the Bois de Boulogne; safe from the prowling thieves who had snooped over him on the quays along the banks of the Seine; hidden from the gendarmes who had nudged him awake with billy clubs in the moonlit groves of the Luxembourg Gardens.

Very nice, he thought, turning his head for another look at the profile of Berlioz cameoed on a huge medallion and mounted on a new marble headstone.

The light of dawn confirmed that the image was a cameo of an older, respectable Berlioz, not the twenty-six-year-old wild man who wrote music with a headful of paregoric, a racing pulse, and a bonfire of lust for a soul.

That ain't the guy who wrote the Symphonie Fantastique, Boone thought. *That's the profile of a middle-aged music teacher.*

Potted plants surrounded the slab athwart the grave, and someone or some organization had recently thrown a bouquet. Probably the same civic-minded bunch that had uprooted the original tombstone and installed a monument.

Nothing good ever lasts, he thought. *Except maybe eternity. If it's good, and if it lasts.*

When the light permitted, he packed his sleeping bag into its stuff sack, broke camp, and wandered around looking for an exit. Once on his feet, he saw that cats had the run of the place. An emaciated gray one guarded the staircase to Zola's grave. A calico slithered through the bars of a windowed mausoleum (presumably in search of mice). A tortoiseshell tom slunk along a balustrade and pounced into a wrought-iron flower cachepot. Boone wondered if a hooded Druid might appear from behind one of the columns and light a pyre beneath the sacrificial animal.

The cold wind blew him up and down dead-end paths, and he got lost in a low-lying hodgepodge of tilted headstones, crumbling limestone vaults, and unkempt concave graves. Chains spalling rust and flaked with verdigris formed cordons around tombs, where replicas of dead dignitaries slept on biers, with their hands clasped on their stone bosoms. Railings sagged with the gravity of centuries around memorials with inscriptions and dates in faint Roman numerals. Some common graves had caved in beneath their tablets, leaving slots, where Boone could peer down into the washed-out earth and see wine bottles, cat droppings, and rubble. Others had sunk, shifting the gravestones and their ornamental sculptures askew.

The famous corpses had their renovated plots, but the rest of the deceased aristocracy were housed in crowded vaults and mausoleum row houses—slurbs of miniature stone mansions huddling together and blocking each other's entrances with toppled crosses and slabs of fallen architraves.

A dust devil danced down the sidewalk twirling a skirt of dead leaves. A piece of tin flashing rattled across a slate roof. Another gust of wind groaned in stone passages.

A wrong turn down an overgrown path took him into a clearing strung with vines and dead tree limbs. He stumbled on a Celtic cross, half submerged in topsoil, then tripped over a statueless pedestal studded with a pair of stone feet broken off at the ankles and followed his sleeping bag into a bramble, where he landed on top of the footless statue. He rolled onto his back and momentarily thrashed around like an upended turtle, until he got hold of a stone bench, realizing as he struggled to his feet that he had discovered the cemetery's junkyard. Headstones, doors from mausoleums, crosses, tablets, statues, and the rubble of desecrated memorials were stacked and scattered around him like dolmens or cairns left by an ancient civilization of Mad Hatters. The shafts of beheaded Ionic columns formed a dead man's colonnade around him, their collapsed entablatures turning to boulders in the grass, the stone foliage of their acanthus capitals clotted with moss and moldering in the weeds.

He wandered further into the maze of building materials from the city of the dead, then gasped and stood motionless, straining to hear again what he swore was a groan, a sob, some human sound, Anubis reading from *The Egyptian Book of the Dead*, Benedictine monks chanting the Day of Wrath. He suddenly realized he would follow this path around one of these sepulchers and into a clearing, where old Hector would be conducting the fifth movement, the witches' Sabbath and the Walpurgis Night, sylphs and sprites dreamily stroking violins, chubby trolls hunkering down around cellos and basses, a hunchback tolling the bell, ghouls and goblins squatting obscenely in a frenzied *danse infernale* around a bier supporting a toppled replica of the Apollo Belvedere, laid out in cold white marble, staring eyeless at the pagan sky.

Boone slashed his way back out through the overgrowth until the dirt path intersected with pavement. He took a shortcut between two headstones, smelled fresh earth and humus, and looked down just in time to keep from walking into an open grave. He peered over the lip of turf and into the dark, bottomless rectangle, feeling his heart beat with the exertion of flight. Next to a heap of clay was a pallet and a newly etched headstone of polished marble. He was afraid to look at the gilded name. Looking up, he saw a whole field of fresh, open graves, with shadows falling on the scarred walls of clay.

While zigzagging carefully through the field of fresh graves, he had a sudden fear that he had died a long time ago, in another country. Yes, he had died, and one of his relatives must have shipped his remains to Montmartre Cemetery. And now his body and soul had been resurrected on Judgment Day, and he was wandering around in a field of graves that had been opened at dawn and had given up their dead. The dead had all known where to go to be judged, but Boone was confused, still dawdling in the material world, out of touch, frightened and lost, until he heard the damned souls congregating in the distance, and knew he belonged with them. As if Judgment Day or eternity was a plane he was about to miss, if he did not hurry.

A stairwell built into a wall under the bridge led him up to a street and back to the land of the living.

He found a patisserie with an espresso machine and warmed himself over coffee and croissants, savoring butter and jam, filling his stomach, and killing hunger pains, glad that he was not interred in Montmartre Cemetery . . . yet. Glad that he had found his room at the Hotel Berlioz and could finish his tour of Paris while awaiting Killigan's arrival.

At 11 a.m., he retrieved his backpack, took the Métro to Opéra, and went to the American Express office for mail. He passed a large outdoor café and cast a casual glance at the patrons. The people at the tables erupted in laughter, staring at him and pointing. Boone blushed and looked behind him, finding a professional mime with an imaginary backpack slung over his shoulder, perfectly mimicking the gait of a corn-fed galoot from Indiana hauling thirty pounds on his shoulder.

The mime hollered a silent "Howdy" and waved, hitching up a pair of imaginary chaps and rolling along, like a bowlegged cowboy fresh from the range.

The crowd roared with laughter and threw coins. Boone dared not speak a word of French or English, lest they laugh even harder.

At the steps to the office, the prospect of mail lifted his spirits. So far, he had received nothing but letters from his girlfriend.

She had written him two letters: one emphatically stating that she would never speak to him or write to him again for any reason, under any circumstances; and another one, two days later, modifying her original decree to allow for periodic communications updating him on her insights into his utter self-indulgence, his beastliness, his fear of women, his terror of growing up, his infantile preoccupation with himself, his sloth, drunkenness, depravity, addiction to drugs, and sexual perversions.

The letter handed to him by the American Express clerk was not one of the tissue-thin blue aerogrammes he was accustomed to getting from Killigan. It was not one of Celinda's blood-red stationery envelopes either. It was a thick white business envelope from America, from Mrs. Marjorie Killigan. Killigan's mom? Boone found three letters inside, the first in a loopy feminine hand:

Dear Boone:

I hope this reaches you. Your mother said you were intending to remain in Paris until you heard from Michael and that you would be picking up mail at this address. She did not have a hotel telephone for you, so I am forced to write you with sad news. Michael is missing from his village in Sierra Leone. I had hoped this was all a terrible mistake, and that perhaps Michael simply had left to meet you in Paris, but as you can see from the copies of these letters, something is very wrong.

Randall called Senator Swanson and says he will fly to Africa himself if he has to. We are all distraught and not sleeping at all. Please, please call us collect if you have absolutely any idea what has happened, or if Michael had mentioned anything at all to you about traveling overland, etc. We are desperate!

Sincerely,
Marjorie Killigan

The second was a photocopy of a typed letter on letterhead, with a logo referencing the U.S. Peace Corps, Sierra Leone Office:

Dear Mrs. Killigan:

This will confirm my overseas telephone conversation with you of this past week. I regret to inform you that, at this time, we are still unable to locate your son, Michael Killigan, anywhere in Sierra Leone. As I described to you in our conversation, he was last seen in his village on October 15 of this year. The circumstances of his disappearance are still under investigation by the Sierra Leonean authorities and the chargé d'affaires of the American Embassy.

I can assure you that everything possible is being done at every level in both governments to locate your son. We are pressing urgently through our contacts with the various Paramount Chiefs and Mende tribal leaders, and we have dispatched couriers to all of our contacts in the Pujehun district where your son was stationed.

Unfortunately, Pujehun is politically unstable at the present time, because of bitterly contested elections for the Paramount Chieftaincy and for several national parliamentary seats. In addition, the fighting in Liberia has spilled across the southern border of Sierra Leone and displaced thousands of civilians. Elections are never a good time in Sierra Leone, but this season is one of the worst in memory. Rioting and looting have broken out in certain areas and some Volunteers were advised to leave the district. It is still unclear whether your son's disappearance is connected in any way with the unrest attending the elections, or whether he had any contact with the dominant political factions.

As I explained to you by phone, we are almost certain that your son is still in-country, as he would not be allowed to leave without obtaining an exit visa and paying the customary fees. The Sierra Leonean Ministry of Immigration has no record of his departure by air or sea from Freetown. Mr. Nathan French, a political officer with our embassy, and a Deputy Minister of Information for Sierra Leone have also traveled to the major border crossings and found no record of an exit visa issued for Michael Killigan. The only other way out of the country would be by bush paths—all but impassable during the rainy season, which has just ended here.

I will notify you immediately of any news concerning your son's whereabouts.

Please know that our thoughts and prayers are with you and your family.

Sincerely,

Paul Stevens
U.S. Peace Corps
Country Director/Sierra Leone

The third document was a copy of a letter written by a person who seemed unable to decide whether to print or write in longhand. The letters were small and poorly formed:

Dear Mrs. Killigan:
I full sorry to disturb you introducting myself for first time with bad news on Mr. Michael who pays school fees for me because I, Moussa Kamara, am servant for him. We do not find Mr. Michael and I cannot see him now for two weeks.

Trouble beaucoup is here for us because bush devils, witchmen, and baboon men have put bad hale medicine and carried bofima into our village and we are all too much afraid. Mr. Michael tried for stopping this business, but he was not able. When he was away, witchmen and bush devils been come and searched Mr. Michael's house looking for pictures snapped with him camera. We were running too fast from them. After, I cannot go back to my village and I cannot find Mr. Michael. They don't find pictures because Mr. Michael done send the picture film for development to a place the name I cannot write if because this letter go to wrong hands. Maybe if I can see what pictures Mr. Michael snapped I can learn the trouble that has found him.

Mr. Michael sometime say I write you if trouble come or sickness come. I look every day for Mr. Michael, until another day I find him.

I think of having good greetings for you and health for you and family health also.

Respect,
Moussa Steven Kamara

A drumroll jolted Boone out of his distressful reading. Two boys in red uniforms stood before him, announcing the arrival of a candy-red hut on a trailer platform drawn by a donkey. A fat man in a red, vaguely martial uniform with tinsel epaulets dismounted the cart and drew a bullwhip out its socket.

Two louvered doors at the rear of the hut opened and disgorged a well-dressed goat onto the sidewalk. A cluster of pedestrians stopped and applauded, laughing at the goat's wardrobe, which consisted of a frilled shirt, a pair of red silk suspenders, a buff Eton jacket, and white silk hose with red garters trussed up just under the goat's hindquarters. Its horns poked through a small black top hat with a silk band and a carnation. The goat climbed atop a small pedestal and bowed.

A juggler threw bowling pins into the air. A boy with a painted face and a leather jerkin lit a sword and swallowed it, sending a plume of black smoke into the air.

The doors of the hut banged open again, and a fat woman in red tights and a buckskin jacket trundled forth. She jutted her chin, displaying a silver goatee, then plopped a ten-gallon hat on her head and hollered "Hee-haw!" with a Texas twang. She walked over to the goat and took a bow. She groomed the goat's beard with a red comb, then groomed hers to match. The crowd roared with approval. The uniformed fat man cracked his bullwhip. The goat reared back onto its hind legs and rubbed goatees with the woman. People laughed hysterically and threw coins into buckets held by the drummer boys.

Boone looked away from the goat and watched the faces of the spectators, as they bared their teeth in snarls of laughter. Their eyes suddenly reminded him of Picasso, who once asked, "Why not put sexual organs in the place of eyes and eyes between the legs?"

He left the crowd and took back streets through twisting alleys of uneven bricks and cobblestones. He crossed bridges, descended into tunnels, rode the Métro, lost himself in the capillaries of transportation networks. The streets were jammed with strangers of all shapes, sizes, and ages: a cripple with a lifeless arm in tow, a man violently scratching his head, as if he had been bitten by something, a woman in love with her shopwindow reflection, children tormenting a dog, lovers on a stone bench groping obliviously.

There was a mange on the skin of the streets, a membrane coating the bricks and stones at pedestrian level. The foundations of buildings were slick with oils from human palms, the masonry seasoned with lungfuls of cigarette smoke and exhaust from the engines of cars and factories. The pores of the very stones were sweetened with spittle, sweaty paw prints, tobacco, scuff marks, shoe polish, and molting human skins. The curbs, benches, and pillars of the sidewalk arcades looked almost as if they had been worn filthy smooth by millions of eyes passing over them.

He found a grimy café with a *Menu Complet* sign, where he crouched over a twenty-franc meal and watched the habitués of the place as they watched him eat.

After the meal, he went out wandering again.

He had left his Indiana apartment looking for adventure, hoping something, anything would happen to him. Before he left, his mother had sat him down in the kitchen where she had nourished him in his youth. She begged him not to go. She had an irrational fear of travel, especially travel to uncivilized countries where the per capita crime rate was a tenth of America's murder rate.

"What if something happens to you?" she asked.

"But, Mom," he had said, "that's why I'm going. I want something to happen to me."

The dragon's teeth sown during his Indiana daydreams were now sprouting nightmares. Was Killigan dead? Was he sick? Kidnapped? Being tortured somewhere by rebels in military fatigues? Cooked over an open fire in a jungle clearing? Bitten by snakes, strangled by boa constrictors?

He took the Métro to Odéon, found a travel agency, and bought a one-way ticket to Freetown, Sierra Leone, on KLM Royal Dutch Airlines. Six hundred dollars. An outrage! He had held himself to one hundred dollars a week since his arrival. Now he was forced to cough up six weeks in Paris for a plane ticket to Sierra Leone, West Africa.

He scoured the bookstores on the Boulevard St.-Michel for African travel books written in English. He found books aplenty on traveling in East Africa, but nothing on West Africa or Sierra Leone. Tourists, it seemed, preferred lions and the Serengeti Plain to poverty and the Sahel.

Even books purporting to be guides on travel in Africa at large barely mentioned Sierra Leone. After devoting a separate chapter to the splendors of Kenya, which sounded like a sort of open-air zoo for Westerners, the authors of *Fielding's Literary Africa* dropped a single page on West Africa in its entirety, and barely a paragraph on Sierra Leone, warning their readers:

Sierra Leone, of the countries we've seen, is undoubtedly the worst. Garbage is piled, without exaggeration, two stories high on the corners of Freetown's streets, when it could be thrown in the ocean only a stone's throw away. . . . West Africans are, from our observations, more emotional, have a lower boiling point, are more aggressive and less disciplined. They do not understand the meaning of the word queue, or line, or turn taking. . . . We found a great animosity toward whites.

"All in all," the authors concluded, "traveling in West Africa is not a 'fun experience.' "

The authors of *Fielding's Literary Africa* moved on without mentioning that Graham Greene wrote *The Heart of the Matter* at the City Hotel in Freetown, or that the trip described in Greene's *Journey Without Maps* began in Sierra Leone. No word either about Syl Cheney-Coker, or any of Sierra Leone's own authors, or its rich oral tradition of story performances.

The passage told him nothing about Sierra Leone and everything about the authors. They were clearly well-bred, "fun"-seeking English people who had long ago mastered the arts of polluting the ocean and waiting patiently in line. They would patiently stand in line all day (so they thought) even if they were starving to death in 100-degree heat and 90 percent humidity, especially if breaking line would somehow draw attention to themselves. They were refined types catering to fun-seeking Americans with the money to spend on travel books. They unwittingly subscribed to the adage that most people can only feel at ease in a foreign country when they are disparaging the inhabitants. The animosity they harvested probably had less to do with the color of their skins than with their insistence that the inhabitants of all foreign countries should behave themselves and act British.

An excellent book by a fellow named Rick Berg, *Travelling Cheaply*, mentioned West Africa only to illustrate a passage on dysentery, observing that a solid shit once a month is a pretty good average for a stay in West Africa. Another guidebook advised him that ten of the world's thirty-six poorest countries could be found in West Africa. Still another warned him that, diamonds aside, disease was Sierra Leone's biggest export.

He finally hit pay dirt in the shadow of Notre Dame at Shakespeare and Company. On a dusty shelf on the second floor, the proprietor dislodged a used copy of a book in English entitled *The Mende of Sierra Leone*, by Kenneth Little. Boone instantly recognized the name of the tribe referenced in the Peace Corps Director's letter and bought the book on the spot.

His last night in Paris, Boone climbed into his sleeping bag under a half-moon and propped himself against Hector's marble monument. He tucked his flashlight under his chin. On one raised knee he placed the letters from Mrs. Killigan, on the other he propped *The Mende of Sierra Leone.*

He reread the letters, circling words as he went: "Pujehun," "witchmen," "hale," "bofima," "bush devils." He read the servant's letter twice and circled the middle paragraph:

> Trouble beaucoup is here for us because bush devils, witchmen, and baboon men have put bad hale medicine and carried bofima into our village and we are all too much afraid. Mr. Michael tried for stopping this business, but he was not able. When he was away, witchmen and bush devils been come and searched Mr. Michael's house looking for pictures snapped with him camera. We were running too fast from them. After, I cannot go back to my village and I cannot find Mr. Michael. They don't find pictures because Mr. Michael done send the picture film for development to a place the name I cannot write if because this letter go to wrong hands. Maybe if I can see what pictures Mr. Michael snapped I can learn the trouble that has found him.

The index in the back of *The Mende of Sierra Leone* had no entry for "Pujehun," "bush," or "devil." "Hale" and "bofima" referred him to "medicine," where he found copious subheadings. He selected " 'bad' medicine men and witchcraft" and flipped to the relevant pages.

The cold marble of Hector's memorial sent shudders through him as he read the passage:

A particularly clear example of the illicit operation of *hale* is provided in the case of *ndilei* medicine. This is a medicine which can be transformed into a boa constrictor by the witch (person) owning it. It is a mineral substance whose Mende name is *tingoi,* and it is hollow inside. It can be bought from its existing owner, if the latter wishes to rid himself of it.

Disposing of it, however, carries a very grave risk, including death, because the medicine becomes an integral part of its temporary owner. This is because the latter becomes virtually the slave of the medicine in return for the work which it does for him, and is slavishly subject to its will. . . .

In terms, then, of the work done, the owner of the *ndilei* and the medicine itself may be regarded as one; since the owner becomes a witch through association with it. He may have acquired it for the purpose of avenging himself on someone who has wronged him. But once under the medicine's power, he is committed to the life of cannibalism which witches lead.

This witch-cum-boa constrictor (*ndile*) works always by night and feeds on the blood of his victims by sucking it vampirelike out of their throats. Usually, his attentions are fatal, and he has the power, also, of causing infantile paralysis in children. The *ndilemoi*'s first step is to secure some article which has any kind of association with his intended victim. This may range from a piece of clothing to anything picked up from the latter's farm. Without it, the witch has no means of attacking the artery. The medicine itself is then buried close to the victim's home—outside in the bush or even at the doorway of his house, in any place from which his house can be seen. From there, it is transformed at the appointed hour into the boa constrictor.

Several pages later, he found *bofima* discussed, and almost decided to cash in his plane ticket and take the 25 percent penalty:

A further very powerful and antisocial medicine of the same kind is the *bofima*. This is made out of the skin from the palm of the human hand and the sole of the foot and the forehead. There are also parts of certain organs, such as the genitals and the liver, as well as a cloth taken from a menstruating woman, and some dust from the ground where a large number of people are accustomed to meet. It also contains some rope taken from a trap from which an animal has escaped; the point of a needle; and a piece of a fowl's coop. . . .

The *bofima* requires periodic "reinvigoration," otherwise it will turn on its owner and destroy him. Some *bofima* medicines have to be renewed annually; others more often. The success and power of this medicine depends on the parts of the body mentioned above. The oil, which is prepared from the fat of the intestines, is used to anoint the *bofima* itself, and is also used as a rubbing medicine to bring good luck and to give the person so treated a fearsome and dignified appearance.

He put his flashlight away and drew the darkness around him with his sleeping bag. The October moon shone on a field of tombstones, where Boone saw witches, fearsome and dignified in appearance, glistening with human fat, wandering among the graves, looking for fresh American body parts in a sleeping bag.

(**3**)

The plane dipped, settling into a rolling tundra of bright clouds, followed by white-out at Boone's window, and then flashes of blue as the wings tore the underside of the cloud bank into swirling white shreds. He watched veils of mist ghost over the wings of the airliner and drift away into seamless sea and sky. Out the window and far below the shoulder of the plane's wing, the sea crawled toward beaches shining like scimitars in the sun. The marinas and wharves gave way to tessellated roofs and buildings, then low-lying bush creeping up into the forested hills, where palms sprouted and roads twisted off into what looked like an empire of solid broccoli tops stretching inland to the horizon.

Boone's travel books advised him that for six months of the year Sierra Leone was drenched with tropical storms, which provided one of the highest annual rainfalls of any country in Africa. The other six months of the year, the streams turned to dust beds, the wells dried up, and the harmattan, a dry wind from the African interior, glazed the rain forests with dust from the Sahara. In recent years, the gross national product, per capita, was $240 in U.S. currency. The average life expectancy was thirty-nine years, with 166 of every 1,000 infants dying each year before they reached their first birthday.

He felt a bump and looked out the window at the drab, single-story terminal of Lungi airport, Sierra Leone, West Africa.

Once in the terminal, he fought off the usual assortment of "guides" and charlatans who wait in airports, train stations, and docks all over the Third World, praying to God in forty languages to please send them a common boob from Indiana. Several smiling broad-shouldered lads in dark blue polyester safari suits—intended to look like some kind of official uniform—asked for his passport and attempted to take his backpack from his shoulder. "We are special travel assistants," they explained in thick accents. "We will help you get through customs and immigration."

Boone refused their services, politely at first, and then rabidly, until the last of the special travel assistants left in search of other prey.

He changed forty dollars into 4,000 leones at a guichet outside the customs office, then rebuffed a squadron of officious baggage handlers who on closer examination turned out to be the same assortment of broad-shouldered special travel assistants, now arrayed in porter's caps and jerkins, instead of blue safari suits.

The group of porter-assistants followed him outside and earnestly warned him that he would be swindled by the taxi drivers unless he let them negotiate his fare into Freetown.

"Drivahs go tief you," said one.

"White man dae pay too much foh taxi," said another.

"Sometime drivah go tief luggage," said another, waving a cautionary finger across his face. "We go able hep you. We go show you oos-kind drivah go take you na Freetown. You put something small-small foh us," he said pointing at the palm of his hand, "and we go able save you money, beaucoup. Notoso?" he asked his fellows, who rendered a chorus of confirmation.

Boone refused in English ("No, thank you"), French ("Non, merci"), and American ("Fuck you!"), until the porters and travel assistants slunk away in groups of twos and threes, glaring at him and loudly recollecting the dire misfortunes of the last seven or eight white men who insisted on arranging their own transportation into Freetown. A few minutes later, he found the taxi stand at the other end of the terminal, where a string of drivers were stashing special travel assistant safari suits, porter's caps, and jerkins into the trunks of their cabs and donning chauffeur's hats.

After ten minutes of tenacious dickering with the drivers, who were snapping their fingers and hissing at him, he closed a deal with one of them for 3,000 leones—down from 7,000—just before a policeman intervened to advise him that the fare into Freetown was set by a municipal ordinance at 2,000 leones.

Once in the car, the driver blithely advised Boone that the ordinance had nothing to do with the going rate for a taxi into Freetown, that the "policeman" was a shill paid by the driver's competitors, and that the deal they had struck for 3,000 leones did not include the cost of the ferry they were about to board. Boone muttered something noncommittal, postponed settling up with the driver until his destination, and craned his head out the window to see what Africa at eight degrees north of the equator looked like.

Hills festooned with palm trees rose over Freetown. His guide-books told him that Portuguese sailors named the place Sierra Leone, or Lion Mountains, in 1462, either because they thought they heard lions roaring in the hills around the bay or because they saw the rump of a lion in the shape of the same hills. Lions live in East Africa, explained the guidebooks, where they can still be seen from inside the confines of an air-conditioned tour bus. In West Africa, there are no lions or air-conditioned tour buses, and the Portuguese sailors probably heard the roar of surf crashing on the bay shores.

Before the Portuguese named the country in 1462, the last his-torical reference to the area came from Hanno, the Carthaginian explorer, who in 500 B.C. surveyed the area from a galley ship and recorded his observations without bothering to name the hills. Dur-ing the 2,000-year interlude, generations of black Africans dreamed and made love in primitive dwellings, spirits roamed the bush paths, rain soaked the earth in the wet season, and the sun boiled it all away in the dry season, trees fell in the forests of Sierra Leone, and if any white men saw these things, they left no papers with black marks describing them. There are no books about what happened before white men came to trade slaves. The great deeds and tra-gedies of the African ancestors were told by the old ones with dim-ming memories who performed stories by firelight in the village baffas.

Boone took a seat on the ferry's deck and tried to look incon-spicuous. *Just act naturally*, he thought. *Like any other white person from Indiana packed onto a ferry with five hundred Africans.* Trouble was, he had no role model. There were no other white people on board from anywhere, much less from Indiana. He wondered how the Colts were doing this season.

After disembarking from the ferry, the taxi took him through the outskirts of Freetown, a sprawling shanty town of some 470,000 inhabitants, the center of what once was a British colony, founded in 1787, when, with the generosity characteristic of civilized white people everywhere, the representatives of the British Empire bought the twenty square miles that make up the heart of Freetown from King Tombo, chief of the Temne tribe, for rum, muskets, and an embroidered waistcoat. English philanthropists talked their governments into starting a Province of Freedom for liberated British slaves. The first boatload of 411 freed British slaves and a hundred whites arrived in 1787. Three years later, 48 settlers were alive to recount the ravages of disease and hostilities with the natives. Another 1,700 ex-slaves from Jamaica and Nova Scotia arrived in 1792. Several decades later, the Americans had the same idea, when a colony of freed slaves had been started in Liberia to the south.

The British ruled Sierra Leone until 1961, when they were defeated by the climate and the backward chaos of botched colonialism, and then left. According to the Krio proverbs, the only weapon used in Sierra Leone's war of liberation from Britain was the mosquito. The headstones of the battle casualties can still be found in the white cemeteries in the hills around Freetown.

Two centuries after Britain founded Freetown and thirty years after she left, Boone Westfall arrived, feeling whiter than milk from an Indiana dairy cow and looking out from his taxi onto a street jammed with bodies so black they seemed to soak up the sunset. The streets of Freetown accommodated two-way traffic only because most of the taxis did not have side mirrors, which allowed them to pass within an inch of one another. Boone's taxi sat motionless while swarms of citizens came and went as they pleased, only begrudging cars when the alternative was imminent physical injury. Old men in skullcaps and threadbare safari shirts smoked clay pipes and laughed at the helpless cars; shirtless teenage boys in rope-belted britches chased each other through stalled traffic; women wrapped in tie-dyed cloths swayed under headloads that would stagger a pack mule; cripples dottered on gnarled crutches; toothless beggars slumped up against storefronts with baskets of coins in their laps, laughing and showing their stained gums; girls in pigtails and blue school smocks chased goats into pens; a policeman in a red beret and sunglasses arbitrated a dispute over a damaged cart.

Everywhere, the pandemonium of human beings in reckless concourse, of parents berating children, of shopkeepers shooing chickens out of their stalls, of police whistles, singing schoolgirls, nattering wives, backfiring taxis, bawling infants, blaring tape players, and barking dogs.

On both sides of the taxi, corrugated-zinc-pan roofs streaked with
rust sloped to the streets from one- and two-story buildings, forming
dark arcades where hordes of black bodies surged and slithered
under ridgepoles strung with charred utensils, stewpots, dead chickens, tobacco leaves, dried fish, and pan scales. Under the zinc-pan
eaves, citizens swashed in and out of shops and verandas and open-
air markets, haggling across makeshift tables of boards and barrels
stacked with secondhand goods, tobacco, peppers, kerosene, rice,
matches, paste jewelry, and warm soft drinks. A crowd of young
men stopped traffic by dancing in the street outside a music store.
The proprietor had turned two speakers streetward to provide free
samples of reggae music to passersby; a placard over the shop door
proclaimed AFRICA SOUNDS in ornate cursive. Eventually, the
crowded streets and ramshackle hovels opened onto a larger avenue
called Siaka Stevens Street, named after the former President of
Sierra Leone and lined with plumed palms.

"De cotton tree dae yonder," said the driver, indicating the biggest
tree Boone had ever seen, in the middle of a roundabout walled in
whitewashed concrete. Far up in the limbs of the crown, he could
see shapes fluttering in the branches like pieces of night confetti.
Kites cut from the cloth of night.

"Witch birds dae," said the driver.

"What kind of birds?" asked Boone.

"Witch birds," the driver repeated. "Beaucoup dae. De tree done
dae five hundred year. I no lie."

The massive tree was bigger than the multistoried buildings in
the center of town, with a trunk the thickness of a good-sized house.
Its branches formed a dense bower, shading the entire traffic circle,
the perimeter sidewalks, and the buildings that cowered under its
limbs.

"If you get four eye, you go able see witch capes hanging from
every limb," said the driver earnestly.

"Four eyes?" asked Boone.

"I tell you!" the driver said. "If you get two eyes only, den you no
go able see ahm. But four eyes go able see ahm."

Boone shrugged his shoulders and mumbled, "Four eyes."

The driver pointed at the cotton tree, unwilling to let the white
man shrug him off. "Look yonder," the driver said. "Do you see
witch capes hanging in that tree?"

Boone saw only the largest assemblage of massive limbs he had seen anywhere and a swarm of huge fluttering birds. "No," he said.

"Den you only get two eye. No more," the driver said. "Witch no dae inside your belly. If a witch be dae, you get four eye and you go see beaucoup witch capes hanging from those limbs. If you pick one, it go bring you magical powers. But if you show it to anyone else, even to another witch, it go kill you."

The driver's formidable store of information on witchcraft and magic seemed to have obliterated his powers of math, for he kept adding a taxi fare of 3,000 leones to a ferry charge of 1,200 leones and coming up with 5,400, excluding special travel assistant fees, portage and baggage fees, taxi negotiation fees, fees for tourist information, and fees he allegedly had paid to expedite their ferry passage, all of which were recounted at great length and liberally waived because the driver was a very generous man with a family of nine starving children and a special place in his heart for white men.

After a bitter quarrel, during which Boone heard about every misfortune that had ever befallen the driver or anyone in his extended family, the driver took 3,500 leones for the taxi fare, including the ferry, and dumped Boone before a storefront with a second-story sign that said "United States Peace Corps." The sidewalk to the only entrance was blocked by a blind man in black glasses, wearing a white skullcap and a Muslim burnoose. The man promptly held out his cup and said, "White man. Peace Koh. Do ya, help me small-small."

"The taxi driver took all my money," Boone said. "Besides, if you're blind, how is it you know I'm white?"

"Africa man no take taxi to Peace Corps house," the blind man said with a laugh. "I sabby dat. You sabby dat? You sabby talk Krio? You no sabby talk Krio? Den I talk to you in English. You no get Salone money? Now American money fine past Salone money. Ih fine-O! Now, I tell you. Do ya, paddy, help me small-small. Let me have some fine-fine American money."

Boone put a spindled American dollar into the cup.

"I tell God tank ya," the blind man said, nimbly fingering the bill. "Your wives will bear you many peekins. And those peekins will bear you many more peekins. You will die with a smile on your face, rocked in the arms of your grandchildren. They will sing you to sleep with songs of your great deeds. Because you have helped me, God will watch over you forever. God made me blind, but he gave me the power to foretell the future, so know that all I have said to you is true. I tell you these things in God's name, and may God pull out my liver and set my hair on fire with lightning if everything I have said is not true."

Boone savored the sheer grandiloquence of the blind man's blessing and followed signs along a sidewalk between two storefronts to a rear entrance of a slanted frame building. After negotiating a set of metal stairs that switchbacked up the rear of the structure, Boone opened a busted screen door and entered a big room aswirl with ceiling fans and partitioned by file cabinets.

He introduced himself to a fortyish woman whose desk was positioned to field requests for information. Boone explained himself and his purpose to her.

"You came all the way from Indiana?" the woman asked.

"I was in Paris when I found out about this," Boone explained. "Michael Killigan's mother wrote to me there."

The woman dolefully shook her head. "We talked to her over the weekend," she said. "I know how concerned you must be about Michael," she added, "but I don't think there's any good you can do in Sierra Leone. The Peace Corps, the American Embassy, the people from USAID, the Canadian, Dutch, and German development agencies, everyone is looking for Michael Killigan. These people know the country. They know the Mende tribe. They know Michael Killigan, his friends, and his haunts. Nobody is more concerned about him than this office and the people at the embassy. If he can be found, they will find him."

The woman pouted and handed him a three-by-five-inch photo of Michael Killigan—skinnier than Boone remembered him—wearing an embroidered African smock and sitting on the veranda of a mud hut surrounded by twenty or thirty villagers of all ages. The Africans were solemn, as if they knew this moment would be preserved on film forever. Killigan's expression was a draw between a smirk and a grimace.

"May I ask where you got that photo?"

"You too, huh?" she said. "Suddenly everyone wants to know about photographs. Last Friday, one of Killigan's servants, Moussa somebody, went to the Peace Corps office in Bo town asking to see the Peace Corps Director. He was told that the Director stays in Freetown. The kid said he had photos he wanted to show the Director. Said he wouldn't turn them over to anybody else. The officer in Bo was finally able to talk him out of one photo by telling him it might help them find Killigan. This week, we got word from the embassy that they're looking for the servant and the photos, and they are mad at us because we let the kid go.

"It's a mess," she said, still peering sadly into the photo. "In years gone by, we have lost Volunteers to illness or snakebite, but this kind of thing has never happened before. Volunteers do not vanish from their villages."

"I have a three-month visa," Boone said. "If nothing else, I can serve as another set of roaming eyes. I can go to Bo or Killigan's village and help look for him and his servant."

The woman shook her head ruefully. "Tromp into the bush by yourself and you'll get frustrated in a hurry," she said. "After that, you'll get sick. The Peace Corps cannot give you medicine or medical care, because you aren't a Volunteer. That leaves native medicine, which is worse than no medicine."

"I've got a three-month supply of chloroquine," Boone said. "I've already had shots for yellow fever, cholera, and typhoid."

"Good for you," the woman said. "Now go downstairs to Dr. Kallon's office and ask him to show you his chart of two hundred and forty other tropical diseases that can blind you, kill you, or put you in bed for three months with lasting kidney, liver, or heart damage. Ask him about schistosomiasis, river blindness, yaws, sleeping sickness, giardiasis, blackwater fever, hepatitis, leprosy, and elephantiasis. As for your malaria medicine, eighty-five percent of the malarial parasites in equatorial Africa are now immune to chloroquine, including *falciparum*, which can give you cerebral malaria and kill you. Nowadays we tell our Volunteers they *will* get malaria if they spend any time in the bush; it's only a matter of how often and what kind."

She put two manila folders into an accordion filer and smiled sadly. "I don't mean to be negative. It's just that, even with the proper training and medical care, living in the bush is unhealthy and dangerous. Elections are coming up, which usually means civil unrest, with a capital U. Refugees are coming across the border from Liberia, and some of the rebels have crossed into Sierra Leone in pursuit. It's not a good time to go out wandering."

"How long have you been here?" Boone asked.

"Three years," the woman said.

"And you're none the worse for wear," he said, hoping she would discern a compliment and give him the information he was about to ask of her.

"I live in Freetown," she said, "not in the bush. When I get sick, I see a doctor who graduated from an American medical school."

"If I get sick," Boone said, "I'll buy a plane ticket home."

The woman grinned and pulled out a nail file. "I can see you know all about the bush," she said. "In the bush, you will be at least ten hours by bush taxi, or *podah-podah*, from Freetown. A *podah-podah* is a Toyota pickup truck with forty Africans and two tons of freight stuffed into it. Killigan's village is twelve hours by *podah-podah*, half of it over roads that would be declared impassable in Indiana. A ride in a *podah-podah* takes stamina; if you were sick, the trip would kill you, and the American Embassy would be sending you back to Indiana in the cargo hold."

"How do Volunteers get to Freetown when they're sick?" Boone wondered out loud.

"Well, it's usually at least two days before we find out about them, and another day or so before we get to them. Then we pick them up in air-conditioned Land-Rovers and bring them back here," she said. "Again, a luxury that would not be provided to you, because you are not a Volunteer."

"What do I have to do to become a Volunteer?" he asked.

"Go back to America and fill out the paperwork," she said. "The Peace Corps does not accept applications from within the host country."

"It can't be that bad," Boone said. "People have been living here for thousands of years."

"Living and dying," she said. "The average life span in the bush is thirty-nine years. The infant mortality rate is fifteen percent in the first year of life. After the British took over, they used to greet one another in the mornings at Freetown by asking, 'How many died last night?' They called Sierra Leone 'the White Man's Grave.' Catholic Missionary Services lost a hundred and nine missionaries in the first twenty-five years of operations. One time, six Catholic fathers were sent in January. By June they were all dead. My advice to you is to stay in Freetown and don't charge into the bush looking for Michael Killigan."

"I'm here," Boone said. "I'll leave after I find him. I'll stay in Freetown long enough to find out where I should start looking, and if it's the bush, I'll go there. Just tell me how to get to Killigan's village, where he was last seen, and maybe who he hung around with," Boone begged.

"I can tell you those things," a voice behind him said.

Boone turned and saw a huge torso in a tie-dyed native shirt filling the doorway to the office. Shaggy hair and a dense beard covered the man's head and face, leaving two brown eyes under an overhanging brow.

"Sam Lewis," the man said, extending a hand of thick fingers, a wrist with a bronze bracelet, and an arm of thick bones with no fat on them. "Agriculture. I'm stationed just outside Pujehun."

"Boone Westfall," said Boone, feeling his palm snag on the welts and calluses of Lewis's hand, and getting a closer look at the imposing bracelet, which consisted of two bronze lizards with adjoining snouts crawling past one another in the hairy scrub of Lewis's forearm, holding themselves in place with prehensile bronze tails.

"It keeps fever away," Lewis said with a grin, noticing Boone's study of his bracelet. "I no get febah since I been wear dis medicine," he said, lapsing into the musical Krio Boone had heard from the taxi driver.

The woman at the desk took a phone call.

"Killigan talked about you," he continued. "You were planning a travel, weren't you?"

"We were," Boone chuckled grimly, "until Killigan disappeared."

"These people can't help you," Lewis said, talking over the woman's telephone conversation, and dismissing the entire office with a backhanded wave. "They know nothing about the bush. They all live in Freetown. On top of that, they're very culturally sensitive, which means they know everything about how things should be and nothing about how they are."

"I need directions to Killigan's village," Boone said.

Lewis motioned for the woman's attention and said, "I'll take him," and pushed Boone toward the door.

"I'm going for my monthly protein fix," he explained. "Why don't you come and eat some *poo-mui* food with me."

"What kind of food?" Boone asked.

"*Poo-mui*," Lewis said. "*Poo* is Mende for 'white' or 'European'; *mui* means 'man' or 'person.' If you go out to the bush in Mendeland, peekins will shout *poo-mui* at you from dawn to dusk, and you'll get plenty sick of it. There's a restaurant in Freetown that serves fried chicken and french fries. There's another one that serves cow beef."

"Cow beef?" Boone repeated.

"Once you get outside Freetown," Lewis explained, " 'beef' means the meat from any animal, usually from bush deer, or from big guinea pigs called 'cutting grass.' They taste kinda like squirrels. Ever eat a squirrel?"

Boone made a face.

"If you want to make sure about what you're eating, ask if it's cow beef."

"Cow beef, got it," said Boone.

"Then they'll lie in your face and tell you it's the sweetest cow beef you've ever had."

Back out on the sidewalk, they found a white female Volunteer waylaid by the same blind beggar.

"I tell God tank ya," the blind man said, shaking coins in his basket. "Your husband will own a huge farm and you will bear many peekins. And those peekins will bear you many more peekins. You will die with a smile on your face, rocked in the arms of your grandchildren. They will sing you to sleep with songs about their favorite grandmother. Because you have helped me, God will watch over you forever. God made me blind, but he gave me the power to foretell the future, so know that all I have said to you is true. I tell you these things in God's name, and may God pull out my spleen and may my enemies walk on my grave if everything I have said is not true."

"Morning-O, pa," Lewis said to the beggar.

"Morning-O, mastah," the beggar replied. "How de body?"

"I tell God tank ya foh it," Lewis said. "How youself?"

"I well," the beggar replied. "How de day go?"

"I fall down, I get up," Lewis said.

"Now meself-self same," said the beggar. "We go see by and by. Next time, you keep something for me, hear me?"

"We go see back," said Lewis.

"That was your first Krio lesson," Lewis said. "When the British dumped boatloads of freed slaves over here in the eighteenth century, the settlers had no common language. They were Africans from different tribes, Jamaicans, slaves who had drifted into London after slavery was declared illegal there in 1772, American slaves who had escaped to Nova Scotia during the Revolutionary War. They were forced to develop a common language out of remembered English, Portuguese, Spanish, Yoruba, bits of French, and whatever else would serve to call a spade a fucking shovel. Blessings and greetings are extremely important. Learn them and do not attempt to transact business without first greeting people. Ask about their families, ask about their health, ask how the day is going, then proceed. The American habit of getting straight down to business is considered very rude."

The restaurant was a dark wooden place lit only by a jukebox playing American music that was twenty-five years out of date: the Kinks, the Beatles, the Velvet Underground, the Moody Blues. Lewis ordered four beers and two platters of food. He swooned and smacked his lips over a meal of soggy fries and tough chicken armored in thick, deep-fried batter. Boone rated the meal far below the fast food he had been eating out of the stalls along the rue de la Huchette in Paris, and picked at the batter in between sips of beer.

"Eat up," Lewis said, washing down a mouthful of fries with half a beer. "You'll get nothing but rice and sauce out in the bush. Rice chop. No cold beer either, because there's no electricity and no refrigerators. Nothing but warm Guinness stout."

Boone forced a few more fries down and wondered what rice chop would taste like if people came all the way to Freetown for deep-fried gristle, batter, and chicken bones. In the course of the meal, he learned that Lewis was on the last leg of a two-year stint in the Peace Corps; that in two years he had had the clap three times, hepatitis twice, and a hot shower once.

"It's my kind of country," Lewis said. "It runs on bribes ('mas-mas,' in Krio, the 'sweet' of office), graft, thievery, witchcraft, and juju. In 1981, the exchange rate was one leone to the dollar. Now it's a hundred leones to the dollar. You can make a fortune trading in three currencies in the black markets at the border. When I came here, two years ago, a cold Star beer was fifty leones. Now it's two hundred leones for a warm one. I used to be able to get a woman outside the casinos at Lumley Beach for the cost of breakfast and a fifty-cent cab fare. Now they've all got diseases, and they want dinner, two hundred leones for the night, breakfast, and cab fare in the morning. The brewery shuts down once a month, and the power goes out in Freetown at least once a night. 'Better no dae,' as they say in Krio," Lewis said. "Better is not there, or nothing good is there."

"You sound like Killigan's letters," Boone said. "But he said the people made the difference. He said the poverty and despair only made them more bighearted. He said he reenlisted because of the people."

Lewis wrinkled his upper lip and snapped his fingers at the waitress.

"That's where your friend and I parted company," he said, giving Boone a hard look. "He spent too much time in his village and not enough time with *poo-muis*. He forgot about civilization, and started thinking these people were noble savages or some goddamn thing."

"What do you mean?" Boone asked, alarmed at the disgust creeping into Lewis's voice.

Lewis banged his beer bottle. "As soon as a Volunteer tells me there might be something to native medicine, or that the bush is really a fucking Garden of Eden, that's when I know they've gotten down on all fours and crossed over to the animal kingdom."

Boone nervously took the restaurant in at a glance and satisfied himself that nobody had heard Lewis over the jukebox.

"Don't get me wrong," Lewis said, in a bland tone that suggested he was unconcerned about being misunderstood. "I like to get down on all fours as much as the next guy, but come morning, I send her home, get up on my hind legs, go back to speaking English, and eat with a knife, fork, and spoon. And it's not a racial thing. It doesn't have a thing to do with skin color. It's not genetics or breeding or Darwinism. It's much simpler than that. Animals live in the bush. When people live in the bush, they turn into animals. Animals with the power of speech."

Boone peeled the label off his Star beer and wondered if Lewis's bitterness ever ripened into outright rage.

"It's a great country," he said, with a tilt of his Star. "Where else can you find beggars, lepers, whores, cripples, and children starving to death in the middle of such exotic beauty and abundant mineral wealth? I've been here almost two years, and I can say with certainty that at least once a day a hungry person has asked me for money. After careful research, I have concluded that starvation builds character. In the beginning, I gave away half my hundred-and-fifty-dollars-a-month salary to starving people, or people who were dying because they couldn't afford antibiotics or rehydration salts. Pretty soon, ten, twenty, thirty people a day were coming to me with their hands out. Their children want foh die, their bellies are empty, they get bad fever, money no dae for medicine, or 'mehricine,' as they say in Krio. I developed a system for rapid appraisal of potential beneficiaries. Adult beggars missing more than seven digits to leprosy automatically qualified for alms from this tender white man, as did blind lepers or blind polio victims with children, limbless people, or mothers with blood-tinged sputum.

"Once I had the citizens in the major-medical adult category, I eyeballed them and decided whether they had ten cents' worth of deformities, or maybe a dollar's worth. I used this system during banking hours, after that I shut the coffers down for the day and refused to give anybody a dime, unless they started dying in a bag of bones at my feet, whereupon I usually concluded that they were already almost dead and my money would be much better spent on the living.

"Star beer!" Lewis hollered, grabbing a bouquet of empty bottles and clanging them at the waitress.

"Every so often, somebody came up to me with a story about how their father 'want foh die' out in some godforsaken village eighty miles out in the bush. How they had to get there before dawn with some *poo-mui* medicine, or the old pa would croak of snakebite, or blackwater fever, or river blindness, or pneumonia. Sometimes they would get down on their hands and knees, touch my foot, dribble tears in the dust, and beg me for lorry fare and money to buy the medicine. Maybe six, seven bucks. A day's wages anyway. At least half the time, I told them to take a hike for yams and bananas. Next day, somebody would tell me that their story was true, and that the old fart had died during the night. Or else I'd give some consumptive, rachitic, old poltroon twenty bucks, only to find out that, instead of a case of tuberculosis or rickets, he'd spent the money on a case of Guinness stout and was hung over in a hammock. After a few months of that, I had to use some of their own wisdom on them. 'How foh do?' I asked, using Krio just like an old pa. 'How for do?' Better translated as 'What can you do?' Indeed. If I bought medicine for every old geezer croaking of snakebite in West Africa, I'd have to fly home tomorrow, and the clinic would be closed for good!

"Make we get Star beer!" Lewis hollered again, this time waving two clanking bouquets of empty bottles.

"And the climate," he said, returning to his conversation. "You drown in a twenty-four-hour waterfall of rain from July to September. The shit comes down in torrents. It carries away children and livestock. By January, you can't find drinking water. You have to pay people a quarter to walk five miles and fetch you a bucket of swamp water. When I lived in Bo, I had a water tower behind my compound that was filled weekly by the German development people. The villagers used to come and sit underneath the tank with little pails, collecting trickles of water that leaked out at the seams. I was pretty nice about the whole thing, and I didn't chase them away. I didn't throw rocks at them, until they started climbing up the stilts and dipping their buckets into the water supply. That truly pissed me off, because half the time the buckets had just been sitting in a heap of warm goat shit. Early on in the dry season, I'd nail them with a few good-sized rocks, and that usually did the trick. But toward the end of the season, when the nearest water was a good five miles off, and swamp water at that, a pail of cold, clean water looked so good to them that they got to thinking it was worth a few lumps on the noggin. So I had to break out the stick I kept behind the door and drive them off like livestock.

"You can't tell them a fucking thing about hygiene or drinking water. It's all hocus-pocus to them. If the water goes bad, it's because some witch in menopause put a hex on the well while everybody was asleep. To them, dirty buckets had about as much to do with it as the fall of the Roman Empire. Health care is more or less left to nature and witchcraft. Deformed children are 'devil spirits' trying to invade the village, so the Sande matrons simply kill them and throw them on the fire. At the other end of life, the old ones get sick, take to their pallets, and die within a week or so. It's a great country."

"You were saying that Killigan spent too much time in his village," interrupted Boone, who was tired of listening to invective.

"Live with animals in the bush, pretty soon you're down on all fours and can't get up again," he said, glowering at his bottle of beer, almost as if he had forgotten Boone was with him.

The waitress, a Krio girl in a headwrap, walked by them once more.

"Say, pa!" Lewis hollered to the proprietor behind the bar. "You no get waitress with better training?"

The waitress sucked her teeth.

"Training dae beaucoup," she said. "You humbug me foh whatin?"

"I no humbug you," Lewis sneered. "I want one Star beer."

"You want beaucoup Star beer," she said. "I no able foh fetch dem so."

"You suck teeth at me? You no respect me better?"

"Na, so you say," she snapped.

"Na, so I know," said Lewis. "For whatin you vex?"

"Something brings something," she said.

"Ah," he said, "the African way. Let's talk proverbs."

"Like brings like," she said.

"If you throw ashes," said Lewis, "ashes will follow you."

"Usai den tie cow, na dae he go eat grass," she countered. "Usai white mahn sit down, na dae he go drink Star beer."

"Pa, do ya, I can get one waitress with better training?"

The bartender came out and shooed the girl off, serving Lewis and Boone another round of Stars.

Lewis glowered after her. "You see what I mean? A simple concept like service is totally foreign to them. Instead, it's something to argue about.

"Anyway, I was saying . . . Oh yeah, one day, your friend, Lamin Kaikai—he preferred his African name. One day, Killigan told me he paid a medicine man to put thunder medicine on his house. Next thing I knew, he was hanging out with Aruna Sisay."

"Who's Haruna Sisay?" Boone interrupted.

"Aruna Sisay," Lewis repeated. "I'm taking you to see him tomorrow. We'll see if he can explain what happened to your buddy. If he doesn't know, he can sure find out. And if you kiss his ass long and hard enough, and pretend he's some kind of superior being because he turned himself into a Mende man, he might tell you where you can start looking."

"Does he speak English?" Boone asked.

"He's American," Lewis said. "Well, he used to be American. He's white, but he's African. He's got three African wives and he speaks fluent Mende. He even speaks deep Mende, or ancient talk, which only the old pas know. Out in the bush, they call him the white Mende man. He came here a long time ago on a grant to do anthropology fieldwork and never went back. He doesn't talk to white people anymore, unless they speak Mende to him and approach him in the African way, with gifts and gestures of respect. That's why Sisay liked your buddy so much, because Killigan took the trouble to learn Mende. If he finds out you're a friend of Killigan's, maybe he'll speak English to you, but don't count on it."

"So the Mendes speak something besides Krio?" asked Boone.

"Krio is the language spoken in Freetown," Lewis explained. "And it's the language used in the market when two people from different tribes are haggling over the price of a cup of rice. You've got eighteen tribes and eighteen different languages in a country a little smaller than South Carolina. When they want to talk to each other, they speak Krio. The Europeans drew the maps, and they didn't give a damn whether the tribes within the borders were speaking the same language or killing each other. The two biggest tribes are the Temne in the north and the Mende in the south and southeast. Where you're going, the people speak Mende. But you'll get along fine if you pick up a little Krio."

"So you think this Aruna Sisay might know something about what happened to Killigan?"

"Maybe," Lewis said. "But like I said, he's African, which means he's not to be trusted. Get information from him if you can, but don't give him any. That's how you survive in this part of the world. Ask questions, listen, but don't talk. Like the rest of these guys, he's into secret society business, and if it serves his purpose, he'll lie to you, and turn your information over to the Poro boys. Lying is a form of polite conversation over here. Lying is considered perfectly OK if you are protecting a secret, and everything's a secret. Witchcraft, bad medicine, putting swears, pulling swears, sex, politics, the Poro Society. It's all secret. If you try to find out about any of it, all you'll get will be lies."

"What's the Poro Society?" asked Boone.

"The men's secret society," Lewis explained. "It's kind of a cross between the Boy Scouts and the Freemasons. It's how young men are initiated into manhood and trained to be warriors, even though, these days, they grow up to be farmers or miners or government clerks. Once a year, the Poro devil comes into the village wearing a mask of palm raffia, with bits of mirrors and amulets attached to it. The devil blows a cow's horn with a lizard skin stretched over the opening. The women and children scatter and bury their faces inside their huts. If a woman sees her reflection in one of the mirrors on the devil's mask, she will become sterile. The devil rounds up all the initiates, and takes them out into the bush for about a month, where the elders give them new names and tribal markings. The markings on their backs are supposedly caused by the Poro spirit, which swallows them like a boa constrictor and separates them from their families. The markings on their temples supposedly appear when they see the Poro spirit. Later, the spirit delivers them back to the village as men with new names. It's a spirit with a mouth, a stomach, and a vagina. It eats children, then gives birth to men.

"Nobody will tell you what happens in the Poro bush, because it's intensely secret. Fowls are sacrificed during the ceremonies, and as the knife is severing the fowl's neck the initiates are warned that the same will happen to them if they ever tell any Poro secrets. During other ceremonies, the initiates are given rice and cautioned that this rice will choke them to death if they ever reveal Poro secrets. If you want to know something about Poro, you can only ask people who have *not* been initiated. And what you get are rumors and the anecdotes collected by anthropologists and missionaries."

Lewis finished his beer.

"It must be pretty rough," he continued, "because every so often, one of the young men doesn't come back. An elder comes to the mother's house and breaks a pot on the ground in front of her, saying, 'You asked us to build pots, we are sorry to say that yours was broken.' Nothing more is ever said about the initiate. No mourning, no grief. He simply disappears."

Lewis rocked back in his chair and went to work on a dish of soft-serve ice cream. "As I said," he added with a mirthless laugh, "animals with speech."

Boone found Lewis's opinions more reprehensible than the described rituals, but he did not risk alienating his only bush guide.

"I should warn you that you'll be going into Moiwo's territory," said Lewis, "and, as you know, it's election time."

"Moiwo?" asked Boone.

"Moiwo's the section chief," Lewis said. "He went to school in England and America, then returned to Sierra Leone with an agenda. His father was the Minister of Finance under the last regime. He lines his pockets with relief money and spends it on limos and women. There's an old Krio saying, 'Monkey works, baboon eats.' Moiwo's the baboon. His monkeys work for him all day, and he sits around and eats. An African big man. Crooked as a dog's hind leg. Now he wants to be Paramount Chief, and it's election time, so he's getting into bad medicine and secret societies. He's definitely way up on top in the Poro business."

"If no one talks about Poro, how come you know so much about it?" asked Boone.

"Most of what I know about Poro, I learned from Michael Killigan," Lewis said. "He met a missionary up around Kenema who knew a lot about Poro. And Killigan used to come back with stories about devil dancers cutting their tongues out, passing them around on plates, then putting them back into their mouths. Or shirts made of magic cloth that could stop bullets. It was great campfire stuff, until he started believing it. After he went through it himself, you couldn't get a word out of him."

"Out of whom?" Boone asked. "After who went through it? The missionary?"

"Killigan," Lewis said, smiling, then wiping it away with the back of his hand. "After Killigan was initiated, he clammed up just like the rest of them. I saw his markings one day. He took off his shirt when we were building a bridge outside of Sumbuya. Never had seen it on a white man. The scars looked kinda purple. Later on, in Bo, I asked him about it. He got up and left me at the saloon. Just the way a dog would leave another dog drinking out of a drain spout. After that, it was common knowledge: Say the word Poro in a bar, in a rest house, at a table in a restaurant, and Killigan would get up and leave."

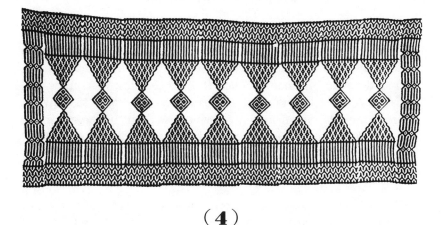

(4)

Randall took the black bundle home from work and opened the box on the kitchen table in front of his wife. Together, they skimmed Michael's last three letters and found no mention of any forthcoming package of artifacts.

"Do you think it means something?" he asked her, pointing at the bundle and wrinkling his nose. "Do you think it's from someone who knows what's happened to Michael? Is it some kind of message? Something evil? Do you suppose it's meant to harm us? Or used to harm Michael?"

Marjorie wearily shook her head, not because she had an opinion about the black egg, but because she recognized her husband's methods. He was a creature of anxiety. Anxiety made him a successful perfectionist at work, and an unbearable pest at home. His favorite technique for acquiring peace of mind in a crisis was to bait her, siccing his fears on her like crazed hounds; her job was to soothe them one by one and send them back tamed, sleeping dogs. He was like a child who could imagine only terrible kingdoms and wicked rulers in the realms of possibility, which she pooh-poohed away, assuring him they would never come to pass.

"It could be poisonous. What if it's some kind of supernatural weapon? A witch doctor's hand grenade? Should we unwrap it and make sure there's not a spider or a snake inside?"

She was preoccupied with her own unspeakable fears and wanted only to hire a domestic to talk to her husband about life's ups and downs.

"You must be worried," he said. "Otherwise you would be telling me not to worry. You think I should be worried, don't you?"

He concluded that his wife's tight-lipped composure was a cover for internal hysteria. The last real tragedy in their lives had been a miscarriage, almost fifteen years ago, a bit of trauma clearly in the female domain. She had handled the whole thing gracefully, and had not allowed her emotional upheaval to interfere with his flawless execution of plan confirmation in what was then the largest single reorganization under Chapter 11 in the southern district of Indiana. But Michael's disappearance was a major tragedy by comparison, and something only Randall could resolve using his contacts in Washington and New York.

"You're very worried, aren't you?" he asked. "You know, the law recognizes something called estoppel by silence," he added, half playfully. "I don't want to get into it in detail, but in certain situations, I would be entitled to conclude from your silence that you agree with me, and later you would be estopped from denying that you agreed with me. You're beyond worried, aren't you? And you think I should be worried too, don't you?"

"Why don't you put this somewhere," she said, pushing the box at him.

Randall took the thing upstairs and stowed it in his closet, up on his gun shelf. Before he put it away, he unwrapped it again and studied it by the closet light. It seemed to reverberate slightly. Its textured surfaces and the patterns on the strips of cloth seemed to swarm under his inspection. The spout looked as if it had been soaked in blood, then baked in a kiln. If the thing was an omen of some kind, he reasoned, then he should hang on to it until he encountered someone who could divine its message.

When he got up the next day, he had two full-time jobs: one, as the best bankruptcy lawyer in the Seventh Circuit, and two, as a desperate parent turned tenacious international private investigator. He worked all morning putting out the usual fires in his bankruptcy practice, cramming a day's work in before lunch, so he could spend the afternoon on the phone to Washington. By day three, he was using Mack as well, to find information about the Peace Corps, Sierra Leone, the embassy there, and the names of people in the State Department who could make things happen in Freetown. By week's end, he had telephoned every relevant official in the State Department and the Peace Corps who would still take his calls.

The sympathetic administrative assistants to senators, congressional staffers, ambassadors, junior ambassadors, and state department bureaucrats offered him only earnest reassurances and extravagant descriptions of everything that was being done, and studiously avoided remarking on how little was being turned up. The telephone calls had given him the illusion that by explaining his tragedy over and over to voices at the other end of telephone lines, eventually he would project his terror and his anxiety somewhere outside himself, where it would then assume manageable proportions, take on the dimensions of just another serious problem that could be solved by doing lots of hard work. He was networking into new circles of power, using his legal contacts and political connections, looking for a capable person who could solve his problems on the promise of a cashier's check or an international money order.

At last, Swanson hooked him up with the American Ambassador in Freetown, who in turn put him on conference call with some kind of chief named Idrissa Moiwo, an African who had been educated in England and America and spoke English. According to the Ambassador, Moiwo was an up-and-comer, about to win an election for something called Paramount Chief. He was the man in charge of Pujehun district, and he personally assured Randall that he would not rest until Michael Killigan was found. When Randall faxed the servant's letter to the American Embassy in Freetown, Chief Moiwo promptly expanded the manhunt to include a search for Michael's servant and the mysterious photographs.

"These photographs may explain everything," Moiwo had said, "if we can get our hands on them."

"There's something else you should know, Mr. Killigan," said the Ambassador. "Apparently, this isn't the first time your son has disappeared."

"It's the first time I've known about," said Randall defensively.

"Turns out that about six months ago or so, your boy joined one of these secret tribal societies," said the Ambassador. "Did he tell you anything about that?"

"He *joined* the tribe?" Randall said. "You're telling me now he thinks he's an African, or some damn thing?"

"He joined the men's secret society of the Mende tribe," said the Ambassador. "It's called the Poro Society. The initiation rites last more than a month. After the rumor came in, we checked around with the Peace Corps people responsible for him, and we found out he 'couldn't be found in his village,' as the local people say, for a month or so, because he was out in the bush getting initiated. The Peace Corps considers Poro and its supernatural politics off-limits. When the field supervisor finally caught up with him, your boy had tribal markings. Poro markings from the sounds of it, but who knows? The villagers don't like telling white people about it."

"Markings?"

"Incisions, small scars around the eyes on the temples. Then there's a pattern of dots on the back."

"Great," said Randall, imagining how his son might look in a power tie and a Hart, Schaffner & Marx suit, presiding over an unsecured creditors committee meeting on the eve of a plan confirmation hearing . . . with *tribal scars* around his eyes.

"These photos," Randall said, abruptly changing the subject away from his son's contributory negligence. "You say these photos may have something to do with his disappearance."

"Cameras can cause trouble in this part of the world," the chief added. "Africans love them and beg to be 'snapped,' but only if they get to keep the photo. Otherwise, they fear a piece of their soul may fall into the wrong hands. Some of the old ones say allowing yourself to be photographed shortens your life."

By way of illustration, the Ambassador faxed Randall the embassy's official warning to tourists not to take photographs:

Local Customs

It is traditional that on festive occasions costumed "devil dance" groups are formed. Usually the devil dance groups will be in the main streets or sections of the city. There are "good" devils and "bad" devils. A "bad" devil can sometimes turn violent and can also incite others in the group to violence. If you see a devil dance group in the street take an alternate street if possible. When driving, if you can't avoid the group, lock your doors, roll up your windows and drive slowly through the group.
DO NOT TAKE PHOTOGRAPHS.

But the chief seemed confident that the servant boy and the photos could be found. Here, at last, was a person who spoke Randall's language, for Moiwo bluntly suggested that money would help, because it would enable him to purchase another vehicle to conduct the search, and would also allow him to show Randall Killigan's generosity to the villagers, and perhaps even provide a reward for valuable information.

Randall sent the money by wire and took the Ambassador's advice that, given the election unrest and the armed revolution in Liberia, no possible good could come of a trip to Freetown. The Ambassador promised to call with any news whatsoever, and would be the first to let Randall know if his presence in Africa would help in the least.

After three days of insistent phone missions to Washington, Randall slumped back into his chair, alone, and stared. All these overseas phone calls and hours on hold to Washington politicos had not produced a single clue to his son's whereabouts.

At home, news of the initiation and tribal markings didn't faze Marjorie in the least, which Randall interpreted as a symptom of her mental deterioration under the strain of the crisis. In bed and unable to sleep, they argued about whether he should fly to Sierra Leone and talk to the Ambassador in person. Marjorie dropped off first, and left Randall in bed at midnight, grinding his teeth over the tribal markings and the secret tribal societies.

He took a warm bath with the latest issue of *Forbes*. Afterward, he found his wife's sleeping medication and poured two of the little blue capsules into the palm of his hand and stared at them. *Why am I taking sleeping medication?* he wondered, almost watching himself take pills he had never taken before. The anxiety was almost choking him. If he could force himself to sleep, maybe that would clear his head for the work that needed to be done tomorrow.

Back in bed, he finally fell into a trance, twitching awake when his heart skipped a beat, or when he remembered the words of the State Department report, and had dreams about his son roaming the bush paths hungry for the souls of witchmen.

Sometime later, he heard a loud, disorienting sound and woke up in a night sweat. His heart boomed in his chest, and the digital clock burned a red 3:34 a.m. into the blackness at his bedside table. He looked up from his bed toward the light of the bay windows, searching for the source of the sound, and saw . . . what could have been just a side effect of the pills.

He saw or dreamed that he saw a bat in his own bedroom. A huge bat. He saw it by the muddy glow from the night light in the corner, just enough visibility to make him wonder if he was of sound mind and vision. At first, he concluded that he was hallucinating, because the thing was so big, with a three- or four-foot wingspan, big enough to darken the bedroom bay windows. He almost felt his ear cup itself and grow toward the fluttering image, straining to hear the whisper of leather wings.

Then it almost deafened him with a loud *thwock!* that sounded like a piece of wood hitting a sounding board. Then *thwock!* again—terrifyingly close to him and so loud he could feel sound rushing around his face like a current.

Randall crawled across the floor to his closet and got a tennis racket (which someone had told him was the best weapon for killing a bat). He crawled over to the bedroom door, snaked his arm up the wall, and turned on the lights, exposing the thing in the sudden garish light of four sixty-watt bulbs in the ceiling fixture.

The bat shot directly overhead, so close he could see the massive span of its fingered wings, its furry torso, its shrieking face, which he glimpsed in one vivid instant, before blinking in terror. It had the head of a dog, or even a small horse, with a hideous, swollen snout, and lips bristling with warts or tumors. The eyes were large, innocent pools of blackness, staring in wonder, almost as if the creature did not quite believe in Randall either.

Randall ducked and blinked, the image of the grotesque head still shining in his memory. Again he heard the faintest rustle of wings, ridiculously delicate when compared to the swooping drama of its flight and the deafening *thwock!* filling his bedroom.

He covered the top of his head with his arms so the beast wouldn't get caught in his hair. When he looked up again, it was gone.

In retrospect, he probably should have awakened Marjorie first, and warned her that there was a bat in the room, and that he was going to turn on the light and kill it. Instead, she woke up terrified and irritated with him. She never even saw the bat. She saw only her husband, standing in his underwear with a tennis racket in his hand, yelling and looking as if he had seen a three-headed dog guarding the gates of hell.

The neighbors heard his yelling, the *thwock!* of the bat, or both, and called the police. The police couldn't find the bat either. They listened patiently while Randall emphatically told them how big it was, that it had a wingspan of at least three feet and a hideous horse's face. He may have caught them winking at each other once, but they were otherwise respectful and polite. They consoled him by telling him that bats always look bigger than they really are. They agreed with him that nothing was uglier than a bat's face. They said that single sightings of birds, bats, squirrels, and other rodents in dwellings were quite common, but if the creatures got into the house, they usually found their way back out again. He was probably rid of the thing and shouldn't worry, they said.

But worry he did. He got back in bed and waited, almost hoping the thing would reappear, because he wanted to know if he had actually seen it. Could an otherwise normal, highly intelligent, well-disciplined, successful attorney wake up in the middle of the night and *imagine* he had seen a winged creature in sumptuous, hideous detail? True, he had been asleep. True, he had taken two of Marjorie's sleeping pills—something he had never done! Maybe it had gotten in somehow and simply *appeared* to be five times bigger because of some trick of refracted light or a short circuit in Randall's racing imagination.

He had no idea where it came from, or where it went. Mental illness was out of the question . . . or was it? Could some metabolic disorder, or an imbalance in brain chemistry, an electrical disturbance, or a freak seizure erupt in one sudden, vivid hallucination, then disappear without a trace? Well, there were traces. Things were . . . shinier, a little brighter. The world looked almost wet, and the surfaces of things seemed overly smooth and bursting with color.

The next day, he settled into a permanent lethargy, punctuated only by catnaps and fits of anxiety. Was his son being held by rebels? Interrogated? Was he already dead? Was he in pain? Was he— Randall—now suffering from mental illness? Shock? Was this bat sighting the first symptom of a serious medical disorder?

His pretrial heart rhythm galloped into a day-of-trial frenzy, even though he had only minor hearings on the horizon. If an intelligent force governed the universe, it had a malicious sense of humor, for it had outfitted Randall, the bankruptcy warlord, with the heart of a neurasthenic invalid. He hated his heart. He wanted to trade it in for the heart of a warrior—one that would not distract him with arrhythmias on the eve of battle. He wanted the heart of the *Challenger* astronaut he had seen on TV, whose pulse was 64 fifteen seconds before takeoff. Instead he was stuck with an erratic ticker that skipped beats, then raced ahead in a string of pounding beats, as if to make up for lost blood. Sometimes it even woke him up at night. During a trial—whether it lasted a week or two months—he could finger his pulse at the artery in his wrist, day or night, and wait less than a minute to feel the world stand still during the skipped beat.

According to his high school buddy, Howard Bean, a prominent neurosurgeon, Randall's skipped heartbeats were harmless arrhythmias. Over the last few years, Randall had seen Bean at the Indiana University Hospital about his heart, and about a host of other physical annoyances, which seemed to have popped up just as Randall was really hitting his stride on his Seventh Circuit campaign. Bean had sent Randall to a cardiologist, who had sent him to a pulmonary function specialist for cardiac testing. . . . It was caused by stress, they said. It did not require medication, but Randall should watch himself.

Randall had told the doctors to go try their quackery on some other helpless duck. He wasn't buying. The episode had confirmed his suspicion that, like everyone else, doctors have an almost irresistible tendency to find what they are looking for. Saying that stress suddenly started causing his heart to skip beats made about as much sense as him showing up with cancer and having them tell him it was because he had entirely too much water in his diet. Stress was the air he had been breathing since day one of law school. Stress separated warriors from boys and girls. Stress was what happened when the dean addressed Randall's entering law school class of two hundred or so young, bright, anal-compulsive, overachieving college graduates and told them in so many words that if they wanted a good job and a lot of money when they got out of law school, they should take infinite pains to be absolutely certain that they were *all* in the top 10 percent of their class. Stress was the gleam in their eyes and the dawning revelation that, though they were unarmed and confined in classrooms and libraries with nothing but paper and books and perhaps writing utensils, they had to eliminate 90 percent of their peers without leaving any marks on the bodies. Under these extreme conditions, Randall the warrior quickly discovered that his intellect was a perfectly serviceable weapon.

And law school was stress kindergarten, because after that, all the really bright, completely anal-compulsive, outrageously overachieving law school graduates who actually *did* wind up in the top 10 percent of their class went on to earn big salaries in huge firms. Once there, the senior partners told these elite intellectual combatants that if they wanted to make partner in less than ten years and swim in sunken tubs full of money, they should take infinite pains to be absolutely certain that they were *all* in the top 10 percent of their associate class by the time they came up for partner. That was stress.

He had to laugh: *Doctors* presuming to lecture *him* about stress? All they had to do was get into med school, and residencies were waiting for them four years later. And what kind of pressure did they work under? If they fucked up on the job, one retired bus driver might croak on the table before he could run up higher hospital bills. You call that stress? If Randall fucked up on the job, entire financial empires could collapse in the space of a two-hour hearing. Institutional investors could shun stocks and kill his client on the basis of a single rumor or a single mistake in a prepackaged Chapter 11 plan. That's stress! And thank God for it, because otherwise, how do you separate really excellent lawyers from simply good ones?

Because Randall hated most doctors, he frequently took his illnesses first to his buddy Bean, who also arranged for any tests to be done on Sundays, typically the only free day in Randall's schedule. The regular doctors were not so accommodating. His family doctor, his cardiologist, his gastroenterologist, and his orthopedic surgeon all thought Randall was a raving hypochondriac, which of course he was not. His doctors were accustomed to treating patients who paid no attention to their health. Their patients were working-class drudges who *liked* being sick, because it meant they could stay home from work. Randall, on the other hand, was obliged to keep a weather eye on his health, because his exceptional career left precious little time for distractions. Even the suspicion of a serious illness could impair his performance in bankruptcy court, so he found it best to eliminate suspicions as they arose. Like the department he ran, his body had to be lean, profitable, and productive, with no slack in the lines for slackers or sickness. Internal organs, like employees, had to be responsive and dependable. Symptoms and performance deficiencies had to be promptly investigated, addressed, and rectified.

•

Dr. Howard Bean was the Chief of Neurosurgery at the Indiana University Hospital. He had square steel-rimmed eyeglasses, a runner's trim physique, and the unflappable mien of a scientist who was amused when the rest of the human race based most of its decisions on phobias and other assumptions that were unsupported by reliable data. Bean specialized in the study of magnetic fields in the brain and their applications for brain surgery. He was flush with lucrative grants from the National Institutes of Health, and was eager to try out the department's new superconducting quantum interference device—a SQUID scan. Because he had set the day aside for research, he wore blue jeans and a white lab coat, and had no plans to see any patients. He had just prepared a volunteer for scanning and had summoned several fellows to help him, when he received word from his secretary that his friend Randall Killigan was in the clinic waiting to see him.

Howard was quite accustomed to Randall airing his medical anxieties—it was a running semi-comic routine—but these sessions usually took the form of late-night phone calls, which Bean patiently fielded as a trusted companion. Until today, Randall's visits to his office had been confined to Sunday afternoons.

Randall was a good friend and highly amusing. A classic example of an exceedingly high intelligence devoted almost exclusively to irrational pursuits and nearly overwhelmed by his own eccentricities, fetishes, and ritualistic behaviors. But in Bean's mind this was a common failing of intelligent laypeople; their woefully inadequate training in math and the hard sciences allowed them to believe in things like the lottery, oat bran, or animal rights. Most of what Bean knew about the legal profession he had learned from Randall. As far as Bean could tell, the law consisted mostly of incantations and time-honored spells which had to be found in something called "precedent" and then recited or set down in documents for judges, who then either took up the chorus of magic words or called forth their own conjurations to dispel those put forth by the attorneys.

But the ironic kettle of contradictions that made Randall the lawyer an amusing friend also made him an abusing patient. Patient Randall had an insane fear of X rays, radiation from CAT scans, any sort of microwave or electromagnetic field. A common superstition, easy enough to deal with under most circumstances, except that patient Randall had an even more insane fear of cancer, so much so that he was truly at peace only after being scanned and shown images that conclusively proved he did not have cancer. Once the scan or the X rays were a month or two behind him, patient Randall came back, afraid that the scan itself may have caused a cell to mutate, and convinced that only another scan or a different, safer diagnostic test could persuade him that he was free of cancer.

Bean found Randall in his waiting room, shouting expletives into the telephone receiver at an operator who had bungled the administration of a four-way conference call. By the time they made it into an examination room, the patient had regained his composure, at least enough for Bean to notice that the arteries of the head and neck no longer stood out and only the major veins were still visible.

"Let me be straightforward about this," Randall said tersely. "Last night, I may have had a serious symptom of some kind."

"Aw, c'mon, Randall," said Bean, taking a seat and kicking his feet up onto a gurney. "Not your heart again. We're putting you on the treadmill twice a year! I have to pay those people time and a half to come in here on Sunday afternoons."

"Fuck you," said Randall. "Who gets you and your partners' taxes done for next to nothing? Who drew up your partnership agreements? Who drafted you a prenuptial agreement so you could get that first marriage out of the way for nothing?"

Bean threw up his hands. "I can't keep running these tests on you every time you get heartburn, Randy. The insurance company's giving me hell and for a good reason: THERE'S NOTHING WRONG WITH YOU! Go back to your office and sue people. No, wait. Take a vacation. Find a hobby that doesn't involve weapons or the martial arts or cussing at people on the phone."

"What about fucking computer games?" said Randall. "What about Tank Commander? That's a hobby. I love Tank Commander."

"More stress," said Bean. "Commanding tank platoons is not relaxing. I've seen you. You look like you're killing snakes with that joystick."

"Look, Howard. I'm not kidding this time. I think something happened to me."

"What? Your back again? I told you the bone scans, the X rays, the lumbar series, everything is negative. I know you read somewhere that cancer frequently presents with lower back pain. But you have been scanned to shreds and there's nothing in there, except spinelessness."

"It's not my back. It's not my heart."

"Your stomach again? Upper GI, lower GI, barium enema, ERCP.

You're clean! The ulcers aren't there yet. Give them a year or two more of this kind of behavior. They'll show up! Maybe you can *will* them into existence if you concentrate on it hard enough."

"It's not my stomach," said Randall.

"Your teeth? Did you quit wearing your bite block to bed? That's a perfect example of how you operate. First it was jaw pain. You swore it was metastatic CA of the mandible. We scanned you. Nothing. The jaw pain didn't go away. We sent you to a dentist, who sent you to an orthodontist. Remember why? Remember what the orthodontist said? '*The* worst case of nocturnal grinding of the teeth that I have seen in my thirty-seven years of orthodontic practice.' His initial clinical impression was that you had gone over your molars with a double-cut machine file."

"My teeth are OK," Randall yelled. "I wear the goddamn bite block every night, OK?"

Bean dropped his feet to the floor and scooted himself foursquare in front of his friend.

"Randy, just once, listen to me. You are under tremendous stress. You work too hard. All day long, you cuss at people on the phone. Every time I call down there, you're swearing at someone on another line. Have you ever listened to yourself? Leave your Dictaphone on sometime. Studies have shown that subjects who cuss on the phone all day secrete excess bile, which makes them bilious, and distempered. Do you want to borrow my copy of *The Anatomy of Melancholy*? You've heard of the four humours? Get at least one. Get a sense of humor and go back to work. All this cussing of yours, all this swearing causes people to dislike you. It makes you splenetic, liverish, phlegmatic, choleric, and some would say just plain full of shit! This in turn causes more stress, and pretty soon stress hens are laying stress eggs everywhere and hatching more stress. Find something relaxing. I know you hate television. So go fishing!"

Planning fishing trips was a standing joke between two guys who didn't have time to order a rod out of a mail-order catalogue, much less squander a whole day boating in some mudhole with their cellular phones, pretending a twelve-pack of beer had relaxed them.

"I'm sure it's a symptom," said Randall. "Nothing like this has ever happened to me before."

"OK," said Howard, grabbing a notepad. "Are we going to do this? I guess we are. Where is the pain?"

"I wish it was pain," said Randall. "I don't have any pain. I saw something. I think it was some kind of hallucination. I'm almost positive I was awake when I saw it."

"Almost positive?" said Howard with a scowl. "Did this happen at night, and were you lying in bed grinding your teeth, with your eyes closed, cussing at people in your dreams?"

"I was awake," said Randall. "I think I woke up because I heard a loud sound. Then I saw a huge bat flying around the light fixture in my bedroom. Nobody else saw it, and we couldn't find the thing afterward."

"You don't need a doctor," said Howard. "You need an exterminator."

"We called one the next day," said Randall. "No bat. No evidence of bats in the attic. No evidence of entry."

Howard sighed mightily. "Randall, bats sometimes get into houses. We had a bat in our bedroom when we first moved into the house."

"How big was your bat?" asked Randall.

"How *big*? It was a bat. You know, like a mouse with wings."

Randall held his head in his hands. "See what I mean? The one I saw was like a *dog* with wings. Big. Huge!"

"You have a ceiling fan in that bedroom, don't you? That's it. You saw the blades of that fan, and the moonlight or maybe a night light made them look like bat wings."

Randall stared into his friend's eyes and swallowed. "Howard, I stood underneath four sixty-watt bulbs and stared this thing in the face," he said levelly. "This wasn't a shadow. This was vivid, you understand? It was as real as you and me. It was hideous, like something out of Africa."

Randall rubbed his face in his hands. "I'm almost afraid to go on about it, because what if it wasn't real? What if I *imagined* something that ugly? It had swollen lips with growths or tumors of some kind all over them. It had fingers in its wings. It had huge, black, wet eyes. I think I even saw my own reflection in them."

Howard's mouth opened.

"Can somebody imagine something so completely out of nothing?" pleaded Randall. "Is there such a thing as one sudden, vivid hallucination? For no reason, out of nowhere? Followed by a return to normal perception?"

"You've had no other visual disturbances?" asked Howard.

"No," said Randall quickly. "Well, I've only seen the one bat. But since that night," he said, his voice trailing off as he looked over Bean's head, "things have a certain shiny quality. Everything seems too . . . bright. Does that make sense? Things are more . . . colorful, or even . . . more beautiful," he said, staring off, briefly sampling and reporting on his perceptions. "Almost like I'm *seeing* more. Can the pupil of your eye get stuck open and admit too much light? So that things look brighter?"

Howard peered into his old friend's face.

"Listen, Howie, I need to forget about this thing. All I want is an explanation, and then I'll be able to put it behind me. Have you ever heard of anything like this before?"

"Perhaps," said Howard gravely. "Usually there is a history of mental illness, especially in your case," he added with a smile. "I'm ruling out schizophrenia and any psychotic episodes. It would be very unusual for someone to experience sudden, vivid hallucinations. Very unusual, but not unheard of."

"So you've heard of something like this happening to a normal person before!?" Randall cried.

"It's very rare," said Howard.

"What is it?" begged Randall. "What causes it?"

Howard shook his head, as if suddenly changing his mind. "Let's go with a wait-and-see plan here. It could be metabolic, it could be psychological. Let's just see if it happens again."

"No," said Randall. "Tell me what you were thinking."

Howard pulled out his appointment book. "Look, this is no different than anything else we've ever done, OK? I always send you to somebody else who actually does the testing, right? But this may, *may* be a neurological problem, so I'm sending you to one of our neurologists. Understand? I'm going to have you see Carolyn Gillis about this and let her decide how to handle it."

Randall was on his feet. "No way. Not in a million years. You think it's something neurological. You are going to tell me what it could be right now, and then we are doing the test before I leave."

Howard closed his appointment book.

"OK," he said, walking away from Randall and toward the door. "You're going to radiology for an MRI scan. Now."

Randall turned white and stared.

"Wait a minute," said Randall. "Why are we getting a scan?"

"What do you mean?" said Howard. "Why do we scan you twice a year? So we can tell you nothing's there. That's why."

"But you always tell me I don't *need* a scan," said Randall suspiciously. "You always emphatically tell me that I do not need a scan. You always say you'll give me your house if there is something there."

"There's nothing there," said Howard. "I just want to be able to *say* there's nothing there and have a scan back me up on it."

.

Forty-five minutes later, two technicians in white lab coats slid Randall's body into a long, smooth tube. Randall told himself it was harmless magnetic resonance imaging, but he suspected that these rays were relatives of carcinogenic electromagnetic fields from power lines, and he could feel deep tumors swelling in the glow of the radiation, like tulip bulbs sprouting in the sun's warmth.

Inside the tube, he felt like Ramses II, slid into his coffin prematurely. Then he heard a whirring sound and had the impression that he was an axle in a wheel, or a cylinder in an orrery or armillary sphere, and some great omniscient device was spinning around him like a turbine, seeing deep inside of him where nothing human had ever ventured, where light had never been, shaving him into cellophane planes to be studied on color computer monitors by scientists.

Back upstairs, he paced the examination room while trying to read an article about computer memory management. Bean came in with a pained expression on his face.

"What?" asked Randall.

"It's inconclusive," said Howard, looking away.

"That's a new one," said Randall with a catch in his voice. "What's inconclusive?"

"There's something there," Bean said, and stopped himself. "Let's be precise. There *may* be something there, but *if* it's there, we don't know what it is."

Gravity sat Randall back in his chair. He felt one skip in his chest, and then the pounding sent heat waves into his face.

"There is no reason to be alarmed," Bean said evenly, looking hard at Randall, "unless we do a different kind of scan and some more tests and actually identify something."

"But what did they see?" said Randall, aghast.

"The people in radiology call them UBOs. An unidentified bright object. The pictures of your MRI scan showed a bright intensity in the deep white matter. But it's nonspecific. They don't know what it is. It could be any number of things, so we will eliminate the possibilities, one by one, by doing specific tests."

"What kind of tests?"

"A CAT scan, an angiogram, a spinal tap, myelography, maybe a positron emission tomography scan . . . But those have to wait until tomorrow."

"Oh, great!" yelled Randall. "Now I can go home with a bright object in my head and lie in bed all night. What do they *think* it is? What do these things usually turn out to be? And how would this bright object make me see a bat?"

"If you were a patient," said Howard, "I wouldn't tell you any of this until I had all my data. The location of the anomaly could, *could* suggest peduncular hallucinosis."

"Which is?" asked Randall without breathing.

"Rare," said Howard. "Very rare. Isn't everything? But knowing how rare something is affords scant comfort once you have it. But you probably don't have it, OK?"

"What is it? What causes it? Is it a virus, or what?"

"The cardinal symptom of peduncular hallucinosis is spontaneous, brilliant hallucinations which present themselves in excruciating detail. It's caused by strokes or injury to the cerebral peduncles or the midbrain near the brain stem, which is where the radiologist saw the bright object in the deep white matter, the UBO."

"Stroke!" Randall said, a skipped beat followed by the trademark pounding. "I haven't had a stroke."

"I hope not," said Howard with a smile that fell just shy of consoling him.

"And I haven't been injured. Nothing's happened to me. No recent trauma."

"Injury is a broad medical term," Howard said. "Any midbrain dysfunction: encephalitis, lesions, craniopharyngioma . . . Injury means anything from an infarct to a blow to the head, to any lesion or . . . neoplasm."

"What?" said Randall. "What's that?"

"Infarct?"

"Neoplasm, you shithead," Randall shouted. "What's a fucking neoplasm? And that thing you said that had 'oma' on the end of it."

"A neoplasm is any new . . . growth," said Howard. "Look, don't let yourself run away with this thing. It's pure speculation until we get data . . ."

"New growth," said Randall, using the wind knocked out of his lungs. "You think I don't know what you're saying! Say it to me, you fuck!"

"Most new growths are benign," said Howard. "OK, not most. *Many* new growths are benign. Well, OK, in the brain, *some* new growths are benign."

Randall suddenly remembered something and started up, causing Howard to lean back in his chair.

"It was a joke you told. We were at a Christmas party," Randall said, staring over Howard's head as if memory were a mountain range spread out across the wall.

"Somebody was saying that their father had something wrong with his heart, and they were complaining because it was a heart attack but the cardiologist wouldn't use those words; he kept telling the family it was a coronary event. And they were like, what's a coronary event? And you defended the cardiologist. You told them how important it is to keep a cardiac patient calm. And afterward, we were riding home in your car, and you said, 'Can you believe those morons? They want their cardiologist to call a heart attack a heart attack. You can just see the patient,' you said. You were clutching your chest, and we were laughing. You said, 'Hey, Doc, what's happening to me?' And then you said, 'You? That's easy. I've seen it a thousand times. You're having a heart attack! But do stay calm.'

"That's what you're doing to me now, isn't it? It's a neospasm or whatever, not a tumor. It's pediculosis or something; it's not a stroke. What the fuck do you think it is? Talk to me!"

"You're panicking over the very small chance that you have a malignancy or a structural defect," said Bean. "I still think it's a fluke, one-time freak of the imagination caused by emotional stress. And the UBO is a false positive. That's what I think."

"*Please* don't say it's stress," said Randall, gritting his teeth and lunging at the neurologist. "Stress makes me high, do you understand? Stress makes me secrete testosterone and endorphins. It's brain candy, OK? I like to make myself sick on the stuff every day, understand?"

"I've known you since you were sixteen," said Howard. "I don't need your history. I'm just telling you that when you start getting older, as we all do, stress can do funny things to you."

"Sure," Randall sneered. "Very funny things. I guess that's why I'm laughing most of the day. It's a big conspiracy with you guys. You never really come clean with the patient. I know. I lie to my clients every day. The truth would kill them!"

"I told you exactly what the radiologist told me," said Bean.

"Sure," Randall said. "I'd love to hear what the radiologist said. 'Looks like a tumor, but the patient is a lawyer, so we better be damn sure before we use the C-word.'"

"He did not say that," argued Bean. "I told you what he said. I explained it using the same terms the people in radar use. It's an unidentified bright object on your MRI scan, and we won't know anything more until we do more tests."

"Right," said Randall with a roll of his eyeballs.

"OK," Howard said suddenly. "I can solve this. I'm calling my radiologist. You'll like him because he cusses a lot, and he has a string of bleeding ulcers to prove it. I'll see that you get unadulterated information from a real expert, the Randall Killigan of Radiology."

Howard pressed a button on one of the phones, raising an announcement of "Switchboard" from the speaker.

"Radar," said Howard.

A ringing tone was followed by another voice. "Radiology," it said.

"This is Bean. Is Ray still on?"

"One moment, please."

"Dr. Rheingold," said a voice.

"Ray, it's Bean. Patient name Killigan. The MRI you did for me this afternoon, what did you find?"

"Bean? I just talked to you half an hour ago. Go away. I told you, I'm dying down here. I'm supposed to be at my kid's birthday party. I already gave you the results."

"Tell them to me again," Howard said with a silent chuckle. "I lost my notes."

A heavy sigh filled the speaker with static. "Bean, I think you should do some research into an aberrant phenomenon you find in everybody except neurosurgeons. It's called *memory*. I read you the guy's MRI not forty-five minutes ago. It's a UBO. A hyperdense signal intensity on the T2-weighted phase in the deep white matter, right midbrain tegmentum and cerebral peduncle. OK? I dictated it. It's being typed up now. It'll be up there in an hour, so you can read it in case you forget it again. UBO, remember? An unidentified bright object. A bright intensity in the deep white matter, to be exact. And this is the Indiana University Medical Center. My staff and I are here to serve you. It was a pleasure working with you and your staff, and I thank you once again, as the referral of your case was most insurance, I mean, most interesting. I have to go, Bean, but I hope my staff and I have the opportunity to assist you in the future."

"One more thing," said Howard with a look at Randall. "Do you think it's a malignancy?"

"Do I what? Did I *say* malignancy? I said a bright intensity in the deep white matter. A UBO, an unidentified bright object, but maybe in your case it's an unidentified hopelessly dull and obtunded object: your brain, Bean."

"But *could it be* a malignancy?" asked Bean.

Silence filled the speaker.

"Bean, I suspect you are up there sitting in a room filled with sunlight, maybe looking out the window at some trees rustling in an autumn breeze. I've been down here in a dark room in the basement looking at ghosts of people's insides since five-thirty this morning. Is it the cocktail hour up there or what? The operative initial in the acronym UBO is U, for unidentified. Unidentified is a complex, obscure medical term that means we don't know what it is. It could be nothing. It could be an arteriovenous malformation, it could be an infarct, it could be a malignant tumor, it could be a benign meningioma, it could be a cyst, it could be a piece of shrapnel from a hand grenade thrown at My Lai, it could be a new computer chip from Intel which was implanted so the guy could use cellular technology without the inconvenience of lugging a phone around. I DON'T KNOW WHAT IT IS. Do you know why I don't know? BECAUSE IT'S UNIDENTIFIED, THAT'S WHY. It could be a napkin ring. It could be Caesar's remains, for all I know. No, wait, it's Brutus's remains, yeah, that's it. No, hold on, it's a bone fragment from the attending neurosurgeon's skull, dating back to a cerebral vascular accident that scattered good Dr. Bean's brains all over the examination room. Further tests may show that it's the Holy Grail. A skull series could detect a piece of the copper astrolabe of Shiraz for all I fucking know, OK?

"But let me take this opportunity to thank you once again for sending us this most interesting referral, and please be aware that our department has recently added a new positron emission tomography scan which will assist us in serving you with the latest technology. Please call me or my staff with more insurance, I mean, with more interesting cases like this one. Let me say thank you once again."

Howard turned off the speakerphone and looked at his friend.

"Dr. Rheingold's bedside manner is really quite professional," said Bean, "but I figured you wouldn't trust that. You heard him. There may be something there, but we don't know what it is. We have to do more tests."

(5)

Outside the restaurant, children took Boone and his drunken escort by their pockets and pulled them toward stalls and mats spread with wares along the sidewalks, where their mothers and sisters, dressed in headwraps and frocks, sold brochettes and pineapple slices, jewelry and flip-flops, groundnuts and fried plantain. White men smelling of alcohol had a way of spreading money around. Boone sensed the excitement in the children, who knew that if they could just strike the proper chord with these white big men, they would be showered in wealth. Sometimes these lugs would give three or four months' pay for a carving that wasn't worth a sick fowl.

Even after his gargantuan repast in the bar, Lewis grazed out of the food stalls, haggling with the ten-year-old girls over the price of their snacks.

"Ten-ten leone? Ih too dear, I tell you. You no go less me small?"

"Na all day long I been sell dem so, mastah. I no go less you small."

"Less me five-five leone," he said. "Let me have the sweet one dae foh five leone."

"Put two leone on top, krabbit man. You too dry eye."

After more unceremonious gorging, they staggered out to the roundabout in search of taxis. Buses, crammed full of black bodies hanging out of glassless windows, streamed out of the roundabouts, blaring African and reggae music; each bus had a young boy with one foot on the running board and a handhold on the luggage rack, calling out the destination of the transport: "Wilbahfoss! Wilbahfoss! Wilbahfoss!"

In the last century, explained Lewis, the mountain villages had two names, one English, one African, and when the villages became suburbs of Freetown, it was the English names that survived: Wilberforce, Leicester, Regent, Gloucester, Leopold, Charlotte, Bathurst, York.

They took a taxi to the Peace Corps rest house, high up in the foothills forested in palms and mahogany, with long, looping roads cut into steep grades, where the British had originally settled to escape the mosquitoes breeding in the low-lying marshes and the poverty breeding in the slums of East Street and Kroo town. When the British left, the European mining company officials, wealthy Lebanese merchants, Sierra Leonean government ministers, and American Embassy or USAID employees moved into the old British neighborhoods and built more whitewashed compounds, gated and fenced, manned by old Krio pas snoozing in their watchmen's hammocks, guarding the Audis and Mercedeses. As Lewis told it, these compounds were staffed with squadrons of servants tending the grounds, keeping house, and minding the children of people with money.

"Labor," he said, "is the cheapest commodity in the country. Cheaper than palm oil, cocoa, coffee, or any of the cash crops. You can hire adults who are willing to work twelve hours a day for the cost of their children's school fees. For a hundred bucks a month, a whole retinue of servants will follow you around, cooking your food, washing your clothes, raising your kids, guarding the house. If you start a company, you can pay good men with strong backs three dollars a day to hack out the tree stumps on your farm with a cutlass or sift through snake-infested swamp mud for diamonds. When the snakes and disease vectors wipe out the workforce, you go back to the villages and hire a new crew."

As they talked, the driver turned off the taxi's ignition and coasted down a sloping stretch of road, swerving to avoid pedestrians and stopped cars. At the bottom of the hill, he restarted the engine for the ascent up the other side.

"Saves gas," Lewis observed, "but it's hell on the brakes, even though brakes are only used as an absolute last resort. Once fuel is burned to get going, nobody wants to squander it all by applying brakes. Most taxis don't have brake pads. You take your life in your hands."

"White man no take life in hand," the driver suddenly said. "White man take drivah's life in hand, notoso?"

After a fifteen-minute journey up into the hills the taxi coasted into the driveway of the Peace Corps rest house. The driver must have been the brother of the one that had brought Boone in from the airport, for they both drove bargains better than they drove their cabs. The haggling started out with the driver at the equivalent of about $1.75 and Lewis at 40 cents. After five minutes of strenuous dickering, the fare was fluctuating between 90 cents and a $1.10, depending upon whether it was customary to charge more for an extra passenger, a bitterly contested sticking point. Finally, the parties insulted one another and broke off negotiations at 100 leones, or one American dollar. Boone resisted the temptation to ask about the going rate for a taxi from the airport.

"All that bickering for sixty cents?" Boone asked.

"It's the principle, not the money," Lewis said. "If you're white they try to stiff you every time."

The rest house sat atop a terrace crudely landscaped with stones, shrubbery, and rock gardens strewn under the trunks of splendid palms. The smell of salt arrived on a faint breeze that stirred the fronded shrubbery and opened winking blue peepholes to the sea. Gecko lizards crept in and out of crevices, their skins the texture of sandpaper and the color of stained glass, their heads atilt with an anxious curiosity, watching the white men with first one eye, then the other, before they disappeared in a blaze of changing colors that seemed to steam off of them and hang in the air like rainbows in a mist.

It was resort weather outside, but the interiors of the rest house offered nothing resembling resort accommodations. The walls were whitewashed concrete stained with rust from window grillworks and slashed screens. A ceiling fan wobbled along on ball bearings that rattled in their races. Upside-down geckos clung to the rafters, motionless, except for their tiny, panting lungs; their black eyes bulging and staring, as if they were interior domesticated gargoyles charged with scaring away intruders.

An old pa, fresh from a nap, greeted them and showed first Lewis, then Boone, to their rooms. Boone's featured a rancid mattress with no frame or box springs, draped in a torn mosquito net. Shredded curtains hung motionless over the window grilles. The fetor of the mattress hung in the air, suspended by humidity so dense it verged on condensation. *Nothing half as nice as the Hotel Berlioz,* he thought, longing for the crisp October mornings he had spent idling among the slumbering corpses.

During the night, he heard taps on the door and girlish voices. "Peace Koh, you want friend? Oo, Peace Koh, you want friend?"

Lewis must have let them in. A skinny girl in a grimy rayon dress appeared at Boone's bedside.

"Peace Koh," she said. "You want friend?"

Her eyes shone in the crooked hollows of her face. Her hair was ratted into tufts clipped with plastic red barrettes.

"No," he said, watching her sit on the side of his bed.

"Whay you wife?" the woman asked.

"I don't have a wife."

"You no get wife? Me, I no get man. I go want make you me friend."

Her left cheekbone must have been broken at one time, along with her nose. On one side of her throat was a raised scar the size and color of a leech. He glanced from her shining eyes to the neckline of the dress, where he could see empty breasts folded and drooping under her hollow clavicle.

"I don't want a friend," said Boone.

She looked down where his eyes had been and touched her scar. "Dirty water self can out fire," she said.

"What?" said Boone, embarrassed that she had so easily seen him appraising her.

"Dirty water self can out fire," she repeated.

He turned his head away from her on the pillow. "I don't know what that means," he said. "I have no money."

He heard giggling from the other room, then hollering from Lewis and laughter from Lewis's consort.

"It's a Krio proverb," Lewis yelled. "Dirty water itself can put out a fire. Make do with what you have. Something is better than nothing. You can't always get what you want. You na gentry man," he said, lapsing into Krio and giggling with his companion. "You get plenty money, now share am, and sex dat sweeteye gal. Keep your raincoat on, though, boy, there's no telling what they got."

She lifted the mosquito net and curled up next to him.

He could still hear Lewis chortling through the wall. "Gentry man say he no get money. Na lie! Botobata!"

"Botobata," Lewis's companion repeated with a snicker.

"What's botobata?" Boone asked wearily.

"Nonsense!" yelled Lewis. "Bullshit! Hogwash! Horsefeathers! Bibble-babble! Twiddle-twaddle! Gibble-gabble! Skimble-skamble! Botobata!"

More laughter.

"Gentry man no get money," Lewis's companion said, sucking her teeth and giggling. "Ay, bo, I no believe ahm. Botobata!"

"Malarkey!" said Lewis. "Pishposh! Bunkum! Piffle! Humbug! Hokum! Hooey! Bosh! Moonshine! Bushwa! Flapdoodle! Fiddle-deedee!"

A breathless pause came through the wall. "Botobata!" they both hollered, pealing laughter and thumping the mattress.

Five minutes later, Boone hazarded a peek over his shoulder and found his partner sleeping. After a while, he heard Lewis grunting through the wall.

"Yeah," he said. "That's fine-O. I like dat too much. Beaucoup bread and jam dae foh you na morning."

At dawn, Boone watched an old pa in ragged shorts and a safari jacket set out a tray of bread, a bowl of margarine, some jelly, and a pot of coffee. Upon closer inspection, the bread was stale and rimed with mold, the margarine was lard dyed yellow, the jelly was see-through pink pectin, and the coffee was a pot of boiled water with a couple measures of coffee grounds stirred into it. The geckos were winding up a night of devouring insects, killing off a few strays before retiring again to the eaves. Boone left the sleeping woman and went out to a table in the common area, where he dipped stale bread into hot brown water.

After a few minutes, she appeared at his elbow, looking even skinnier by day.

"You keep something for me?" she said, putting out her hand. "I no get money."

Boone gave her two hundred leones. She put one piece of bread in her pocket and another in her mouth and left.

In the shower, the hot and cold taps both delivered freezing cold water. He clenched his teeth and got out before he had finished washing.

After Boone emerged, Lewis went in, and spent fifteen minutes under the arctic spray contentedly singing "Roland the Headless Thompson Gunner," by Warren Zevon.

After breakfast, a taxi took them back into Freetown and dropped them at the massive cotton tree. Lewis advised that in this part of the world the cotton tree was a landmark, that it had been a land-mark since the Portuguese had landed, and that slaves had been traded in the shade of its limbs. Then he gave his charge a sly look, and asked, "What do you think of all the capes hanging from the limbs? Aren't they beautiful?"

"Right," said Boone. "Capes."

"Well den," Lewis said with a laugh, "you no get four eye."

They went to a lorry park next to an open-air market, where they were promptly set upon by hordes of children trying to sell them everything from cakes and chewing gum to jewelry, fingernail clip-pers, and key rings.

"Do you have a wallet?" Lewis asked.

"Money belt," said Boone.

"Congratulations. Experienced travelers use money belts; tourists with wallets get tiefed by the Tiefmahn," said Lewis, exaggerating his Krio. "The best pickpockets in the world live in Sierra Leone. I had a billfold stolen out of a pair of button-down Army pants. Women Volunteers have had money taken from their bras in the middle of the market. If you sleep in a room with bars on the windows, they'll steal your shirt with a fishing pole and a hook. Thieves are celeb-rities, famous for their daring and cunning, as long as they don't get caught. God help them if they get caught."

"What happens to them if they get caught?"

"It ain't pretty," said Lewis. "It makes Shirley Jackson's 'The Lottery' look like high tea."

The *podah-podah* for Pujehun was a small Japanese pickup, with a sheet-metal canopy and a luggage rack over a truck bed fitted out with wooden benches. Bob Marley's portrait was daubed on each door, and painted on the flap of the canopy overhead were the words LIVELY UP YOUSELF. The tires were as smooth as the dirt road, and Boone saw no hope for friction between the two surfaces.

Lewis got into a rhubarb with the driver, who had tried to charge them double. Lewis maintained it was because they were white; the driver pleaded that he had just made an innocent mistake. The driver gave a signal, and the loading process began. Boone followed several Africans onto the sheltered truck bed and took a seat on a wooden bench worn as smooth as a bone.

He discovered a latent claustrophobia as the driver escorted ten or twelve more adults—with as many children, goats, and chickens—into the lorry and onto the benches. The women wore tie-dyed gara cloths and headwraps. The children wore nothing, except small leather pouches of "medicine" tied to their arms and waists with strings. Some of them had huge umbilical hernias, which sprouted from their navels like bananas.

After the humans were loaded, in came bundles of hairy cassava roots, baskets of kola nuts, burlap bags, a woven cage containing two chickens ("fowl," the woman said, as she passed them to Boone, who relayed them on into the truck bed), another goat (this one had busted horns, was afflicted with mange, and had a sightless white eye bulging out of its socket), a basket of dried fish ("bonga"), a jug of petrol, a gallon of orange palm oil, a rack of Guinness stout bottles filled with kerosene and stoppered with waxed paper, several fifty-pound bags of rice, a case of motor oil, a roll of steel screen, stewpots filled with more dried fish, a bolt of country cloth, another jug of palm oil, a fardel of unknown shrubbery, a box of tools, a bald spare tire worn through to the fabric on one rim, more peekins passed from hand to hand until claimed by relatives, four fence posts, a spool of baling wire, a bag of cement, a rusted coffeepot stuffed with twine, a satchel of plastic thongs, and three dead chickens ("dead fowl") bound to a stick by their feet.

No sooner had all the bodies and goods been packed into the back of the lorry than in came a stream of soft bundles and bags, which the occupants wedged into every available crevice, until the lorry was packed as tightly as a golf ball. If everyone took a deep breath simultaneously, Boone thought, the ribs of the canopy would buckle like tin.

Meanwhile, the luggage rack on top was stacked eight feet high with bags of rice and peanuts, baskets of cocoa beans, more bolts of country cloth, and bundles of clothing and palm raffia. Young boys—"bobos," Lewis called them—ranging in age from ten to sixteen, helped load the lorry in exchange for reduced fare and a perch high atop the mounded luggage racks. Boone wondered if it might be safer on top, for he could then at least jump off if the thing tipped over.

The passengers bore the prolonged loading process with patience. An older woman engaged Lewis in an exchange which included a nod of her head in Boone's direction. Boone could make out the words "*poo-mui*," "belly," "run," and "peekin," after which the passenger compartment—Lewis included—erupted in laughter.

"What happened?" Boone asked, feeling his rib cage displace several parcels when he drew a speaking breath.

"She says she hopes you aren't another *poo-mui* with dysentery whose belly runs like a small peekin's, or else we'll be stopping and unloading all morning. Apparently the last *poo-mui* she rode with had to get out every five miles to trot into the bush and let his belly run."

Boone imagined the ordeal of unpacking the entire rear of the lorry and shifting the other passengers enough to create an opening large enough for an adult to exit; he shuddered at the magnitude of the task and the logistics of packing and repacking the three-dimensional jigsaw puzzle of cargo pieces.

"She says white men have the bellies of children, and that they are constantly sick with fever, runny belly, or headache. She wants to know if white people lie in bed sick all day in the land of *Poo*, and how they manage to stay so sick when they have so many powerful medicines and magical machines."

Once on the road, the passengers fell into a stupor induced by the concurrent forces of heat, overcrowding, bone shock, sweat, noise, and the odors of humans and animals. Every hill was a laborious fifteen-mile-per-hour ascent, during which the two-liter aluminum engine surged and groaned with no result other than a redoubling of the oily smoke wafting back into the ascending lorry. The ensuing descent was punctuated by the shrill whinny of padless brakes, the thud of ruts in the truck bed, and the creaking of welded joints in the canopy overhead. Each time the lorry bobbed and swayed up onto two wheels, the bobos atop the mountain of parcels screamed with terror and delight.

By midday, the inside of the *podah-podah* was a hothouse of sweating flesh. The humans and animals instinctively realized that the environment was unbearable and responded by lapsing into artificial comas. Everyone apparently had mastered the art of self-hypnosis, even Boone's Peace Corps escort. Boone tried it in spurts, but came to each time a child screamed or an animal defecated on the truck bed.

Sweat streamed into his lap, evaporated, and clung to him. The ruts in the laterite road were transmitted without interruption to the bones of his pelvis, as if the lorry's bench had been bolted directly to the axle. His shins suddenly broke out in a ferocious itch: the impulse to gouge them was so powerful that his fingernails would have produced an immediate bloodletting, except that he was pinioned on either side by sweating Africans.

The goat with the mooneye wormed his head up between the cage of fowls and a burlap bag and brayed at Boone, studying the white man with its blank eye.

The eye—white as milk, but swirling with the colors of a pearl—mesmerized him. The goat blinked, and a pale blue lid slid over the mooneye. As Boone stared through his misery, the eye acquired a wicked gleam, and the goat's braying became urgent and expressive, almost as phatic as human speech. In a trance of heat exhaustion and misery, Boone stared into the swollen, chatoyant eyeball and listened to the brays of the goat, as if the eye, or the goat, or an evil spirit within the goat was speaking to him in tongues, telling him in an ancient, arcane language: *You're an animal just like me*, the goat said. *You used to eat off vinyl countertops in an air-conditioned kitchen. Not anymore. Welcome to Wild Kingdom, white boy. Stick around. Maybe we can fix you up with an eye that looks just like mine.*

The goat brayed satanically, then took to butting children in an effort to vent misery with its head. A boy squatting in the center of the lorry bed scolded the goat, then casually upended it and tied its hooves together with cords. The child scowled, then parted a forest of human legs and shoved the goat under a bench.

Through the ribs of the lorry's canopy, Boone saw another planet consisting of a laterite road dropped like a thread in a sea of chlorophyll. Every half hour or so, the driver and the three bobos riding up front yelled, "Beef! Beef!" and swerved violently on the rutted highway, as knee-high animals scurried from under the wheels of the *podah-podah* and into the bush. These were bush deer the size of cocker spaniels, called duikers, or the fat rodents called cutting grass. Boone thought the driver was swerving to avoid the animals. Until one time the cry of "Beef!" went up and the axle welded to Boone's pelvis registered a soft thump. The driver pulled over, ran back along the highway, and came back swinging the carcass of a bush deer aloft and shouting jubilantly, "Beef!" One of the bobos dismounted, bound the hind legs, and handed the carcass aloft.

At the roadside villages, Boone saw black skin and brown dirt, structures made out of mud and dead vegetable matter, hemmed in on all sides by impenetrable green. The bodies had risen up out of the earth, cleared some of the green away, and built huts with zinc-pan roofs to live in. Other than the ubiquitous green of the bush, color appeared only in clothing. Gara cloths, robes, headwraps, and the lappas used to bind children to the backs of women provided a tie-dyed riot of colors and patterns.

After nine hours, Boone's joints locked up and blood no longer made it below his waist. Just before sunset, Lewis hollered ahead through the windowless cab and the lorry slowed.

"Get out at the junction," Lewis said. "Walk up the dirt path about a mile. You'll see people coming in from the farms. When you see them, say, 'Cusheo, paddy.' Hello, friend."

Boone stifled the urge to panic. "I thought you were coming with me."

"If you show up with me," Lewis advised, "Sisay might tell us both to get lost. If you show up alone and helpless and tell him you're a friend of Michael Killigan, he will never turn you out. Don't mention my name," he added. "You'll have an easier time of it."

"Cusheo, paddy," Boone repeated.

"Cusheo!" the passengers sang out with a laugh. "How de body?"

"Good," said Lewis. "After that, say, 'I no sabby talk Krio. I want make you show me usai dat white Mende man, Aruna Sisay, dae.' "

Boone repeated the words and jumbled them. The lorry riders laughed uproariously.

"How about just 'Usai Aruna Sisay,' " Lewis said. " 'Usai' means 'which side' or 'where.' If you need a place to stay, come back to this junction in the morning and wait for a *podah-podah* going south. Tell the driver you want to go to Pujehun."

Lewis spoke briefly to one of the women.

"You just bought that speckled fowl in the wicker cage to your right," Lewis said. "You also bought three kola nuts. When you get out, give her four hundred leones and take the fowl and the kola nuts to Aruna Sisay as gifts. Don't ever go to an African's house without bringing a present with you."

At the junction, the bobos opened a hole in the passenger compartment big enough to disgorge the *poo-mui*. His legs barely functioned, but he managed to pay the woman, and was handed the caged fowl and three smooth, pinkish, kidney-shaped kola nuts the size of throwing rocks. The bobos handed down his back-pack. The vulture-eyed goat crawled a goodbye from under the bench, and the passengers cried, "Cusheo, paddy!"

As the *podah-podah* pulled away, Lewis hollered out, "Stay in the village and don't go in the bush!"

Boone stooped to gather his backpack and gifts and jumped when he heard the sound of a human voice.

"Meestah West fall," the voice said, splitting Boone's name in two.

A small boy stood no more than fifteen feet from him. Either Boone had missed seeing the boy's approach, which was unlikely given the distance from the road to the bush path, or the boy had appeared like a hallucination.

He looked just shy of ten years. The fly of his dusty shorts had been sewn shut, and the waist puckered on each side where his belt loops had been tied together to take in the slack. One bare foot, gray with dust, stood on the other, and one skinny arm flopped over the top of his head dangling fingers that lazily scratched an ear. He twisted from side to side without moving his stacked feet. As soon as Boone looked into his big eyes, he looked away.

"Meestah West fall," the boy said again.

Boone was dumbfounded.

"Meestah Aruna say come," the boy said.

Before Boone could respond, the boy folded his legs into a squat, crawled under the backpack, and stood up with it balancing on his head.

"I'll carry that," Boone protested. "It's too big for you." But the boy was already walking away from him, his upper body perfectly steady under the pack, while his skinny legs crept up a rutted ascending path into the bush.

In short order, the path became a tunnel through a bower fronded with palm trees and strung with hairy vines the thickness of suspension cables. The humidity absorbed all ambient sound, as in a carpeted room with heavy drapes, leaving only the sough of their lungs and the thud of their feet on the earth. The screech and chatter of birds and animals seemed always just ahead of them, until Boone realized that the creatures were everywhere, and they simply fell silent in the bow wave and wake of the passing human disturbance. Every so often, he heard delicate rustling behind the curtain of bush, but he followed the lead of his diminutive guide and ignored it.

After a steady fifteen-minute walk, they met women and children straggling in from the farms on intersecting footpaths. Boone acquired an entourage of peekins carrying platters and buckets on their heads, crying, "*Poo-mui! Poo-mui!*" in high-pitched voices. When he lifted his arm to wave hello to them, they sagged behind the skirts of women and giggled in terror. When he dropped his arm and resumed walking, he could hear them creeping up behind him, daring one another to touch him.

At last the tunnel opened into a wide clearing surrounded by towering palms. Mud huts with thatched roofs and small houses of whitewashed concrete huddled in groups around dusty, interlocking common areas.

The boy bobbed gracefully up and down under the backpack and led Boone into a series of dirt courtyards. A woman wrapped in a lappa pounded rice in a mortar carved from a stump. Goats and chickens scattered before them, and children gathered to watch the parade pass.

As Boone entered the first courtyard, rock music greeted his ears, but he was unable to localize the source in the scramble of huts. Before he could name the tune, an orange Frisbee sailed over a cluster of thatched roofs, and a teenager in a University of Wisconsin T-shirt emerged from an adjoining courtyard in pursuit. The kid outran the Frisbee and caught it six inches off the ground, then executed a brilliant backhand return toss over the thatched roofs.

Boone caught glimpses of the adjoining courtyards through the passageways between huts. The music grew louder as he followed his guide between two wattle-and-daub compounds and emerged into a another sunny courtyard, where a huge boom box was mounted on a stump. In the middle of the village of Nymuhun, Sierra Leone, twenty miles southeast of Bo, in equatorial West Africa, Boone heard the Grateful Dead slip into the refrain to "Cumberland Blues."

He had trouble integrating Jerry Garcia's banjo licks with the scene in the courtyard, where he nearly fell over a naked child wearing leather amulets and chasing chickens off a patch of cement where cocoa beans were drying in the sun. Toothless old mas in headties stared out at him from the shadows of mud verandas. A mother suckled an infant on a stoop, while another child screamed in the dust at her feet.

His guide walked past the boom box and onto the veranda of an L-shaped house on the far side of the courtyard. One whitewashed wall of the L had been frescoed with an exact replica of the skeleton crowned with roses from the Grateful Dead's *Skull & Roses* album, another contained an equally precise rendering of the wreath of roses from *American Beauty*. Over a red door was a net with a piece of bamboo cane, and under it, in bold black letters: "Deadheads Unite."

The red door opened and a hairy blond man in a University of Wisconsin T-shirt, madras Bermuda shorts, and running shoes strolled out onto the veranda with his hands in his pockets. His clothes wafted on a gaunt frame, which would have seemed almost unhealthy but for the light in his eyes, the color in his cheeks, and the musculature evident in his torso. A formidable necklace of cowrie shells, animal teeth, and bones depended from his neck, along with a leather pouch, tightly lashed with a thong. On the skin of each of his temples were fan arrangements of short incisions, tribal markings opening outward in the direction of vision.

"Excuse me," Boone said, "I'm looking for the University of Wisconsin."

"We are no longer affiliated with that institution," the man said with a smile and a twinkle of blue eyes behind rimless granny glasses.

"Boone Westfall," said Boone, taking the man's hand.

"Aruna Sisay," said the man. "We will, however, proudly display any logo or message on one hundred percent cotton T-shirts, as long as the T-shirts are provided free of charge," he added, glancing down at his shirt.

"These are for you," Boone said, holding out the caged fowl and the kola nuts.

"Right hand only," Sisay said, making an unpleasant face and looking at the kola nuts in Boone's left hand.

"What?" asked Boone, setting the cage down and transferring the nuts to his right hand.

"Gift giving is important, but the first thing to remember is that it's done with the right hand. In this part of the world, your left hand is used for one thing, cleaning yourself after using the latrine. Do not touch people with your left hand. Do not touch your mouth, face, or any utensils with your left hand."

Boone presented first the fowl, then the kola nuts, thinking that he didn't mind going through this hand ritual once because it was kind of cute, but it wasn't something he intended to make a point of remembering for the duration of his stay.

"If you shake hands with an elder or an important person, you may grasp your right wrist with your left hand," he added. "It's a gesture of respect, kind of like a double handshake."

Clusters of children were forming in the perimeters of the courtyard, and whispers of *poo-mui* were rising to a chant.

"Let's hide inside until dusk," said Sisay, motioning Boone toward the compound. "First, your room," he said, opening a door into a separate room with one wall common to the compound, "at least for tonight."

Inside was a dark rectangle with a roof over low rafters. A square, screenless window with hooked shutters opened onto the courtyard. A tick mattress ran the length of the end wall, and a table with a hurricane lamp occupied most of the common wall, leaving just enough space for the two of them to turn around and exit.

A separate door led from the veranda to the main living area—behind the skull and roses wall—where he found clean, modest quarters fitted out as a study or a library, but with a bed and cane chairs included and a shelf with eating utensils.

"I have wives and children," said Sisay, "but they stay in another compound."

Boone politely ignored the uxorial plural and toured the premises instead. "Books," he said, peering around a corner and into a darkened room fitted out with long, crowded shelves. "Lots of them." As his eyes grew accustomed to the shadows, he could make out the moldering bindings of dead volumes. The spines of the hardbacks were blighted with mildew, and the paperbacks were clumps of stained pulp with rounded edges.

"My books have all rotted, or been eaten by rats and cockroaches," Sisay said. "I can't say I miss them. You'll find the rest of them in the latrine, and feel free to use them. I do. When I want a good story, I go out to the baffa at night and watch the storytellers perform. They tell better stories than the ones you find embalmed in print. Even the same story is different every time, because it's told by a different person, or the crowd is in a different mood. The audience, you see, assists in the telling of the tale."

"Lots of anthropology," Boone said, still looking over the shelves and making out a few of the titles.

"I was a graduate student," Sisay said. "I came here to study the Mende tribe of Sierra Leone." He gestured toward one of the cane chairs for Boone, then took a seat for himself in the lotus position on the earthen floor. "I gave up on anthropology quite a while ago. As you'll soon discover, it is impossible for a white man to study the Mende people, because they are constantly absorbed in studying him. Someday I may return to America and study the savage, violent, unspeakably greedy people who live there, but first I have to work up the courage."

Boone could not tell where Sisay's self-mockery ended and his bemusement with the rest of the world began.

Sisay fingered the pouch around his neck. "I turned my Claude Lévi-Strauss books over to the villagers some years ago. Portions of *Structural Anthropology* turned up as far away as Sulima beach, which borders on Liberia, where the pages are still being used and reused to wrap five-cent orders of peanuts, or "groundnuts," as they are called in Salone. A mori man—a kind of textual medicine man—up in Kenema folds individual pages from Lévi-Strauss's *Totemism* into compact squares, sews them into leather pouches, and attaches them around the waists, wrists, and ankles of peekins to protect them from witches who transform themselves into fruit bats, owls, and boa constrictors at night and swallow the limbs of infants, causing paralysis. You probably thought polio was caused by a virus," he said with an arid smile.

"The Fula man out on the highway wraps kola nuts in pages from *A View from Afar*. *Nothing* is thrown away. There's no garbage problem, because there is no garbage. Nothing is wasted here, except people. Only *poo-muis* throw things away. And if a *poo-mui* throws a page of a book away after eating his groundnuts, I can promise you that a villager will be two steps behind him to retrieve the precious paper to wrap something else in."

Boone's impatience surfaced, and he decided to at least begin the task of bringing this oddball's attention to the problem at hand. "I'm really here to . . ." Boone began.

"I know why you're here," Sisay said. "You're looking for Lamin Kaikai. You went to the American Embassy or the Peace Corps. They probably told you that the entire country is a mess, and the development agencies and embassies know even less than usual about what's going on out in the bush. They told you the gangsters from Liberia are making incursions into the south of Sierra Leone, and the country is swarming with refugees and mercenaries. They told you what elections mean in this country. They may even have told you about our section chief, Idrissa Moiwo, his electioneering methods, and his bitter struggle to wrest the Paramount Chieftaincy from Chief Kabba Lundo, who has held the office for fifty years. Then somebody told you about me. But it had to be somebody who lives in the bush, because all the white people in Freetown who have heard about me think I'm some kind of deviant or lunatic. That leaves Volunteers, and it had to be a Volunteer who's been here long enough to know that the Western relief organizations and government agencies don't know anything about the bush. Probably somebody whose tour is almost up. Probably somebody from Bo District or Pujehun District, where they'd hear about me. I'm gonna guess Sam Lewis out of Pujehun, or Kent Garrison out of Bo. No, not Garrison, he'd have sent you to his buddy who's the Speaker for the Paramount Chief in the district. It was Lewis, and he didn't come with you because he knew I wouldn't let him stay here for more than five minutes. He told you I knew your friend and that I spoke Mende."

"The white Mende man," Boone said. "He said you might have information that the Peace Corps and the government can't get. Native information."

"Information is a white word," Sisay said. "You can get information at the U.S. Embassy from overfed white guys wearing suits and sitting in front of computer screens. An African would correctly conclude that the *poo-muis* in the embassy know about only one thing: computer screens. If you can get past the few proud galoots with shaved heads who stand in the bulletproof booths and operate the buzz-bolt locks, you'll be seen by someone with information."

Boone watched Sisay sneering in the dim light and realized he was in the keeping of another misanthrope. Lewis hated Africans. This guy hated Americans, which didn't strike him as a characteristic that would be useful in finding his buddy.

"You don't need information. You need to *know*. You need *vision*. You don't come into that kind of knowledge by dropping in for a week and asking a few questions. When you need to know something in this part of Africa, you hire a looking-around man," he said, pronouncing it in Krio with a hard "g" as "looking-ground mahn." "A diviner," he continued, "one part priest, one part psychiatrist, and one part fortune teller. How do you think I knew you were coming?" he asked with a grin.

"A crystal ball, I suppose," said Boone.

Sisay shook his head. "Stones. The looking-around man threw stones, and the stones said you were coming."

"I'll bite," said Boone. "Where does one find a looking-around man?" He decided to humor this character, privately concluding that Sisay had eaten acid one time too many back in his Grateful Dead days.

"You pay money," said Sisay. "You have to try them out until you find one who's not a charlatan and who knows what he's doing. One simple test is to hide one of your belongings in a secret place where it will be difficult to find. Then tell the looking-around man to find it for you. Some of them can tell you where it is without even leaving the room, but they are expensive. It also takes time, because you have to bring the good ones in from up-country, which means you have to send a messenger and wait for a reply, and then wait for your appointment. It's called West African Internal Time, also known by its acronym: WAIT. Over here, you don't kill time, it kills you. Especially if you're a *poo-mui*."

"A white person," Boone said.

Sisay went over to a covered pail and removed the lid. He ladled water into two cups and handed one to Boone.

"That's one translation," said Sisay. "But then you would be hard put to explain why the Mende call African-American Volunteers *poo-muis* and are uncharacteristically aloof toward them. When the tours of African-Americans come over here wearing their kente cloths and clutching a copy of *Roots*, they are warmly received as long-lost brothers and sisters, as long as they stay in Freetown and meet with Sierra Leoneans from the Ministry of Culture. If they come out here to the villages, they will be coolly received as *poo-muis* in black skins. The loneliest people you will meet in Sierra Leone are African-American Volunteers stationed in villages.

"*Poo* means 'white' or 'modern' or 'European,' but it's more of a personality trait than a color. *Mui* means 'person.' But some say that in old or 'deep' Mende, *pu* means 'to add' or 'to acquire,' which is what Americans and Europeans do best. So some would translate *poo-mui* as 'greedy person' or maybe 'selfish person.' To the Mende, you and I are *poo-muis*. We constantly and effortlessly *acquire* new and better possessions, presumably because we have access to powerful medicines."

Here was a guy who left his calling back in the States, thought

Boone. *How many of these lectures did he have and what good could possibly come from them?*

"My guess is that you have more money in traveler's checks right now than most of these people will earn and spend in their entire lives."

Great, thought Boone. *Now he's going to ask me how much money I have.*

"You must imagine how far your eyes would bug out of your head if someone came to visit you in America and pulled more cash out of his billfold than you make in three years."

It might not be much money at all depending on how many years I have to listen to speeches about the desperate poverty of the Mende people.

"That's how these people feel when they hear about white people buying plane tickets for seven hundred dollars. It's inconceivable. Three years' salary for a plane ticket! Even the diamond diggers average only the equivalent of about three or four hundred dollars a year, and they are wealthy indeed."

Sisay drank from his cup; Boone stared down at his.

"Is the water . . . safe?" asked Boone.

"No," said Sisay, "but there's nothing you can do about it. Use caution for the first couple of weeks. You'll get sick four or five times, you'll have runny belly for a month or two, and then you and the parasites will settle down in a happy symbiosis."

"Months? I don't plan on being here for months," Boone said, thinking that he would be lucky to live a month if he had to stay in a place like this.

"Just WAIT and see," said Sisay with a grin. "You may stay at my place for one or two nights, but if you plan to stay any longer, arrangements will have to be made."

Boone quickly protested that he did not wish to inconvenience Sisay in any way.

Sisay dismissed him with a wave of his hand. "I'm not talking about convenience," he said. "If you decide to stay here for any length of time you will need a grandfather and a name."

"A grandfather?" Boone asked.

"And an African name," Sisay said. "As you'll soon discover, you are now part of a community. You'll spend very little time alone, and the rest of the time, everyone in the village will be in your business, and you will be in theirs."

Joining a family and whiling the days away in enforced conviviality with smiling natives did not quite fit in with what he wanted to accomplish during his stay, but Boone wondered if joining a family would permit him to enlist more help from his "relatives."

"Without a name and a grandfather, you don't really have a social identity. The villagers have no frame of reference for you. Whose son are you? Who is responsible for you? To whom should they address their compliments or complaints about you? Without a family, you are just an unsettling enigma, rolling around like a stray white chess piece in a game of checkers. It will take you at least two months to find your friend," he said, "unless he shows up of his own accord. I'll set up the naming ceremony."

No need to make any decisions in these parts, thought Boone. *This mother hen will do it for me, if I let him.*

"What makes you think it will take so long?" asked Boone. "Do you have some idea of what happened?"

"I'm not sure what happened," Sisay said, "but in this country it's a safe bet that it's either witchcraft or politics, or, more likely, it's both. Not only is there trouble in the south with the Liberian rebels making incursions into the country, it's also election time. During elections, the entire country erupts in anxiety, and sometimes violence, at the prospect of power changing hands. Certain secret societies take measures to obtain *power*, a sort of palpable essence, which can be accumulated and wielded by medicine men. Members of these secret and illegal societies—the Baboon Society or the Leopard Society—supposedly transform themselves into animals—Baboon Men or Leopard Men—then go in search of victims for sacrifice. Powerful charms and fetishes are made from the flesh of human victims. But the *medicine* needs to be 'replenished,' or 'fed,' or it loses its potency. It's been going on since the last century, and probably even before that. The British cleaned house every ten years or so by holding Leopard and Baboon trials in Freetown and hanging all the society members from public gallows. On top of that, during elections, the practice of witchcraft rises to a fever pitch, because everyone is putting swears on each other to obtain an advantage over their political enemies. Once a swear is let loose and its intended victim hears about it, a counter-swear must be effected as protection, and so on."

LSD, thought Boone. *Lots of LSD followed by lots of malarial delusions. After that, he probably fell in love with a woman who believes in all this voodoo. Somebody or something had damaged the guy's psyche.*

Boone finally blinked, opened his mouth, and produced a question. "People . . . *believe* in this stuff?"

"Of course," Sisay said.

"And people openly practice witchcraft?"

"Witchcraft is prevalent," said Sisay, "but it is technically illegal. People do, however, openly protect themselves from witches, which is legal . . . and prudent."

He pointed toward the rafters over the door to the veranda, where Boone saw a small red net spread neatly above the lintel with a strip of bamboo cane suspended in the webbing.

"The net is called *kondo-bomei*, witch net; it will catch any witch that tries to enter the house. The bamboo is called *kondo-gbandei*, witch gun; it will shoot the witch and kill it."

"You believe in that?" Boone asked with a half laugh.

"I don't believe in anything," said Sisay with absolute conviction. "I'm only interested in results. You don't have to worry about *kondo-gbandei*," he said, pointing at the red net and giving Boone a chilly smile, "unless you are a witch."

"Right," said Boone, "I'm a witch," feeling Sisay's eyes on him and not liking it, "and you're Merlin, I suppose."

"White people usually want to know if witchcraft is *true*," he said. "Whatever that means. They think science is somehow *true*. They forget that the West puts all of its faith in science, not because it is true, but because it *works*. Who cares if science is true, so long as it makes your car go and heats your house? Who cares if witchcraft is true, so long as it destroys your enemies and protects your crops? I assure you that in this country witchcraft works."

"So Killigan's been abducted by politicians or witches, is that it?"

"I said witchcraft, politics, or both," said Sisay. "And you're not drinking your water."

Boone stared into his cup. "No matter how long it takes to find Killigan, I think I'll stay with my water tablets," he said.

"You'll have a problem there," said Sisay. "I don't care what you do in my house, but you are going to be traveling about. You will be staying with others. It would be the height of bad manners to refuse water from your hosts. A Mende man simply will not understand. If you insist on purifying your water in another village, you will be implying that you believe their water has been tainted by witchcraft, which, as we all know, is the most common cause of waterborne diseases. Imagine how you would feel if you invited people over to your house in America for dinner, and they asked you if they could purify your food before eating it."

"Well, what do you expect me to do?" asked Boone. "Get sick on purpose?"

Sisay's eyes traveled the length of Boone's frame. "You have plenty of money. You should have no trouble feeding yourself and a colony of parasites, if they should move in. You could stand to lose a little weight anyway. If you're going to travel through parts of the world where people are starving to death, don't you think it's a bit unseemly to be overweight? I mean, how does it feel walking around in this country where starvation gnaws on everyone's elbow, knowing that you come from a country full of fat people trying to lose weight? I can think of even better reasons to lose weight. Over there in Liberia, after the rebel factions took power, they shot all the fat people on the assumption that anybody fat must have been working for the government. Probably a safe assumption in this part of the world."

Boone examined his stomach. "I had my insurance updated before I left America. I was exactly normal for my height."

"Normal back there is overfed over here," he said dismissively. "As for Killigan's whereabouts, there's another possibility we haven't discussed. I know you came here to find Michael Killigan, but have you wondered whether he wants to be found?"

"Meaning?" said Boone. "He would be hiding?"

"If he really wanted to disappear, there are plenty of places you can only get to by bush path, parts of the country where people still scream and run away when they see a white man."

"From whom would he be hiding?"

"Real or imagined enemies," said Sisay. "I was getting worried about him. He was becoming . . . marginal, I guess you would say. Too African," he added with a smile, "which is what they still say about me. The more he mediated disputes among the village people, the development agencies, and the Peace Corps, the more he became involved in local politics, and the more he disliked white people. He was getting squeezed. The Peace Corps explicitly forbids political activity, but the development agencies and government ministries funded by the development agencies kept giving him more and more power because he was a rare creature, a white man who spoke fluent Mende. He moved easily among the village, the bush, and the world of the white development agencies, where there is money, lots of money, and lots of corruption. Being too African probably isn't dangerous, but being too honest is. If the Dutch send a hundred bags of cement from Bo to Makeni to build a bridge, you can bet that only sixty or seventy will arrive, and that the official in Makeni will simply sign off on the receipt, and the missing cement goes . . . to certain powerful people.

"When Killigan started working on those projects, he had his own men at the work site counting, and if a hundred bags of cement did not arrive, he raised hell until he found the person responsible and fired him. Meanwhile, each time he successfully planned and completed a project, he was held in higher esteem by the villagers. His reputation was spreading. But the certain powerful people were missing their bags of cement."

"It's a nice theory," said Boone, "but I have information that there was some kind of raid on his village by witches or Baboon Men or something."

"There was a funeral in his village," said Sisay. "The raid could have been election business, terrorism directed at Kabba Lundo, the Paramount Chief, who also lives in Ndevehun, or the chaos could have erupted because a *Ndogbojusui* was sighted."

"A what?" asked Boone.

"Dog-bo-joo-shwee," Sisay enunciated slowly, "a bush devil. Tomorrow, I will take you to see Pa Gigba, who was in Ndevehun when all of this happened. I don't know how much he will tell us, but I know he was there. And yes, Baboon Men have been sighted, and not just in Killigan's village. Like I said, it's election time."

"Witches, Baboon Men, and now bush devils," sighed Boone. "Any other creatures you haven't told me about?"

"Americans," said Sisay, without laughing. "Lebanese. British. Germans. The diamond miners. The murderers who own the mining companies. They are the most fearsome creatures in the bush. A bush devil is nothing compared to them."

"OK," said Boone, "I get the message. I'm not here to reform Western civilization; I'm looking for my best friend. What is a bush devil?"

"What is a regular devil?" asked Sisay, mocking him with a quick grin. "A *Ndogbojusui* is a spirit who lives on top of a mountain by day, and at night roams the bush paths looking for straggling hunters or other wanderers who are foolish enough to travel alone in the

bush at dusk. Like most genies and devils, *Ndogbojusui* are white,"
Sisay added, with an almost imperceptible pause. "A bush devil
usually has white hair and a long white beard, but he can change
his shape at will. He attempts to trick travelers by asking them
questions and by charming them into going with him into the bush,
where those who follow him are lost forever. Some anthropologists
speculate that the original bush devils were the Portuguese who
'tricked' hunters and travelers into following them, and then sold
them as slaves at the docks in Freetown."

"This mythology stuff is interesting, and if I was here on vacation
I'd listen to it by the hour," Boone said, "but it doesn't tell me how
to find Michael Killigan."

"No," Sisay said, "but it might keep you from getting lost. You
seem far too impatient to learn anything about the bush, so I'll keep
it simple: Do not go into the bush at night. Ever. For any reason.
Plan your journeys so that you end up in a village well before dark.
Even in daylight, you must be careful in the bush. Anyone traveling
alone in the bush is not to be trusted. If you meet a lone hunter or
a solitary traveler, be polite, but keep your distance, do not engage
the person in conversation or follow them. Don't eat anything they
may offer you. If you meet a beautiful woman, do not touch her or
accept any gifts from her. Understand? It's not like the woods or
the wilderness back home. It's not just a place . . ."

"I suppose *Ndogbojusui* is how the natives explain missing persons over here," Boone said, convinced that Lewis had steered him
into the keeping of a psychotic Deadhead. "Again, it's interesting,
but I need to know if Michael Killigan is lost, or if somebody kidnapped him, or . . . injured him, or what? I have a letter from one
of his servants," Boone said, suddenly recalling Lewis's advice from
the restaurant in Freetown: *Don't trust him. Ask questions, listen,
but don't talk. That's how you survive in this part of the world.* "I
should say I *saw* a letter from one of his servants. Killigan's mother
showed it to me in Paris. It talked about bad medicine and witchmen
coming to the village while Killigan wasn't there," he ventured,
deciding for the moment to keep the mention of photographs to
himself. "It was a letter from his servant. Moussa . . ."

"Moussa Kamara," Sisay interrupted. "Pa Gigba is Moussa Kamara's uncle, and as I said, Gigba was in Killigan's village when
this disturbance occurred."

"Well, great. We can talk to Gigba first," Boone said, "but then I plan to go to Killigan's village and talk to this Moussa guy, and take it from there."

"You can go to Ndevehun if you like," said Sisay, "but you won't be able to talk to Moussa Kamara."

"I suppose that's forbidden," said Boone sarcastically, "or I suppose he's a witch or a bush devil."

"According to the section chief, who sent word to our village chief," said Sisay, "Moussa Kamara is dead. They found him a week ago outside Ndevehun hanging from a cotton tree. Somebody slit his belly open and stuffed him with hot peppers. They found a live gecko sewn inside his mouth."

(6)

The Origin of White People

Long ago, there lived a man with two wives. One year, his big wife told him that she could no longer bear working with the new wife on the same farm. The big wife wanted her own farm. To keep peace among his wives, the man went to find more bush for his wives to farm. He went all the way to England looking for more bush. There he bought a vast farm of *poo-mui* bush, wrapped it in newspaper, set it on his head, and carried it home to his wives.

The man divided the bush into two farms: one for his big wife and one for the new wife. Though he tried not to show it, the man favored the new wife over his big wife. The new wife was young, and her breasts were round and full of milk. Everyone in the village knew that the new wife was a "love wife," because the man had gotten almost nothing from her parents. The man spent much more time brushing the new wife's farm with his cutlass, and only brushed his big wife's farm when it was too overgrown to manage.

The big wife became jealous. When the husband gave his wives the seed rice to plow, the big wife told the younger one that the rice should be boiled and dried in the sun before planting it. Despite this trick, the new wife's parboiled rice somehow grew into thick pods. The big wife gnashed her teeth with jealousy. She hired a coven of witches to put a curse on the new wife's farm. She and the other witches turned themselves into the large rodents known in Mendeland as "cutting grasses" and ate the young wife's rice. Each night, the big wife and the witches went to the farm, took off their human skins, put them in a lake at the edge of the farm, dressed themselves in cutting grass skins, and ate the girl's rice.

"Human skin go off," the witches chanted. "Cutting grass skin come on."

Morning after morning, the new wife found her rice crop ravaged, until finally she went to consult a looking-around man to find out who was destroying her rice crop. The looking-around man cast stones and told her that the big wife and her coven of witches were changing themselves into cutting grasses every night and eating the rice on the young wife's farm.

"To stop her," the looking-around man advised, "buy twenty bags of pepper, take them down to the lake at the edge of your farm, grind the pepper up, and pour it into the lake." The girl did as she had been instructed.

That night, the big wife led her coven of cutting grasses to the young wife's farm. They put their human skins in the peppered lake, put on their cutting grass skins, and gorged themselves all through the night on rice. At first light, they went back to the lake, took their human skins from the peppered water, and put them on their bodies.

"Cutting grass skin go off," they chanted. "Human skin come on."

Soon the pepper started to burn. As her human skin caught fire, the big wife and head of the cutting grasses began to cry, "Human skin go off! Human skin go off!"

In the morning, when the new wife and others from the village came to the farm, they found the big wife and her coven of witches standing by the lake at the end of the farm, with their bellies full of rice and their skins removed, leaving only a plump whiteness.

These skinless witches were the first white people. All white people came from them.

Jenisa waded into the stream and spread her family's clothes on a flat washing rock. Her co-wives, Amida and Mariamu, stood next to her, knee-deep in the tug of the stream's current and the spume of suds from palm-oil soap. Their conversation was punctuated by soft grunts of effort and the thud and squish of soapy garments pounding heavy stones. The sun had settled below the palm trees, and Jenisa could hear the shouts and songs of people returning from the bush farms. The long shadows of mango and pearwood trees fell across the water on either side of the rock where the women brooked their clothes. The drone of huge, carnivorous flies and the chatter of birds echoed in the tunnel of bush overhanging the stream. Muddy water rushed over the washing rock in twisted rivulets and tore itself into white tassels of soapsuds and foam.

Amida and Mariamu were complaining about how the day's work

had been assigned by Yotta, the big wife of their common husband, the powerful section chief, Idrissa Moiwo. They made fun of her fat behind, called "waist" in Krio, and the smell of her genitals, called "private."

"Ai O!" said Amida. "Dat big wife Yotta, ihn business strangah. Look ihn waist spread like bush cow yone."

"To God," said Mariamu. "And ihn private dae smell like rotten fish bonga. You no know whatin dat woman dae do na night. She dae wash ihn waist wit sansan and sapo. Still it get dat rank scent."

"Imagine," added Jenisa, "she dae expect us foh brook ihn drawers. I no able. Dat fish bonga scent dae go 'pon person tae it no dae come out. I no know whatin make dat wife man take ahm."

"Den say she been fine-fine befoh traday, O. Ihn body been fresh, ihn face fine. But usai she done wowo tae dat ugly dancing devil, Kongoli, self dae 'fraid ahm. Ihn nose flat like benni cake."

"I been hear dat. She been get one boyfriend wi ihnself no de wash. Una been sabby dat yella pa wi been dae sell den haf-haf ting dem na ya?"

"Pa Mustapha?"

"Na ihm."

"Lawd have massi. Dat pa dae, he been dirty like whatin. All dem peekin dem been mock ihm foh dat. Ihn dirty one."

"Well, Yotta done meet up ihn matches. Mastah and Missus Rank!"

They all laughed bitterly and pretended they were beating Yotta with their washing stones, until Mariamu warned of the approach of Fati, Yotta's daughter and spy.

Jenisa, Amida, and Mariamu all hated Yotta, and so did Fati. But whenever it suited her schemes, Fati told Yotta everything her mates said about the big wife. Then Yotta would retaliate by spreading stories about the men her mates were sleeping with, and why their children either died or received poor training, whereas hers were models of Mende rectitude who respected their mother and served their father. Yotta's stories would then filter back to the young wives, who would point out Yotta's infidelities and speculate about her real motives for spreading lies about her mates. And the gossip went in and out of the *mawes*, up and down the banks of the stream where clothes were brooked, out along the lines of women bearing head-loads in from the outlying farms, and back into the markets.

In Krio, the word for this kind of vicious, backbiting gossip is *congosa;* it is rumormongering designed to poison hearts and trigger palavers. When the men gossiped, it was called village planning, or "hanging heads," though, except for a pronounced emphasis on the profit angle, the content of the conversations was the same.

Jenisa moved to the other side of the washing rock, so that her lengthening shadow would not fall on the deeper parts of the stream. A turtle or, worse, a crocodile could swallow her shadow if she was not careful. Just a short time ago, Amida, her mate and close friend, had seen a *Njaloi,* a genie with a brilliant gem set in his forehead, swimming deep in this stream. The light from the *Njaloi's* stone had blinded Amida, and the genie called to her to come under the water, and promised he would take her to a cave filled with a vast treasure. The whole village talked excitedly about the sighting for days, and, at night, in the baffa, by the light of a single hurricane lamp, Amida's aunt again told the story of how, when she was a small girl bathing with her mother in the stream, a water genie, a *tingowei,* appeared to her as a long golden chain lying on a rock. While she was admiring the golden chain, the *tingowei* stole her shadow. The aunt said that without her shadow she became instantly dizzy and fell into the water. The genie dragged her down and took her to a cave filled with treasure and showed her an evil white spirit, a thing so horrible she could not now describe it, for if she was successful in her description, anyone who heard it would be unable to forget the terrible image. It promised to give her towns filled with treasures if she would agree to do things that were so terrible, a person hearing of them would never again trust anyone wearing a human shape. Only a powerful medicine finally allowed her to put the hideous thing out of her mind.

The stream was a dangerous place, frequented by mermaids, genies, and capricious spirits that liked nothing better than making people insane or saddling them with curses and misfortunes. The stream was visited only in groups, and then only to bathe or to brook clothes.

When Fati joined them at the washing rock, she brought news of the arrival of a white stranger, word of which was spreading through the community of huts and *mawes* like vibrations traveling along a delicate spider's web, touched at one point by the intruder.

"White strangah been come," said Fati.

Fati was Yotta the big wife's daughter, but because Amida and Jenisa were nearly the same age as Fati, they all behaved as sisters to one another and as daughters of Yotta. Only Mariamu was older, being the second wife of their husband, the section chief.

"Usai dat white man come out?" Jenisa asked.

"I think say he American man. He been come out na Freetown," Fati replied. "I no see ahm. I been dae brook me clothes, when I hear he been come, jus now."

"Whatin he been come na hya foh do?" Amida asked, winking at Jenisa.

"Den say he come foh find dat Peace Koh man. Den say dat Peace Koh man done go wakka-wakka. Dey no see ahm. He done go alackey. Trouble dae, beaucoup. Water roof. Better no dae."

"Peace no dae inside the country. Dese rebels been come out Liberia with bloody hands and put bad medicine na Salone."

News of the white man's arrival made Jenisa's heart beat faster, and she shared her excitement by returning Amida's knowing glance. As Jenisa's confidante, Amida knew that a looking-around man had told Jenisa that a white stranger would come to the village and give her a gift that would change her life. This gave Jenisa hope that her hard life of sorrow and despair might soon change for the better. She was twenty years old, and still she had no children of her own. Her charmed life as the young, beautiful, new wife of Section Chief Moiwo had become a Mende woman's nightmare— she had lost two children in childbirth, and *Ngewo*, the Mende god, was taking his time in sending her more.

All her life had been spent in preparation for bearing and raising children, and now she had none. When Jenisa was still a child, her mother took her aside and told her that her father was so proud of her, he had decided to give her as a wife to Section Chief Moiwo, a man whose farms were so vast he could feed the entire village. She would also go to school, because Moiwo had been to school in England and America and wanted a clever, educated, new wife. So, while she was still very young, she went to live in Section Chief Moiwo's compound under the care and training of his big wife, Yotta. She obeyed Yotta, even though Yotta was cruel and jealous of the pretty girl who would one day be a new wife for her husband. She entered the Sande Society, the woman's secret society, full of joy and eager to become a woman. In the Sande bush, a special sequestered place near her village, she was trained by the woman whose name she now bore. She went into the Sande bush with her sisters and her cousins, and left her childish ways and her childhood name behind. All trace of man was removed from her private, and she was born Jenisa, the most beautiful and best-trained woman to emerge in all her finery from the Sande bush. Her skin glistened with scented oils. The entire village gave her gifts, and she proudly danced and sang for her admiring elders.

Before they cut the man part out of her, the matrons had showed her the eyeball of a fish. And her Sande mother said to her, over and over, "Enter this fish and swim far below your pain." The drums beat and blood pounded in her head, and her grandmothers removed the small stick of maleness from her. The pain happened somewhere far above her. She bore it easily, and proudly, according to her training, and gloried in the greatest moment of her life. She was now one with her sisters, a pure woman, ready for marriage and childbirth. Even before she left the Sande bush, the matrons had let it be known all over the village that she was first in her class, daughter of a big man, and already given as wife to a section chief.

In the Sande bush, she had learned how to serve her husband. She had learned the arts of loving a man, of bearing children, of weaving, of dancing, and music making. She learned that her love for the wife man must always be complete, but not unconditional. For, the matrons had told her, the wife man, too, must love his wives completely and treat them with respect. If this was not the case and her husband ever mistreated her, then the Sande matrons had ways of bringing these misbehaving husbands into line, first by complaining to the big men in Poro, the men's secret society, and second, if necessary, by afflicting bad husbands with genital atrocities. For instance, no man may see what happens in the Sande bush. Those intrepid men who dare spy on Sande proceedings suddenly develop hideous deformities of the private: hydrocele, elephantiasis, hernias, and swollen testicles.

Soon after her wife man took her as his new wife, she heard delicious rumors that she was a "love wife," meaning, even though the marriage had obvious practical benefits for both her father and the section chief, the women of the village said that Moiwo would have taken her even if her parents had had nothing, because she was young and clever and very beautiful. Yotta's jealousy grew by the day, but Jenisa managed to be both modest and tactful. She learned early that most women were jealous of her, because she was clever and beautiful; Yotta's jealousy was sharper only because

Yotta wanted to be the big wife, as well as the best-loved wife of her husband. Jenisa gave Yotta her due as the big wife, but was not slow to exploit the wife man's infatuation with her as the new young wife.

She took no sexual pleasure from Moiwo's climbing on her to make children, but she enjoyed influencing the way things were run in the compound just by whispering things in his ear. If Yotta made some ridiculous rule, and enforced it only to make the lives of the young wives miserable, Jenisa found that it could be changed with a whisper. If she wanted some special treat or a new dress, a whisper brought it to her. More than anything, she wanted to give the section chief a child, for this would make her father big with pride and her wife man even happier. But after the first year, during which it seemed that Moiwo was always wanting her when it was her turn to stay with him, he stopped sending for her, or if he sent for her, he did not love with her, but only spoke of work to be done around the compound, of relations to be cared for, and crops to be looked after. This was normal, the Sande matrons told her. Her Sande mother told her that a man's love is like a big splash in the river, but a woman's is a strong and steady current. She kept herself busy and flirted with young men to pass the time. If she fancied one of the young village men, she knew she could make him love her, but she was waiting for the right one.

She pounded more clothes on the washing rock and realized her thoughts were racing away from her, like the soap in the stream.

Her co-wives laughed, beat the clothes, complained of Yotta's insufferable ways, and worked.

All of her co-wives had love men because their wife man had five wives in two villages, and he was always gone to another village, to Freetown, or even to America, and it was clear that he wanted as many sons and daughters as possible, the first as laborers for his farms, the second as a means of acquiring ownership interests in more farms through marriage. It also seemed that he did not care *how* these children came about, as long as any woman damage fines were paid in money or servitude to him.

But Jenisa decided that if she was going to take a love man, she wanted a very special one. Not the misfits her co-wives had taken up with. Yotta's love man, Pa Mustapha, "Mastah Rank," was the laughingstock of the village, because he never washed himself.

Mariamu had a love man who could barely see because of river blindness. Amida had two love men, both young soccer players who were always fighting and drinking palm wine.

She bided her time, until she met a white Peace Corps man—Mistah Michael—whose Mende name was Lamin Kaikai, and who came to the village one day to see Mistah Aruna Sisay on business. Here was a love man! She quickly learned that even though this *poo-mui* had money spilling out of his pockets, he had no wives or children! He didn't need wives or children to work his farms. He didn't need farms, because he had bank accounts full of money all over the world! This Lamin Kaikai's skin shone like the sun, and he had a fine and beautiful body. He was a "sportsmahn" and wore magic shoes that made him run like the wind. But even when the village boys made him take off the magic shoes before racing him, he always won, probably because of some other hidden medicine. His pockets were full of medicines that were capable of protecting from every evil and bestowing every comfort on him and on those he loved.

And even though he was a *poo-mui*, he spoke her language and loved her people, and her people loved him. She knew when she first met him that she could have him, because he openly admired her training and she felt his eyes on her skin. He teased her, and she teased him back. He mocked her with a Mende proverb, and she promptly bested him with a better one in front of a crowd on her veranda.

He came again and again to see Mistah Sisay, until one time she had found Lamin sitting alone on the veranda. She wanted to touch the beautiful yellow hair on his arms. She had asked him why African women always want to touch the hair on the arms of *poo-mui* men.

"Because it makes them pregnant," Lamin had said with a laugh and a funny face.

"Pregnant with whatin?" she had said, besting him again. "A white bush pig?"

They both had laughed and she smoothed the hair on his arm.

"I would like to see what this yellow hair looks like in the moon-light," she had said, and that night she did.

Six weeks later, she was the happiest Mende woman in Sierra Leone, for she knew she would be having the *poo-mui*'s child, and what a child that would be! She would be the envy of every woman in the village; even her husband would probably be delighted, so she had thought, because she had grown up in his house, watching his co-wives love with whomever they pleased. The village men did not ask too many questions about their wives' suspicious pregnancies, only because as far as anyone knew they came from the wife man's loins and no other. She learned too late that this pretense would be impossible if she delivered a mulatto child. For whatever reason, her wife man went into a rage when he learned that his young love wife lost a child because of unconfessed adultery.

One child had been born dead. A second child lived for only two days, when it was killed in its sleep by a witch. When the first peekin died in childbirth, Jenisa took a splinter and placed it under the little finger of the stillborn's left hand, so that if her second child was born with a scar under the same finger, she would know that it was a witch child trying to come back into the world. When she had difficult labor with the second child, the Sande matrons, the leaders of the women's secret society, told her the child probably was not coming out because of unconfessed adultery. If not adultery, then a witch was holding the child inside. They dragged Jenisa about the birthing hut and beat on her belly with sticks, chastising the witch and calling it names. Finally, they concluded that no witch could hold up under such blows, and that either Jenisa had committed adultery and had not confessed it to her husband, or a bad medicine man or jujuman, called a *hale-nyamubla* in Mende, had taken an egg from a sitting hen and had buried it in an anthill to put a swear on her. This would place her in "stocks," and she would be unable to deliver the child, and would, instead, die. Her only hope, the Sande matrons told her, was to confess and hope that adultery was the cause of her problems.

Jenisa dared not reveal her love man. Her wife man had many powerful, illegal medicines and used them freely to destroy his adversaries. So instead of confessing to loving with Lamin, she told the Sande matrons that she had been loving with Vande, Pa Gigba's son, which was true, in the sense that she had once loved with him before she was married.

Minutes after this confession, the child was born. She was afraid its color would give her away, but no whiteness appeared in its skin, though she knew it was Lamin's child. It died before its naming day, before Jenisa could take it out into the morning sun on the third day, spit on its forehead, and pronounce, "Resemble me in all my ways and deeds, being named after me."

She wrapped the tiny body in leaves, sat on a mound of earth that had been dug away from under a banana tree, and pushed the child backward into the grave, to avoid any witch spirit that may have killed it. She did not cry, because her grandmother had told her that a mother's tears for her dead infant would scald its skin. God gives; God takes away. The infant was not meant to be a person.

The Sande matrons said that the witch must have come in the night and eaten the baby from the inside out. They shook their heads, clucked their tongues, and wondered how, after all that good Sande Society training, a young wife could be stupid enough to try childbirth without first confessing adultery to her husband.

On the evening of the third day after the child's death, the town crier walked around the village and announced, "Everybody listen! Everybody listen! The man who is loving with the young wife of Section Chief Moiwo had better come forward or he will be sworn. Should he not show himself before tomorrow, a powerful medicine will search him out and take revenge on him. His testicles will shrivel like cocoa pods in the sun! His liver will turn to dust! If he tries to sleep, his heart will stop! If he tries to go by water, spirits will overturn his boat and drown him! If he reaches for his wife, he will embrace a corpse! If he goes into the bush, snakes will bite him and the boa constrictor will strangle him! If he tries to think or speak, his mind will be crazed until he is insane! Such are the swears that will be put on the man who is loving Section Chief Moiwo's young wife if he does not come forward and admit woman damage."

This announcement brought forth both of Amida's boyfriends, and later a protesting Vande, who swore he had not touched Jenisa since before her marrying day and was bewildered by the accusations of the looking-around man, who claimed to have knowledge of Vande's woman damage. Late into the night and on into the early morning, the court *barri* was filled with men from all the families, drunk on palm wine, and swept up in a classic West African palaver over the appropriate fines to be assessed against the three offenders for woman damage. All three young men ended up having to work for many months on Moiwo's farms to pay off large fines. But Vande escaped his debt by leaving for Freetown. One of Amida's lovers stayed, and told Amida in their secret meeting place that he would work forever on Section Chief Moiwo's farm if it meant he could hold her each night in his arms.

Jenisa was afraid she would lose another child to witchcraft or bad medicine, because her secret lover did not reveal himself and the swear had been let loose. What if the swear found him or her and bestowed some new calamity on them? Then she had learned that her love man had chased a *Ndogbojusui* into the bush outside his village of Ndevehun and had disappeared. The rumors were that he had gone crazy, as white men sometimes do, but she did not believe them.

Why was there so much evil in the world? If her ancestors were watching over her, why did they let these terrible things happen? Had she done something to offend them? Had someone in her family failed to perform the proper sacrifices and offerings, or otherwise shown disrespect? Perhaps her ancestors were hungry, and she had not given them enough food? Adultery explained nothing. Other women had three, four, five, or more healthy children with no troubles. They too had lovers, because they were the third and fourth wives of old men, but they had only strong boys and beautiful daughters to show their husbands.

The ancestors were supposed to intervene on her behalf and ask *Ngewo*, the father of all the Mende, to help her bear strong, healthy children, and to bless her with food to feed them. Instead, *Ngewo* allowed witches to take her children from her and fill her heart with bitter sorrow. Already, Amida had overheard Yotta, the big wife, asking other wives in the village if they thought Jenisa herself was a witch because two of her children had been taken. The loss of a third would be almost conclusive evidence of witchcraft, and Jenisa would be the first suspect. For everyone knows that a witch must supply her coven with fresh infants to eat, sometimes even her own.

To discover the source of her troubles, Jenisa had saved money for months, skimming pennies from her sales of palm oil in the market and saving them in the pouch under her bed. Then she had paid the money to a very powerful looking-around man, who moved stones on a board and cast cowrie shells. The looking-around man told her that a woman in the village—a widow who had not remarried and had not observed the rituals of purification after her husband's death—had put a swear on her. Jenisa knew at once the identity of her enemy.

The woman's name was Luba and her husband had fallen out of a palm tree during the last rainy season and had died. A spitting cobra, waiting for him in the palm tree, had blinded him with its venom and bit his face, and the men in the village said that as he fell from the tree, he screamed "Luba!," his big wife's name, and died when he struck the ground.

As a Mende woman, and as one of the man's three wives, Luba had to be washed of him before she could take another husband or love with another man. The water that was used to wash the soles of the dead man's feet was saved. Luba and the other bereaved wives were kept apart from the rest of the village and did not see or speak to anyone. Three days after her husband's death, an old woman poured the water on the ground in front of his house. The old woman then made mud with a pestle from the wet earth. Luba and her mates were summoned. The old woman took each wife by the hair and dragged her through the house. Another old woman followed, driving each widow ahead of her, in turn. When they arrived again at the front door of the house, each wife put her face close to the mud and shouted to her husband, "Husband of mine, I am in trouble!" Then the mud was smeared on the bodies of the grieving widows and baskets were hung by strings from their heads. Sympathizers filled the baskets with gifts, and the brothers of the dead man who were interested in taking a particular wife gave that one a big gift. But the widow Luba received only tokens, and no brother gave her a big gift. Everyone knew that none of the dead man's brothers wanted her.

Luba and the other wives accompanied the old woman into the bush, where each wife rested her head on a plantain tree. The old woman knocked down the tree with a pestling log and made a dish of boiled plantain, which they ate that evening for their food. Luba and her mates were smeared with mud again and dressed in rags, so that their husband's spirit would no longer desire them. Other women stayed with the widows to prevent them from sleeping that night, for if they slept, their husband might slip back in to stay with them.

The next day, Luba and her mates went to the river and washed away the last thing that belonged to their husband: the dust from the soles of his feet. She and the other widows were then to have remained in the dead man's compound for forty days, during which time their hair was shaved off and the sisters of the dead husband cursed them and told their dead brother that he would be a fool to linger in this world for such vile, ugly women.

But before ten days had passed, there were rumors that Luba was sneaking out of the compound at night and was loving with Sherrif, one of the dead man's brothers, out in the bush. Then there was talk that she had also slept with another brother, Alimami, also in the bush. With her hair shorn and wearing muddy rags, she sexed the brothers of her dead husband on land their fathers had farmed. She disgraced herself and then bewitched her husband's brothers into desecrating the family farm and their dead brother's wife. Crops no longer grew on the farm. But Luba did not care. Her only pleasure was in knowing she had defiled those who thought they were her betters: *You did not want me enough to put a big gift in my funeral basket, but you sexed me in the bush when your brother was barely ten days dead. You spilled your human seed on the land that feeds your families.*

And if her infernal sexing kept her husband from crossing the river to the village of white sands, Luba did not care. Her utter depravity was more powerful than any wandering spirit.

Now Luba lived alone in a shed. She still wore rags and kept her head shaved. The village children said that they had seen Luba change herself into a leopard and hide in the bush behind the latrines. On moonless nights, they could see Luba's orange eyes floating in the darkness. Their grandmothers told them that if they followed those orange eyes into the bush, they would be lost forever. Always, they would see the orange eyes just ahead of them, until they found themselves lost in trackless, eternal bush, and then a bush devil would trick them, or a witch wearing the shape of an animal would fall on them, paralyze them, suck blood from their throats, and eat them from the inside out.

As soon as the looking-around man told Jenisa about the swear that Luba had let loose on her, the chaos and tragedy of her life made perfect, terrible sense. A swear! The Sande matrons were right; Jenisa had committed adultery, but it was her enemy's swear that had killed her children and brought trouble, sorrow, and death into her life.

It was useless to ask why Luba had put her in stocks and had turned a swear loose on her. One might as well ask why driver ants bite people. A woman who would sex her dead husband's brothers in the bush during her mourning time would do anything. Luba's vile behavior had probably sent her husband to the evil place of everlasting hunger, where the dead till barren soil with their elbows and gnaw their own knees in savage hunger. If so, Luba would laugh out loud. Such a woman probably put swears on people just so she could shriek with delight while watching them suffer.

Jenisa needed protection. She needed a powerful medicine to kill her enemy. She borrowed large sums of money and consulted the looking-around man again and again. There were so many questions. Was Luba a witch? Some said yes. Some said her husband had screamed her name as he fell from the tree because he had recognized her in the shape of the spitting cobra. What kind of swear had Luba let loose on her? Simple protection was probably not enough; Jenisa needed to attack and kill her enemy with a more powerful swear. If Jenisa could kill Luba with a powerful medicine, would it also "pull" Luba's swear? This kind of bad medicine was illegal. How was it done without others finding out about it? Should she tell her wife man about Luba and what the looking-around man had told her? But her wife man, the chief, had been to school in England and America. He got very angry when his wives spent money on looking-around men and medicine men. He believed in white medicine, which was very powerful in curing afflictions that came from God, but was useless in protecting one from witchcraft and swears.

She had heard stories of powerful witch-hunting cults from the north who had bound a confessed witch and carried her into the bush. The witch hunters dug a shallow grave and buried the witch alive, throwing stones and garbage in on top of her until she died. But the witch's shade came back to haunt the village. Confined to its human shape, the witch was far less dangerous than its shade. The living, human shape was the shade's roost or cage. When the human shape was killed, the shade escaped and could no longer be trapped or harmed, except by witchfinders. Once free, the shade took its revenge by flying about the village and settling its weight on the faces of sleeping people. The witch hunters were called back again; this time a powerful witchfinder captured the witch's shade in the shape of a lizard and tied it safely inside a leather bag. Though the cults were very effective, they cost more money than she had ever seen.

The looking-around man told Jenisa that to remove Luba's swear, Jenisa had to cook a meal and serve it to a white stranger, who would then give her a gift. The looking-around man told her to bring the white stranger's gift back to him, and he would make a very powerful and dangerous medicine from it that would kill her enemy.

Jenisa rested her stone on the washing rock and fingered the horn of a bush deer, which she wore on a leather string around her neck, and prayed. She remembered the story her father had told her when he had given her the horn filled with medicine and told her never to eat the meat of *mbende*, the bush deer. His great-grandfather— now one of the fathers who are remembered, called *kekeni* when prayers and sacrifices are offered—was bathing in this stream, when an alligator seized him in its jaws and carried him to a cave underneath the bank of the stream. Her ancestor had no way out of the cave, because a wall of water rushed past the opening and would drown any man who tried to swim through it. The alligator left the ancestor in the cave and went to tell its family about the sweet human beef he would be serving them for dinner that night. But on the bank above the cave, a bush deer was about to give birth. The pains of her labor were so great that she stamped and stamped her hooves on the bank, until she stamped so hard that one of her hooves broke through to the cave below. The ancestor clawed at the hole until it was big enough, then climbed out of the cave to safety. After he was free, he summoned his family to the bank of the stream and announced, "Look, alligators almost ate me, but I was saved by the bush deer. These bush deer are now our brothers and sisters, and we must return their favor by never eating them again."

The next morning, she went with her family to the praying place at the foot of the cotton tree. The praying man arrived and spoke to the ancestors on the family's behalf. Jenisa's father brought forth a cooked fowl and a pot of rice.

"Oh, fathers and grandfathers, see the big pot we have brought you to eat. Watch over us. Keep safe our wives and our children. Keep our chiefs safe. Take care of us. Too many infants have died before their mothers could hold them in their arms. Our little bobos are being bitten by snakes. People have drowned in the rivers. We beg you to keep us safe from these misfortunes. Please keep us safe. See the big pot of sweet food we have brought for you."

The praying man poured water on the ground. "Fathers and grandfathers, here is some water for you to wash your hands. Now you may eat the rice."

The praying man mixed portions of the food with red palm oil on a banana leaf and placed it on a sacred stone.

Oh, fathers and grandfathers, Jenisa prayed, turning the horn of medicine over in her fingers, *let my thoughts reach you. Keep my love man safe. Keep my wife man safe. Protect me from my enemy and give me healthy children.*

(7)

Randall spent a sleepless night pondering the unidentified bright object in his deep white matter. The terminology sounded almost astrophysical, except it described inner space. His. Testing was scheduled to resume at 8 a.m. Meanwhile, he was supposed to go home, forget about the bright object in his brain, and sleep. Right. While Bean and Rheingold and the other doctors were at home dreaming about tax-sheltered annuities, Randall stared at the ceiling, grinding his teeth, certain that his brain tumor was seeding his bloodstream with metastatic satellites. He had an almost irresistible urge to do a total backup of all his software and data files onto a mini data cartridge capable of holding 400 megabytes of compressed data. He could carry it in his breast pocket, just in case he could take it with him.

He waited for the bat to show again, almost hoping it would, so he could get a better look at it. But then, what for? Either way he was in trouble. If there was a bright object in his deep white matter causing him to hallucinate, it was probably a brain tumor that would kill him in six months. If the bright object was a false positive, and there was nothing organically wrong with him, then he was a stranger to his own imagination. He would spend the rest of his life waiting around for newer, weirder, and more private hallucinations to move in with him and crowd out the rest of the world. At night, he would stare into the darkness and watch giant, repulsive bats appear out of thin air.

At four in the morning, he called Mack's extension at Sterling and left a voice mail: "The CEO of Nimrod Products just called me from some place in California. He's a friend and a client. His wife has come down with something called peduncular hallucinosis. The family gets their estate planning done upstairs. Get on the computers and find me some medical dope on peduncular hallucinosis. Bill it to my personal matters file, and I'll allocate the time later."

At eight o'clock, he returned to the Radiology Department at the Medical Center and gave his name to a clerk who sat behind a sliding glass panel. She gave him a big paper cup filled with contrast solution and pointed at a vinyl bench in the hallway. Randall held his nose and drank it, certain that the stuff would probably set off airport metal detectors and make Geiger counters natter at high frequency.

Normally, technicians conducted the scan, then provided the doctors with films to read. But this meant that Randall often had to wait for the results to be read by a radiologist and reported to his doctor, who would then report them to Bean. This time, Randall insisted that Bean be *at* the scan with a radiologist, so that when it was over, the doctors could walk right out of the booth and tell him what they had seen.

Scan time came and went, and still Bean failed to show. Randall waited, feeling a huge tumor swelling inside his skull, causing increased cranial pressure, wrath at Bean and the technicians, and desperate fear. Finally, a technician came out and told him that Dr. Bean was stuck inside someone else's brain with a surgical team and a lot of complications. Bean's message was for Randall to go ahead and be scanned, then wait for the results like everyone else.

Two technicians fetched Randall from the vinyl bench. If they already knew about the UBO, their manner didn't show it. They helped him onto a table that had an eight-foot doughnut at the head of it, with a hole for him and the table to slide through. First, they injected radioactive dye into his arm.

"More dye, for contrast," they told him with a smile.

"It's harmless," they said, wearing goggles, lead aprons, and black rubber gloves.

"Nothing to be afraid of," they told him, via microphone from a booth with three-foot-thick lead walls.

"You get more radiation from a sunburn," a bromide they presumably could not offer their skin cancer patients.

Randall usually argued with them about how much contrast fluid he had to drink and how much radioactive glop they were injecting into his arm. But this time, he was passive and agreeable. They positioned his head in the doughnut and then ran back to their booth. A small red light flashed, the tray moved in increments, slowly and precisely feeding him through the doughnut. Again the whirring sounds of some huge hydraulic engine spinning around him, punctuated by soft clicks whenever radiation was released. He could ̄ see one of the monitors in the booth, a colorful representation of a vertical slice of torso—probably his—with heads on white lab coats staring into it.

After twenty minutes, the technicians came out of the booth.

"You guys watched it on those monitors while the scan was being done, didn't you?" asked Randall.

"Yes," they said. "We did."

"Well," he stammered. "Did you see anything?"

Their faces instantly froze in precisely neutral expressions.

"We are not permitted to disclose test results," said one.

"Your doctor will provide you with the results," said the other. "We are not physicians. We are not permitted to evaluate or interpret results. We just obtain the scan and send it on videotape to the radiologist, who . . ."

"*I know that,*" Randall said, clenching his teeth. "But you know damn well if it was positive for anything, or negative, or whatever," he said, flashing them a humble smile, which failed to alter their precisely neutral expressions.

"Sorry," they said in a precisely neutral tone of voice.

"Very sorry, I'll bet," growled Randall.

Although their expressions did not change, Randall was suddenly convinced that they had just seen a huge brain tumor in living color on his scan, and now they were hiding it from him. Sure. At least once a week for years, these guys had seen tumors light up like alien warships all over their monitors. They had practiced this routine hundreds of times. Just walk out of the booth, keep your face straight, and try not to think about how you are talking to a guy who doesn't know he is going to be dead in six months.

When he left the room and closed the door, Randall felt them shake their heads behind him. As he walked down the hall, he imagined them going back into their booth for a second look. *Did you see the size of that thing?* they were probably saying. *Way past graveyard ugly!*

Next, he was due up in Bean's office for a spinal tap. In the hallways, he passed people whose fortunes had already been told.

A young couple beaming over an ultrasound photo of their unborn child. A stone-faced mother and father grimly towing a bald little girl. A stroke victim fidgeting in a wheelchair.

Two nurses prepared him for the spinal tap, something he'd never had before. He was at once grateful for another source of information about his condition and apprehensive about potentially dangerous side effects, like severing his spinal cord on a misguided syringe. The sting started at the base of his spine and spread up to the back of his neck. Afterward he seemed able to walk, but his toes tingled, probably a nerve or something they sliced in there. Or maybe all these dyes they were shooting into his blood were pickling him like a frog in fixative.

Back in Howard's office, the secretary told him that Howard had been in an emergency aneurysm repair since six that morning. A very complicated case. Could take hours.

"Is there any way you can call down and get me the results of that scan?" asked Randall, feeling like he was going to cry, or throw up blood, or discharge electricity, or give off radiation, erupt in some new way, because he had never been so afraid.

"I'm sorry," she said. "Only physicians are allowed to disclose test results to the patients. A pretty hard-and-fast rule around here. No exceptions."

"But my doctor is in surgery," said Randall, swallowing his nausea. "He could be in surgery all day, and I'm not going to be able to get . . . I want to know everything is OK, so I can go back to work."

"Sorry," she said, with a look that said she wasn't the least bit sorry. "Rules. You'll have to be a big boy and follow them."

Randall chewed on his fingernails for forty-five minutes until Bean showed up and hustled him into a consultation room.

"Where were you!?" Randall yelled.

"Do you really want to know?" asked Bean. "It's called standstill. We put a fifty-two-year-old aneurysm repair into hypothermic arrest, disconnected his heart, hooked him to a bypass pump, refrigerated his blood, and took his brain down to sixty degrees so we could go in and repair the aneurysm without him bleeding to death. Cold brains use less oxygen and blood than warm ones, so we just disconnected everything for ten or twenty minutes. After we clamped off the aneurysm, we hooked his heart back up to his major vessels, jump-started him, and prayed like mad that the thing would take a charge. Pretty standard stuff, really, but before you get pissed off, may I suggest that this patient, for a short time, needed me more than you did."

"OK, OK. I'm selfish. So what'd the scan show?"

"Angiography negative," said Bean. "It is not an arterio-venous malformation."

"Forget arterio-veno!" shouted Randall. "Is it a fucking brain tumor?"

"I don't know," said Howard softly. "Too deep for a CAT scan. We'll repeat the MRI, but nine times out of ten, you just get another UBO and nothing new."

"What about the spinal fluid?"

Bean sighed. "Elevated protein," he said.

"Which means," said Randall.

"It's nonspecific," said Bean, shifting in his chair and jittering his leg. "It could be an infection . . . Could be a . . . lesion . . ."

"Could be a brain tumor the size of an asteroid," said Randall. "You don't know shit from toilet paper, do you?" he shouted, leaping out of his chair and marching up and down, glaring at his friend. "Now what? More tests, I suppose?"

"Probably not," said Bean levelly. "Look, you *made* me your attending physician," he said. "I'm trying to be objective and do what I would do if you were any other patient. If you don't like my treatment, go see Carolyn!"

"I'm not any other patient," Randall yelled, marching some more. "What am I supposed to do? Go home and forget about it? Think about garbage or something?"

"We usually have to just wait and see," pleaded Howard. "Keep a close eye out for any symptoms and if something happens we'll be all over it. An infection usually gets better and goes away."

"And a tumor?" Randall croaked.

"Usually grows until we can see it," said Bean, "or until it begins causing other symptoms."

"Like a blinding headache, right?" said Randall. "Double vision, and the stone-cold comfort that you won't have to put up with it for long, right?"

"Look," said Bean. "Think about it. You're working ninety hours a week. OK, that's normal. Then your kid disappears in Africa. You can't sleep. You take some sleeping pills and wake up two hours later and see something that at first looks very weird, then it's gone.

Sounds like a one-time, hypnagogic hallucination. At worst, a freak occipital lobe seizure. It probably won't happen again. If I were you, I'd think real hard about whether you saw *something* that just looked different under the circumstances. And I'm talking to you as your friend, not your neurosurgeon."

Randall held his head in his hands.

"Go to work," said Bean. "Think about what I said tonight. Talk it over with Marjorie. If you want to talk some more, call me, no matter how late it is, OK?"

•

Randall breezed through the Sterling lobby as he always did, without saying hello to anyone, unless they were on the compensation committee. He switched on his computer and answered the blinking message from his secretary, who had a list of bankruptcy people to call, and one message from Senator Swanson, who had left the name and telephone number of Warren Holmes, the same bureaucrat who had called Randall on the first day of his son's disappearance.

He stabbed the button on his phone that connected him to Mack.

"Sir," Mack said, with a supercilious chuckle.

"Call that expert witness service we use," said Randall. "I need an expert on bats."

"Bats," said Mack. "Baseball bats?"

"Winged, nocturnal mammals," said Randall. "And I'm not talking about the sonar stuff. I'm interested in the different kinds of bats. If they ever make noises that people can hear. Where they live. How big they can get. What's the biggest kind, and so on."

"Morphology," said Mack. "I'll bet there's such a thing as a bat morphologist."

"Whatever. Tell him I've got a case I might need to use him on. Get him on the line, and then hook me up with him," said Randall. "Today."

"Mr. Bilksteen on four. Beach Cove," said his secretary over the intercom.

Randall normally would not have even returned a call from the likes of Bilksteen, but he had a sudden, sentimental craving for the familiar pleasures of kicking opposing counsel's ass around the bankruptcy court.

"Bilksteen," Randall said, jabbing the speakerphone button with his broadsword and settling back into his swivel chair.

"Pick up, you piece of shit," said Bilksteen bitterly.

"Are you still alive?" asked Randall. "Somebody said they saw you in hell having whiskey and cracked ice with the devil. I figured you for dead. I don't mean to have you on speaker, but my hands are full. I'm editing a bill we're sending to Comco Banks for one of those ridiculous lift-stay motions we were talking about just the other day. Hold on a second," said Randall.

An office courier came into Randall's office and placed a firm newsletter in his hands; Randall fed it to Benjy, and pushed it on through the bear's alimentary canal with his broadsword.

"Wait a second," said Randall. "Now that I get a closer look at this statement of services. This bill is for the Beach Cove case! That's your case, isn't it, Bilk?"

"If you believe in anything," pleaded Bilksteen. "If you believe in anything that would ever allow you to help another human being in trouble, I'm asking you . . . please, give me a deal, give me *any* deal I can take to the limited partners. Even if they won't take it in a million years, just give me something. I could at least go back with something . . . and a little of my self-respect."

"You mean, do you a favor?" asked Randall. "Please, no begging. It gives me heart trouble. Doing you a favor would be inconsistent with my client's interest. Comco writes my checks, not Beach Cove, and I hope you are not offering to write me checks," said Randall.

"You're the one who belongs in hell," said Bilksteen.

"Are you threatening me with punishment in the afterlife?" asked Randall. "This is bankruptcy. Pull yourself together. And once you get yourself together, if you're still ashamed to show your face in bankruptcy court, then try implementing some of those new Japanese management techniques that are supposed to be so good for firm culture and whatnot. You could start by publicly disemboweling yourself in front of the courthouse, to atone for your abysmal incompetence as a bankruptcy lawyer."

"I mean it," pleaded Bilksteen. "Any deal. Any deal at all."

"I'm adding this phone call to the bill," said Randall, "and we are approaching the second increment of billable time."

"If you don't care about me," said Bilksteen, "think about the limited partners. Some of them put their kids' college money into this thing."

Randall disconnected Bilksteen and punched the number of Mr. Warren Holmes, some kind of cultural relations officer with the State Department according to the voice mail messages. He beeped his way through the usual automated answering obstacle course, cursing himself for not telling his secretary to get the guy on the line.

Finally he reached Holmes, who reminded him of their first conversation and reintroduced himself—a good friend of Senator Swanson, eager to help in any way he could, particularly if Randall had questions about native matters, which apparently Mrs. Killigan had been calling Senator Swanson about. Randall listened with half an ear, while Holmes tried to impress him with his qualifications.

"My training was in the hard sciences," said Holmes, "but then I went into anthropology, and from there to foreign service. I was stationed at various embassies in Africa for almost ten years. Senator Swanson said you had some witchcraft questions."

"My wife tells me there's some suspicion of witchcraft, some kind of juju, or gris-gris, or whatever they call it," Randall said. "We have certain letters from my son's servant that said something about witchmen and bush devils. What do you know about this kind of supernatural stuff?"

"Well, Mr. Killigan," said Holmes with a polite sigh, "it takes some doing to answer that kind of a question. It's not a simple thing. Before you can explain things like witchcraft, you have to understand the African mind."

"If understanding the African mind will help me find my son," said Randall, "I'm listening."

"I used to be with the embassy in Ouagadougou, in what was then Upper Volta," Holmes continued. "Now it's called Burkina Faso, or some damn thing. I studied these people for years. They're primitives. They don't understand things the way we do. When something out of the ordinary occurs, they have to invent explanations to account for it."

"Because they are superstitious," Randall inserted helpfully.

"Exactly," said Holmes. "I stayed in a village for a couple of weeks over there. And while I was there, one of the men went crazy. He started seeing things at night, screaming, he stopped eating, he didn't make any sense when he talked. All the other villagers tried to tell me that the man had a witch in his belly, and that the witch was gradually taking over his soul."

Holmes laughed derisively into the phone. "They actually believe that some kind of being or force could enter a person and assume control of his personality. They don't realize that the universe obeys perfectly rational laws of science. Instead, they make the whole thing up as they go along."

"Christ," said Randall, secretly wondering just what it was the man had seen at night that had made him scream.

"They don't realize that the crazy person is probably just afflicted with a garden-variety acute hebephrenia with a lithium-resistant bipolar component, most likely caused by synaptic dysfunction in the pineal body, resulting in elevated serotonin levels and proportionately increased stimulation of neuroreceptors in the hippocampus and the amygdala. Know what I mean?"

Randall was still imagining what a person might act like if a force or a being was taking over his personality. Would the person be aware of the force?

"Of course I know what you mean," snapped Randall. "Psychiatry. Or neurology, or whatever."

"Now. Why don't Africans know what makes people go crazy? Because they know nothing about brain chemistry and metabolic disorders. Because they don't have positron emission tomography, or superconducting quantum interference devices, or single-photon emission computerized tomography. Does that sound like witchcraft? Hell no. That's science. And you can take it to the bank."

Randall was hearing every other word. How, he wondered, would such a being or force present itself?

"What else do you have for me?" he asked irritably.

"That's not the half of it," Holmes said. "They think the entire world is full of invisible spirits, and these spirits live right there with them on the land, appearing to them in dreams and influencing everything that happens in the village. They think they live and dream in some kind of force field, inhabited by demons, witches, devils, genies, sorcerers, and disgruntled ancestors. Any strange or significant place, or any huge or odd object or being—animals, trees, waterfalls, places of ritual—can have a spirit, or a witch. Can you believe it? They're so ignorant and superstitious, they don't realize that everything is actually made up of molecules, consisting of electrons, muons, and neutrinos in orbit around atomic nuclei, together with protons, neutrons, pi mesons, mesons, baryons, kaons, and hadrons, all held together by gluons and made up of quarks of all 'colors' and 'flavors': up quarks, down quarks, top quarks, bottom quarks, anti-quarks, strange quarks, mirror-image quarks, and charmed quarks. Know what I mean?"

"Physics," said Randall, "of course."

"Of course, no one's ever 'seen' these elementary particles in any pedestrian sense of the word, but we 'know' they are there, because we've bombarded them with other elementary particles and observed certain indirect behaviors . . . and, just as you might suspect, all of these particles conform to perfectly rational laws of physics. Does that sound like witchcraft? No, praise God. That's quantum mechanics, and solid enough to build a house on. So let these African villagers go ahead and think spirits run everything, we know better, right?"

"Right," said Randall.

"See, the difference between us and them is that when something out of the ordinary happens over there, they have to invent an explanation, stories, myths, tales of old. Over here, we know that nothing is out of the ordinary, because someone, somewhere, has a perfectly rational scientific explanation for what happened, so we don't have to invent any stories. And frankly, I sleep better because of it."

"Me too," said Randall.

"They think a Great Spirit named *Ngewo*, who lived in a cave, made the world and made all the men and women and animals in the world. Over here, we have scientific evidence. We *know* that the universe really came from a single infinitely dense point of matter, which exploded in the big bang a hundred or so billion years ago. Now, if I had to choose between a story about a spirit in a cave and another one about a single infinitely dense point of matter exploding billions of years ago, I don't have to tell you which one I'd put my faith in."

"Yeah," said Randall.

Mack's intercom light lit up.

"Thanks for the information," said Randall. "I'd like to have my secretary or my wife fax you a copy of that servant's letter, so you can take a look at the description he has of these witchmen coming into the village."

"That would be fine," said Holmes.

Randall turned Holmes over to his secretary, with instructions to get Holmes's fax number, call his wife, and have her fax a copy of the servant's letter. Then he stabbed Mack's intercom light.

"Yeah," said Randall.

"Bat man on line three," said Mack Saplinger over the intercom. "University of California at San Diego. His name is Dr. Veldkamp, Ph.D. in zoology, with a heavy emphasis on you know what. He doesn't speak much English. It's mostly Latin, until he hears the word 'money.' I told him we might need an expert witness on bats, and that you were a lawyer with some bat questions. He said he'd talk to you if he could charge the same hourly rate you do."

"Put him through."

Mack confirmed the connection and hung up.

"Professor Veldkamp," said Randall breezily, "I trust my associate gave you some idea of what we're after. It's really quite a peculiar case, but I guess in my twenty-some years of lawyering, I've used every other kind of expert witness, so why not a bat expert?"

"I hope I can help," said the professor. "Mr. Saplinger gave me your address, so you'll be receiving my résumé and monographs of my journal articles. I'm also the author of two books: *The Ecology of the Dwarf Epauletted Fruit Bat* and *Bat Morphology*. I received my training at the University of Chicago, under Dr. Blanford."

"Right. That's exactly what we need. See, we have a guy who's trying to give away a lot of money. A *lot* of money. I'll stay away from legal terminology, if you stay away from bat terminology. The rich guy—let's call him Midas—has hired us to set up a series of big, complex trusts for him. But one of his would-be heirs—let's call him Harry—is trying to stop Midas and us from giving away the money, because Harry says Midas is incompetent. Nuts. And one of the reasons Harry says Midas is nuts is because Midas claims that one night he saw a big bat. A *huge* bat. I mean, Midas claims this thing had at least a four- or five-foot wingspan. Big! Now, I've got plenty of brainsick clients who tell me all kinds of daffy stories about money, but I've never had one with a bat story, so I'll ask you: Do bats come with wingspans the width of Volkswagens?"

"Of course," said Veldkamp. "Bats have wingspans ranging from five centimeters, about the size of a butterfly, to just under two meters, almost the armspread of a human being. They weigh anywhere from two grams to twelve hundred grams, or three pounds. But where did, uh, Midas see this bat?"

"In his bedroom," said Randall, "in the middle of the night. But he got a pretty good look at it, because he turned on the lights and tried to kill it with a tennis racket."

"I meant, what part of the world? What country?"

"Does that make a difference?"

"No," demurred the professor. "Maybe it doesn't make any difference. Maybe bats are the same everywhere, just like laws. It doesn't matter whether you live in Madagascar or Marin County, the bats and the parking ordinances are the same, right?" He chuckled. "The largest bat in North America is the mastiff bat, *Molossidae eumops*, with a wingspan of about a foot and a half. If Midas was vacationing in Papua New Guinea with some cannibals, he could have seen a flying fox, *Pteropus*, which is more around the size you're talking about, wingspans of one and a half to two meters."

"Let's see," Randall said, "two meters . . ."

"About six feet," said Veldkamp. "Once you get over two feet, you're almost certainly talking Old World. And you're almost certainly dealing with *Megachiroptera*, as opposed to *Microchiroptera*."

"You can't use Latin on the witness stand," said Randall. "Jurors hate it."

"Old World fruit bats. They live in Eurasia, Australia, and Africa. Big, fruit-eating bats," said Veldkamp, "as opposed to other bats, including New World fruit bats, which are much smaller, and different in other ways. Many zoologists speculate that the big Old World fruit bats have an entirely different ancestry than regular bats, because the large fruit bats for the most part do not echolocate."

"Echo . . ." said Randall.

"Echolocate," the professor repeated. "They don't use sonar to hunt and navigate. The big fruit bats see with large, animal-like eyes; most of them don't emit the ultrasonic sounds you've probably heard so much about."

"Fruit bats don't make noise, then?" Randall said. "Because . . ."

"I didn't say that," the professor interrupted. "Bats make some noises, including squeaks and chirps audible to the human ear, but echolocation is almost always ultrasonic, which means humans can't hear it. It's how bats *see*."

"I know that," said Randall. "But this bat made a loud, almost percussive sound . . . definitely audible to the human ear . . . or so Midas said. Like really loud castanets or something. Kind of like a loud *thwock*, Midas says. See, that's another reason Harry says

Midas is nuts, because Harry claims that bats make only noises that humans can't hear, which of course would mean that if Midas *heard* a bat making loud *thwock* noises, then he must be too nuts to handle his money. Belfry syndrome, I guess you might call it."

"Some fruit bats make loud, low-frequency sounds audible to the human ear," said Veldkamp. "The loud *thwock*, that's definitely a fruit bat, and a very special kind of fruit bat. Probably *Hypsignathus monstrosus*, from what you've described to me, since it's known for its distinctively loud voice. Very interesting creatures. They are quite large frugivores, with wingspans well over three feet. They are the so-called hammer-headed or horse-faced bat."

"Yeah!" said Randall, almost too enthusiastically. "It looked like a horse, or a dog's head, with wings!"

"It has a grotesque, swollen muzzle and its lips are covered with wartlike growths."

"That's it!" said Randall. "That's the bat . . . I mean, the one Midas described."

"It has a large, well-developed larynx—almost a sounding board really—for making those distinctive *thwock* sounds."

"That's it! Then he's not crazy," Randall said. "He just found a *hypsig*-whatever in his house."

"If he found a fruit bat with a wingspan of more than two feet, he lives in Asia, Australia, or Africa," said Veldkamp. "If he found *Hypsignathus*, or the horse-faced bat, in his house, then he lives in Africa. Central Africa or West Africa."

Randall swallowed. "He lives in Indianapolis."

Professor Veldkamp chuckled into Randall's ear. "I would love to be an expert witness for you, Mr. Killigan, but I am afraid that there is no way I could convince a jury that a sane person could find an Old World fruit bat with a wingspan of five feet in his bedroom in Indianapolis, unless he put it there himself."

"I see," Randall said, staring into the sea blue of his computer screen. "Maybe I'll call Midas and check on some of those measurements and . . . some of the other stuff. Maybe he's taking medication or something."

"Maybe," said Veldkamp. "If he wants to say he saw it in Indiana, get him down to about a foot, foot and a half tops. And, more important, get rid of the loud *thwock* sound, OK? Otherwise, he was traveling in West Africa when he saw it."

"I'll be back in touch," said Randall.

A ring-again call came through as soon as his line opened.

"I've got that Nimrod medical stuff you wanted," said Mack over the speaker.

"Nimrod?" said Randall blankly.

"The CEO's wife," Mack said. "I've got it right here. My guess is that she's seeing things and she can't sleep at night."

"Get on with it," said Randall.

"*Annals of Neurology*," said Mack. "May 1990. 'Peduncular Hallucinosis Associated with Isolated Infarction of the Substantia Nigra Pars Reticulata.' " He paused and chuckled. "Already I can tell you she won't like the bill. In law as in medicine, mouthfuls of Latin mean the bill is going up."

"Talk," barked Randall.

"Here's another one. *Neurology*. October 1983. 'Peduncular Hallucinations Caused by Brain-Stem Compression.' Peduncular hallucinations are vivid, colored visual images of people, animals, plants, scenes, or geometric patterns, usually associated with brainstem lesions of vascular and infectious etiology."

"The *Annals* article gives a history of the disease. They used to think it was a dissociated state of sleep in which the visual hallucinations were dreams occurring in a state of relative wakefulness. Another guy, Van Bogaert or some such, says peduncular hallucinosis is a state of ego dissolution with loss of the ability to distinguish external reality from imagination.

"Hello?" said Mack.

"I'm here," said Randall, feeling his ego dissolve and seep through his imagination into external reality.

"So, if she has peduncular hallucinosis, it would seem that she has a vascular lesion, an infectious lesion, or a craniopharyngioma, which is a tumor of the . . ."

"What kind of tests do they run on people to find out what's causing it?" asked Randall, not wanting to hear about tumors just now.

"CAT scans and MRIs mostly," said Mack. "But before those were invented, they usually had to wait for an autopsy. As near as I can tell, nobody really knows how or why midbrain lesions disturb sleep or give rise to visual hallucinations. Sleep is disturbed, intense visual hallucinations occur, the guy dies about six months later, and when they open his head and scoop it out, they find midbrain lesions."

Modem lights blinked, and messages flashed across the top of his computer screen. He recognized his stockbroker's logo graphic followed by a streamer of bright white letters: "Get happy! Merck up 6½ on steady volume."

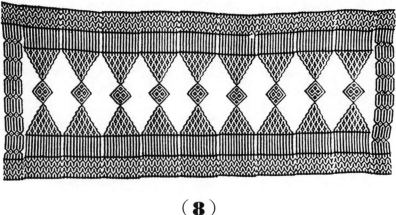

(**8**)

Boone woke from a sleep as deep and dank as death, shrouded in the bone-white cloud of his mosquito net, steeped in his sweaty sleeping bag, and raw from the prickles of the tick mattress. Had he heard a man shouting, or had he dreamed it?

"ALLAH AKBAR! ALLAH AKBAR! ALLAH AKBAR!"

In the foredawn silence, a voice bawled the vowels out in the full-throated sonority of a town crier, punctuated by the thud of a drum. Someone stirred on Sisay's side of the wall.

"Sisay," Boone said, in a voice he hoped would make it up the cement wall, over the din from outside, under the zinc-pan roof, and into Sisay's quarters. "Someone is shouting outside. It may be an emergency or something. I can't tell. Is something wrong?"

"Only with you," Sisay said. "It's morning and you're still in bed."

"But the yelling," Boone said. "What is he saying? What time is it?"

"I can see you're a real world traveler," said Sisay derisively. "Half the planet has been hearing 'Allah akbar' five times a day for the last thirteen hundred years, and you've never even heard it once."

"I'm from Indiana," Boone protested. "You know, one of those American high school graduates who can't find Africa on a map of the world."

"The village muezzin is filling his lungs with the mighty breath of Allah and is calling the men to morning prayers. He is telling you, in Arabic, that God is great. That's one translation. God is most mighty is another. When I was new to the country, I asked a wise old pa to translate 'Allah akbar' for me. He told me it means God is very, very big."

"What time is it?"

"Morning time."

"ALLAH AKBAR! ALLAH AKBAR! ALLAH AKBAR!"

This time the bellowing was so loud it reverberated in Boone's open, empty aluminum canteen, setting up a dissonant, antiphonal moan.

"Consider yourself blessed," Sisay advised. "In many villages, they use battery-powered bullhorns to tell people just how big God is."

Boone heard sandaled feet scuffling across woven mats in the next room.

"I'll be back in half an hour," he said, banging the screen door behind him.

Boone turned over and listened to Sisay greeting other villagers on their way to prayers.

"Morning-O, Mistah Aruna. How de body?"

"I tell God tank ya," Sisay replied.

"Na de *poo-mui* stranger, he no come foh morning prayers?" a voice asked.

"Na America he been come out," Sisay explained. "America man, he no pray." Then in a loud voice Boone felt was directed at his window, Sisay said, "In America they pray to television sets and video display terminals."

"Vee-dee-oh dees-play tah-me-nahls," a voice repeated.

"Whatin tele-vish-ee-ohn?" asked another voice.

"Na foh make you stupid," said Sisay. "Foh make you eyes big, and you brain small. Foh make you greedy too much. Foh make you one greedy big eye. Naim dat."

"ALLAH AKBAR! ALLAH AKBAR! ALLAH AKBAR!"

As soon as the muezzin left off, Boone drifted back into a doze populated by hooded figures calling from minarets. Then he heard what sounded like a soul shrieking in the seventh rung of Dante's Hell, where the violent and the bestial gnaw their flesh in a river of boiling blood. *What now?* he wondered. He had already been awakened during the night by a "palaver," which, according to Sisay, had arisen out of a woman damage case. Some of the young men in the village had slept with two young wives of the section chief, which gave the chief the right to seek healthy fines for woman damage. The actual offense had occurred some time ago, but last night Moiwo's representative and the young men and their extended families stayed up half the night in the neighboring *barri* arguing about the amount of labor required to discharge the fines.

Geckos had also kept him up most of the night. The geckos he had seen in Freetown were apparently an urban, domesticated variety; these village geckos were far more aggressive. They rattled the underside of the zinc-pan roof through the night—saurian warriors marauding and devouring their weight in insects. And now in the first light of dawn, he could see them wearing green and orange war paint, streaking across the ceiling like iridescent lightning bolts, preying godlessly on the orders of the insects, their mouths crusty with the guts of night killings.

Again he heard wraiths of hell braying in terror and agony. *Roosters*, he suddenly concluded. *Cocks crowing.* Not just any cocks, though. Not the Old MacDonald cock-a-doodle-doo American barnyard domestics. These shrieking voices were as old as time and crowing with the terror of the first and last dawn. In the blender of his hypnopompic imagination, the cocks grew human voices and began a horrid chorus in strophe and antistrophe: "The world ends today!" squawked one forlorn soul, with a rasping wail from a throat that would be slit before sundown. "The world ends today!" cried another in the same anguished squall that passioned the night when Peter denied Christ. "Never heard of the guy!" another repeated thrice, with the squawk of a doomed parakeet in a collapsed mine shaft. "Who's he?" crowed one in rut, mounting a hen from behind and drawing blood from her neck with its beak. It was the cry of Nature taking God's name in vain and devouring itself in a rage of famine.

After the cocks left off, a dozen infants with dry bellies took over, sending up a rondo of bloodcurdling squalls for milk from the breasts of mothers who were in no apparent hurry to feed them. Boone listened to the jabber of women and children in neighboring dwellings, their voices twining like strands in a communal fabric, with distinctive aural patches forming at various dwellings within earshot. A husband and wife quarreled to the left of him. Several women argued over a howling infant to his right. A small boy sang songs to his brothers and sisters behind. The infant's howling changed to choking, accompanied by the excited chatter of the women in attendance.

In the courtyard outside his window, small children had gathered with trays, calling out the virtues of their wares:

"I got de sweet benny seed cake."

"I got de fine-fine kola nut."

"De sweet orange ih dae foh you. Three foh five cent. No moh."

He heard sandals scuffling across the veranda, followed by the squeak and clatter of a falling pot handle.

"Kong, kong," said a female voice at the door to Sisay's quarters.

Boone opened his door and found a young woman bearing a pot, a platter of cakes, and two canteen cups.

"Is that coffee?" he asked hopefully.

"Ih dae," she said, setting the coffee and cups on the concrete knee wall of the veranda. "Fine-fine cakes dae," she added, lowering a platter of fried dough and sesame seed cakes. She was plump, but still shapely and graceful. He watched her pour coffee into cups.

"Whay you name?" she asked with a grin, looking over her shoulder and catching him in the act of admiring her.

"Boone," he said. "Boone Westfall."

"Usai you come out so?"

"What?" said Boone.

She smiled apologetically and covered her mouth. Then she straightened, assumed the posture of a child reciting her school lessons, and said in careful, exaggerated English, "Where you come from?"

"America," said Boone.

"A name, Jenisa," she said. "A yam young wife to Section Chief Moiwo. He say me send you dis food foh welcahm you na Salone."

"Tell him thank you very much," said Boone. "I'd like very much to meet him. Does he live here, in this village?"

"He is a big man," she said. "He has many houses. Sometime he stay na hya. Sometime he stay na Ndevehun. Sometime he stay Freetown. Sometime he stay Bo. Na elections dae come. He go wakka-wakka, talking for elections. He go wan make ihnself Paramount Chief. He no hya foh sometime. Naim dat."

Her eyes went from Boone to his backpack.

"Whay you wife?"

"I don't have a wife," he said.

"Na lie you dae lie," she said. "You get beaucoup wife na America."

"I don't have a wife. I've never been married."

"You think me stupid? You wan wash me face foh me? You get beaucoup wife dae na America. Whatin na you come na hya foh do?"

"I am looking for my friend. Michael Killigan. He is a Peace Corps Volunteer."

"Peace Koh," she repeated. "I sabby ihm. Den say he been come out Ndevehun."

"What do they say happened to him?"

"I no know. Dey no see ahm," she said. "Den say he been go alackey."

"Alackey?" Boone asked.

"He craze. He done run off. Den say he come out Ndevehun. Dey no go able foh see ahm. Better no dae inside Ndevehun."

"What can you tell me about something called *hale* medicine?" Boone asked.

"*Hale?*" she said, pouring brown water into one of the cups. "Na medicine. Which kind *hale?*"

"How about the kind of *hale* that witchmen or bush devils use?" he said.

She averted her eyes. "I no know," she said, setting the pot back onto the tray with a clatter. "I no know."

Her eyes fell on the table with the hurricane lamp and personal items he had strewn there.

"What ees thees?" she said, picking up a stick applicator of mosquito repellent.

"It's mosquito repellent," he said, again admiring the look of her. "It keeps mosquitoes away." Then, noting the fascination shining in her eyes: "Would you like to have it?"

"I can have it?" she asked eagerly.

"Sure," said Boone. "And maybe you can do something for me?"

"Whatin?" she asked.

"Some people say that witchmen or bush devils came to my friend's village and did something to him with *hale*, or took him away into the bush. Have you ever heard about anything like that happening before?"

"I no understand," she said. "I no know." She slipped the repellent into her lappa and wiped her hands. "Better no dae," she said, becoming distressed. "I dae go." She put her hand on the door latch and showed him her round, black Mende face. Her nostrils flared slightly with emotion, and one tear beaded in the corner of her eye.

"Could you ask around for me," said Boone, "and see if that sort of thing ever happens to white men? And maybe where these witches and devils hide out or meet?"

"I no understand," she said, her eyes widening. "I no get word for talk. I dae go."

She rounded the corner of the veranda and disappeared into the adjoining courtyard.

Apparently, all over Sierra Leone, coffee was brewed by dumping grounds in a pot of water and boiling it. It fell to the coffee drinker to sip the hot water out of the cup and leave the sediment behind. Boone fingered a cake, and found a small, sealed white envelope under the cakes. Neatly printed with a fountain pen on watermarked bond was the following message:

We can help you find your brother, if you will feed the medicine.
Don't speak about this with *anyone* until we meet. I will reach you.
Idrissa Moiwo
Section Chief

Boone heard the sounds of men returning from prayers. He stuffed the paper into his pocket and ate another cake. He heard Sisay's voice briefly, before it was drowned out by the braying of domestic animals, the clatter of utensils on stones, and the continued choking and howling of the neighboring infants. He was relieved to see his host.

"The babies," Boone said with a wince, "are they sick or what?"

"Noisy, aren't they?" said Sisay. "And you want to know why? Well, for simplicity's sake, let's say we're hearing six kids scream their lungs out. According to the field studies, one is bawling because he will die of dysentery or malnutrition before his first birthday, another has the same afflictions but will make it past his first birthday, only to die of something else before his fifth, the other four are howling because they are enraged at the prospect of spending their infancy sucking on dry dugs, sweltering in mud huts, and listening to the death rattles of their cousins."

Sisay cocked his head and listened to more wailing and choking. "However, just now, I think we are hearing young Fatmata and her sister Nyanda choking her little Borboh with cassava pap. A Mende mother is taught to force-feed her infant until its stomach is 'hard,' whatever that means. It's a senseless custom, but the women swear by it. The first year I was here, an infant 'stopped breathing' shortly after one of these feeding sessions. No connection between that and the cassava packing, of course."

The sputtering and gagging continued, punctuated with screams of anguish when the infant managed a breath.

"And you just let it happen?" Boone asked, not bothering to conceal his exasperation.

"No," said Sisay. "I tried to tell them that it was a poor nutritional regimen. I told them the babies could choke to death from being force-fed. I said I knew of no possible benefit to be gained from cramming food down an infant's throat."

"And?"

"They ignored me. What would a white man know about raising a Mende peekin in the bush?"

The infant hacked and spat, coughed, choked, gagged, and let out a shriek, followed by the nattering of women, presumably telling each other the best technique for force-feeding an infant.

"I can't stand it," Boone said. "I have to do something."

"That makes me nervous," said Sisay. "That's when white people are most dangerous. When they try to make things 'better' for Africans. When white people are trying to enslave Africans or rob them, the Africans usually know just what to do. They've dealt with slave traders, invaders, and plunderers for centuries. They usually quench the world's thirst for slaves by capturing some of their enemies and selling them to the slave traders. But when white people come in with a lot of money or 'know-how' and try to make things 'better,' that's when things really go to hell. Why can't white people just visit? Why must they always meddle? It's as if you were invited to dinner at someone's house and during your brief visit you insisted on rearranging all the furniture in the house to suit your tastes."

The infant gagged violently and choked.

"But you can't just sit here and let a helpless infant choke to death, can you?"

"I can," Sisay said. "Maybe you can't. Maybe you should go see what you can do. Some of the women Volunteers down south tried to do something about it. Like most white people, they fancied themselves as some kind of cultural police. They were quite upset with the way the Sande matrons trained young women: the mandatory clitoridectomies during the initiation rituals, the force-feeding of infants, the polygamy, the brutal manual labor for women, while the men drink palm wine and gamble. The Volunteers held clinics for the village women and tried to convince them that the Sande matrons were part of an ageless male conspiracy to devalue and enslave women. The Volunteers announced that the Sande Society initiation, which young girls are taught to anticipate with great joy and excitement, was nothing but genital mutilation and brainwashing, designed to turn women into chattel kept by men.

"The Mende women said, in essence, 'Thanks for your opinion, but we've been doing things this way for thousands of years, and we don't need you to come in and tell us what to do with our bodies,' an argument which one would think might appeal to these *poo-mui* feminists. But no such luck. They stepped up their cultural chauvinism and did everything they could to rearrange the furniture during their visit.

"A few of the Volunteers were actually making progress, and by that I mean some of the more educated women at least started listening to them . . . until the word got out."

"The word?"

"Somebody made the mistake of telling one of the village women about abortion rights, and it was over. The next time the women organized their clinic, one of the Sande matrons took the floor and said, in essence, 'These *poo-mui* women are trying to tell you that initiation is harmful and bad, that we should tell our husbands they can have only one wife, and that we should not force-feed our peekins. Guess what? In America, they let medicine men cut healthy peekins out of their mothers' bellies, then they throw the peekins into latrines. How's that for savagery?'

"So much for the clinic. The Volunteers had to be reassigned, because the village women thought the *poo-mui* women were witches trying to trick them out of their children so they could take them into the bush and eat them."

More sputtering, coughing, hacking.

"Nothing is simple when it comes to mixing cultures," Sisay said. "That's why many people argue that Africa would be better off if you and your countrymen just . . . left, and took your money and your 'good' intentions with you."

"Kong, kong," came from the wooden door, this time male voices.

Two men appeared wearing Muslim burnooses and skullcaps. Sisay introduced them, and each of them bestowed a kola nut on Boone, which he learned was to bring him good luck during his stay in Sierra Leone. After exchanging greetings for a good half an hour, the men went on their way, and Boone bit into one of the kola nuts, finding the texture of a damp macadamia nut and a taste so violently bitter it seemed to absorb every trace of moisture in his mouth.

"What the hell is it?" asked Boone with puckered lips and a screwed-up face.

"Caffeine, nicotine, and aspirin all found in the same nut. It's given as a gift of greeting or farewell, as medicine, or primarily as a stimulant to keep hungry people working when there is nothing to eat, or to keep devil dancers going all night and into the next day. You took too big of a bite. You'll get quite a buzz off even a nibble or two."

"It tastes like a macadamia nut pickled in turpentine."

Sisay sat on the floor and took a bite.

"More trouble in the village," he said. "Mama Saso miscarried a set of twins last night, which will make things very touchy around here for a while. The birth of these twins had been foretold in a dream, but now they are dead. Twins have special cultic powers. They can foretell the future and protect the family from witches. But now, of course, the villagers are saying that the witches ate these twins before they could be born."

"What isn't caused by witches?" asked Boone.

"The Mende will stoically accept almost any hardship," said Sisay. "But when an abnormally high number of infants start to die, it's usually because of witchcraft."

He went to the water pail and served up two cups of water.

The most annoying thing about his host, Boone thought, was the way he pointedly omitted expressing disapproval of anything native, especially witchcraft, or this barbaric stuffing of infant bellies. He also had displayed a respect for native medicines, even though, according to Lewis, the native cures for such things as snakebite were not nearly as effective as the antivenin found in the clinics.

Boone was suddenly tired—perhaps because the kola-nut buzz had worn off—and was thinking about retiring to his room for a nap before lunch.

"I have arranged the naming ceremony," Sisay said, interrupting his inclinations to rest alone for a while. "Bring a gift for your father. Do you have any cigarettes, another T-shirt, or anything else in your immense American backpack that you could bestow upon your father as a gift?"

"No cigarettes," Boone said. "But I have several tobacco pipes."

"The perfect gift," said Sisay, "and not by chance. Your ancestors are looking out for you."

Boone rummaged and grumbled, deciding that this relentless gifting of authority figures who suddenly wanted to be related to him would get old fast, unless he put his foot down, preferably in his host's mouth during one of his speeches. The entire cultural history of the village was being played out for him, while hours, days—two days!—were almost gone. In America, a missing person was an emergency. Here, there were more important things to do, like pretend you are related to somebody you never saw before.

Boone selected the most battered of his three briar pipes and took along a small pouch of terrible French tobacco.

He followed his host through the meandering courtyards of the village, where the workday was under way. Women in groups of three or four, some with children strapped to them, pestled rice by lifting eight-foot logs and dropping them into mortars carved from tree stumps. Steady and rhythmic as human derricks, they sang to the thud of wood on rice on wood. Others winnowed the husks from the kernels by tossing the pulverized rice with fans, allowing the shredded hulls to flutter off like insect wings in the morning breeze. A small peekin with a goatee of bluish breast milk bounced in his mother's lap, slinging her sagging breasts about by the dugs like a drunkard with the nozzles of two tapped kegs in hand. A naked boy zealously guarded a patch of poured cement, where cocoa beans were drying in the sun, pelting marauding chickens with stones. Boone later learned the peekin's zeal was inspired by the prospect of a meal if he did his job, and nothing for supper if his mother found roosters in the cocoa beans.

Boone wandered over to a group of women hulling rice and greeted a scrawny grandma who looked as if the effort of hoisting the huge pestle would kill her before lunch.

She laughed and smiled, until he put his hands on the pole and offered to hull a little while for her.

A look of horror broke out on her face and she called her relatives to come share her apparent indignation.

Boone hulled a few times to show them what he had in mind.

Their mouths fell open. They shouted. They stared, their eyes bloodshot with shock and disbelief. The old woman screamed with a vile look. She was insulted and enraged. She looked like she was getting ready to spit in his face, as if he had just asked her to go to bed with him, or to watch him go to the bathroom.

The women quickly decided, *poo-mui* guest or no, they would take matters into their own hands. Two of them took the pestle from him and the rest of them pushed him away angrily, shouting at him and calling for Sisay to please take control of his stranger.

"What the fuck are you doing?" Sisay yelled, pulling him away from them.

"I was trying to help," said Boone, shrugging him off. "She looked tired and sweaty and too old for the job."

Behind him the women were now in a circle pointing at him and calling their neighbors out of their houses to hear about the *poo-mui*'s outrageous behavior.

"Hulling rice is women's work," said Sisay. "Now they think you are mentally ill. And you touched the thing with your left hand!"

"I was trying to help," said Boone.

"You failed," said Sisay. "A man doing women's work is about as acceptable as cross-dressing over here. You would have made a better first impression if you'd come out of your room wearing a negligee. Now they are saying you grabbed the pestle because you don't have a penis."

His host seemed truly upset, but Boone cared less and less. He was on the verge of leaving the village to find this Moiwo fellow and see what "feeding the medicine" was all about. For now, he followed his host through the courtyards, around wells, and under shaded baffas, waving at the citizenry and hoping the naming ceremony would be a short one. Emaciated, ancient women sat in shaded verandas, batting flies away from their faces, while peekins braided their grandmothers' hair and listened to the ancestral songs. An old pa wobbled one of his last teeth out of its socket and held the bloody enamel gem in his fingertips, considering it philosophically. One woman was so decrepit, she sat alone in a dark, shaded corner, her arms wrapped around the folded bones of her legs. She coughed softly into her kneecaps. When she called to the white men in Mende, Boone saw bare gums stained orange by kola nuts. She gestured at them with a fingerless hand, a stump with smooth, rounded knobs where the digits belonged.

Sisay greeted her, then shrugged his shoulders, gestured at Boone, and spoke Mende, continuing on his way.

"What did she want?" Boone asked.

"Medicine," he said. "The old ones all think you have medicine and snuff because you are white. Every once in a while, one will follow you all day, like a stray, asking everybody you visit with if you gave them any snuff. The old grandmas love snuff. The British used to hand it out like candy."

"What happened to her? Where did she find a piece of machinery that could do that to her hand?"

"Hands plural," Sisay said. "Leprosy. There are no machines around here. No gas or electricity. Plenty of diseases, though."

Until Lewis had mentioned lepers in Freetown, Boone thought leprosy had gone out with chariot races and the fall of the Roman Empire, but he was afraid to show his ignorance.

"I know what you're thinking," said Sisay. "It's still quite common in the Third World, but you don't hear about it much anymore, because white people don't get it. You need dark, overcrowded, unsanitary conditions. Nine people sleeping in one room with chickens, goats, and a few peekins. We also still have lots of polio, measles, whooping cough, and a dozen other diseases that have been eradicated where you come from. You probably won't get any of those, but don't worry, you will get malaria, whether you take the chloroquine or not. You can bet on that. It's the common cold of West Africa."

"How bad is it?" asked Boone.

"I don't know whether it's the high fevers or the chloroquine you take to get rid of it," said Sisay, "but you'll see things . . . like the inside of your soul. The first time is the worst. You'll be so hot, they'll be frying eggs on you."

"I'm taking the prophylactic," said Boone. "That should protect me for a week or two."

"It might brighten up your fever delusions a little bit," said Sisay with a threatening laugh, "but it won't protect you."

They arrived at a compound several courtyards distant, and Sisay tapped on the door.

"Kong, kong," he said. "Mistah Aruna done come foh name ihn strangah."

A man in a clean safari-style shirt, matching pants, and sandals greeted them and introduced himself as a schoolteacher. He showed them into a single large room, darkened by drawn shutters, with a cooking fire in one corner and ten or twelve tick mattresses arranged around the perimeters. Small curtains or stacks of chests and boxes separated some of the berths into private cubicles. Bundles and bags hung from the tie beams, along with cutlasses and rusted farm implements. On one wall hung a calendar from 1957 showing the snow-capped Grand Tetons; on another was a stained and tattered poster of Ronald Reagan, the actor, circa 1940, gift-wrapping a carton of Chesterfield cigarettes and smoking a fag. Ron was advising, "I send cartons of Chesterfields to all my friends . . . What better Christmas gift?" Hard by Ron's poster was a glossy of an African couple romantically sharing a glass of Guinness stout. The look on the woman's face was calculated to separate a male of any race, color, or creed from a day's pay for two bottles of Guinness stout.

The three men took seats on a hardened mud floor. After introductions the teacher interviewed Boone briefly on the particulars of his visit, then poured what looked like dirty dishwater out of a brown jug into four cups. A woman in a headwrap and a lappa emerged from the shadows and ladled rice and sauce onto plates. Then the teacher took the pot and ladled food onto a plate-sized leaf, setting that portion aside, together with a bowl of water. He closed his eyes, and spoke Mende, while pouring one of the cups of dirty dishwater slowly onto the dirt floor.

"What's he doing?" asked Boone.

"The ancestors are gathering to celebrate your naming day," said Sisay.

Boone looked askance into the shadows. "Their ancestors or my ancestors?"

"Your American ancestors live in Indiana," Sisay said, "and they probably stopped having anything to do with you long ago, because you do not honor them, or feed them. Today, your African ancestors are gathering to baptize you as a new member of their family and to share in this meal."

"These gathering ancestors," Boone said, again scouting the interior of the hut. "I'm assuming they are dead, right? So they don't actually eat or drink, do they? I mean, it's symbolic or something, right?"

The teacher laughed. "If the ancestors did not eat or drink, I am quite sure we would not be wasting real food and good palm wine on them."

Sisay and the teacher shook their heads and commiserated with one another on the incongruous stupidity of white people.

"The teacher is preparing food and pouring libation for them. The rice has been cooked in red palm oil with no pepper. The dead hate pepper. The teacher is telling the ancestors that, if they will intervene for you and ask Our Father, *Ngewo*, to keep you safe and to help you find your brother, you will return and offer them a big pot of sweet upland rice and a cooked fowl."

The teacher offered Boone a cup of the dirty dishwater and handed another to Sisay. Sisay and the teacher drank. Boone stared into his cup.

The teacher is handing me hemlock, thought Boone, mentally mocking the monotonous piety of Sisay's tone.

"Palm wine," Sisay said.

"Is it . . . ?"

"Why don't you put some of your water tablets in it before you drink it," he said acidly, then added, "And if you do that, you can pack and take the next *podah-podah* to Pujehun and stay with Sam Lewis."

Boone thought that sounded like a fine idea. He pretended to take a swallow, smiling broadly, though he discovered that the stuff not only looked like dirty dishwater, it tasted like it too.

Sisay set his cup aside and rose. "You, and you alone, must be the first person to hear your name. I'll wait outside."

Once Sisay had gone, the teacher handed Boone another cup of palm wine. "Your name is Gutawa Sisay," he said solemnly. "You are Pa Ansumana Sisay's grandson and the brother of Mistah Aruna Sisay. *Hota gama hota ta mamaloi mia.* A stranger's stranger is the grandchild of the host. I have asked that our prayers and our offerings reach *Ngewo*. I have asked that they reach *Kenei* Amadu and *Kenei* Nduawo and all our forefathers who have crossed the waters and stay in the bosom of *Ngewo*. From this day forward, you will never be alone. Whether you are traveling in this world or in the village of white sands across the waters, your ancestors will be with you. They will be watching you. When you are sleeping, your ancestors will appear to you in dreams. When you suffer, they will hear your prayers. When you need *Ngewo*'s help because you are in trouble, they will take your part and speak to Him on your behalf. When you are hungry, they will see that your farm gives you crops and that fish swim into your nets. When you are in pain, they will make you strong and teach you to bear it. When you are afraid, they will give you courage. And when you are alone on your deathbed and remembering your sweet life of dancing and feasting, they will be with you. They will greet you when you cross the waters and go to the village of white sands, where you will live with them forever in the bosom of *Ngewo*."

The teacher filled the cups with more palm wine, then called out, "Mistah Aruna! Come, look you brothah, Gutawa Sisay, done come."

Sisay reappeared in the doorway and spoke Mende to the teacher, who promptly rose to his feet. Then, turning to Boone, Sisay said, "Get up. Your grandfather is coming."

Sisay stepped back from the door and motioned to Boone, reminding him to grasp his right wrist with his left hand as a gesture of respect.

A backlit silhouette in a short-sleeved tunic barely filled the doorway that both Boone and Sisay had stooped to enter. Pa Ansumana Sisay entered the quarters with the gait of an aged man who was still used to having things his way. He greeted the teacher and the white men in quiet musical Mende, acknowledging Boone's two-handed handshake with a hoot of merriment and a nod of approval to Sisay. A threadbare skullcap sat lightly on his baldness, and a clay pipe was held in place by ragged molars. In the firelight, his face was a graven image, cratered by the elements and undiagnosed skin disorders—the eyes set in small, dark caverns over a bluff Mende nose that was as broad as the snout of an ox.

The face belonged on a statue peering down from a pedestal or from the second story of a cathedral, the features masterfully exaggerated by a sculptor. Words were unnecessary. Let young mortals use words. Pa Ansumana had only to lift his stately head, as black and weathered as a crag of obsidian. It said: I have survived seven decades of witchcraft, politics, cholera, floods, droughts, military coups, famine, tribal wars, failed crops, court cases, fines, squabbling with relatives, dysentery, falls from palm trees, riots, taxes, tainted water, corrupt Paramount Chiefs, poverty, thieves, deadly swears, driver ants, secret societies, yellow fever, government men, leopards, white mining speculators, intestinal parasites, the British, snakebite, chronic malaria, and bush devils . . . What have you done?

His age put everyone on notice that they were dealing with a force of nature and a powerful human being who had surpassed insurmountable odds in a land where most people died before their fortieth birthday. His enemies were all dead, and their debts to him had been paid by their survivors. He was well into his second set of wives—six of them—with as many farms, tended by legions of children, grandchildren, and boyfriends to his junior wives, all owing ultimate fealty to Pa Ansumana. Swears bounced off him like rubber bullets from toy guns. He knew more about witchcraft than witches, more about secret societies than the headmen, and more about the bush than bush devils. When the well was tainted by witchcraft or poor sanitary techniques, whole compounds took to their pallets with fever and dysentery, infants died, robust diamond miners were laid low in latrines for days on end, but Pa Ansumana belched, rubbed his tummy, picked up his cutlass, and went out to brush his farms.

"This is your grandfather," Sisay said. "He is your grandfather because he is my father and you are my stranger. Therefore, you are now my little brother. Michael Killigan is a good man and a good friend. His friend is my brother. But I must warn you," he said. "You must never do anything to shame me or to shame my father. Understand?"

Boone nodded and wondered what would happen to him if he inadvertently shamed Sisay or Pa Ansumana.

Pa Ansumana looked upon his new grandson with twinkling eyes and said, "*Nyandengo!*"

Boone presented the pipe and tobacco, and his grandfather's eyes gleamed with appreciation.

"*Nyandengo!*" This was followed by more Mende spoken to Sisay.

Then Pa Ansumana turned and lifted his arms, placing his hands over Boone's head. Boone looked up and saw gnarled muscles spangled with veins, swaddled in creased black skin, scaly as a tortoise's. He felt compelled to kneel or bow, as Pa Ansumana summoned the Mende God, *Ngewo*, with the familiarity of an Old Testament prophet entreating Yahweh, and bestowed Mende blessings on his new grandson.

> "*Ngewo i bi mahugbe.*
> *Ngewo i bi lamagbate panda.*
> *Ngewo i bi yama gole.*
> *Ngewo i bi go a ndileli nya hangoi hu.*
> *Ngewo i bi go a ndevu hu guha.*
> *Ngewo i bi go a ndenga*
> *Ngewo i bi go a gbotoa.*"

"God take care of you," translated Sisay. "God walk you well (safe journey). God keep you in a good way. God give you a clean face (good fortune). God give you peace after I am dead. God give you long life. God give you children. God give you many blessings."

Boone suddenly felt charmed, convinced that this man had the power to bless him and approach God on his behalf.

"He says you are a good grandson, and that I have trained you very well, that this is a very fine gift that would make any grandfather's heart big with pride. He is very happy you are here and happy you will be his grandson."

"Tell him I am happy and honored to be his grandson," said Boone.

News of Boone's African name spread quickly, and his neighbors were anxious to try it out on him. Everywhere he went, citizens sang out from the verandas, "Afternoon-O, Mistah Gutawa. How de body?"

When he answered in Krio and allowed how he told God thank you for it, they laughed and slapped their thighs.

A troop of adolescents arrived at Sisay's compound and called him "Mastah Gutawa," which rubbed his American civil rights sensibilities the wrong way. They wanted to sweep his room, brook his clothes, fetch water for bathing and drinking, and cook his food. Among them, he recognized the woman named Jenisa, who had brought him his morning coffee and cakes.

He proudly told them that he would not be needing help with these activities, as he was quite capable of looking after them himself. He was not the sort of white man who wanted African people to do menial labor for him, and he had no intention of hiring them as servants. One of the youngsters comprehended the gist of Boone's message and explained it to his companions, causing their faces to contort in distress and disappointment.

"Mastah? You no go hire us foh work?"

"I am not your master," Boone said. "Do you understand? I'm just a person, like you. Not a master."

They looked at each other in dismay.

"Mastah, we no understand whatin you dae talk."

"I am not your master," he repeated. "Do you understand?"

"Yes, mastah," they said disconsolately.

"You don't understand," he said, becoming equally distressed. "I am not your master. Do not call me master."

"Yes, mastah," they said in unison.

He threw up his hands. They hung their heads and walked away grumbling.

Sisay watched the entire exchange from the veranda, shaking his head, the usual derisive twist adorning the corners of his mouth.

"Congratulations," he said. "You just told six kids whose pas make about two hundred bucks a year that they can't have any of your money, even though it's all but spilling out of your pockets."

"But they wanted to be my servants!" Boone protested. "They were calling me their master."

"You can't live here without spreading some of that money around. You're a millionaire. Enjoy yourself. Share the wealth. For twenty-five cents, someone will clean your room. During the dry season, for a dime, someone else will walk two miles for you to get a bucket of water for you to bathe in. For fifty cents, someone will cook you a meal and serve it to you. Nobody here is going to admire you for not hiring servants. You'll just be thought of as unbelievably stingy, a krabbit man, as they say in Krio."

"But I don't want servants," he complained. "I don't like to be waited on."

"Think of yourself as a major corporation," said Sisay, rising from the hammock. "You can't come into town and not hire anyone. It just won't work. You can think about it, Mistah Gutawa Sisay, on your way to meet your neighbors and ask after your friend."

Sisay picked up the chicken and a sack of onions and handed them to Boone. "Fowl," he said, handing him the chicken. "Yabbas," he added, passing him the sack of onions. "Pa Gigba is in from the fields. He was in Killigan's village for a funeral on the day Michael Killigan disappeared. Follow me with your sambas."

Dusk was upon the village. The boom box was cranked up again, this time putting out "Sugar Magnolia." Sisay led Boone across a neighboring courtyard, past a well and a thatched gazebo, and into another courtyard, where they approached a hut with a flap of canvas for a door.

Sisay called through the flap in Mende and voices came from within. Several peekins banged open the flap and stared at Boone. *"Poo-mui! Poo-mui!"*

Sisay spoke more Mende, and a male voice inside the hut responded. A stream of chattering women and children emerged. Sisay held the flap back and waved Boone into the hut.

Inside was a mud-walled den of chaos, lit by a kerosene lantern and filled with squawking chickens, more naked children, a dog, dirty plates in a bucket, and bundles of bedding. The rafters were strung with belongings and implements. The lantern scattered swollen shadows of people and objects.

An old pa in a white stocking cap and a Bart Simpson T-shirt rose out of the shadows and half stood under the low ceiling to take Boone's hand. The man spoke Mende to Boone. Boone nodded and smiled.

Geckos chased cockroaches in the bevels of the smooth earthen floor; chickens chased the geckos; an old ma chased the chickens; and the food chain came full circle when a cockroach clambered onto an untended dish of rice.

"Give him the sambas," said Sisay, smiling at Pa Gigba.

Boone presented the fowl, careful to use his right hand, and followed with the onions.

"*Nyandengo!*" Pa Gigba cried, showing crooked teeth set in gray gums. "Sweet yabbas!"

"Pa Gigba traveled to Ndevehun, the village where Lamin Kaikai, Michael Killigan, lives," said Sisay. "He attended the funeral of his niece there some weeks ago, and saw Michael Killigan before he disappeared."

Pa Gigba spoke Mende and motioned at a patch of earthen floor. He kicked a trough of bananas aside and removed a small child from the area. He said something in Mende to the child, and the child bowed its head and shuffled off.

Sisay promptly squatted, and Boone gingerly lowered himself onto the ground, not sure that he wanted to assume a cross-legged squat in such a place, afraid a chicken or a peekin might flounder into his lap.

Sisay and Gigba exchanged pleasantries and asked after one another's families for a good half an hour. Boone sighed loudly and studied the interior of the place, wondering if it would be impolite for him to pull out his Swiss Army knife and cut his fingernails.

Finally, Boone heard the words "Mistah Lamin" and "Ndevehun."

"*Sabu gbiina,*" the man said anxiously. "Kaikai no dae. Better no dae."

"What?" Boone asked curtly. "Kaikai is Killigan's African name, right?"

"Oh," said Sisay sarcastically, "I thought you were interrupting to ask Pa Gigba how his family is doing. I thought you were about to ask if his wives, sons, and daughters are healthy, and how the harvest is going for him this year. I should have known better."

"My best friend is missing and probably in some kind of trouble," Boone said with a clenched smile. "I'm here to find him. Does this guy know anything, or not?"

Sisay took a deep breath and fixed a baleful eye on his companion.

"Maybe I should just tell all the villagers to drop everything they are doing. Leave their cutlasses on the farms, let the sick children die in the huts, forget the harvest, and assemble for a meeting in the *barri*, so we can all devote ourselves to the only task that is really important to the welfare of the village," he said, *"finding the poo-mui's friend!"*

Pa Gigba picked a toenail, as if he was embarrassed to be witnessing anger between *poo-muis*.

"If we find Michael Killigan, the first thing I have to talk to him about is training *you!* 'Sabu gbiina' is Mende," Sisay explained. " 'Better no dae' is Krio. They mean the same thing. Better—good —is not there, or nothing good is there. Yes, Kaikai is Killigan's African name." Sisay looked at the Mende man again. "He says Killigan is not there, nothing good is there. Only bad news. Only evil."

"What kind of evil?" Boone asked.

Sisay spoke again.

"*Ndogbojusui*," the man said. "*Hale nyamubla, honei, ndile-mui. Koliblah.*"

Sisay waited for elaboration, but none was forthcoming. The old pa quietly stared at his feet, peeking once at Sisay, hoping the white men were satisfied and the conversation was over.

Sisay pronounced the words slowly for Boone's benefit. "As I've already told you, 'Dog-bo-joo-shwee,' is 'bush devil.' 'Ha-lay,' is 'medicine,' " he said. " 'Nya-moo-blah' is 'bad' or 'evil,' so 'evil medicine.' 'Ho-nay' is 'witch spirit,' and 'ndee-lay-mui' is a witch who takes on the form of a person or animal. 'Koliblah' are Leopard people, or Baboon people, people who take on the shape of animals."

Sisay again spoke to the man, repeating each of the Mende words.

The old pa responded by offering Sisay and Boone a plastic Esso oil jug smeared with grime and dirt. Sisay accepted two cups from Pa Gigba and poured what looked like more dirty dishwater from the jug into the cups, handing one to Boone, and filling a third cup for the old pa. Without thinking, Boone examined the palm wine, because he thought he had seen a foreign object flow out of the jug and into his cup. Then he smelled something sour and sniffed the cup, wrinkling his nose at the odor.

"Make another face like that," Sisay said without a trace of humor in his voice, "and you are on your own."

His glare of intense indignation startled Boone. "Pa Gigba risked his life climbing a palm tree so he could make this palm wine and offer it to his guests. Once he climbs a hundred feet up into the palm, it's not uncommon to find a mamba snake waiting for him. It's palm wine. Drink it and like it, or you will be insulting this man, and shaming me."

Boone was suddenly damn sick of being told how to eat and drink, whom to hire, how to shake hands, what time to get up in the morning, and what gifts to give and to whom. He resolved to take the next *podah-podah* to Killigan's village and do his own investigating. And if he was not welcome there, he would go stay with Sam Lewis in Pujehun. Meanwhile, he was all but certain that Pa Gigba knew something about Killigan's disappearance, so he drank the thing to the dregs and held his cup out for more.

"Does all this evil business have anything to do with Killigan disappearing?" Boone asked, gritting his teeth, while toasting Pa Gigba with another swig.

Pa Gigba shrugged his shoulders, drank, and held out his cup.

"He knows nothing about bad medicine or witches," Sisay said.

The man interrupted Sisay and again shrugged with a palms-up gesture of helplessness.

"He knows absolutely nothing about such things," Sisay continued. "Furthermore, he doesn't know of anyone who *does* know about such things. He can tell us nothing about what happened in the village, except that nothing good is there."

Boone kept his eyes on the old pa, but, at least on the subjects of bad medicine and witches, the man clearly did not want their eyes to meet.

"Can't he just tell us whether all of this witch business has anything to do with Killigan's disappearance?"

Sisay spoke Mende; the man shook his head and stared at the floor.

"He knows nothing," Sisay said.

"Bullshit," Boone said. "He looks like a kid with a joint who's just been told to empty his pockets."

"You're acting very *poo-mui*," Sisay said sharply, the curl of his lip indicating that this was no compliment. "There's a lesson in this for you, if you can step out of your two-hundred-dollar hiking boots and go barefoot for just a day or two."

Pa Gigba poured more palm wine into Sisay's cup.

"I have an African proverb for you," Sisay said, still suppressing a sneer. "The Krios call them *paluibles*. If television hasn't already obliterated your story sense, you might learn something."

Sisay straightened his back and settled his hams into the dirt floor:

"A hunter was out chasing game through the bush, when he stubbed his toe on a human skull, half sunk into the earth. 'What is this?' exclaimed the hunter. 'How did you get here?'

" 'Talking got me here,' the skull replied mysteriously.

"The hunter was astounded and ran back to his village, telling everyone he met about the talking skull. After a time, the chief heard about the talking skull and ordered the hunter to take him to see it. The hunter took the chief into the bush, found the skull, and asked it, 'How did you get here?'

"The skull said nothing. The hunter stubbed his toe on the skull, and said, 'What is this? How did you get here?' repeating exactly his previous words to the skull. The skull said nothing. The chief became very angry, accused the hunter of lying, and ordered his men to chop off the hunter's head on the spot.

"After the bloody work was done and the chief had gone, the skull spoke again. 'How did you get here?' it asked the hunter's head.

" 'Talking got me here,' the hunter replied."

Sisay set his cup on the ground in front of his legs.

"Talking about witchcraft has a way of getting you accused of witchcraft. That goes for *poo-muis* too," he said, impassively delivering a chilling look. Boone had a sudden intuition that Sisay would do little to intervene if a white boy from Indiana was mistakenly accused of witchcraft.

"This man has lost children to witchcraft. Witches sent army ants swarming through his house for two years. He dug a moat around the house and filled it with kerosene and poison at a cost of about two years' salary. But nothing could stop the ants. They simply built bridges out of their dead and kept on coming. Someone worked a medicine called *tilei* against his wife, and it ate away her nose. *Ngelegba*—'thunder medicine'—destroyed his father's house, because his father supported the wrong candidate for Paramount Chief. Now you come in here and demand to know about witchcraft?

"If you want to find out what happened to Michael Killigan, you've got a long sit-down ahead of you. These people have many secrets, most of which *I* do not know after living here for fourteen years. Don't expect to storm in here and spend a week investigating a culture that has kept its secrets for thousands of years. You will go home with nothing."

"May I ask one thing," Boone said impatiently. "Are we talking about witches or bush devils, and does it make a difference?"

Sisay translated, then turned to speak to Boone. The old pa interrupted them, speaking Mende.

"When he was a young man," Sisay said, "he was hunting in the bush with his father. It was twilight and they got lost while pursuing a wounded bush deer. A *Ndogbojusui*, an old man with yellow hair and white skin, just like yours, appeared in the path before him. At first, they thought it was the spirit of a dead ancestor, but then it spoke to them and asked, 'Usai you come out so?' or 'Where do you come from?' Then they knew it was a *Ndogbojusui* because of its white skin, and because it began, not by greeting them in the Mende fashion, but by asking them questions, which is how a *Ndogbojusui* discovers the thoughts of its victims. His father had told him many times how to deal with the questions of the *Ndogbojusui*. One must never reveal what one is thinking, one must instead be stubborn, contrary, and best the *Ndogbojusui* at its own game. If the *Ndogbojusui* gets the upper hand in the exchange, even for a moment, then it will trick its victim into following it deep into the bush, where the poor soul will be lost forever. 'Usai you come out so?' the *Ndogbojusui* repeated. 'Na the moon I come out, jus now,' his father replied. 'How do you fetch water from the well?' asked *Ndogbojusui*. 'With a fishing net,' his father said. 'How you go sex woman?' asked *Ndogbojusui*. 'With a blade of grass,' said his father. And with that, the *Ndogbojusui* stamped his foot and disappeared."

"So at least we know he knows something about bush devils," Boone said with a glance at his translator, getting the sickening feeling that his questions seemed only to provide the occasion for lengthy stories having almost nothing to do with the topic under discussion.

The old pa looked from Boone to Sisay and back again. Sisay

leaned forward and fingered the pouch around his neck, speaking quiet, urgent Mende.

The old pa rose slowly, went to the flap over the door, and looked out into the courtyard. He spoke Mende and left.

"He is inspecting his house," said Sisay, "checking for witches in the form of fruit bats hiding in the rafters and eavesdropping."

So far, Boone thought, it was the mental hygiene of the occupants that needed inspecting. He could not decide whether to humor them along or leave.

The old pa returned and took his seat, speaking Mende in a hushed voice.

During pauses in the old pa's speech, Sisay translated for Boone.

"What he is going to tell us was told to him by others who saw what has been happening. Other than what he has heard, he knows nothing about what has happened."

The old pa rose again and peeked through a crack between the flap and the mud doorframe. Then he returned to his seat and spoke Mende in a low, urgent voice, while Sisay translated.

"Two children died suddenly in the village, and the blacksmith and a mori man suspected witchcraft. Several days later, while the families were mourning, a witch was seen in the village. It came into the village in the shape of a young girl who said she had come from Pujehun for the funeral rites. Later in the day, a villager saw the woman take an article of clothing belonging to someone in the village, presumably to get control over its owner. The villager watched the young woman hide the clothing and other articles in a bush. The villager promptly told the chief of the woman's suspicious behavior. When the chief and two elders looked into the bush, they found a snake swimming in a bucket of blood and, next to it, a pile of stones equal in number to the huts in the village."

Sisay paused and the man looked from Boone to Sisay again. Sisay nodded and said something in Mende.

"The villagers set up a cry and chased the woman. But on the path out of the village, she turned abruptly and looked back at her pursuers and the village. People saw the sun burning in her eyes. Two huts burst into flames, and the woman escaped into the bush. When the fires were controlled, the villagers followed the path taken by the witch and found the fresh skin of a huge boa constrictor lying in the path just outside the village."

The man continued, slipping back and forth from Krio to Mende, Sisay roughly translating in the wake stirred up by the man's distressed words.

"The villager who told the chief about the girl became paralyzed soon after and died. It was widely believed that someone foolishly killed the witch. As everyone knows, a dead witch is far more dangerous than a live one, because the spirit of a dead witch can roam free without worrying about returning to its human form. According to the villager's neighbors, the shade of the dead witch settled on the man's face while he was sleeping. He woke up paralyzed and screamed, helplessly watching as the witch smothered him to death.

"The villager's family gave the ngua-mui—the probing man— permission to examine the intestines of the informer. The spleen was removed from the corpse and dropped into a bucket of water mixed with herbs. The spleen sank to the bottom, proving that the spirit of a witch had entered the man and killed him. The villager was buried under a mound of stones. A stake was driven through the grave to prevent the witch spirit from wandering and harming other people, but as is often the case, the shade of the dead witch returned again and again to terrorize the village."

"But what about Killigan?" said Boone, again having the sickening feeling that these people were incapable of linear discourse, and that every conversation was a walk in the bush.

"Killigan was not in the village at the time, but his house was ransacked or looted. Pa does not know who went through the house. Other dwellings were also looted, so it is hard to say if Killigan's was targeted."

Pa Gigba again rose. This time he left his hut, and Boone could hear him walking softly around it. Then he returned, took his seat, and whispered to Sisay in Mende.

"His nephew, Moussa Kamara, has photos, pictures snapped by Michael Killigan. Bad men want these photos."

The old man touched Sisay's arm and placed a finger over his lips. He turned toward Boone and implored him desperately for something.

"What's he saying?" Boone urged.

"He's"—Sisay paused—"talking about the photos, I think. I'm not sure."

"Photos of whom?" asked Boone. "What are they?"

Pa Gigba grimaced, then moaned and covered his ears.

"He doesn't know," said Sisay. "He can't say."

The old pa looked earnestly into Boone's eyes and spoke at length, nodding, as if he was assuring Boone that he could help him and that everything would be fine.

"What about that?" asked Boone. "What was that?"

"He says he doesn't know where your brother is," Sisay repeated. "He can't say."

Boone thought the translation was far shorter than the original conversation and didn't match the look on Pa Gigba's face. But Sisay, who seemed to take umbrage at the slightest breach of manners, would almost certainly throw him out of the village if Boone challenged his understanding of Mende.

"Ask him if he has any idea at all where my brother is or what happened to him."

Sisay rendered what sounded like a statement instead of a question.

The old pa resolutely shook his head, as if he now regretted even letting them into his house.

"The conversation is finished," said Sisay.

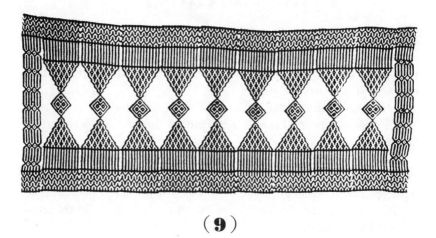

(**9**)

Boone's trip to Killigan's village was postponed by a storm system that moved through his bowels with the ferocity of a tropical cloudburst. His fourth day in Africa was spent deep in the interior of a remote, unmapped equatorial latrine exploring the dark incontinent.

It was a wattle-and-daub shed with a door of unpainted planks and no window—one of a long row of pan-roofed outhouses that backed up into the bush about twenty yards from the edge of the village. Each family compound—or *mawe*—had its own latrine, built according to Peace Corps specifications. Inside was an earthen floor and a wooden platform with a ragged, dark hole in the middle. Sisay had shown him the facilities, and stressed the importance of replacing the lid—a wooden disk with a handle—to keep the flies from carrying human excrement around the village. On either side of the hole, smooth, shiny impressions of human feet had been worn into the wood. Sunlight shafted in through chinks in the mud walls and illuminated motes of dust—or maybe they were protozoa— buffeted about by powerful odors and adrift in the soup of West African humidity.

The first time Boone squatted and peered into the hole, he realized his psychology professors had been right in asserting that there is some inexorable, subliminal association between shit and death. The interior of the latrine had a sense of place as powerful as any grave or altar. Something other than an intense odor emanated from the dark hole. Was it a sound? A subaudible vibration? The thrumming of cryptozoa assiduously turning shit back into dirt? Or was he hearing only movements in the symphony of the bowel?

On one corner of the wooden platform was a stack of past issues of *The Guardian*, an international newspaper of tissue-thin pages offering selections from *Le Monde* and *The Washington Post*. There were also several stacks of semi-bound volumes from Sisay's decomposing library; they were spineless, and whole sections had been torn from their bindings and mixed in with others. He found pages of Rilke crosshatched with a tour guide to Mali, Hemingway jammed in with a collection of essays on International Development, Kierkegaard, a manual on installing hand pumps for wells, Thomas Pynchon, Frazer's *Golden Bough*, Kurt Vonnegut, a Peace Corps health manual, Gaston Bachelard—all reduced to toilet paper— some of it better than others. The acid-free paper tended to make for a sturdy but abrasive product; the moldering paperbacks had a softer, more absorbent texture—apparently also the consensus of the other members of Sisay's compound, as the paperbacks were ravaged, whereas some of the bound volumes were left almost wholly intact.

But *The Guardian* was clearly the favored product, and after experimenting, Boone found out why. It provided low abrasion, absorbency, and a fascinating perspective on ten-year-old world events. While Boone's bowels evacuated quarts of precious fluid from his system, he read about Britain's successes in the Falklands or the Contras' valiant maneuvers against the women and children of Nicaragua. While waiting for another knot to form in his abdomen, he read all about Jimmy Carter's moral equivalent of war, the release of hostages in Teheran, and the promises of supply-side economics. Ultimately, history followed dysentery into the hole, and Boone stood, took one step toward the door, and felt another knot form in his lower abdomen. He wearily settled back into a squat over the black hole and fingered another *Guardian*, cursing softly between cramps and peristaltic convulsions, listening to the schloop and plip-plop of shit landing in the chthonic darkness below.

If shit and death had something in common, it was somewhere down that dark hole—an invisible node where scatology intersected with eschatology, where saprophytes gorged on sap, where man met manure, where the human became humus, where brain, bone, and heart were swallowed by the earth and moldered back into minerals and elements.

He tried a page of Bachelard. Too stiff. The poetics of shit. Maybe human beings are simply composters, biological garbage disposals designed to accelerate the transformation of plants and animals back into soil, the same way leaves turn to mulch faster if they are ground up first.

He had the Western compulsion to name the bug. Was it giardiasis? Common amoebic dysentery? Some other unnamed, unclassified microbe? Maybe it was cholera, in which case he wouldn't have to worry about anything much longer.

After the eighth trip in the space of an afternoon, he complained to Sisay about the difficulty of defecating into an open hole with no toilet seat to rest his hams upon. According to Sisay, who showed no compassion whatsoever for his plight, it was time for Boone to pay the fiddler for having lived his life in antiseptic American kitchens and bathrooms. Eating sterilized food and drinking chlorinated water had rendered his intestines utterly helpless against even the most harmless Third World bacteria. There was nothing for it but to acquire resistance the old-fashioned way. Even sickness, it seemed, was Boone's fault, America's fault, and the African climate was blameless.

"I take it this doesn't happen to you anymore," said Boone. "You're immune, or you've adapted, or whatever."

"I was sick on and off for the first year or so," he admitted. "Now I get sick only when I go back to America. After five years here, I went back for about a week. I was standing in somebody's kitchen in Rochester, New York. My American friends were shoveling platefuls of leftover food into the garbage disposal. I threw up all over the counter. I had forgotten what perfectly good food looked like going down the drain to the sewer. It was like watching a disgustingly drunk billionaire burn hundred-dollar bills in front of beggars.

"Next day, I resolved to sit on my mother's front porch and soak up some American village life, to remind myself of what I had left behind. It was Saturday. My mother's next-door neighbor, a well-groomed, weight-gifted, vertically challenged accountant named Dave, brought out a leaf blower, a lawn mower, a leaf grinder, a mulcher, an edger, and a weed trimmer. He worked all day, making a terrific racket, chopping, trimming, and spraying toxins on a small patch of ground, which produced absolutely no food, only grass. The rest of the world spent the day standing in swamp water trying to grow a few mouthfuls of rice, while Dave sat on his porch with a cold beer admiring his chemical lawn. Sickening? You bet. It was time to go back to Africa."

Sisay offered only a change in technique. He squatted on his calves for Boone, and gave him a "look, no hands" gesture. "It's really quite comfortable after a couple weeks of practice. But until then, you're going to be too weak to develop new muscles, so try this instead."

He picked up one of his straight-back chairs and removed the seat, leaving a bare wooden frame. "I think you should just move in up there for a day or two. Why keep trudging back and forth? Spend a day or two and really get to know yourself."

He poured a foil packet of UNICEF rehydration salts into a plastic jug of water and handed it to Boone, along with the seatless chair. "Don't stay out past dark, though," he said. "There's a witch who hangs out behind the latrines in the shape of a leopard. You don't want to be mixing it up with her."

Boone noticed another disturbing phenomenon in the form of ulcers that appeared on his arms and legs. He showed them to Sisay, who shook his head and remarked, "Tropical sores. You've been scratching your mosquito bites."

"Doesn't everybody?" Boone rejoindered.

He had discovered (too late) a number of gaping holes in his mosquito net—holes so large they had created a kind of mosquito trap, allowing mosquitoes in, but not out, so they could suck his blood all night and inject him with who knows what kind of diseases. By the time he found them in the morning, they were as fat as ticks, and were taking after-dinner naps in the gossamer folds of his mosquito net. When he killed them, they left gouts of his own blood in the netting. Then he had unconsciously scratched the bites, the way he had learned to do in the land of his birth, and had turned the itching welts into small wounds. In America, when the skin broke, a scab formed, and the lesion healed in a matter of days. All well and good in the U.S.A., where the environment is so sterile, you can eat off any given floor, or perform open-heart surgery in the bathroom, because the surfaces have all been sterilized by cleansers and disinfectants, until nothing remains but a refreshing medicinal odor. The worst thing wounds are exposed to in America are photons from a TV set.

The regimen backfired in West Africa. There, scratching a mosquito bite opened a hole in the protective envelope of the skin, exposing the interiors of his body to the contagion called air; for air in equatorial Africa is nine-tenths humidity, teeming with airborne microbes in suspension, just waiting to sink their cell walls into an enfeebled white organism. In three days' time, the tiny pinpricks became suppurating, festering, gaping holes the size of fifty-cent pieces. Dolor, tumor, rubor, thermor galore!

"Protein is very scarce in these parts," Sisay said. "You shouldn't waste fuel mending unnecessary bullet holes."

Sisay advised him that the only way to halt the cratering process was to boil water twice a day, wash the sores, douse them with hydrogen peroxide, then daub them with antiseptics. This required a trip to the village Fula man, who operated a pharmacy, convenience store, kerosene filling station, and hardware store all out of a shack the size of a toll booth. After obtaining the antiseptics, Sisay took him on a brief tour of the surrounding farms.

Boone followed, the muscles in his legs twitching and heat flashes reverberating painfully in his open sores.

They came almost at once on an old pa wearing nothing but rags and leggings and a stocking cap, beating a small stone dwarf with a leather scourge. The pa cursed and swore in a language Sisay claimed no one understood or had ever heard before. Every now and again, the pa hauled off and kicked the thing with all his might, then danced around the farm holding his toe and howling in agony, glowering at the stone dwarf, as if it had maliciously smote him with a stone limb.

"That's Pa Usman and his *nomoloi*," said Sisay. "Mende farmers have been digging up prehistoric soapstone statues of dwarves on their farms for as long as anyone can remember. They are depictions of the *tumbusia*, the spirits of dwarves who farmed this land before the Mende people came. Because these dwarves were the original owners of the land, they are jealous of the current Mende owners, and they sometimes take revenge by preventing crops from growing. Then the farmer must threaten or cajole the peevish *nomoloi* to enlist its cooperation. Sometimes the *nomoloi* accepts the sacrifices offered to it and will zealously watch over the crops and prevent vermin, thieves, and witches from traversing upon the land; other times the *nomoloi* stubbornly refuses all gifts and thwarts the farmer's every effort to grow food on the land. That's when it must be whipped, which is what Pa Usman is doing as we speak."

As they drew near, Pa Usman kicked the dwarf once more, then howled and hopped around the field, glaring over his shoulder at the dwarf and shouting harsh syllables at it. He had a tatterdemalion stocking cap, which looked as though he threw it up in the morning and stepped under it. The cap appeared to have two layers, with gaping holes in each layer that somehow never intersected, so that his head remained covered. The ornamental fuzzball which adorns the peak of such hats had long ago severed all its moorings, except for one tenuous thread that provided enough slack for the fuzzball to bobble about somewhere above Pa Usman's ear.

"Afternoon-O, Pa," said Sisay.

Pa Usman made harsh guttural sounds and pointed at the dwarf, showing Sisay and Boone a look of unmitigated contempt. He ended his diatribe by spitting a thick wad of kola-nut paste onto the dwarf and kicking it ferociously. His face contorted in pain and disbelief, as if he was shocked to discover that he had again stubbed his toe, and that somehow the blow must have been administered by the stone dwarf.

His shirt was made of mosquito netting, with holes slashed in the back of it. For leggings he had an oversized pair of walking shorts with the crotch ripped out so that it hung free like a loincloth or a short zippered skirt. A rope held it closely at the waist.

He picked up the leather scourge and showed it to the dwarf, making menacing guttural sounds.

"Pa Usman is . . . different," said Sisay, as they watched the old pa violently flog the dwarf. "I think he's gone a little overboard in his relationship with this *nomoloi*. He carries it with him in a box and feeds it at meals, disciplines it as if it were a willful child, and prays to it at night. He's had particularly good success recently by serving it Coca-Cola just before bedtime, which you can get—warm, of course—at the Fula shack."

Pa Usman threw the scourge aside, pointed to the dwarf, sweat coursing down his gnarled arm and dribbling off the tip of his finger.

"He lives alone in a shack made entirely out of zinc pan," said Sisay. "All the other villagers think the shack has baked his brains and made him crazy. But they still feed him when his crops won't grow."

As Sisay spoke, Usman pointed again at the dwarf and nodded smugly at the white men, as if he had finally taught the thing a lesson. Then he hauled off for one last good kick, and stared in amazed disbelief, as he grabbed his foot and danced around the *nomoloi*.

"What is he saying?" asked Boone, wishing he could tie the old pa's feet together and spare him the loss of his toes.

"No one knows," said Sisay. "He's a Mende man. Always was and always will be. But some time ago, after fever took his wife, he started speaking in a language that no one understands. It's not Mende, not Temne, not Koranko, not deep Mende . . . No one knows what he's saying. Except maybe his *nomoloi*."

Sisay took Boone back to the village and taught him how to treat tropical sores. First, the technique of the bucket bath, or how to take a shower in one bucket of water, which was the way white men bathed. Boone was shown to a small outdoor stall at the fringe of the compound, where he was given one bucket of water, one cup, and soap. His instructions were, first, to wet in preparation for washing: one cup for the head, two cups for the torso, one front, one back, one cup for each arm, one cup for the "private," one cup for each leg. Next, lather generously with soap, and rinse using the same number of cups. Sixteen cups in all, or one gallon of well water.

Africans bathed in the streams and rivers, where they picked up schistosomiasis, a parasite that incubates in freshwater snails, until it gets the opportunity to burrow into a human host, where it takes up residence with colonies of hookworms, whipworms, giant intestinal roundworms, tapeworms, threadworms, amoebas, flukes, trichina, spirochetes, plasmodia, mycobacteria, and a host of other parasites which inhabit humans living in warm moist climates, turning them into savage planets teeming with colonies of organisms. The parasites are astute ecologists, though; they usually do not quite kill the bodies they inhabit, carefully leaving just enough blood and nutrients to allow their lethargic hosts to find food and sleep in a hammock, while they go carousing in the bloodstream and intestines, dining out on the proceeds. In America, humans usually are not food for worms until they die; in Africa, the worms move in early and stake their claims in advance of the big day.

On his way back out to the latrine—one arm crooked in the seatless chair, the other cradling the jug of rehydration salts—he had to walk by several families huddled around cooking fires. The villagers tried out his new name a few times, and he replied, using the few stock Mende greetings that Sisay had taught him.

Every common Mende expression had its Krio equivalent, and Sisay had painstakingly translated both versions of the most likely greetings, blessings, and requests for assistance. The most common greeting, the Mende equivalent of "How are you?" is expressed in

Krio as "How de body?" or "How is the body?" The Krio response, "I tell God tank ya," is heard thousands of times an hour all over Sierra Leone. The Mende equivalent of "How de body?" is *"Bo bi gahun,"* and the response is *"Kaye ii Ngewo ma,"* or "There is no fault on God," literally: "There is no rust on God," also heard and used by every Mende citizen dozens of times a day, and commonly understood to mean that God is keeping me healthy, or I am living proof of God's goodness.

Boone got plenty of mileage out of *"Kaye ii Ngewo ma,"* pronounced something like "Kiyangowoma." No matter what anyone said to him, Boone replied, *"Kaye ii Ngewo ma."* The reaction from the clusters of Mende spectators was invariably jocular disbelief, followed by an exclamation, such as "Ai O!" and a slapping of knees and thighs. *Too funny. Another white man trying to talk Mende.*

But when the villagers saw him staggering latrineward with the chair and the jug, they knew he had runny belly, so they did not ask how his body was (for no one wanted to hear that there was in fact at least some rust on God). Instead, they said, "Oh sha," a Krio expression of condolence, which seemed to communicate a compassion for the sick that stopped short of pity.

"Oh sha," the children called softly from their mothers' laps when they heard about the *poo-mui*'s gastrointestinal misfortunes.

"Oh sha," said the mothers and young wives. "Mistah Gutawa's belly dae run. Mehrisine no dae foh mend ahm. He no feel better."

"Oh sha," said the toothless grandmas. "Poor Mistah Gutawa's belly dae run like small peekin. Sickness been come 'pon him tae he no able for eat."

"Oh sha, Mistah Gutawa. Leh God mend you, yaaa!"

By the time evening settled over the village, the latrine felt a lot like a second home to him. There was his room attached to Sisay's place, the veranda where he visited briefly with other villagers, played with children, ate bananas, listened to infants screaming; then there was his shit bungalow, where he spent the better part of the day, sitting in his seatless chair, shaking with the rigors of dysentery.

He was intimately acquainted with the wattle-and-daub walls of the latrine: the wasp's nest under the eave, the shadows of the stick rafters, the well-worn bevel between the boards where the cockroaches came and went, the slightly larger cranny where a huge but well-behaved spider hung out. The subtle changes in earth tones in different parts of the wall, where clay of a different place or a different season must have been used—all nuances of place, a place he came to know in the same way a victim learns the moods and quirks of his tormentor's personality, or an invalid learns the patterns of the cracks in the ceiling he stares at all day.

He passed the time feeding the spider driver ants and wounded cockroaches, fascinated by the creature's ruthless efficiency in pithing its prey, injecting venom that liquefied the innards of the victim, then siphoning out the guts. He sipped from the rubber jug of rehydration fluids and lit a candle to keep him company and serve as a reading light during his shit vigil.

He had plenty of time to think about just how he had arrived at this pass. He had nothing but the noblest of motives, but maybe he had erred in selecting his method. What good could he do for Killigan, or anyone else for that matter, when he was stranded in a latrine, waiting to be killed by equatorial parasites? Maybe he could have done more good by staying in Freetown, or even by staying in America. Why was he letting an ex-Deadhead tell him what to do? Did he really have to use African methods? Based on what he had seen so far, they were nothing more than superstitions of the most disorganized kind, consisting of swears, charms, curses, and taboos having no organized application or function. What could he possibly learn by consulting a looking-around man, or by staying in this village taking orders from a radical expatriate with three wives and a chip on his shoulder for his own kind?

Each knot in the lower abdomen, each tremor of nausea, each aimless blast of fecalia took fluids, nutrients, strength, and hope from him. He tore a page out of a book called *Paths Toward a Clearing*, by Michael Jackson, and read it by candlelight:

Traditional African thought tends to construe the unconscious as a force-field *exterior* to a person's immediate awareness. It is not so much a region of the mind as a region in space, the inscrutable realm of night and of the wilderness, filled with bush spirits, witches, sorcerers, and enemies.

He was getting weaker. He could feel his pulse beating in the swollen craters surrounding his tropical sores. His hamstrings twitched (probably from dehydration), his scalp oozed sweat, and his asshole caught fire in its cradle over the black hole. This was not a part of the world where he wanted to be dependent on others. He had seen enough to know that in this country people had a habit of shrugging their shoulders at the thought of death or disease taking their neighbors. Already, he had heard the expression "Ihn want foh die" more than once, in reference to a sick villager or an elder approaching death. It was a passing observation, delivered in the same tone of voice one might use in America to say, "He wants to go shopping at the mall."

Death was as random as the placement of the mud huts, as common as a stray stool, as insignificant as a mosquito bite. It was as quick as a mamba snake, as slow as tuberculosis tubercles sprouting in the lung.

Boone imagined himself dying on a tick mattress with a bunch of old pas standing around scratching their heads, while Sisay told him to wait another hour or two, until the witch doctor answered his beeper. Before long, he would be praying again, another sign of just how bad things were. *God is very big*, he thought. *Very, very big*, he hoped. *Big enough to absorb all of this and more. Big enough to protect his best friend from rebels or juju men or the corrupt bureaucrats missing bags of cement.*

When not in his room or in his latrine bungalow, Boone was with villagers, or they were with him. Each morning, he stepped out of his semi-private room and waded into a stream, a swamp, a forest of humanity, and for the rest of the day, he was never alone. If he went into his room, happy faces appeared in a row at his window, "*Poo-mui! Poo-mui!*" If he dozed off in the hammock, he woke up in a bird's nest of small African heads chirping, "*Poo-mui! Poo-mui!*" If he left anything out of his backpack, it was promptly seized and passed around for examination, comment, and above all questions.

"What is this?"

"How is it made?"

"What does it do?"

"How much does it cost?"

He was alone only when moving his bowels or sleeping; the rest of life was lived constantly and relentlessly in the company of others, and the others had no concept of or respect for solitude. Sisay was never alone either, but he welcomed company and spent the day singing, telling proverbs, and laughing. When Sisay spoke to villagers, the sour world-weariness disappeared from his voice; his face came to life and his eyes lit up. Whether he was addressing a toddler or a senile adult, he gave total attention to that person. A conversation was something people had in England. A discussion was something you had with white people. What Sisay had with his extended Mende family was raillery, jokes, stories, spoofs, insults, wild conceits, extrapolations from proverbs, and Krio parables. The Mendes howled and shook one another and laughed insanely. No matter how many times they had seen it, they still could not believe a white man could do such things with their language. With the notable exception of several renowned missionaries, a white man had never thought enough of the Mende, their language, and their way of life to actually stay and live among them.

Whether he was besting witty elders or being bested by a twelve-year-old diamond digger, he never dropped the ball, he constantly redoubled the joke, turned it back on itself, turned it back on himself if need be, anything to keep the ironic farce in motion. If Sisay tried to leave the village, it always took him a good hour or two just to make it to the path leading out, because he had to stop and jaw with each conclave on each veranda—mainly joking back and forth in Mende. Most conversations consisted of jokes, blessings, or proverbs:

If you have a big cock, tell the tailor before he sews your pants.

Don't put your finger in someone's mouth and then hit them on top of the head.

Love is like the lard in soup: it is only sweet when it is hot.

A hen with chicks does not jump over a fire.

Love is like an egg—if you want to fully enjoy it, you should not hold it too hard or too lightly.

One finger cannot catch lice.

Nothing went further than a good spoof, pun, bluff, witticism—it was the national pastime. And in the evening, the favorite entertainment seemed to consist of verbal jousting. Two clever comedians began by insulting each other, then matched wits before an audience, who rated the performance of the contestants by laughing or shouting after each verbal thrust, parry, and riposte. The contest ended when one of the wags managed such a scintillating display of repartee that his opponent was speechless in the face of the crowd's roar of approval.

Boone laughed along with the audience, even though he did not understand enough Krio to comprehend all of what was said. It was enough to watch what appeared to be an argument erupt into laughter and thigh slapping from a steadily growing knot of spectators. Altogether, he felt like the most aloof, unsociable, and unaffectionate person in the world. An emotional runt. They laughed and kissed one another, blessed one another back and forth, teased each other. And Boone sat watching, or rose wearily and went to his shithouse.

Hunger is the best sauce, according to the Krio proverb, and despite his disorders of the belly, Boone always had plenty of hunger sauce by day's end. Each evening, they ate one large meal of rice and sauce served on a large communal platter, from which Boone, Sisay, Sisay's three wives, his five peekins, and guests all ate using their right hands. The first night, Boone had noticed everyone freely picking their teeth while digesting their food and savoring the after-dinner conversation, so he had absentmindedly reached up and picked a piece of gristle out of his teeth with his left thumbnail, causing everyone present to turn their heads aside and retch.

"That's your bathroom hand," Sisay had reminded him, while holding his nose in mock disgust. "Remember?"

Every evening, the smell of food or the sight of a steaming pot of chop being carried to the *poo-muis'* quarters also brought out the beggars, the blind, widows, widowers, and other social strays, who showed up coincidentally just as dinner was served, and were promptly welcomed, seated, and fed by Sisay and his family. Even at meals in other *mawes* in the village, Boone noticed that no matter how poor his host, or how ill he could afford feeding an extra mouth, the sudden appearance of a remote relative, who just happened to be visiting a friend, always prompted an invitation to dinner, and the invitation was always accepted. Sisay had told him that, although a Mende man will almost always scowl at the burden of feeding yet another relative, the food will be served. He will complain about it to his relatives; he will grouse about it to his wife, the chief, the beggar's other remote relatives who steered the hungry person in his direction, but the food will not be denied. Or as Lewis had remarked in Freetown, "Asking a Mende man to stop being generous with his food is like asking him to stop lying—an impossible request."

The head male of each *mawe* apportioned the meat, favoring the *poo-muis* with large portions, followed by progressively smaller portions to other males, smaller still for women, and none at all for the children. Once weaned from mothers and the force feedings, Sisay had explained, peekins had to fend for themselves at mealtimes, for they received almost nothing in the way of a serving, and instead subsisted on whatever fell on the floor, was left on the plates or in the pots, or whatever they could cadge from doting adults, who were disinclined to waste food on unproductive family members.

The head male then gave a signal and the scrimmage was on for food, which usually disappeared just as Boone was reaching for his second mouthful. He had a terrible habit of chewing his food slowly, searching carefully with his teeth for bits of bone, gravel, or gristle. Eventually, they realized he was as helpless as a peekin with no training, so they took mercy on him and set aside a small section of the platter at the beginning of each meal for him; then they gorged on the rest of the platter, finished it, and stared irritably at the reserved portion, while Boone worked his way slowly through it.

The secret, Sisay had advised, was to swallow without chewing, and without stopping to breathe, until you had packed in as much as possible during the crucial first three minutes. After the initial frenzy, rough territorial partitions of the rice usually had been tacitly agreed upon, and one could slack off for a few breaths.

After dinner, Boone visited his latrine. At dusk, he staggered back to Sisay's compound and curled up on the floor in his sleeping bag, feverish and trembling.

"Oh sha," said Sisay.

"Fuck you," said Boone. "I figure it's either the water or the palm wine."

"It's neither," said Sisay. "It's your delicate digestive tract. You didn't have to join the human race. You could have stayed in America, where five percent of the world's population consumes seventy-five percent of the world's resources."

They were interrupted by visitors, including Pa Ansumana, who had a couple of grandsons in tow, Dowda and Alfa. The grandsons expressed their condolences, and Boone watched them explain his condition to Pa Ansumana. His father indicated his understanding with a grunt, then showed Boone his flexed arm and a fist, as if to say, "Be strong, or you are no son of mine."

Boone decided to sit up.

The two grandsons pulled a pile of *National Geographics* out of the study and began examining the pages. Apparently, this was a nightly ritual in Sisay's compound. The young men of the village stopped by after their farming or diamond digging and went through old issues, selecting photographs, showing them to Sisay, who would then explain them in Mende or Krio.

The men lit pipes. Sisay provided a clay ashtray, which contained several of Boone's used pipe cleaners.

"What ees thees foh?" asked one of the grandsons, fingering a used pipe cleaner that was well gaumed with resin and carbon.

"It is for cleaning the pipe," Boone said, making pipe-reaming motions.

Dowda examined the pipe cleaner intently. "I see," he said. "And then how do you clean this"—holding the pipe cleaner up—"after it has cleaned the pipe?" he asked, rolling the pipe cleaner between his fingers and the ball of his thumb, showing Boone how the tar and resin made his fingers stick together.

Boone smiled indulgently and explained that pipe cleaners were meant to be used only once and then discarded.

After this was translated, the grandson and Pa Ansumana both huddled over the pipe cleaner, studying it even harder, and occasionally wiping their fingers on his sleeping bag. They spoke Mende together on the matter, the young miner going through the motions of reaming out the pipe and holding it in the direction of the fire. Finally Pa Ansumana seemed to grasp the idea of a pipe cleaner that was to be used once and discarded. A smile glimmered in his eyes, a kind of delight in the absurdity, the extravagant pointlessness of having such a well-constructed wire tool meticulously fitted out with absorbent fibers and plastic bristles, all created by a machine several oceans away for the fleeting, profligate purpose of cleaning one pipe, one time, and then thrown away.

After a couple more headshakings and muttered exchanges between grandfather and grandson, both men turned toward Boone, and the grandson, with purposeful seriousness, asked, "Why?"

Boone wanted to be honest, but he could tell that the Africans were on the verge of concluding that a man who could afford the luxury of squandering meticulously machine-crafted pipe cleaners probably had whole kingdoms at his disposal, as well as twelve wives, three farms, armies of servants, and a backpack full of extremely powerful medicines.

"Well," Boone said, "it's too difficult to clean a dirty pipe cleaner, and they are made very cheaply by a machine. They are *meant* to be thrown away."

"How much?" Dowda asked.

"How much for what?" Boone rejoindered.

"How much one pipe cleaner?"

"They don't sell them one by one," said Boone, doing a mime of a shopkeeper distributing single pipe cleaners to a queue of eager customers. "They sell them in packets . . . bundles." He showed them a packet by way of illustration.

"How much packet?" asked the young man.

Boone quickly converted $1.69 into leones and gave Dowda the figure.

Dowda entered into another excited exchange with the old pa.

"What now?" Boone asked.

Sisay produced a sigh. "He's telling his grandfather that a day's pay will buy two bundles of pipe cleaners, and from there they are trying to figure out the cost of one pipe cleaner. It's kind of like those sportswriters who figure out how much Michael Jordan gets paid per free throw or per minute of play."

Pa Ansumana chuckled, shook his head, and spoke Mende.

"What did he say?" asked Boone.

"He said, if you live long enough, you will see everything."

"What ees thees?" asked one of the young men, showing Sisay a photograph of a man in a suit holding a fan-shaped aluminum reflector under his chin and soaking up rays with his face. The caption below the photo said: "Manhattan Commuters Sunbathe on the Run While Waiting for a Bus."

The explanation, all in Krio, took the better part of twenty minutes, because the reflector and its purpose had to be explained, as well as the concept of a white man wanting to darken his skin by exposing it to the sun. This took some doing, for if, as they knew, a white man would be crazy to turn himself black, then he must be half crazy if he wanted to turn himself brown.

As Sisay spoke, they were interrupted by a racket that was even worse than the woman damage palaver of his first night in the village. Sisay froze and for a split second his usual smirk tightened into a grimace that told Boone this was no ordinary village palaver. He and his guests rose from the floor to meet the commotion before it reached his door. Boone heard the crowd calling Sisay's name, the wailing of women, and the shouts of angry men.

Sisay opened the door onto a moonless night, with the courtyard lit only by the guttering flames of swinging hurricane lamps. A crowd of villagers swept up to the steps to the veranda, shouting and quarreling in Mende and Krio. Children hid behind the knee walls of the courtyard and the lappas of their mothers. Old pas shouted at one another over the din, losing their dignity to panic.

Boone searched the crowd for a focal point and found none, until the mass of black bodies parted, and three men appeared bearing a limp body, and behind them a man pinioned and escorted by two strong men. The captive was bandoliered in ammunition and charms. Amulets, the teeth and bones of animals, pouches, and cartridge belts hung from his neck and shoulders.

The man was arrayed before Sisay, as if to give testimony, and the apparently dead body was placed at his feet, the head propped up by a stone. When the bearers of the body stepped back from their cargo, the crowd gasped at the face of death.

Pa Gigba! The wailing of women rent the night air, and the men resumed quarreling, some of them appeared to be accusing the captive man and some defending him.

A shiver swept up his spine and pringled the hair at the back of his neck when Boone recognized the face of old Pa Gigba, the bloodied Bart Simpson T-shirt now up around his neck—the old pa who had been in Ndevehun the day Killigan had vanished. Just off-center in Gigba's forehead was a powder-burned hole plugged with coagulated blood. Where his right ear belonged there was an excavation in the flesh and clumps of gouted blood, still oozing with serous fluid and new blood.

It was the first fresh dead body Boone had ever seen.

"Death is come!" a woman shrieked. "Death is come! Death is come!" cried the women and children, some collapsing on the ground and hiding their faces in terror and anguish.

"You killed this man with this gun, notoso?" a man cried showing the hunter a gun.

"I killed a leopard," the hunter retorted with the ferocity of a man defending his life. "Section Chief Moiwo hire me foh hunting. He say, 'Lahai, do ya, kill me some sweet beef this day.' I say, 'Yes, Chief Moiwo, God willing, I find you the sweet one this day.' Chief Moiwo been give me two cartridge, like usual, and I been go bush. Dae, I been see one leopard. Ihn come at me just when evening been come. Ihn come at me strong, foh eat me!"

"Na lie!" a man said, accosting the hunter. "Lie! You dae lie!"

The hunter tore his right arm free of his escort and opened his bloody, clenched fist in the light of the hurricane lamps. "I no lie! Look dae! Look dae and see! I no lie!" He held his palm up and showed the crowd the furry, vesseled, triangular ear of a jungle cat. "I cut-cut de ear befoh de man change back. I killed a witch! Dees man was traveling trew de bush in leopard shape. I kill ihm, and ihm change back. I been see dis ting!" the man shouted, pointing at his eyes. "My eyes no get fault! As I cut de ear, the man been change back to ihn human shape."

The crowd disintegrated into dark fringes of wailing women, clusters of children covering their eyes and shrieking at the night sky, and factions of men hanging heads, shambling slowly away from the body, muttering forebodings of witch business in the village.

Pa Ansumana descended the steps of the veranda and faced the hunter over the lifeless body of Pa Gigba. He put out his hand and spoke Mende to the hunter. The hunter placed the leopard's ear— a crumpled flap of fur and skin, scabbed in black where the ear had been severed—in Pa Ansumana's palm. The old man stooped to one knee and fitted the animal ear to the wound in the side of Pa Gigba's head, where a dark gout of clotted blood still seeped trickles of bright red.

He returned the bush cat's ear to the hunter, and took a lamp from one of the men, holding it out and above to inspect the corpse.

Boone too inspected the body, and shook with fear or the early tremors of a greater illness, gathering like a storm in his foreconscious. The night air passed through him in a frigid tinge of fever and raised gooseflesh on him. He must have stood up too quickly when the alarm had sounded, then went swimming in the crowd's hysteria. Blood pounding in his eyeballs made his field of vision vibrate, as he stared at the torchlight and shadows dartling on the dead man's features—a mask of skin sagging into the skull—almost shriveling into the snout of an animal.

He put an arm out and staggered, pinpoints of light teeming like maggots in the furry black collar constricting his field of vision. He remembered men speaking Mende and hoisting him by the armpits, before his head fell back into blackness.

He woke up in his sleeping bag on Sisay's floor.

"If you are well enough to travel tomorrow," Sisay said urgently, "you should. This is bad. The village is in total upheaval. First Mama Saso's twins, now this! There will be an investigation. Pa Gigba will be examined for signs of witchcraft. The *ngua-mui*, the washing and probing man, will open his abdomen, remove the spleen, and place it in a bucket of water mixed with special herbs. If it floats, Pa Gigba is not a witch, and the hunter will not be believed. He will be tried for murder before the Paramount Chief. If the spleen sinks, Gigba is a witch, the hunter is telling the truth, and you and I are in serious trouble," he said, meeting Boone's eyes and holding them.

"Witches are even more powerful after they are dead," he said. "But, more likely, the spleen will neither sink nor float, but will settle somewhere in the middle of the bucket, meaning malign influences were present but were not in total control of him."

Boone's eyes widened and his head shook in total exasperation.

"The old pas will hang heads in the court *barri* for days before deciding what to do. Assuming he's not a witch, there will be a funeral. All of this is going to be complicated by the presence of a white stranger, which is why, if you're able, you should travel."

"I will," said Boone, hoisting himself onto an elbow.

"Tomorrow is the last Friday of the month, which is payday for Peace Corps Volunteers," he explained. "Every Volunteer left in the southern district will ride their motorcycle into Bo tomorrow and get their check. They'll all be at the Thirsty Soul Saloon in Bo, which is where white people get drunk on the weekends. It's less than an hour by bush taxi. I suggest you spend the weekend there, and see if the Peace Corps has been able to learn anything new. I doubt it, but you may stumble onto something. When you return, I'll have a looking-around man here for you. A good one. His name is Sam-King Kebbie. He is a blacksmith from Kenema. He's not a charlatan. He knows what he's doing."

"Where can I find this Section Chief Moiwo?" asked Boone.

Sisay looked at him suddenly.

"What do you want with him?" he asked.

"Nothing," Boone said. "I'd just like to meet him. If he's the section chief, maybe he can help us."

"He's running for election," said Sisay darkly. "He won't help you, unless you happen to have a lot of money, in which case he'll offer to help and take the money. He's probably in Bo too. But I wouldn't go looking for him. People get . . . funny when they are running for election."

"If I run into him," Boone said, "I'll just introduce myself and see what happens."

"My advice would be to not run into him," said Sisay, cocking his head and listening to another argument somewhere out in the courtyard.

•

That night, the toothless, fingerless old grandma who had asked Boone for medicine sat on her veranda with her grandchildren, who were crying and still terrified by the sight of Pa Gigba's corpse. Grandma Dembe told them why children cry themselves to sleep at night and the story of how the ugly toad of Death came into the world.

"Every night we die," she said, "and every morning we rise from the dead. Every night infants cry because they feel night coming on, they feel death coming on. They writhe like snakes in their anguish. Some are more clever than others, and it is the clever ones who scream the loudest, for they fear sleep the most. They are afraid that if they die and go to sleep, they will never wake up again. They do not know that they will wake up in the morning feeling better.

"It is the same when people know they must die. They live a long life, and then they cry and beg and writhe like snakes in their anguish when the time comes to die. They are afraid they will die and go to sleep forever, instead of waking up the next day, across the river, in the village with white sands.

"And that is why infants cry themselves to sleep at night," said Grandma Dembe.

"How did the ugly toad of Death come into the world?" asked one of the children.

"*Ngewo* made a man and a woman," Grandma Dembe said. "*Ngewo* gave the man and the woman all they wanted. But every time he gave them something, they wanted more: first food, then fire, then animals, then tools, then medicines.

"At that time, the ugly toad of Death did not haunt men. Instead, God sent his servants to collect living people when their time was spent. But one day, a proud man refused to go with God's servants, though he was politely asked several times. God sent Mr. Sickness to get hold of the proud man and shake him with fevers.

" 'Mr. Sickness has caught me, but I can't see him,' the man cried, and he could not move.

" 'You have lived long enough,' said Mr. Sickness. 'It is time for you to go.' But the man refused.

"The next day, God sent the ugly toad of Death to bring the man caught by Mr. Sickness. The man died and was buried.

"Mr. Sickness and the ugly toad of Death stayed in the world to catch and bring those who will not come when they are called."

(10)

Mack wheeled a stack of documents in on a cart.

"Here's DropCo Steel," he said with a proud flourish, indicating several foot-high stacks of crosshatched documents. "Petition, proposed cash collateral orders, schedule of affairs, creditor matrix, list of twenty largest creditors, and memoranda in support. After you sign them, I'll box them and cab them over."

Randall selected a document from the top of the heap and flipped through it.

"You have a floater for a secretary, today," he said, studying the signature page.

"I do," said Mack. "Sally's sick. How did you know?"

"No secretary in this department would print a document for my signature on 25 percent cotton bond paper. Tell her to redo it on 100 percent bond."

"Redo the whole set?" Mack asked.

"We can't file them like this," Randall said, "can we? Tell her to print them again. And tell her I want four blank lines between the body and the signature line. She's only got three here," he complained, pointing at the signature block.

Mack left with his cart and his tail between his legs.

A single trill from the phone announced an in-house call.

"Killigan," said a voice over the intercom, "Stone. I'm down here in the War Room working on the Swintex case. I'm deep into section 507. Seems like I remember a partnership retreat. I think we were both shitfaced at the time," Stone continued, "but I remember you telling me that Thomas Aquinas would have to come back as a bankruptcy lawyer before anybody could really understand all the

things you could do to a creditor using 507. You were doing Mag-
netron or Metalink at the time. I think you were in front of Judge
Baxter in the southern district."

"Magnalink," said Randall with a sentimental chuckle. "They
were holding their ankles and begging for mercy."

Stone laughed. "You said you found a way to skin an unsecured
creditor, leaving nothing but vital organs and a nervous system
behind." He giggled. "They were still alive, you said. They were still
conscious, but they were absolutely powerless to do anything but
scream themselves to death."

"Magnalink," said Randall. "Talk about fun."

"I need to know how you did it," said Stone. "I've got a guy on
the other side who's asking for it. I want to crush his skull, but I
need him left alive so we can use him to deal with the other creditors
in his class."

"Go into the Magnalink directory. I think it's on the F drive of
the token ring server," said Randall. "Look at the plan confirmation
documents. In the meantime, think about it this way. Section 1129
is the sun. Section 507 is the moon. If you align them just so, it's
like an eclipse. There's a penumbra. That's where you want to be.
Read it first, and then I'll come up and explain it to you. We'll have
this guy breathing through a hole in his neck before he knows what
hit him."

"Thanks, boss," said Stone.

"Mention it," said Randall. "Preferably to the Swintex CEO.
They've got a sister corporation in Chicago on the verge of going
under. We could use that work. Tell him we saved him a bundle
in fees by hitching him a ride on the Magnalink documents."

Randall hung up the phone and wistfully wondered why all of
life couldn't be as simple and as immediately rewarding as a thriving
bankruptcy practice unfettered by administrative meddling. But
such vocational glows were becoming increasingly short-lived and
infrequent. The department was straining at the seams of the usual
managed chaos. The tumor scare, the time out for the tests, the
phone calls to Washington, all of it was showing up in his concentration and his performance. His career-building cases were at least
temporarily in the hands of junior partners and associates. Actually
trusting them could only lead to trouble. If a minion turned on him,
mistakes could be made (using the political passive), it could be let
known that Randall wasn't quite riding herd on his cases the way

he usually did, and other lawyers were doing most of the work. Actually confiding in the other partners was out of the question. He had learned early never to reveal his true thoughts or let them get the upper hand in any exchange. Instead, when confronted, he was stubborn, contrary, and quick to beat them at their own game.

The management committee had received a report that Randall was becoming too volatile. That at least one big client had suggested they might look around for the same bankruptcy expertise in another lawyer with more stability of mood and manner. This, he knew, was a false report, intentionally leaked, probably by somebody drawing a bead on him from behind. The substance of the rumor was the kind of bullshit a bull shits when it has eaten bullshit. Somebody was fucking with him and getting ready to suggest he was being distracted by events in his personal life. This was Firm Code used to identify weakness and an inability to swear allegiance body and soul to the partnership. He decided it was time again to plant the rumor that he was leaving with a tribe of Sterling warriors unless the committees got off his back and let him get on with the business of commercial warfare.

Meanwhile, Africa was an expanding continent taking up more and more of his day, swelling the wrong columns in his performance profile with hours of nonbillable time. He had kept in close contact with the American Ambassador in Freetown, who in turn was in touch, from time to time, with the section chief, to whom Randall was writing checks. This Moiwo fellow seemed quite confident that Michael was alive and off in the bush being initiated into some magic cult of sorcerers or diviners, some mystical gig, the description of which fit his kid like a glove. There was abundant hope that he would turn up in one piece, which was not to say that he was out of danger. Dabbling in this sort of magic always carried risk, said the embassy people, especially at election time.

At home, things were even worse than at work. Marjorie took the pronouncements of the section chief regarding Michael's possible safety as an answer to the prayers she had been buying from a convent of cloistered nuns. Her belief in the power of prayer was so strong that she commissioned custom-designed prayers fashioned by experts, in this case monastic nuns, insiders who spent their lives in transports of devotion to God. These women left the material world at age eighteen and never looked back. Randall remembered them from his Catholic youth. They were sanctified and full of grace and gave undivided attention to God. In their presence, even Randall, the indifferent Catholic, momentarily suspended his belief that money was the only thing you could count on in a crisis. Here were very different creatures indeed, for they passionately believed in something not described anywhere in the Uniform Commercial Code. They were a highly specialized breed. If the cause was a worthy one, these cloistered nuns could touch God's sleeve and whisper into his bended ear.

He saw the prayer money when his monthly bank statement came over the modem, passed across his screen, and into the predefined categories of his personal financial software. When he pressed Marjorie for details, he learned that the prayers were for Michael, and not a word of prayer to protect him from a potential brain tumor. Why? Because she didn't believe he had a brain tumor, she explained. She went so far as to frankly admit that she thought he was a hypochondriac.

Very low. Age was giving her fangs and claws, and he was discovering a host of mental blemishes. He had put up with her irritating complaints about how he supposedly had been almost intolerable lately, that he ranted and raved and raced from one worry to the other, that he was allegedly panicking, "heartsick," she said, about his scans and Michael's disappearance. He reasoned with his loudest, best voice, explaining his special medical needs to her one by one. But after he finished, she walked him over to the desk where she kept track of the family health insurance and asked him in a nice way if he would go with her to see a psychiatrist, a doctor recommended by a family friend of hers. Randall decided to pacify her and go along. He thought of it as a way of helping her confront her own need for professional counseling.

Once he got there, he found out the guy was not a doctor at all, but a Ph.D. in psychology who called himself a doctor. Randall looked at his watch and realized that he was going to be stuck in a small room with his wife and a patronizing dweeb in a sport coat and turtleneck for an hour. The good doctor kept throwing out phrases like "marital dynamics" and "dysfunctional codependency," which Randall instantly recognized as *billing* words, or words that one charged by the hour to explain. What did this overeducated Dutch uncle who made his living by nodding his head think Randall did all day? Randall could tell that Dr. Dweeb was anxious to find marital troubles, which would mean referral to a marriage counselor and a cut of the fee.

After forty-five minutes of pussyfooting around, the untenured academic made his move and pulled a shiv out of his sock.

"Marjorie is very concerned about your health and your happiness," he said. "I think that's one of the reasons she wanted you to come here with her today."

Dweeb smiled so hard his dental work showed. He bowed his head, and looked up at Randall. The good doctor's benevolence and selflessness threatened Randall's airway. A platter might come in handy if all that genuine concern started dripping off his face. Randall kept his hand on his wallet.

"Some of the events I've heard you and Marjorie discuss here today sound like you're having an understandably difficult and stressful time coping with your son's disappearance," he said. "No one blames you for your feelings of loss and anxiety. Indeed, it would be unnatural if you did not find this a stressful and trying time. Sometimes anxiety and stress manifest themselves in unpredictable ways, sometimes the fear takes on a life of its own, and the stress-afflicted person exhibits an anxious flight of ideas, a symptom that can be quite trying for a spouse. Do you use alcohol to relieve stress?"

Marjorie avoided Randall's sudden black stare.

This was an assassination attempt, with the dweeb as the hit man, and she was using Randall's money to pay for the job.

"Out of concern for you," continued Dweeb, "Marjorie also has advised me that lately you've had more than the usual number of physical complaints, and that you had a brief episode of nocturnal disorientation."

This brought Randall up short on the lip of a cliff overlooking the abyss of outright betrayal. *So that's the game*, he realized, always amazed when people had even worse motives than he, the cynosure of cynicism, could imagine. *Your wife tells me you're nuts, and she's hired me to help you*, which in essence was this amateur's pitch. The guy was hiring himself out as a private investigator of Randall's private life. Here was a "doctor" who needed to be sued. Wasn't this a solicitation of some kind, reeking of a professional conflict of interest? He had a sudden urge to see this man's children on the street lamenting the day that their dad had stepped into the shadow of Randall Killigan.

He nearly exploded, thinking about how some clerk in the outer office was probably taking an imprint of his insurance card even as he sat there. He had a few things to say, but he was smart enough to keep his mouth shut. A sudden premonition of divorce court swam before his eyes, with the dweeb taking the stand, dressed in a suit and tie for the occasion. Ambush! He could see the raiding party coming into formation on the high ground around him, scavengers looking for ammunition, which, if he didn't watch himself, would fall out of his mouth and into their laps.

The internal effort nearly killed him, but he kept his counsel.

As a parting volley, Dweeb smoothly weaved in another reference to the "flight of ideas," which he solemnly proclaimed could be alleviated by the proper administration of certain medications.

Randall bit his tongue and mentally drafted a letter he would send after he was safely out of enemy artillery range:

Dear Camp Counselor Dweeb:
Regarding our one and only meeting and your pitiful attempt to extort money from me using that pataphysical, pseudoscientific drivel you bill out as psychological counseling.

I have three relevant observations:
(1) You make 35 grand a year.
(2) I make 500 grand a year.
(3) One of us has a mental problem.

Yours very truly,
Randall Killigan, Esq.

This flight business was a new one on Randall, or so he thought, until he asked the doctor exactly what it was. Dweeb described the flight of ideas as a "rambling from subject to subject in a wearisome harangue, with nothing but superficial associative connections holding the topics of conversation together."

Randall looked at his wife and waited patiently for elaboration.

"That's it?" he had asked. "A rambling harangue held together by superficial associations?" He looked again at his wife. "Let me ask you something, Doctor. Are you married? And if so, have you ever tried to read the paper while your wife's on the phone? You want to hear a rambling harangue held together by superficial associations?"

Randall went home shaking his head, once again amazed at the kind of blather people lined up to pay for by the hour. Did he need to lose an afternoon at the office and pay some transactional analyst to tell him about the flight of ideas? He had half a mind to hire his own trigger man to look into Marjorie's mental health. Her ideas had been flapping around loose like kites in a storm since the first day he had met her! So it's *flighty ideas* they're worried about? Well, if they meant to get a handle on the notions gusting around inside Marjorie's skull, they had better round up the varsity falconry squad and bring on the toils and meshes! If he asked her a simple question, her ideas scattered, spooking themselves like birds without a single feather in common, a symptom the good doctor would have to agree was especially trying for her spouse.

He could not even imagine living inside such a mental state. His ideas were orderly and rectilinear.

That night, he lay his head on his pillow, closed his eyes, and listened to her piloting her ideas madly through the airspace surrounding his head. In his mind's eye, he could see each garish, flaffing idea winging aloft: a coot, a booby, a loon, a cuckoo, a cockatoo, a barnacle goose, a fool duck, a crow, a dodo, a goatsucker, a buzzard, a grouse, a gull, a jackdaw, a kite, a laughing jackass, a mockingbird . . . Scattershot flocks spreading out against the sky, unfurling in swirling skeins, disintegrating helixes, always breaking formations and converging again—a soaring, panicking, unstructured stimulus. Sparrows bolting in innocent terror. Dithering woodcocks, turkeys galloping just off the runway, peacocks riffling their awesome fanfares of color . . . The flur of pigeons wheeling around steeples, alighting on the beveled edges of bells, setting up whispering tintinnabulations in the belfries, where slumbering bats hung from the traceries, grinning like gargoyles, waiting for night, to riot and swoop and snag their bony, winged claws in the hair of madmen, screeching in high-decibel, eldritch sonars tracking insects . . . so shrilly that only the insane can hear them. Bats sleeping in cracks, fissures, sulci, fossi, sulculi . . . Bats in the oculi of domes. Bats shitting guano all over the spandrels, the stained glass and flying buttresses, the five classical orders, and even the noble statues!

Randall yawned and pumped his pillow. *At least I'm not crazy,* he thought. *At least one of us is not flying ideas around like dodo birds. You'd have to be daffier than old Daffy himself to get caught*

up in something like the flight of ideas. But the bat was never far
from his thoughts. It had now almost become a part of his personality. He could no longer stand up before the chief bankruptcy judge
in the southern district of Indiana as a simon-pure and single-
minded warrior, because a voice in the back of his head was saying,
"Your honor, I stand before you, not as a devoted officer of the court,
an instrument of commercial litigation, and a warlord of the Code,
but as a man who saw a West African bat with a four-foot wingspan
in his bedroom." It subtly undermined his self-confidence, in the
same manner that he imagined illegal drugs or secret sex crimes
compromised the performance of otherwise competent profession-
als, because these people knew they were living lies, they had a
Jekyll personality they showed to their clients, but Hyde was always
giggling over their shoulder.

Analysis of the problem did not help any. He turned it over in his
mind, at night, after his wife had gone to sleep. Would thinking
about it somehow bring the thing back? He knew no ordinary,
rational explanation could account for the bat's appearance, so
he explored—dabbled, really—in extraordinary, irrational explanations. Either his mind, his universe, or both had produced a hideous
aberration: Had it come from within, or from without? Had he
hallucinated the thing into being? Was it some confluence of nightmare and sleeping medication? Had the rational universe ruptured
and issued some inexplicable freak?

He flirted with believing in the supernatural, but the supernatural
was even more frightening than brain tumors. If there were supernatural events, they were probably populated by supernatural
beings who operated somewhere outside the jurisdiction of the
bankruptcy court. It could mean afterlife, maybe even . . . all the
things he had forgotten about after leaving his position as head altar
boy at St. Dymphna's Cathedral some forty years ago. Once out of
grade school, he had wisely and heavily invested in science, reason,
and money. But if he could admit at least the possibility of miracles
or occult phenomena, it might allow him to blame the bat on something outside himself. As it was, reason and science relentlessly
turned his suspicions inward. He could not reorder the material
universe to account for a West African bat in his Indiana bedroom:
The only remaining variable in the equation was Randall Killigan.

And if Randall Killigan had a brain tumor, the investing could
become even more intense and conflicted. His odds would be very

bad, and odds that low bring out the gambler in everyone. He re-called the spirit, if not the letter, of Pascal's Wager, which he con-formed to his own reduced circumstances: Even a 5 percent chance that God exists starts looking better than a 3 percent chance of living five years. Which made him think about rearranging his portfolio.

After Marjorie fell asleep, he reached over to his nightstand and grabbed his Bankruptcy Code. Whenever he had a big case coming up, a confirmation hearing, a hearing on a lift-stay motion, or any other dispositive proceeding, instead of girding his loins and painting his face, he prepared himself, late at night, by studying the Code. After the clamor and the smoke of the daily battles had cleared, after everyone else had gone to bed, after his opponents had gone home to weaken themselves with alcohol or distract themselves with women or children, after it was absolutely quiet, Randall sat up absorbed in the Code, the source of all his power.

In any bankruptcy proceeding, no matter how big or how much money was involved, the parties usually ended up arguing over the meaning of a mere six or seven sections of the Code that were crucial to the disposition of assets in that particular case. Randall already knew most of those sections by heart, but early in his career he discovered that if, on the eve of battle, he read those crucial pro-visions, over and over, ten or twenty times, late into the night, and on into the morning, he often discovered some new relationship between them, some new bit of legislative history, or an obscure but creative judicial gloss on one of the clauses, which in turn affected the provision and its relationship to the other provisions in that section, and ultimately the relationship of the section to the other sections and to the Code itself, which in turn led to another theory of the case, and before he knew it—almost as if by magic—he discovered an entirely new method for destroying his client's adversaries and recapturing the assets that had wrongfully been taken on a fraudulent promise to repay.

Randall was Magister Ludi, the Code was his glass-bead game. Everyone knew the sections and the provisions in the sections, but it was the *relationships* between them that only the masters under-stood. When an eager young associate bounded into his office, all wild-eyed about some new interpretation of a provision that appeared to mean that vast sums of money would soon flow out of the bank-ruptcy court and onto their clients' ledgers, Randall loved to kick back in his chair and laugh. "That's pretty good, boy," he would say, "but take a look at section 507. It directly contradicts your theory, and there is no such thing as a contradiction in the Code. It's already been picked over by thousands of lawyers and legislators who had big money at stake and who have judicially interpreted it and legislatively modified it until it is a thing of perfect symmetry. Go read 507, and then we'll talk."

Armed with his late-night Code revelations, Randall destroyed the lives of devious debtors. Of course, he would take all the property he could get his hands on and see that it was returned to his client, the bank. Of course, he would sue them so hard they landed in the emergency room clutching their chests. The common folk who spent their lives in front of TV sets thought Randall was greedy or wicked or both. They did not understand that if debtors were allowed to break their promises and defraud banks of money, pretty soon the banks would have no money to lend! No one would be able to get a loan! They didn't understand how things worked, because they had been bewitched by television, and were too lazy to understand the fundamental truths of commercial litigation.

When Randall was on his feet in the bankruptcy court, the world was simple and Manichaean. Creditors were businesslike, law-abiding institutions that lent money to borrowers on a promise to repay at a set rate of interest. The borrower freely assented to the terms of repayment and had signed notes, contracts, and personal guarantees to that effect. Then, one day, the borrower said, "I changed my mind. I'm breaking my promise. I am not going to pay the money back."

People once trusted each other. There was a thing called honor. There was no money and no laws, only a man's word. People said things like "You have my word on it," or "He is as good as his word." But then society got bigger, and all the innocent, well-meaning citizens couldn't know absolutely everyone they were dealing with, so they developed an anonymous warrant, a symbol of their good intentions. Instead of favors and promises, people relied on money. If money took the place of favors and promises, then what are debtors? They are people who selfishly subvert the symbols of good faith and promises. They *owe*, usually because they were able to defraud others. They come to the bank and gladly take our money, our good intentions, our good faith, and squander it on selfish and unprofitable ventures. Are they filled with remorse, now that they have defiled our good faith? Do they keep their promise to repay? No, they repay our good faith, our promises, our good intentions by lying, cheating, deceiving, fabricating records, writing bad checks, debasing and undermining the entire system of good faith. And who pays for them?

Needless to say, the speech was altered slightly when he agreed to represent the debtor.

As he was turning these things over in his mind he noticed the closet door was open. The closet light operated off a door switch and so was on, throwing a yellow nimbus on the pale interior crowded with his empty clothes. Who would wear those clothes if his bright object turned out to be a brain tumor? As he stared at the wall and thought of Marjorie crying only for herself at his funeral, he saw one shadow pass like a film across the white wall. Had he imagined it? He heard one faint tap, a drop of liquid striking the wood floor, then another, forming a single pit-a-pat. For no reason at all, he suddenly heard bat professor Veldkamp's words chuckling in his ear: *I am afraid that there is no way I could convince a jury that a sane person could find an Old World fruit bat with a wingspan of five feet in his bedroom in Indianapolis, unless he put it there himself.*

Randall moved swiftly, but took care not to awaken the enemy sleeping next to him. His heart lurched and throttled into overdrive as he went to the closet and flung it open, ready to duck if anything flew out. Nothing did. He stepped into the closet with his back to the closet light and pulled the box down into his own shadow. He set in on a low bench, reached in, and took the bundle in his hands.

Instead of screaming, he took a single gasp for air when his fingers stuck in viscous ooze. He dropped the box and held the bundle up into the light, watching fresh blood stream in rivulets over his hands, down his forearms, and onto the floor, where he had heard the drops fall. He hyperventilated through his teeth and stared at the bloody bundle. More than blood, he feared that if a scream escaped from him, his wife would find him standing in the closet holding a dry bundle of rags with his head stuck in some private hallucination. *Then what?*

He set the sticky bundle back in the box and cleaned up the puddle of blood with a stack of paper tissues. He flushed them down the toilet and washed his trembling hands in the sink, watching pink-tinged water pool in the flutes of the sink and course to the drain's black hole.

Not even Bean was going to hear about this. Visual bat hallucinations, maybe. But tactile? Auditory? Even olfactory hallucinations? Because a suffocating stench came off the thing in waves, smelling like death, rotten blood, and musty dollar bills. He instinctively realized that, real or unreal, showing this poultice from hell to his wife or Bean or anyone else would be a confession of mental illness. If it was real, they would think he had made it himself. If it was not real, then it was another hideous specter that only he could see.

He needed proof that this was not another freak of his rupturing imagination. He needed objective verification of this thing's constituent elements before he would proceed. Laboratory analysis, that was the solution. He needed disinterested scientists to examine the thing and tell him what it was. Mack would know where to send it. The firm had running accounts with labs for testing in product liability cases.

And what if the lab said it was an old bundle of rags from Africa? What if Bean's lab said he was seeing and feeling a private nightmare, a hallucinatory solipsism created by his own neurological disorders? Maybe it was the aura before a seizure.

Something real was happening, but only to him. Maybe it was his bright object growing fingers into the soil of his brain.

(11)

Bo—which means "the potter's clay"—is the capital of Mendeland and is situated in the lower midsection of Sierra Leone almost equidistant from Freetown on the west coast and Sierra Leone's border with Liberia to the east. Bo grew from nothing around an ill-fated railroad that once joined the hinterlands to Freetown and hence the world. Since the mid-1960s, when a former President decided the country did not need a railroad, the rusting, overgrown tracks have stood as a monument to failed human endeavor in a country and a continent jinxed by colonialism, witchcraft, political disasters, and corruption.

With a population of 40,000, Bo remained—even without the railroad—the third-largest city in Sierra Leone, consisting primarily of dusty roads lined with shacks, where tailors pedaled at their sewing machines, Fula men and other petty traders sold matches, cigarettes, and aspirin, matrons of chophouses served platefuls of rice and sauce, and bartenders sold tepid beer out of kerosene-powered refrigerators. The roads wound into roundabouts with small markets or lorry parks, then spun out again into a sprawl of ramshackle buildings and pan-roofed arcades. Taxis roamed the roads, coasting down hills with their engines switched off whenever possible. In dusty trails on each side of the roads, strings of women and children bore headloads and buckets, led goats, and shouted *"Poo-mui!"* at the passing white man.

As it turned out, what Sisay had called a "bush taxi" was nothing more than the first car or truck to come along with room for a passenger and a driver willing to negotiate a fare. Boone simply stood at the side of the road with a cupped supine palm, which in

Sierra Leone means: *How about a lift? I'm willing to pay.* Within half an hour, he had a ride from a Sierra Leonean government employee who spoke Krio so quickly and used so many proverbs and slang expressions that conversation was impossible. The man was not Mende, so Boone's prolific *Kaye ii Ngewo ma*'s were politely ignored. They rode in silence, except for an occasional burst of Krio from the driver, and an awkward shrug from Boone, followed by irritation at each other's inability to understand plain English. Still, compared to the *podah-podah*, the bush taxi was luxurious. He was dropped off at the intersection of Damballa Road and Fenton Road, across from a prosperous Lebanese market, at the doorstep of an institution Peace Corps Volunteers have been patronizing since President Kennedy sent them to Sierra Leone in the 1960s.

The Thirsty Soul Saloon began as a counter facing out into a roofed concrete veranda, open on three sides, where tables of planks and barrels were flanked by long benches. The clientele consisted of white people—Peace Corps Volunteers, USAID workers, European development workers, British, Dutch, and Canadian Volunteers, and the occasional diamond prospectors, though their tastes ran more to the casinos, discos, and resort hotels along the beaches in Freetown. Now and again, a black African came in—a government clerk or a low-level administrator from one of the development companies—ready to piss a week's pay away on a drunk with white people, who drank twice as much on less than half a day's pay.

The place had previously been as accessible as an open-air beer market, where white people came to water their livers and to maunder over their *poo-mui* concerns—things like cold sodas, potable water, air conditioning, antimalarial medications, decent tobacco, cow beef, soap, and toilet paper. But the accessibility of the saloon led to a phenomenon known among the *poo-mui* as "beggar creep." Of an evening, when the *poo-muis* gathered and fell into lubricated conversation, hungry children and beggars surrounded the establishment, standing haggard and shiftless in the open archways, sometimes calling softly, sometimes hissing in the Arabic fashion, trying to attract the attention of the white people without annoying them.

"Do ya, paddy, let we have ten cents."

"White mahn, look me empty belly. I no get notting foh eat."

They raised their eyebrows imploringly, or indicated paralyzed limbs or missing fingers, coughed demonstratively into bloody rags, or showed the patrons empty bottles of medicine that would not be refilled without a contribution. As the afternoon wore on into evening and the drinking and conversation grew more riotous, the beggars, of necessity, crept closer, lest they be shut out by the din and the failing light and the ever duller sensibilities of the clientele. Soon mendicants were touching the patrons' bended elbows and falling down on the ground in desperate supplication, where they blocked the passage of waitresses and generally obstructed the flow of Star beer and commerce.

The proprietor, a Krio with a Mende mother, from whom he had inherited his warrior's temper, could spend only so much time kicking beggars across the floor and driving them ahead of him with an old golf club, given to him by a white man for just this purpose. Ultimately, he sealed off the open arches with heavy steel mesh, keeping the riffraff at bay, allowing the white people to drink in peace, and leaving a single entrance to the Thirsty Soul, which could be monitored from the bar. But the caged arcades still filled with beggars, their britches hitched up with rope belts, zippered flies torn asunder, T-shirts stained and caps torn. Their mouths looked like talking wounds sown with broken teeth. They crawled up and down the mesh, pantomiming their needs through the rusty iron webwork, pleading for leones over the songs and laughter of the white people.

Every now and again, the proprietor came out and doused them with a bucket of water.

Boone made his way down a row of Honda dirt bikes parked outside and into the bar area, which was populated by young whites in tie-dyed native shirts, drinking in clusters, calling out to one another across the plank-and-barrel tables. He was amazed to find Sam Lewis sitting at a table with a writing pad and a plate of food fenced in by empty bottles of Star beer.

Lewis waved at him nonchalantly, and seemed not the least surprised to see him.

"Ain't it funny how white people run into each other in this country," he said, dropping a chicken bone back into a bed of rice and palm oil. "Sit and drink," he said, pointing at the bench across from him. "Or have some chop, if you want," he added, giving the plate a nudge.

Boone's bowels were still rumbling with the effluvia of his latrine vigils, and the thought of food caused his intestines to buckle and knot with vapor lock. He guessed that during the rest of his stay in Sierra Leone, he would always be acutely aware of the distance to the nearest latrine.

"What's that?" he asked, indicating Lewis's paperwork.

"I'm getting out soon," said Lewis, still writing. "And I think I've got a job lined up with a couple of Lebanese smug—I mean, diamond miners. The Shahadi brothers out east in Koidu, Kono District. But I'm covering all the bases. I understand the employment situation is grim back in the States, and many of the Volunteers are jobless for months upon return. So I'm writing ahead to potential employers there, just in case my mining job falls through. This particular letter will also be published in our local newsletter for Bo Province Volunteers and will serve as a model résumé and job query letter for departing Volunteers who are in search of employment.

"Here," said Lewis, lifting freshly scribbled pieces of notebook paper dribbled with sweat and beer and handing them to Boone. "Tell me what you think."

Mr. Samuel B. Lewis
United States Peace Corps
Pujehun
Sierra Leone, West Africa

Mr. U. R. Grasping
President and Chief Executive Officer
Crapulent Manufacturing Corp.
1212 Mammon Drive
Porcine, Wisconsin

Re: Application for Employment with Crapulent Manufacturing

Dear Mr. Grasping:
As my résumé indicates, I majored in behavioral psychology, graduated with a bachelor of arts, and then went straight into the Peace Corps, where I have been an Agriculture Volunteer for almost two years. You may be tempted to conclude that the only practical skill I have acquired is how to grow rice in bush swamps. It's true, I have no experience in the American business world and no knowledge of widgets or any of the other products manufactured by Crapulent. However, I do have an extensive background in dealing with greedy, ruthless people who are as dumb as pig iron and who don't care about anybody but themselves, all of which I feel make me uniquely suited

for a position with your company. After all, for the last two years, I have been living quite prosperously in one of the poorest countries in the world. If I can extract food, sexual favors, precious stones and minerals, illegal drugs, and money from these people, who have an average annual income of around $240, just think what I will do to your customers. I have a nimble sense of humor, I am pleasant when approached, I am prompt, courteous, hold my liquor, and work very well with others, especially attractive young women.

In the course of my travels, I have become something of a fanatic about the reproductive rites of women. I have made myself a skilled lingualist in subtropical female languages and can speak fluently to the better-looking ladies of many different cultures and countries. I realize this last skill may not have immediate on-the-job application, but it is one of those intangibles that will contribute to corporate goodwill and the company's persona, once I get at all the girls whose husbands don't speak the same language to them at home, if you take my meaning. Even if you don't take it, suffice it to say that I'm talking about quality of life, corporate culture, and boosting morale in the workplace.

I am a veritable human turbine when it comes to willpower and self-discipline, as evidenced by my having frequently and repeatedly used every recreational drug known to man, without once having a problem with addiction or dependency. I follow a daily spartan regimen of exercise and diet, I quit drinking every night at midnight, and I'm up next day at the whack of dong.

Although I work very hard, I am also a family man, with dozens of children in many different African countries and several different states, not to mention a set of twins in Thailand, issuing from a 48-hour layover in Bangkok. Nothing was more important to me than the mothers of these children. So, although I will work myself to the bone for the good of the company, rest assured that I will always find time to be active in the community and to continue being a father to unborn children.

I look forward to putting my formidable talents to work for you at Crapulent, and I eagerly await your reply.

Yours very truly,
Samuel B. Lewis

"Don't worry about the handwriting," Lewis said. "I'll have one of the girls in the Bo office type it up for me. Do you think it's too strong?" he asked, taking another pull on a Star, concern furrowing his brow. "I can't be bashful about my strengths, but I don't want to seem immodest either."

"I think it's you," said Boone.

"Here," Lewis said, shoving a plate of bones, skin, and grease at Boone, "have a piece of chicken."

Boone surveyed the plate for a limb that had not already been gnawed on and settled on a drumstick half concealed by rice and palm oil.

"I have to warn you, though," Lewis said. "It's an experimental undertaking. My cook brought me the thing this morning after it was killed by a snake. Don't ask me what kind, she couldn't say. All we know is that a snake bit the chicken and it died. I brought it here, and they cooked it up for me out back. Now, you tell me: Is it OK to eat a chicken that has been killed by a poisonous snake?"

"I don't know," Boone confessed.

"I don't either," said Lewis, "but we'll find out pretty soon, won't we? Because I just ate the whole thing."

"Why didn't you ask one of the villagers?"

"Ask a villager?" Lewis said. "Are you kidding? I'd ask a villager if I should be in long bonds or tax-free munis before I'd ask them about what's safe to eat."

Boone gently returned the drumstick to its position on the plate. "I'll pass," he demurred.

"It sure tastes good," said Lewis, stripping the last bone of meat in two bites and pouring half a bottle of beer in behind it.

Suddenly, Lewis sat bolt upright and clutched his throat. His eyes bulged and he showed Boone a mouthful of shredded chicken. Volunteers at the surrounding tables turned and stared.

"It's the snake venom!" Lewis hollered. "It's taking effect! Quick, before I die, I want to make one last woman . . . I mean wish."

The patrons burst out laughing and shot bottle caps at Lewis.

"Well, say, gang," Lewis crowed, "what say we get all fucked up and talk about our feelings? Star beer!"

Boone decided to test the depths of his irritable bowels with a cold Star. Lewis fell into a bottle cap shooting contest with two other Volunteers, wagering that they could hit an empty kerosene can at forty paces. Bets were placed and money came out on the table.

Dark fingers appeared in the grillwork, followed by heavy breathing at the sight of so much money in plain view and about to be won or lost on the flick of a bottle cap.

"Mastah, I beg. Let we have ten cents. Do ya, I beg."

"White man, I no get notting foh eat. Febah been make me wife want foh die. I no get food foh me peekins. I pray God, let we have five leone, no moh."

Lewis shot a bottle cap, missed the kerosene can, drank half a Star, and shoved the money at his opponent. He surveyed the gallery of mendicants hanging on the grille.

"Is it only male beggars today? Where are all the women beggars? Let we get some women beggars, do ya. How about some sweet-eye gal beggars, pa, you can do that for me?"

This earned Lewis a round of censure from the other Volunteers and facefuls of unmitigated disgust from the women among them.

"Never mind about the female beggars, pa," Lewis said, beaming at the women Volunteers. "These *poo-mui* gals look like dey like me too much. Look, see ahm! Dey go want make me be dae boy-friend."

Over another round, he introduced Boone to ten or twelve other white people, American Volunteers warming up for something they called *Poo-mui* Night, which, if the tales of *Poo-mui* Nights gone by were any indication, sounded like a cross between Saturnalia and hog-killing time.

Boone met Joe from Duluth, Bill from Phoenix, Mary from Ta-coma, Helen and Frank from Billings, who came over as a husband-and-wife Peace Corps team and were divorced within six months of their stay, Harry from Minneapolis, Pete from some place in New Jersey . . . a blur of young white people in embroidered African shirts, American shorts, and plastic thongs. They hailed each other by their African names and mixed Valley girl and post-surf-punk slang with Mende and Krio sayings. "Totally awesome" came out hard by "Better no dae" or "Peace no dae inside de country."

Everyone knew about Killigan's disappearance, but no one had so much as a rumor of what had happened to him, nor did they offer Boone any advice on how to find him. After introducing them, Lewis gave Boone the lowdown on the person as he or she walked away to rejoin the revelry in progress.

"That's Frank Nation," he said, "formerly of Frank and Helen fame." He indicated an emaciated balding Volunteer, who appeared stooped with age and saddened by a lifetime of sorrow at the age of no more than thirty.

"He used to be married to Helen, the skank yonder in the denim skirt," said Lewis, indicating a not unattractive, somewhat thick-boned brunette. "The one with the sturdy, homegrown set of briskets flopping around loose inside the tie-dyed T-shirt.

"She divorced Frank, and you'll get a high-decibel account of just why if you ever get within her considerable broadcasting area. When they first got to their village, she must have tied old Frank down out there, then done brain surgery on him with her voice-activated trepanning device. The guy looked like he'd had a lobotomy by the time he got away from her."

Three planks away, Helen filled the ear of a British Volunteer, her voice shrilling easily over the beer-hall ruckus and the imprecations of the beggars. One sample and Boone knew that Helen was what Schopenhauer had in mind when he said that the amount of noise which anyone can bear undisturbed stands in inverse proportion to his mental capacity.

"She's nice to look at, but she won't do nothing for you, no matter how hard you breathe on her. She's here for the Third World experience. She's busy discovering a village that never existed until she arrived to experience it and give it deep meaning. She's into multiculturalism and hates dead white males, because they have been enslaving and debasing women for centuries. The history of Western civilization began right around the day she was born. All the art, history, music, literature, and philosophy before her time are really just spoors left by an ageless conspiracy of white male animals who roamed the earth with the dinosaurs of old and kept themselves busy making war, getting drunk, and enslaving and debasing women. She'd rather listen to some spasm band out in the bush banging on rusty saws than to Mozart or Elvis Costello. If it weren't for white males conspiring against the truth and beauty of the Third World, and enslaving and debasing women, she believes, we would be teaching our children about Bob Marley and Gloria Steinem instead of Beethoven and Kant. Just look ahead a couple hundred years; all the longhaired musicians will be tuning up the cellos and violins at the Vienna Philharmonic, chalking up and getting ready to tear into a version of 'No Woman, No Cry,' and instead of reading what Plato had to say about the soul, we'll be memorizing Gloria's immortal insights on self-esteem.

"Helen wanted to start Western civilization over with the heretofore missing radical-feminist component. She kicked things off by marrying Frank, so she could use him as Exhibit A whenever she got into an argument about the natural superiority of women. Anything men can do, she can do better. Take, for instance, enslaving and debasing her husband. Did someone say pathetic? Just look at the guy! Do I need to say any more about men? What a pitiful creature of his own fears and inadequacies! Do you want to hit him, or just watch Helen do it for you?

"She's got vision," Lewis said. "I've never seen such a clear-sighted creature in my life. She understands the central truth: That men are animals, and women are reptiles. I agree with everything she says, and I have been begging her every Friday night for months and months to please go with me over to the rest house after the saloon closes, so she can enslave and debase me, but she won't hear of it."

Lewis and Boone tipped their Stars and had another gander at Helen.

"After Helen," Lewis continued, "Frank lost all sense of judgment. First he went bush with a vengeance, then he made the mistake of falling for a village girl and married her in a tribal ceremony. Then he tried to take her home to America. This girl had never even been to Freetown before, for the love of Christ, and this fool wanted to take her to see his parents in Manhattan . . . that's New York, not Kansas. After that, he figured they would go settle down in Iowa or Missouri or Kansas, I guess, someplace quiet and not too fast for her. He really thought he could do this. As I said, his brain had been damaged by prolonged exposure to certain frequencies.

"The noise and disorder of Freetown nearly killed his new bride. Just getting her out to Lungi airport was like dragging a damned soul by its hair through the gates of hell. She thought the buildings were on fire because the sun was glaring in the plate-glass windows. She thought the people swarming in the streets were at war with each other and would soon turn on her. At the airport, Frank fed her tranquilizers for the plane flight, so she slept through most of that. But then she woke up at La Guardia and went into shock.

"Forty-eight hours later, Frank and his African bride were back in her village," said Lewis. "Now old Frank's got the look of somebody who bites himself and likes a good head banging now and then in the privacy of his own mud hut. He's living out in some half acre of hell, with four dozen African relatives feasting off him like leeches, while he slowly goes insane. Wait until you hear about his 'research,' " Lewis said, making quote marks with his fingers, his tone a mix of scorn and pity. "Poor bastard's gone off his feed. He don't even drink beer anymore. You'd think he'd at least go back to the States and get his head shrunk."

"Maybe he likes it here," said Boone, watching Frank stare glumly into a plate of rice chop.

"Right," said Lewis, "that's why he has that incandescent smile."

A scuffle occurred at the entrance to the saloon as clutches of vendors vied for admission. The proprietor allowed in two groundnut girls, a woman with a platter of cakes, and a crippled beggar who got about on a square of three-quarter-inch plywood fitted out with casters.

"OK," continued Lewis. "At the other table, the tall skinny guy with the red beard is Bill Sutter from Phoenix. He's an anthropologist studying famine. A real disaster groupie. He goes to places where there are droughts and famines, and records data on the physiological processes that accompany starvation. All the villagers know him; he's always bending over people collecting blood samples and vital signs before they die. He also collects blood samples from dying tribes so that their genetic codes can be preserved and studied by future genealogists. He reminds me of those missionaries who used to baptize people who were dying of thirst. He's well funded too, but he spends all the money on instruments to assist him in the collection and analysis of data on the patterns and processes of starvation.

"Sitting with him is Otto," said Lewis, indicating a stout, blowsy man in khakis surrounded by an arc of empty Stars. "He's with the German development company. He's going back down to the Sewa River to see about rebuilding a bridge that's been torn down twice already. About three years ago, he found the villagers using a rope-way ferry to pull themselves and their produce back and forth across the river and decided a bridge would make their lives a lot easier. Of course, he didn't speak any Mende and barely any Krio at all, but from what little he could make out, the inhabitants seemed to agree that, indeed, a bridge would make their lives a lot easier. So Otto put in for the money to build the bridge, and his request was approved because, coincidentally, the bridge would also make it easier for the rutile, bauxite, diamond, and timber companies to get equipment to the work sites.

"What the villagers didn't tell him was that, although a bridge would make their lives a lot easier and they were quite capable of building one themselves, they did not do so because a bridge would also make it a lot easier for a particularly notorious bush devil to cross the river at night and terrorize the villages on the east bank of the Sewa. As it was, the ferry did not run after dusk, and the bush devil had no way of crossing the river after dark . . . until Otto built his bridge.

"The villagers were much too polite and deferential to the wisdom of *poo-muis* to disagree with him or stand in the way of his project. They simply let him finish his important work, then tore it down the day after he left. A year later he went back, this time to *educate* the people first, then build the bridge. And after weeks of head bobbing as an interpreter described the social and economic advantages of a bridge over the Sewa, and more head bobbing as the interpreter explained how bush devils were make-believe creatures who could not be allowed to obstruct progress and prosperity, everyone agreed that a bridge made all the sense in the world.

"Three months later Otto had another bridge up. Two days after he left, the villagers had it down again. When pressed, the villagers confessed that they agreed with everything the *poo-mui* had said. Furthermore, he seemed so sincere and devoted that they had let him build his bridge, because they could see how much the project meant to him and could not find it in their hearts to keep him from his dream. What harm could there be in letting him build the bridge? Chances were, he'd go back to the land of *Poo* and would never know if the bridge had been torn down. Hadn't they done the same for the *poo-mui* who so desperately wanted to dig a well in the middle of an unmarked graveyard? Wasn't it easier just to let him dig the well and then not use it?"

More Volunteers streamed into the Thirsty Soul and more beggars adorned the mesh. The conversation at the tables was buoyed up by the steady flow of Star beer, allowing all the Volunteers to float their concerns about "the Killigan thing." The favored method for dealing with the anxiety it created was to suggest that this kind of thing had never happened before, and that the best explanation was that he had crossed into the realm of politics, which, together with drugs, was absolutely forbidden by the Peace Corps. Drug abuse is a bit easier to define than political activity, and though several Volunteers got tossed out each year for buying or selling Nigerian marijuana, nobody in recent memory had ever been expelled for political activity, and the Volunteers were unsure about the elements of the crime. Political activity was one of those things the Peace Corps Director of Sierra Leone would instantly recognize without having to define it, the way certain Supreme Court Justices were unwilling or unable to define pornography, preferring instead to remark, "I know it when I see it."

There was speculation about raids by Liberian rebels. Fifty years after the British first repatriated freed slaves by sending them to Sierra Leone, freed American slaves tried the same idea to the south and founded Liberia in 1822. The capital, Monrovia, was named after James Monroe, and America managed to keep its hand in things, until Liberia became an American outpost, communications station, and Voice of America broadcasting center for all of Africa. Even the currency—U.S. dollars—was American, and the country was dominated by large U.S. rubber, timber, and mining companies, with Firestone the largest employer and landowner. Most recently, the Reagan administration bribed Liberia's former President, Samuel K. Doe, a member of the Krahn tribe, with the usual foreign aid, but Doe loved blood and tribal warfare more than money. Heavily into witchcraft and bad medicine, Doe once gave the CIA Director, William Webster, a pouch of magic dust. (There was no word about what Webster had done with the stuff, but some said he intended to use it in a run for the presidency in 1996.)

When an army commander from the Gio tribe tried to overthrow him, Doe had the rebel publicly disemboweled. Then he dispatched his Krahn soldiers to Gio villages, where they randomly machine-gunned and bayoneted civilians in retribution. The massacre ignited the tribal war still raging all over Liberia. It also allowed the infamous Charles Taylor to start his own country in the middle of Liberia, with his own army of teenagers toting automatic weapons, his own currency, and the power to sell protection and access to the mines to U.S. and European corporations.

Harry from Minnesota had recently crossed over from Liberia and had seen the rebels at their checkpoints, fifteen-year-old bobos with automatic weapons. Body parts were strewn in ditches at the side of the road. Krahn civilians were being interrogated, then executed, in huts on either side of the checkpoints.

Killigan's village was farther north than the rebels had ever ventured, but they were becoming more aggressive by the week. Killigan had administered at least one program that had distributed aid to Krahn refugees. So the fear was that a raid to capture Krahn refugees may have also netted one of their benefactors.

The thought of his buddy being interrogated by teenage rebels gave Boone a case of nausea and anxiety, which he promptly treated with more Star beer. He was on the verge of concluding that he had blundered into the upper circles of hell, and there was nothing for it but to drink from the river Lethe and turn himself into a barnacle on the Stygian wharves of West Africa.

Some Volunteers felt the Liberian scenario was entirely too far-fetched and instead suspected that any intrigue had originated in-country, and that Killigan must have blundered into one of many exploits and disputes that erupted all over the countryside during elections. There was speculation that he had somehow interfered with diamond smuggling, the most lucrative trade in the country, run by networks of criminals and corrupt politicians—Ministers of the Interior who extended an open palm and looked the other way when they received enough foreign currency. If the diamonds mined in the deep mines of the Kono District were exported through official channels, the country would be one of the wealthiest in Africa. Instead, the diamonds were smuggled across porous borders, leaving bribes in the pockets of a handful of venal government officials and nothing in the national treasury.

Lewis, whom Boone had learned to respect as having an almost infallible eye for the despicable motive in any confrontation, subscribed to the latter theory, but he left to water the ground out back before he finished his exposition.

Frank Nation drifted over to keep Boone company and (Boone later concluded) to glom on to an unwitting victim. The haggard, stoop-shouldered youth took a seat across from Boone and stared into his cola.

"Sam says you're living in a village up north," said Boone, deciding conversation was probably the best policy.

Frank slowly lifted a pair of eyes that seemed to be set in the sockets of a flesh-toned skull.

"I used to be in the Peace Corps, but then I sort of had to stay in-country," he said. "So I found work with some graduate students in international development who wanted me to do fieldwork and research for them."

"What kind of research?" asked Boone, doing all he could to keep Frank from returning like a genie to his cola bottle.

"The causes and origins of poverty in the Third World."

"Interesting," Boone said, again losing Frank's gaze to the fizz of warm soda. "Was this for a thesis or a dissertation of some kind?"

"A thesis on what?" Frank said, looking up suddenly, as if Boone had just asked him the most ridiculous question in the history of Western civilization.

"I don't know," Boone said. "I just . . . thought . . ."

"What's there to write about?" he asked Boone, demanding an answer. "What's there to say? I can summarize all of my research and conclusions in one sentence."

Boone looked away in search of something to notice in the crowd of *poo-mui* revelers, because the tone of Frank's voice and the deranged look in his eyes convinced him that the less he knew about Frank's research, the better.

"The people in the First World are eating the children of the Third World every night for dinner," he said, staring at Boone, as if he expected this statement to elicit a critique from his listener.

"That's . . . unusual," said Boone. "But I don't know what it means."

"Cannibalism," said Frank. "You are what you eat; but they aren't, because we eat it all; therefore we are eating them."

"But . . ." Boone began.

"Ever hear of the pineal body?"

"The what?" Boone asked, staring hard at two eyes lit up with conviction.

"The pineal body," Frank repeated. "It's a small conical body arising from the third ventricle in the human brain. In the Middle Ages, scientists said it was the seat of the soul. A little later, they said it was a vestigial third eye. Then they said it was an endocrine gland. Before long, they'll conclude that it's really all three."

A certain giddiness came over Boone, as if Frank's dementia was catching, or the Star beer was doing its work. He looked for Lewis and wondered how much more unhinged discourse old Frank had in him.

"Seeing used to be an active sense," Frank explained. "The pineal body used to emit its own internal ray, which together with the sun's light made all of creation shimmer like a tapestry illuminated by light from the seat of the soul. Then they invented television, and the preponderance of artificial light caused the pineal body to atrophy, and we lost our ability to see nature by the light of our own internal ray. That's why only so-called primitive people can see the spirit world, because they still have active pineal bodies."

"I see," said Boone.

"Ever been out in the bush at night?" asked Frank, as if this was a prerequisite to understanding his theories.

"I have," Frank said, without waiting for an answer. "But it's nothing you can tell anybody about. You wouldn't believe me anyway."

"Try me," said Boone.

"Go out to the bush late at night. If you don't have a soul, you won't be able to see. The moon won't help you. You can only see by the light of your own internal ray. It's one way to find out if your pineal body still works."

"What's your medication . . . I mean, what's your motivation for continuing this research?"

Boone saw Lewis at the bar gathering a bouquet of Star bottlenecks with his knuckles and coming to the rescue.

"Boys," he said, "you're probably trying to solve the problems of the First, Second, Third, and Fourth Worlds. And I have a Star beer for each one of them. Be careful, though," he said to Boone. "You shouldn't overindulge in this part of the world. Back home, if you have a few too many, you can step into a nice, clean, air-conditioned bathroom and talk to Ralph on the big white telephone. Over here, you have to get down on your knees and hang your head over a hole in the ground and hope you don't lose your balance."

Lewis distributed Stars and tipped one toward the ceiling. Frank crept off in search of other prey. Boone watched the beggars crawling the steel mesh.

"What did Sisay say you should do?" Lewis said as soon as he had Boone alone at the table.

"I'm to consult with a looking-around man when I return. Some witch doctor from Kenema who is going to help me find Michael Killigan."

"A fortune teller," Lewis said, taking a deliberative swig on his Star. "These diviners and looking-around men are small-time astrologists compared to the medicine old Sisay uses when he's in trouble. What's he doing? Starting you out slow? Ask him about thunder medicine. If you had one of those thunder boys show up in Killigan's village and announce that thunder medicine was going to be turned loose on whoever knows anything about Killigan but ain't saying, my guess is they'd come out of the bush on their hands and knees. I can't believe he's pissing around with a diviner. Ask him about real medicine. The bad stuff. For starters, ask him what's in that bag around his neck. Ask him why he lives in the bush instead of going back to America."

"As near as I can tell," Boone said, "he likes living in the village. He's happy."

"You bet he's happy. He's pinching himself every morning he's so happy," Lewis said, wrinkling his lips in disgust.

"What's wrong with him being happy in the bush?" asked Boone.

"Let me help you out," Lewis said. "You said he's happy, right? You and I are citizens of the world? We understand each other, don't we? I don't care how long he's lived here, he's still basically an American male, right? If he's an American male and he's happy, what does that tell you? He ain't watching the Super Bowl or the NBA playoffs, is he? OK. That means he's either getting laid or making money, right?"

Boone shrugged his shoulders and said, "Not necessarily."

"Whaddaya mean, not necessarily?" said Lewis. "He ain't into drugs, is he?"

"Not that I know of," Boone confessed. "I think he's just very happy here."

"If he's *very* happy, he's got to be getting laid *and* making money, which might explain why he would want to live in a snake-infested hothouse of a country full of parasites and terrible food. OK, he's *very* happy. Why does he like it? Power, that's why. He's running half the country. He's into that Poro shit up to his eyebrows. Did you see his markings? Did you see that pouch around his neck? Probably full of snake heads and body parts. He's a killer shark in a little pond. I'll tell you why he likes it. He's got three wives and a lot of land. He's got armies of people working for him on his farms. All he has to do is go for a walk every once in a while and wave to all the pickaninnies out slaving in his fields. He puts on a big front, like he's sworn off American greed and embraced the life of a simple bush farmer. Botobata. The guy is a power broker. Talk about big men. He's up there. He's connected.

"Put yourself in his position. Let's say you decided to go bush and settle down here. Let's do a little simple math. You probably got at least a couple grand in traveler's checks. OK, you can rent a four-room house and compound for about a hundred twenty dollars a year. You can't buy land. Nobody can, because the dead ancestors own it all, but you can rent all the land you can farm for five bucks an acre. OK, you can get a wife for thirty-three dollars. You can get a *good* wife for about fifty bucks. And you can get the cream of the crop—big teats, no diseases, a young tight one with good training —for under a hundred. And good training over here means she does what she's told, you understand? OK, you pay her family a hundred bucks, and that means she has to serve you for the rest of your life. She can't divorce you unless you beat her too much in public. You can beat her senseless in the privacy of your own home, but not in front of her own family. It's some kind of honor thing I don't remember.

"OK, that's only the beginning! Because, guess what? You can buy as many as you want! Let's say you got four wives: Fatmata, Adima, Sallay, and Fatu. OK, let's say you want Fatmata to salute the flag on Friday nights, and on Saturdays you want Adima to get down on her hands and knees and bark like a dog. You got it! Sunday, Sallay plays the flute while humming 'The Star-Spangled Banner,' and Monday Fatu takes it from behind with a smile on her face. You got it! Next week, if you're in the mood, you can dip them all in palm oil and pretend like you're an axle with eight nippled ball bearings. Am I making sense?"

"You are disgusting," said Boone, unable to suppress a grimace of revulsion.

"I know," said Lewis. "And you selflessly spend time with me because you want to show me how to be a better person. OK, while you're in the compound purging fluids from your tubes, you got droves of big Africans out working your farms for you and sifting mud in the swamps looking for diamonds. Why? You're white and you got money! Are you getting the picture yet? This ain't suburban Indiana, pal. Women are chattel, got it? Livestock. Beasts of the field. These people are starving, illiterate stiffs who would praise God for the chance to earn five cents washing your feet. You na mastah, OK? Understand? You're a master and there's nothing you can do about it. And if you try and pretend like you're not a master, these beggars are not flattered or impressed, or enlightened. No, they are shocked and annoyed at your bizarre behavior, not to mention pissed off because you won't give them any of your money."

"You're worse than disgusting," said Boone.

"I know," he said again. "And the thought that I might be leading a virtuous person like you astray causes me almost unbearable personal anguish."

"So if we all acted like you, nothing would ever change here. These people would remain in bondage."

"Who's holding them in bondage? Go home if their way of life offends your Western notions of human dignity. I guess in America they'd all be free, right? Free to squat in some East St. Louis tenement watching Oprah on a rent-to-own TV, only thirty-nine dollars and ninety-nine cents for sixty months.

"You're operating under the assumption that, one, you could change things, and, two, that what you have to offer is better. Sure, it's better for you, it's what you grew up on. It's like asking a fish if he'd like to grow legs and walk on land. You can't teach these people anything about your way of life. You can't set up an American outpost over here and expect them to start building shopping malls, delivering pizzas, and suing each other just because you think it works for you and yours. Look at the bright side. Once you get outside of Freetown, there's no television over here. None. Talk about progress! These people have never wasted so much as a single hour staring at dots of light on a square screen. No books either. Let the rest of the world sit around staring at black marks on paper. There's work to be done here. People are too busy farming and getting laid for that."

"I think you're both nuts," Boone said. "He tells me about bush devils and witches. You tell me about thunder and bags of medicine. As usual, nobody can tell me what all of these superstitions have to do with Killigan's disappearance."

"I can help you there," Lewis said. "But you ain't gonna like it."

He hollered at the proprietor for two more Stars. Boone had the sickening feeling that Lewis was prepping him with a tranquilizer before administering the bad news.

"Moiwo," said Lewis. "I did a little asking around."

"The name keeps coming up," Boone said, remembering the girl who brought him his coffee, and the note.

"Monkey works, baboon eats, didn't I tell you? Now, it's election time, he's getting into body parts, if you know what I mean. Ritual cannibalism. And the leftovers are used to make the most powerful medicines in the country. Some say he's been to see the Baboon Men."

"Oh, great," said Boone, "more creatures. What's a Baboon Man?"

"I call 'em monkey men," said Lewis. "They come out right before election time, looking for victims to feed to their medicines. African gangsters wearing chimpanzee heads and skins."

"I thought you said they were baboons?"

"They are. In Krio, baboon means chimpanzee."

"Oh," said Boone, frowning into his beer. "Well, then, what do they call baboons?"

"Gorillas," said Lewis, firing off a bottle cap and drilling the kerosene can he had missed twice before. "Gorilla is Krio for baboon."

"Well, then . . ." Boone began.

"They don't have any," said Lewis. "There are no gorillas in West Africa. As for big apes, there's just you and me."

"You know, if we rounded up all these devils and witches and Baboon People in a zoo, we could charge admission and make a killing."

"Your friend had run-ins with Moiwo," said Lewis. "That's known. Not that Moiwo would ever do anything to a white man. Not directly anyway. Not even he would be that greedy. But the scary part would be if your buddy crossed Moiwo, and Moiwo decided to use some witch medicine or Baboon medicine on him. That would be . . ." Lewis stopped for a breath and a serious look into Boone's eyes. "Bad. Real bad. Worse than thunder medicine. Maybe even worse than witchcraft and *ndilei*."

"I've read about that," said Boone, "in a book about the Mende I found in Paris. What is it?"

"*Ndilei* is a bundle of rags or animal skins with a piece of red mineral substance called *tingoi* stuck into it. It's buried or planted in a person's house, and then later it turns into a bat or a boa constrictor . . . It's *bad* medicine. Ask old Sisay about *ndilei* medicine for Christ sake, or how about . . ." Lewis leaned over and whispered, "*Bofima.*" His lips opened in a wicked slit. "Yeah, lay that one on him. See what he has to say about *bofima.*"

Someone started a boom box going with *poo-mui* music at the next table, and the Thirsty Soul rang with the sounds of Talking Heads, *Once in a Lifetime.*

The ruckus caused Lewis to whirl and fire a bottle cap at the offender.

"I'm having a conversation here," he hollered over the lyrics.

A diamond miner stooped over the table and motioned at Lewis. "There are some girls waiting for us," he said, motioning toward the entrance, where a cluster of smiling young women in lappas hissed and waved at the white men. "How many do you want?"

"Whaddaya mean, how many do I want?" Lewis roared, Star foam flecking his lips. "As many as hell will hold and the devil will ask in for a drink! Round 'em up! We'll pay the freight! When inflation gets to where I have to think about how many women we're getting for the night, it's time to leave this country!"

Someone sneaked the volume back up on Talking Heads.

A piercing shriek rent the air and silenced the clamor of bottles, the buzz of conversation, and the boom box.

"WHY DON'T YOU DISGUSTING ANIMALS LEAVE THOSE POOR WOMEN ALONE!!" The voice sounded like one of the Erinyes fresh from the long ride out of hell.

It was Helen, on her feet and ready to draw male blood.

Lewis staggered off of his bench and gestured expansively at Helen, as if he were about to ask her for a dance.

"Helen, my dear," he slurred, "honey, darling, sweetie. You misunderstand me. I am a feminist. I'm defending these women's rights! I'm talking about *choice*, Helen! I don't have to tell you how important that is! As I understand our previous conversations," he said, with a drunken flourish of a Star, "these women have the right to control their own bodies. They have the right to choose when and whether to bear children, without any interference from me . . . or you, correct?"

Lewis staggered over to the entrance and led one of the African prostitutes into the Thirsty Soul. The woman smiled, then looked back at her companions and laughed.

Lewis stood her at the head of Helen's table and said, "Evening-O, missy. Whay your wife man?"

"Ah no get wife mahn," the woman said.

"You no get wife man?" said Lewis. "I no get wife. Whatin you come find na hya?"

The woman smiled and again looked back at her companions. "Ah come na hya foh make you me friend."

"Ahh!" Lewis said, winking at her. "You go want make me your friend?"

"Yes," she said. "Ah go want make you me friend too much. Let we go now," she added, holding out her hand.

"Wait, small-small, missy, do ya," he said. "Whatin go happen if you make me your friend, and one small peekin come out?"

The woman raised her hand and smiled behind it. "Ah want one small peekin too much," she said with a giggle.

"Thank you, missy!" howled Lewis. "That will be all! I'll be along shortly!"

He showed the woman back to the door and then waltzed by Helen.

"It's different, you pig," she said, "and you know it."

"You're right, Helen, it is different. In your case, we're talking about your right to control your own body, and in her case, we're talking about her right to control her own body. That is different."

Helen threw money on the table and headed for the door.

"Fortunately, my fellow Americans," said Lewis, raising his voice so Helen could hear him on the way to her dirt bike, "we are staying in a country that does not put any laws on this woman's body. So if anybody has a video camera, you might want to bring it along, and I'll see if she chooses to control her own body and use it to make some first-class porno movies."

More Star beer arrived. Lewis took his seat and banged the table with a new Star.

"How'd I do?" he said, drooling out of one corner of his mouth.

A crowd of Africans ran up Tikongo Road, laughing and clapping their hands, leading a jeep filled with uniformed Africans.

"Well, look at that," said Lewis. "The villagers always warned me that if you tell a story about a snake and use its name, it will answer the call and eventually appear."

"Who's that?" asked Boone.

"Section Chief Moiwo," Lewis said, "and his entourage. Don't worry, you won't have any trouble picking him out. Just look for the guy who gets the most food out the deal."

Boone rose to peer over the tops of the beggars, who began hissing and gesticulating, trying to pull his gaze down a notch.

Moiwo stood on the haunches of a well-fed pachyderm that rolled under his khaki shorts. As he waved and smiled, his belly strained at the seams and buttons of his safari suit. A policeman's cap heavily gallooned with gold braids rode low over a pair of black lenses and rims that hid his eyes from the sun and the world. He had an oversized head that seemed to be unevenly swollen, as if his skin had been upholstered to his skull and the fat had swollen into his face, featuring it with curious lobes and pouches. When he smiled, he showed a row of perfect white teeth. He gestured expansively with his arms, while shouting into a megaphone. Gold pinky rings set with stones flashed in the sunlight.

"Electioneering," said Lewis.

Other uniformed men stood on the running boards of the jeep and appeared to be scanning the crowd, like nervous Secret Service men. Finally one of them raised his arm, then several others followed, talking excitedly and pointing into the gathering crowd.

A commotion arose beyond the steel mesh, in the direction the men were pointing. A table of wares clattered to the ground, the woman with cakes and the groundnut girls scooped their products into basins or aprons and protected them against the developing fray. Citizens of all ages converged on the intersection where a knot of people were engaged in a heated argument.

"Tiefmahn!" someone hollered from the shops opposite the saloon, off in the direction where Moiwo's men were pointing. "Tiefmahn!"

A young man leapt from the tailgate of Moiwo's jeep and raced by one of the saloon's archways, pausing just long enough to shout "Tiefmahn!" to the patrons within. Another young man in rags stepped off the tailgate with a covered birdcage and joined the press of vendors at the entrance to the saloon.

The cry went up from the perimeters of a gathering throng of people who had restrained one young man and were beating and kicking him.

"Hmm," said Lewis, turning his sweating Star in his fingers. "Looks like one of Moiwo's boys spotted a tiefmahn. You're in for a show now."

"Tiefmahn!"

An old ma in a headwrap, whom Boone took to be the aggrieved party and victim of a petty theft, was administering blows about the thief's head with a porcelain basin. When the thief raised his arms to block her blows, men on either side of him pinned them to his sides. Several other adults pushed the thief and his captors back and forth, giving him a box to the ears or a poke in the eye when he was passed over to their side of the gauntlet.

"Tiefmahn!" shouted the little children who ducked under the legs of the adults and kicked the thief's shins or poked his legs with sticks.

The white Volunteers in the saloon rose and idled at the vacated archways of the saloon, taking in the spectacle with the halfhearted interest of football fans watching a preseason baseball game.

Lewis did not move from his seat at the table.

Boone half stood in a crouch, long enough to see the thief fall from view.

"Will they kill him?" Boone said, trying to be nonchalant like everyone else.

"Sometimes," Lewis said with a yawn, "but not usually. It depends what he tried to steal and if he's ever been caught before. If he's a repeat offender, they'll probably beat him up so bad he'll look dead, but he'll still be breathing. Sometimes they play possum on you too, because they know there's no fun in beating a dead thief. Then the police will come and take him to jail. If somebody in his family has money, they'll send along a bribe, and in two or three days' time, the thief will mysteriously escape. If no one in his family has money, the police will beat him to death out of sheer boredom and irritation."

Boone wondered for a moment what impact he might have if he left the saloon and tried to stop the beating. The crowd was now well into feeding on its frenzy and so large that he would succeed in getting nowhere near the action, nor would he even be heard above the furor.

As he watched, the crowd hoisted the thief back onto his feet and held his arms and legs, which emboldened the more timid members of the crowd to surge forward and deliver the blows they had been saving in their fear of getting too close. Soon, a ring of people formed, looking almost like dancers at a hoedown, except for the violence breaking out in their faces, balancing themselves with interlocked arms, freeing their legs and feet for kicking.

"It's a great country," Lewis said. "Instant justice. No lawyers, no judges, no wasted tax money."

"Instant brutality," said Boone.

A flatbed truck fenced with slats of wood and barbed wire made its way through the crowd, beeping its horn and gently nudging bodies aside with its bumper, until it ground to a halt in front of the saloon. Two uniformed Africans dismounted from the truck bed, rolled the limp thief onto his belly, bound his arms and legs behind him, and hoisted him up to two other uniforms reaching over the slats of the truck bed. As soon as the body cleared the barbed wire, it was dropped like a sandbag onto the truck bed, and the truck commenced beeping its horn and crawling through the dispersing crowd.

The proprietor showed the two groundnut girls and the woman with cakes out, and admitted a woman selling paste jewelry and the boy with the covered birdcage.

"About these medicines," Boone said, still sickened by the sight of the beating. "Is there any way to make sense of them?"

Lewis blurred in Boone's vision and slurred his speech. "There are two kinds of medicine. Legal and illegal. The most powerful legal medicine is thunder medicine. You can have a medicine man put thunder medicine on your house to protect it from thieves and to let everyone know that they'll be struck dead if they harm your property. That's legal, but it's expensive, and it requires the attendance of the Paramount Chief to make certain that it's properly controlled and not misdirected against innocent people. But if you're up against illegal medicine, the really bad stuff, you won't get anywhere, unless you get some of your own that's badder than the stuff they have. The most powerful illegal medicine is *bofima*. But it's a dangerous business, because you can't use the *bofima* unless you *own* it, and once owned, it enters into a kind of relationship with its owner. The owner has to 'feed' the medicine every so often to 'recharge' its powers. But it can get out of hand."

"What does the medicine eat?" asked Boone.

"Human fat," said Lewis. "*Bofima* is a pouch containing skin from the palms of the hands, the soles of the feet, and the forehead, best obtained while the victim is still alive. Then you add a cloth from a menstruating woman, some dust from the ground where a large number of people are accustomed to meet, a needle, a piece of fowl coop wire, a piece of rope used in a trap from which an animal has escaped, and whatever else is in the Baboon cookbook that year, and you have *bofima*. But, as I said, it only lasts so long before it needs to be fed again."

"What do they do with the *bofima*?"

"Anything they want," said Lewis, "because as soon as people hear about it they are thoroughly terrorized and will pay any amount of money or offer any privilege to escape the medicine's power. But aside from using it to put curses and swears on your enemies, it's used to guide men through difficult or dangerous endeavors, like getting elected to high office. The pouch has seven strings on it with a hook attached to each string. It's cast into the bush on a moonless night and pulled slowly back out. The head Baboon Man then interprets the tug of the thing and studies whatever snagged in the hooks, and the group conducts itself according to the omens. Every time a new member joins, he must provide the next victim to feed the *bofima*."

"Did Killigan tell you about *bofima*, the way he told you about Poro?"

"Actually, no," Lewis said, looking down the neck of his Star. "I had a spot of trouble last year up around Makeni. Some pretty bad trouble and . . ."

"You used *bofima*?"

"Only once," he said, "I got it from somebody else, and I unloaded it, without any ill effects, before it was feeding time."

"You consulted it by casting it in the bush?"

"Not really," said Lewis. "A guy working on one of my farm projects tried to poison me. Twice. Some unreimbursed woman damage he claimed I'd done on him. The second time he poisoned me, I was medevacked back to the States for three weeks. He was having one of the women in my cook's *mawe* put insecticide in the sauce for my rice chop. As you know, the stuff is so hot you'd never know if it was laced with cyanide. I was as sick as a dead dog for weeks."

"So you used the *bofima* to . . . get revenge?" Boone asked.

"What would you do? I killed the son of a bitch. Internal hemorrhage. Just what the doctor ordered. They brought him to me on a pallet. He had blood coming out of him every which way. It was leaking out around his eyeballs, for Christ's sake. He lived just long enough to tell everybody that I had killed him with bad medicine, which was just fine, because nobody else has tried to poison me since."

The beggars returned to the archways, fresh from the momentary diversion of the thief's beating, pleading for money and attention from the white people. The bobo with the covered birdcage negotiated in thick Krio with Volunteers at the next table. Lewis was getting so deep into Star he would soon need diving equipment. He glowered, then waved off the beggars.

The bobo stood between Boone and Lewis at the head of their table and set the covered birdcage between them.

"We don't want no tropical birds," said Lewis.

The boy wore a Muslim skullcap and rags. His teeth were stained orange by kola-nut paste, and one eye stared blank white, unsighted by river blindness.

The boy bartered with Lewis.

"Hah!" shouted Lewis. "That's one I haven't heard before. He says that in this cage he has a captured human soul, which he will allow us to see for the modest price of five hundred leones."

Boone felt something stir under the cover. The boy showed orange teeth in a smile, and cajoled Lewis.

"He says that inside this cage is the soul of a twin who did not properly bury his father or honor his father's memory. When the twin died, his soul flew through the bush in search of his father's grave, which of course he could not find because he had not properly buried his father and had not visited the grave or left food or libations there for his ancestor."

The boy smiled again and the white eye seemed to roll in its socket and develop a bluish cast.

"I'll pay half, if you pay the other half," said Lewis to Boone. "It's about five bucks American."

"OK," said Boone, watching the cage shudder with the movement of whatever was inside.

The boy removed the cover of the cage with the flourish of a magician. Inside, Boone saw what looked like a small human skeleton wrapped in white fur, with waxy, fingered wings spread-eagled and the pinions clipped to the bars of the cage. The white wings met at a torso that was pale and almost translucent, marbled with blue veins. The head, too, was pure white, with large oval ears ribbed in pearl gray. The snout was a wrinkled bivalve of bone-white cartilage, the mouth pink with small, sharp teeth open in a violent, silent shriek.

"That's no fucking soul," scowled Lewis. "It's an albino bat. I've seen that before. Soul of a twin. My ass! Deal's off."

The boy protested loudly and held out his hand, demanding payment, first from Lewis, then from Boone.

"Don't pay him," shouted Lewis. "Listen, bobo, I ain't no exchange student out here for the weekend from Freetown. I've been here two fucking years too long to get clipped by some bobo with a bat in a birdcage. Out!"

The proprietor hurried over with his golf club and threatened the boy, who gathered up his cage and shouted at Lewis and Boone. The boy fixed his one good eye in a baleful stare, first on Lewis, then on Boone, spitting words at the white men with teeth and tongue.

"Oh, shit," Lewis howled facetiously. "We're in trouble now. He's cursing us. He's putting a West African swear on us. I'm terrified! Yeah, right, if we travel in the bush we will be lost forever, if we try to eat we will choke on our food, I've heard it all before. Here," he shouted. "Try this one! Fuck you! How's that for a curse? That's an American curse for you, you little shit!"

The proprietor drove the boy and his covered cage through the entrance and shook the golf club after him.

"I could swear that was one of Moiwo's bobos," said Lewis. "I'm sure of it. What's he doing conning white men?"

The caged walls of the Thirsty Soul rattled with renewed vigor. The beggars had watched a prize of five hundred leones almost get paid over for nothing more than a glimpse of a white bat; now, to their minds, the money was up for grabs as surplus cash burning holes in the pockets of reckless *poo-mui* speculators.

Lewis banged the table in a rage.

"Do you think I could have just five minutes of peace and quiet?" he yelled, shooting a bottle cap into the steel mesh. "Seven days a week I live out in a village hovel listening to the ageless whine of poverty, the despair, the stupidity, the fantastic superstitions, the squalor and the misery. Once, just once a week, I come to this modest establishment to spend a short while with my fellow Americans, tasting libations and sharing our common heritage."

The saloon crowd fell silent, with only scattered chuckles. The chorus from the beggars lulled to a murmur of do-ya's.

"You know, the Americans have a saying that describes this," shouted Lewis. "It's called invading my space. That's what you people are doing, that's right, an invasion of my space, this space you see here where I'm settled in on my duff trying to enjoy myself has been invaded. An invasion by you, the invaders, exhibiting invasive and invasionary behavior and brimming with invasiveness. The Lord said the poor have always been with us, but do they have to invade my space? Do they have to dun me night and day for money? And after I get home to America, I'll probably turn on the TV, and there you'll be! Starving all over my living room. And you know what I'm going to do? I'm going to change the channel, that's what. You know why? Because I don't like looking at you. Go starve somewhere else. I am not starving, and I don't want to sit around imagining what it would be like. So get lost!

"May I hollow out just one patch of land here? Just these hundred or so square feet? I'll call it Little America. Do you suppose I could come once a week to *Poo-mui* Night, in the Thirsty Soul Saloon, in this Little America I made, kick back, and relax for a few hours? Is that asking too much? I guess so! That's going overboard! I'm set upon by beggars! Go away! Sure, I've got money, and guess what? You can't have any of it!

"You know what you people need?" Lewis hollered. "Exercise and the right kind of breakfast. I'm not talking about living longer, that's pretty much out of the question anywhere on this blighted continent. I'm talking about *feeling* better. If you all jogged, ate more fruits and vegetables, and less fat, and got in touch with your inner child, you'd all *feel* a lot better about yourselves. I'm talking about self-esteem!"

"Mastah, I no sabby whatin this esteem you talk. Do ya, I beg, lemme have ten cent. Me wife get febah, de peekins get notting foh eat. To God I pray, mastah, help me small-small."

"You probably think you've got it rough, don't ya?" Lewis howled. "Sure, the wife's sick, the kids got nothing to eat. Tell me something new! How would you like to live in the poorer sections of some of our American cities? Some of those people have nothing but a black-and-white TV to watch. Everybody else has color TVs. What do you think of that?"

"Mastah, I no sabby whatin dese TV you talk. Do ya let we have ten cent."

"You no sabby is right," said Lewis. "You don't know how lucky you are!"

Boone's vision blurred again, and his stomach turned, either announcing another binge of dysentery or simply registering his opinion of Lewis's sense of humor. Just as he thought about heading back to the rest house for some sleep, the proprietor appeared at his elbow and pointed toward the entrance of the Thirsty Soul.

A groundnut girl in a headwrap held a folded piece of paper toward him. Boone walked over to the entrance and knelt down beside her.

"Moussa noto tiefmahn," she said, big tears forming in the corners of her eyes. "He say me give dese papers Mistah Gutawa Sisay."

"Who?" Boone said, gently touching her elbow.

"Moussa Kamara," she said. "Dey been beat ihn foh a tiefmahn. He noto tiefmahn. He been come nya hya foh give you dese paper. He no tief any person. Dat Baboon Man Moiwo lie and say Moussa a tiefmahn. Moussa noto tiefmahn."

"Lewis!" called Boone.

Lewis swaggered over, and the two of them took the groundnut girl outside, where it was quieter. Lewis and she spoke Krio at length. Finally, he took the paper from her and handed it to Boone.

"She claims that man was not a tiefman." Lewis scowled, almost falling over in his drunkenness. "She claims that was Moussa Kamara, Killigan's servant. He was coming to see you. She claims Moiwo's men fingered him for a tiefman, then stood around while the whole town beat him to death."

"Moussa Kamara is dead," said Boone.

"I know that," said Lewis. "I was sitting right next to you."

"No," Boone retorted. "That could not have been Moussa Kamara. He was killed several weeks ago. Sisay said they hung him from a tree outside Killigan's village and stuffed him with pepper. He had a live gecko sewn into his mouth."

Lewis stooped down for some more animated Krio with the groundnut girl.

"She says the man who was just beaten to death as a tiefman was Moussa Kamara, Michael Killigan's servant. And that he was coming to see you. As soon as he knew that Moiwo's boys had spotted him, he tried to get away, but they called him a tiefman and the crowd got him instead."

Lewis gave the girl money and asked her more questions.

Boone opened the paper and drew near the lights from the Thirsty Soul. In the handwriting he would recognize anywhere was a message that at once filled him with hope and crushed him with despair:

This bobo is my servant, Moussa Kamara. He will lead you to me. Do not cooperate with anyone else. Trust no one. Do not tell anyone about this message. Do not tell anyone where you are going. Make sure you are not followed.

M.K.

(12)

Randall arose before Dweeb's ally and went out to his front lawn for *The New York Times,* national edition. His head still throbbed with visions of the bloody bundle. What passed for sleep had been no more than a vacillation between waking and sleeping nightmares. He had unconsciously lived his whole life assuming there was an external world, an internal life of the mind, and between them, he guessed, were his eyes. Now the boundaries were dissolving. Either his imagination was gushing out of his eye sockets and filling the external world with phantoms, or freaks of nature were freely swooping in through the open windows of his soul and taking over.

On his way outside, he half expected to float like an astronaut or see all the clocks in the house melt. He spied the sky-blue sleeve of the *Times* nestled in its usual spot next to the silver maple. Maybe the headline would read: "Bloody Bundle Shocks, Confounds Prominent Midwestern Bankruptcy Lawyer."

He read the paper at the kitchen table and tried to remember the Our Father, but he kept getting the words mixed up with the Hail Mary. He skipped the business section, ignored a lingerie ad, and lingered instead on a story about ragpickers living on the streets of Calcutta. They made their living by scouring garbage dumps all day for bits of plastic and paper, which they collected in bundles and sold for pennies to middlemen. A woman wrapped in a sari squatted on a patch of concrete with her two children—they stared out of the news photo with weary, soulful eyes.

Randall felt a sudden kinship with them, now that he too had been touched by despair. He asked himself if he would be willing to live under such conditions in exchange for having his son returned to him safe and sound, in exchange for not having a brain tumor, in exchange for having the world returned to a stable, predictable place. He concluded that, even if he did find his son, it would only be a matter of time before Michael would get wind of the pavement people in Calcutta and would then run off to join them. He tried to imagine himself cleansed of tumors and sitting in front of his hovel in Calcutta.

Maybe saying prayers would help. Maybe he should cross his fingers, bless himself, throw salt over his shoulder, knock wood. Maybe he should get down and crawl on his hands and knees in case there was some supernatural being in charge of the universe who might notice Randall's abject humiliation and dispense a little pity his way.

A brain tumor would, in all likelihood, kill him in less than a year, to say nothing of ruining his chances for being elected Chairman of the American Institute of Bankruptcy Lawyers.

Maybe he should forget the formalities and just go to church. St. Dymphna's was less than three blocks from his front door. *Do they even have daily mass anymore? Does anyone go these days?* Even if they didn't have mass, he could throw himself on the flagstones of the unfamiliar temple, a revenant altar boy trying to relearn the syntax of prayer, clawing at the floor of his thoughts, pleading for the love of God for the strength to bear whatever was happening to him.

.

The main door to the cathedral was locked, so Randall drew the collar of his coat closer and walked the long journey around the nave, up and down wheelchair ramps to the side door and into the soaring interior of St. Dymphna's Cathedral. It was a Gothic replica, designed to tip the head of the visitor back and lift the eyes to heaven. Light and harmonic shadows filled the ribbed, groined ceiling vaults, creating patterns almost as beautiful as the internal cohesion of the Bankruptcy Code, or the symmetrical ribbing of a bat's wing.

Twenty-seven years ago, Father Macaunahay had presided over the sacrament of matrimony marrying Randall Steven Killigan to Marjorie Cecilia Newstead. During the ceremony, Randall had let his eyes drift up to fingered vaults tinted pink by the rose windows of the transept, and had recalled how nothing had changed since his First Communion, since his Confirmation, since his altar boy days, when he had served mass at least once a day, with funerals and weddings thrown in to boot. The building was exactly the same, relentlessly and eerily just as he had left it, redolent with beeswax and incense, odors still lingering after forty years.

Randall Killigan in church! Perhaps it is possible to be wide awake and dreaming at the same time. Maybe it wasn't real, maybe it was only a place in his mind, which would explain why it never changed. On a bet, he could probably go up the stairs behind the sacristy and find the cavernous, marmoreal lofts of rosewood closets, probably still strung with cassocks and surplices, and fitted out with kneelers, where he had bowed his head and practiced reciting his Latin responses: "*Confiteor Deo omnipotenti* . . ." The same ornate marble railing where he had knelt to receive his First Communion still spanned the front of the cathedral. The small brass gate through which he had walked up onto the altar for his Confirmation, the beginning of the natural progression from Soldier of Christ to bankruptcy lawyer.

Everything was almost exactly the same, and would be the same, even if he came back in his sixties looking to bury his mother, or a friend, or looking to have his marriage annulled. On Judgment Day, he would probably find the place pretty much as is. He would be summoned from the grave by a voice of thunder, called to the pulpit, and ordered to proclaim his offenses against humanity to a congregation of friends, family, lawyers, and judges. Maybe an archangel would stand at the pulpit and summon Randall Steven Killigan forward to read his bankruptcy briefs aloud to the congregation of souls.

"Could you tell us a little bit more about debtor-in-possession financing?" the angel would say. "We would love to hear all about it."

His next thought was: *Where is everybody?* The early-morning masses in his altar boy days drew a crowd of at least a hundred. Here, scattered far and wide in the vast echoing expanses of the nave, were maybe ten or twelve elderly citizens—the men with bald heads and canes, the women with curved spines and tinted hair. To the last man and woman, they looked as if they might not show next week.

Faces mottled with age spots and frail, gray heads fitted out with flesh-colored hearing aids briefly glanced up at his passing. In small smiles and polite glances they showed him they knew why he had come: He was nursing some private tragedy—could they see it in his face?—cancer, or the loss of a loved one. Otherwise, why would an outwardly healthy, middle-aged man in a tailored suit show up at six o'clock mass on a Tuesday? Then again, if the church was not real, then the beings standing around him were apparitions from his dreams, spectral incarnations of his impulses and fears: faceless authority figures, former lovers, friends he had betrayed under extenuating circumstances, his son, his wife . . . His grandparents. Teachers who had expected better things of him.

He sensed his presence being noted as someone no one recognized, and as the only member of the congregation under sixty-five and still able to safely operate a can opener. The priest was bound to notice him too, as someone who had never been there before. Maybe Randall could talk to the priest afterward. He was in fine shape: *wanting* to talk to a priest? What do these guys *make* a year? Poverty? Chastity? Obedience? A place to sleep and eat, free scotch, and the respect of the community, in exchange for preaching to the converted—stand up there saying things people already knew, but didn't quite want to believe. Their job was to talk to guys like Randall, who were falling apart.

He knelt, bowed his head, and tried to pray. Then he heard everyone stand and the priest—a man Randall had never seen before (he was half expecting Father Macaunahay)—began:

"In the name of the Father, and of the Son, and of the Holy Spirit."

Randall said "Amen" along with everyone else, and promptly felt like a fraud.

He imagined that the entire congregation had heard his Amen and knew by its wavering tone and its uncertain enunciation that it was the Amen of a man who last went to mass twenty-seven years ago, at his wedding.

The priest was overweight. For some reason, Randall wanted him to be discalced and wearing a coarse garment, gaunt and haunted, gentle, with big moist eyes, just this side of a hallucination, nourished only by locusts and honey. Randall saw a mystic, a gentle teacher, who would place a hand on Randall's head and cast out his raging anxiety, maybe send it into a herd of plaintiffs' lawyers, who could then charge down the hill and throw themselves into the river.

Instead, the priest was stout and portly, and spoke of God's love with the stolidity of an estate-planning lawyer.

The priest and the congregation then began to pray together:

"I confess to almighty God,
and to you my brothers and sisters,
that I have sinned through my own fault
in my thoughts and in my words,
in what I have done, and in what I have failed to do . . ."

Of course, he knew none of the words. And he could not find the prayer in the daily missalette, because they didn't call it the *Confiteor* anymore, so he mumbled along, slurring and humming the words in a rough approximation of what was being said. His eyes followed bundles of pilasters aloft to the soaring vaults again, until a yawn blurred his vision with tears of exhaustion.

The man standing several yards down in the same pew bore an uncanny resemblance to Randall's grandfather, may he rest in peace. Randall had a sudden premonition that he would come and help him find his place in the missalette. With a benevolent smile, the man would gently thumb through Randall's book, and stop at the appropriate page. There, in the ornamented initials of an illuminated manuscript, it would say: THIS IS NOT A DREAM.

"Glory to God in the highest,
and peace to his people on earth
Lord God, heavenly King,
almighty God and Father,
we worship you, we give you thanks,
we praise you for your glory."

Maybe figures in the congregation would begin turning in groups of two or three, studying the bankruptcy lawyer with looks of solemn disgust, abhorring him for the monsters he had raised in the privacy of his own soul, predatory creatures he had husbanded, then turned loose on the world. The people wanted to stay as far away as possible, but close enough to get a look at what sort of man could take such delight in the misfortunes of others . . .

The priest began the reading of the Gospel:

*"Just then the disciples came up to Jesus with the question: Who
is of greatest importance in the kingdom of God? He called a little
child over and stood him in their midst and said: I assure you,
unless you change and become like little children, you will not enter
the kingdom of God. Whoever makes himself lowly, becoming like
this child, is of greatest importance in that heavenly reign.*

*"See that you never despise one of these little ones. I assure you,
their angels in heaven constantly behold my heavenly Father's face."*

Change and become like little children, he thought. That's rich.
He had a pretty good idea what would happen to child Randall if
he was representing the bank in a nasty single-asset case, where
the loans were guaranteed personally by the husband and wife, and
the bank was after the house, the car, bank accounts, stock, the
playground equipment in the backyard . . . and child Randall would
come in advising everyone that they must all become like little
children.

"We must love and trust each other," he might advise. "Aren't
we all brothers and sisters?"

"You hold him down," one of the other lawyers would say, "I'll
cut the meat off of him."

His remains would be bezoars in the intestines of his predatory
opponents. Ritual cannibalism. The Rite of Spring Lawyering. He'd
be tied down on an altar somewhere, listening to them discuss
methods: "Do you think we can get his heart out fast enough, so
we can see it beat a couple of times before it stops?"

Making himself lowly and loving his neighbor were out of the
question. Randall could no more go around loving his neighbor in
bankruptcy court than Hector could have kissed Achilles on the
cheek at the gates of Troy and invited him to go skinny-dipping in
the wine-dark sea, while rosy-fingered dawn broke in the east . . .
Let compassion pop into his head just once, for even an instant,
and his head would be off and rolling around the courtroom, and
some other warrior of the Code would be astride his vanquished
Christian remains, washing his hands in Randall's blood, and filling
his lungs with a cry of victory.

The priest interrupted Randall's thoughts with a sermon. Smiling
down from the pulpit, with his thumbs tucked into his cinctured
alb, the priest looked out over the congregation and rested his eyes
on Randall Steven Killigan.

He knows, thought Randall.

"You must *change*," the priest said, taking in the believers with his arms, "and become like little children. Make yourselves *lowly!* Most of us look to the scriptures for comfort and understanding. We would rather understand our lives than change them. Changing them takes work. We would rather mull over scriptural platitudes, things we can nod along with and go home saying, 'It's just as I thought. I was right all along.' But that's not the message here. The message is *change*. Lower ourselves. Become like little children, full of wonder and awe."

Change? For forty years he had been thinking through the wilderness of being. The paths and convergences that had brought him here were as various and complex as the nerves in his brain. At each juncture, he had made a selection, and each selection became a part of his being, as if living in the world a certain way could actually alter the synaptic structures of his brain; could maybe even rearrange or alter the constituent elements of the soul. So that in the afterlife the soul of a gambler would actually "look" different than the soul of Mother Teresa, and different than the soul of a bankruptcy lawyer.

Having selected the life of a bankruptcy warrior, he was now capable of certain thoughts, and not others. Quite without thinking, he had succeeded too well at self-discipline, producing an irreversible state of being. Happiness and peace of mind were no longer feasible, for instance, unless he was billing out at least 2,200 hours a year. If an angel of the Lord showed him the death of his son, the betrayal by his wife, eternal damnation self-selected by the warlord, showed him how each decision had led him willy-nilly down each juncture in the paths of being, he would still be helpless to change himself and go back.

He had no idea where these thoughts came from; he knew only that they were symptoms of weakness, of possible mental instability, of an organic disturbance, possibly a neoplasm, or some other bright object in his deep white matter. If he did not resolve this problem soon, he feared that the daily, obsessive anxiety would permanently alter his brain chemistry. Maybe he would wake up endowed with an ability to hear the high-frequency sonar screams of bats. Soon he would start to make crucial mistakes. He would mishandle one major bankruptcy, and that client would go away mad. A year later they would all be gone. "*He used to be the best goddamn bankruptcy lawyer in the Seventh Circuit,"* they would say. *"Then things took a bad turn. You were hearing about personal problems. It's always chicken and egg when drinking's involved, but I think he lost a son, his only son."*

He turned his attention back to the priest's sermon.

"Those here who are parents have a special knowledge of what it means to become like little children," said the priest. "We were children once. And now we are mothers and fathers, grandmothers and grandfathers. And how desperately we love our children. Not more than our spouses, but with an equally powerful love of a different kind. And when that love is returned, we are filled with joy, with the happiness known only to mothers and fathers.

"But when that love is not returned. When our son or daughter turns away from us in hatred or selfishness. How bitter our hearts! For then we become like the shepherd Jesus told us about who had ninety-nine sheep to watch over on the hillside and left them all to find and rescue the one helpless stray . . . Think of your pain if you were spurned by your own son or daughter, or maybe one of your children has been seriously ill, to the point where their life was endangered. How desperate and helpless your pain. How choked with bitterness and fear of losing your precious child forever!

"Let us imagine now in our hearts that desperate pain of love we have for our children when they are lost, or they have turned from us in anger. That is how your Father in heaven feels each time you turn away from him, or speak in anger to your brothers and sisters on earth, or take advantage of them in their weakness or ignorance. You spurn our Father in heaven, showing him only your hatred and selfishness!"

Did he see a bat a few nights ago? A huge bat! With his own two eyes, by the light of four light bulbs, in his own bedroom? Did he hold some bleeding freak of nature in his own two hands last night? And was he now hearing a sermon that was clearly written for him? He looked again into the soaring vaults, now washed in the pastel tints of morning sunlight diffusing through stained glass, maybe coming in through the north windows like the divine light in paintings of Gothic cathedrals.

His eighth-grade teacher—a shriveled, meanspirited nun with dentures that looked like a linebacker's mouth guard—had told him that the universe was one big miracle, one big expression of God's will, as if God had exhaled, and out came the universe in a storm of spectacular cosmic events. But because people lived, breathed, ate, and saw the miracle every day, all day, they thought it was routine. They could no longer look at the world with the eyes of the first human. (Think of what that first human saw! And with no words to help him!) Everything had been poisoned by preconceptions and expectations. They imagined it was subject to the pathetic laws and theorems they imposed upon it. Soon miracles consisted only of the unexpected, instead of the inexplicable—for ultimately nothing can be explained . . . she had said. And even if they could see Creation with the eyes of the first human, their heartbeats would rise (like Rilke's thunder!) and kill them.

He was here only because he could not bear to think that his son's disappearance was just another accident in a universe of colliding molecules. His own perceptions had so terrified him that he had sought shelter in the refuge of the weak. He was regressing to an earlier stage of psychological development. Half Catholic. Once the good nuns installed the basic components, no matter how many times he redid the wiring, there would always be certain phantom circuits that still carried religious impulses, cryptopsychic filaments extremely sensitive to the least . . . vibration or disturbance: deaths, times of sorrow, life-threatening illnesses . . . prompting a reversion to ritualistic processing behaviors . . .

> *"We believe in one God,*
> *the Father, the Almighty,*
> *maker of heaven and earth,*
> *of all that is seen and unseen."*

Randall was able to find this prayer, entitled "Profession of Faith," which long ago he had learned as "The Creed." He read it with feeling and sentiment for his schoolboy days.

"God from God, Light from Light, true God from true God, begotten, not made, one in Being with the Father."

Maybe Judgment Day would be like a section 2004 examination of the creditors in a Chapter 11 bankruptcy. Maybe he was deteriorating mentally. That's why he had turned to prayer, night hallucinations, and other symptoms of mental instability.

"On the third day, he rose again in fulfillment of the Scriptures: he ascended into heaven and is seated at the right hand of the

*Father. He will come again in glory to judge the living and the dead,
and his kingdom will have no end."*

The priest began a litany of prayers for various parishioners and
special causes, paying special attention to people who had *tithed*,
or given a tenth of their incomes to the Church.

"And we pray, O Lord," the priest added solemnly, "for our President. We do not know the exact state of his health at this time.
But we ask you, Lord, for his safe recovery."

What happened to the President? Randall almost said aloud. The
President was abroad, Randall knew. He was halfway across the
world with an entourage of American watch manufacturers. They
were all in Switzerland demanding that Swiss people buy American-
made watches, instead of unfairly selling Swiss-made watches to
American consumers, while refusing to open Swiss markets to
American watch manufacturers. Randall had seen the President on
the six o'clock news, in high dudgeon with several American watch-
manufacturing executives. "This is the very essence of an unfair
trade practice," the President had said. "Americans buy quality
Swiss watches; but the Swiss do not reciprocate by buying
American-made watches, even though watches made in America
are priced competitively."

Randall had seen the morning *Times*, but something must have
happened after last night's printing of the national edition. He stifled
the impulse to lean over the two empty pews and tap the shoulder
of an elderly parishioner on the off chance that maybe she was
picking up the news on those hearing aids that were squeaking
with feedback.

The President had a heart condition. He must have had a coronary. That's it! A heart attack was the most logical explanation! The
Merck! In two hours, the stock market was going to open in New
York and plunge straight down a steep slope to hell. Maybe he could
slip out and call his broker at home. Maybe he could buy options
to cover his position, a basket of puts, or maybe even a straight short
sale. Would that be easier or harder than just trying to dump the
stock? If he tried to dump it, there would be no buyers, and he
would end up getting a sale after it had dropped 30 percent in price.
No, he was better off getting in line to buy options and betting on
a fall.

Could he go any lower? Thinking about money at a time like this?

He should simply trust God, he realized, and calmed himself. After all, he was in church. God would take care of him, his Merck, and his son. What if he was a ragpicker in Calcutta? What if he grew a brain tumor? Would he care about the Merck then? Of course he would, because if his time was up, then his wife and his son were going to need all the money they could get. No more fat checks from the law firm. But God knew that, didn't He? God would take care of that.

Maybe Randall was remembering how to pray. Yeah. He should just kind of . . . let go and trust God. Just become . . . like a child. Just place himself at the mercy of his Father in heaven.

Maybe a straight short sale? No way. Who would be stupid enough to buy it?

> "And so, Father, we bring you these gifts.
> We ask you to make them holy by the
>   power of your Spirit,
> that they may become the body and blood
> of your Son, our Lord Jesus Christ . . ."

Maybe God would help him find his son if he sold all the Merck and gave the money to the poor.

> "On the night he was betrayed,
>   he took bread and gave you thanks and
>   praise.
> He broke the bread, gave it to his
>   disciples, and said:
>
> Take this, all of you, and eat it:
>   this is my body which will be given up for you."

How many times had he rung the handbell as an altar boy at just this moment: the elevation of the Host? No bells rang now. There were no altar boys. These days they were probably all gang members. They went to rock concerts and knew all about sex, violence, and alcohol, instead of the consecration of bread and wine into the blood and body of Christ.

Take this, all of you, and eat it, he repeated silently. He felt like a person from a foreign country who had never been to mass, had never even *heard* of mass. The Eucharist suddenly struck him as a primitive, savage ritual. He imagined what it would sound like to have an American Catholic explain it to him. *It's like a sacrifice, an offering. But it's a mystery too. See, the priest changes the bread and wine into the body and blood of Christ. Then we eat it and drink it. But the bread and wine, they aren't just symbols, they BECOME the body and blood of Christ. Trans . . . Transmutation? No. Transubstantiation. Yeah, that's the word. There's another word that means you're eating God. Theo . . . Theophany? No, that's mystical experience. Theophagy, that's it. It means the sacrificial eating of a god. Sounds like a term paper:* The Central Role of Eating in Sacrificial Rituals. *Primitives used to do it, to get power, which the Catholics call grace. But wait?* he thought, interrupting his own imaginary explanation. Christ was a man too. He was sitting at the table with other men when he broke the bread. Eat my body. Drink my blood. He was telling other men to take his body and eat it. That's not theophagy, that's . . . And his thoughts came full circle to his son, probably chased through the bush by cannibals, heathens in loincloths, with bones through their noses. Why couldn't his son have just stayed home and gone to law school? On the other hand, what if Michael had gone to law school and had not graduated in the top 10 percent of his class? Cannibalism might look pretty good . . .

> *"When supper was ended, he took the cup.*
> *Again he gave you thanks and praise,*
> *gave the cup to his disciples, and said:*
>
> *Take this, all of you, and drink from it:*
> *this is the cup of my blood,*
> *the blood of the new and everlasting covenant.*
> *It will be shed for you and for all*
> *so that sins may be forgiven.*
> *Do this in memory of me."*

Randall decided to risk Communion, even though he knew he could be committing a mortal sin if he was not absolutely convinced that he was eating the body of Christ. He was not eating *symbols* of the body and blood of Christ as the pagan Episcopalians believed. No, the bread and wine actually *changed into* the body and blood of our Lord Jesus Christ. Not the historical Jesus, but the entire Person just the same. He remembered actually believing this with all his heart, and thought he might manage to do so again, if it would help him regain control . . .

He hurried to the front of the church, so he would be among the first in line, leaving only two elderly women between him and where he knew the priest would stand to distribute Christ's body in pieces of bread and his blood from communal cups of wine. Neither of these elderly women, Randall reasoned, could have any fatal viruses, and thus he could safely share the cup of the new and everlasting covenant with them.

"Body of Christ," said the priest, placing the Host in Randall's hand.

"Amen," said Randall, wondering when they'd stopped just putting the Host in your mouth for you. For he recalled it used to be a sin to touch the Host. He had done it once as a boy, quite without thinking, and had held the finger and stared at it for days, expecting it to wither. They probably had to change the method for distributing the Host after they lost the altar boys to gangs and rock concerts. Nobody to hold the silver paten under your chin.

"Blood of Christ," said a layperson, wiping the lip of the cup and offering it to Randall.

"Amen," he said, appreciating the hygienic efforts of the wine distributor, surprised by the taste of wine this early in the morning.

Randall knelt, bowed his head, and prayed that his son would be found. That he did not have a brain tumor. That there was some perfectly harmless explanation for the night disturbances. That God would convince Marjorie not to turn against him. That God would please keep the President healthy. Or if that was not to be granted, then that the stock market would not crash, or if that was not to be granted, then that the Merck miraculously would not fall along with the rest of the market. Or, failing all of the above, that he would be able to place an order for a whole bunch of puts and calls and other stock options to protect his Merck holdings, in which case, his prayers would require some modification, because he would then be asking for the Merck to precipitously decline, then stabilize long enough for him to sell his puts, whereupon it should then rise to above its present level, so he could sell his calls.

We ask this through Christ Our Lord, Amen.

But if God was hearing all of this, would He be quite annoyed and disappointed in Randall's preoccupation with money? Would He be insulted that the celebration of the mass had reminded Randall of cannibalism? Maybe God would think it was funny? Probably not. Laughter is satanic. It was invented after the Fall. God cannot laugh. Nowhere in the scriptures could Randall recall it saying, "God laughed and said, 'Why, that's the funniest thing I ever heard!' " The scriptures are full of desperate half-wits, birdbrains, madmen, tax collectors, con artists, and obtuse fishermen. Every page contains at least one gaffe by some thick-witted apostle, but nowhere do the scriptures say, "Jesus laughed and said, 'Oh, horse-feathers, Peter! Go jump in the Dead Sea!' " Maybe God cannot laugh because everything makes perfect sense to Him. No non-sense, no irony, no absurdity, no contradiction . . . To God, Groucho Marx was just another human thing making noises with his mouth. No wry, divine smiles, no sloppy raspberries. Not a day goes by without Him thinking: *That's not funny.*

"Let us pause for a moment," the priest said, "and contemplate God's love, accepting it into our hearts. For if we can do that, it will give every second of our short lives a divine purpose: serving Him."

This, Randall realized, was true. The overfed priest spoke the truth. Randall had lived his life indirectly serving God as a bankruptcy lawyer. By enforcing the law of the U.S. Bankruptcy Code, Randall was helping the world to be a stable and fair place. For what was the Code but a means to wipe the slate clean of failed endeavors, to assign any assets to the most deserving creditors, according to strict rules, and start anew? It was a law passed by Congress and the President, and Randall's job was to make sure that his clients understood what they were entitled to under the Code and that any debtors guilty of fraud were caught and punished. Would God tolerate fraud? No way! God hated swindlers and money changers. And Randall served God by making damn sure that fraudulent debtors paid in this life and the next. He might as well be a missionary for Christ's Church and get credit for all the good he's doing in the world.

Randall would serve God by making enough money so that his grandchildren would one day bear witness to Christ's love, privately educated, and raised in the glory of His love.

"The mass is ended. Go in peace."

"Thanks be to God."

Refreshed and full of grace, Randall was ready to go back to work casting lots for garments.

On his way out, he walked by an arrangement of three wooden closets, which he instantly recognized as the confessional, where he had knelt as an eight-year-old and confessed his sins, courageously admitting to crimes against humanity like telling a lie or hitting his sister.

Randall noticed a small green light over the priest's door, looking like a console light on a heavy appliance indicating the power was on; he realized that a priest was in there waiting to hear confessions.

On impulse, he opened the door and found the same red leather kneeler, the same cedar closet, a little wider than an upright coffin, upholstered in velvet instead of satin, the same purple curtain covering the sliding panel, closed when the priest was hearing the sins of the penitent in the other booth.

Randall went in, shut the door, and sat in darkness, staring into the shadowy veil in front of him. The hatch slid open.

"Bless me, Father, for I have sinned," said Randall, saying the words, almost without remembering them. "My last confession was . . . about forty or so years ago. I can't remember exactly."

He paused and heard the priest clear his throat.

"I also don't remember the exact words I'm supposed to say," said Randall, "but I'm in trouble, and I think my son's in trouble, and I may need help . . ."

"Do you want to reconcile yourself with God?" asked the priest, his voice textured with age and compassion.

"Yes," said Randall. "I think so, but I'm not sure about the sacraments, you understand. I think I just need help, because I'm so . . ."

"Do you intend to confess your sins to me and to God?" asked the old priest quietly.

Intend? thought Randall, seizing upon the word, and realizing again the naive impunity with which laypeople use words that are fraught with complex legal implications. *Intent* was an essential ingredient of *fraud*, the F-word of bankruptcy parlance. *Intentional* fraud could wipe out assets, nullify safe harbors and the protection of statutes, result in punitive damages. Do I *intend* to confess my sins to you and to God? Was it permissible to request that certain terms be defined before he gave an answer?

"I think so," said Randall, privately wondering if the doctrine of unclean hands, which barred wrongdoers from seeking redress in the courts of equity, might also bar him from petitioning God for assistance.

"What are your sins?" asked the priest.

"I am unsure about the rules, so I don't know exactly which ones I may have . . . not abided by. Have they changed or anything in the last few decades?"

"Do you love God?"

"I do," said Randall. "I think I do. I haven't thought much about it, until recently. But once I started thinking about it again, I kind of thought to myself that if God exists, which He probably does, I would love Him. And maybe if there was even a small chance He could help me . . . Then I would need His help."

"Do you love your neighbor?"

"My neighbor?" asked Randall. "You mean, other people? Do I love other people? Yes, I do, I think, when it's permitted. I mean, you can't go around loving opposing counsel, for instance. That would be a violation of the Code of Professional Ethics, because it would not be in my client's best interests. But generally, in the theoretical sense, I would say that yes, I love others, in a manner of speaking, within certain limits, consistent with various statutes, codes, and rules of court.

"This loving business," he continued. "I know it's desirable in terms of long-range planning, but my problem is more immediate. My son is missing in Africa. My only son, and I . . . Well, I may have a very serious illness. A brain tumor. I might die, or if I don't die, then it's something psychological. I might go insane, because mysterious . . . things are happening to me."

"You are afraid," said the priest.

Randall held his breath and mastered a rogue emotion, which threatened to bolt from his stables and make an ass of him.

"Yes," he admitted, hearing his voice crack nonetheless. It was time to go. Crying in the presence of a priest was even more humiliating than a brain tumor. Pretty soon he would break down and look for consolation in the Beatitudes: *Don't worry about being poor in spirit and weak, it means you're blessed!*

"Fear of death," said the priest. "No one can face that alone."

Randall looked down where a shaft of dim light fell through the veil onto his vesseled hand. He moved his own fingers, watching them from afar, wondering what they would look like when they were attached to a dead man whose eyes were empty sockets.

"You won't be alone," said the priest. "No matter what happens to you or your son, God the Father will be with you. And if God is calling you away from this world, only your body will perish, your soul will be with Him . . . if you have faith."

"Faith," repeated Randall, "in . . ."

"In God," said the priest patiently, "in eternal life, in the resurrection of the body, in life everlasting."

If he had a soul, Randall was unsure about whether he wanted it to survive him, unless he could have control over it, some kind of estate planning, or perhaps a durable power of attorney. Would his soul linger about his body and reminisce? Would it flee in terror into an eternal hell of its own making? Would it attend the funeral and savor the heaving bosoms of women who had loved him? Or disappear into the aether, mixing it up with lower-order souls who had never been to law school or medical school? Would a soul so situated be able to receive supplementary updates to the Code and to the Bankruptcy Reporters?

And what would the afterlife be like? What parts of his interior life would survive? Maybe it was all the same, here and hereafter. Maybe on the other side the laws were even more complex, with statutory histories covering all of eternity. Computerized research could serve up parallel authorities from other galaxies. He could eternally update the software of massive computer systems, giving him access to all the information in the universe by doing term searches of infinite complexity.

Maybe bankruptcy would go on forever, and he would always be the best bankruptcy lawyer in the universe, alone and unchallenged, feared by all, unwilling to indulge himself in the pleasures of the afterlife, because they might compromise his concentration and his technique.

Nothing but fond hopes, he realized. Death would be the end of his career. He felt the unidentified bright object in his deep white matter swell with multiplying cells. They were reproducing in a deadly geometrical progression. The tumor was throwing off colonies of cells, which were migrating to his lungs, his liver, his bones . . .

Brain tumor or no, there was only so much time left in his life. It was measured in seconds separating him from death. He could spend them making war in bankruptcy court, looking for his son, taking a hot bath, eating cookies . . . or praying.

"Father, I . . . am afraid I might be dying," he whispered. "I guess I just need to know what I'm supposed to do."

The priest sighed gently. "First make a full confession," he said. "Then we will pray together."

"Confession of what?" pleaded Randall. "I haven't killed anyone or committed adultery or anything . . . so, I mean . . ."

"Have you intentionally *harmed* anyone?" asked the priest.

Of course, Randall thought, *that's my job!*

"No," he said, "only in bankruptcy court. Only if they tried to harm my client first. Self-defense, I guess."

"I'm sure you can help your clients without harming other people," said the priest. "Can't you?"

Sure, thought Randall, *and a guitar mass probably would have ended the Siege of Leningrad.*

How was he supposed to convey the unmitigated savagery of a contested fee-application hearing to this old man who sat in a box all day listening to people moan about sins?

"I suppose so," said Randall.

"When you use your talents to help other people, you are serving God the Father," said the priest. "When you use your talents to harm others, you are turning away from God. That's what sin is. So if you recall any specific occasions when you used your talents to harm others, those would be sins you should confess now."

Now? thought Randall. *How much time do we have? A definition of "harm" would help.*

Maybe he could expedite things by offering to make a sizable tax-deductible donation.

Randall coughed. "Nothing specific comes to mind, Father, but I see what you are saying. I should just try to *help* people more."

"Yes," said the priest. "Find Christ in others."

"Uh-uh," said Randall.

"Then death will hold no terrors for you," said the priest.

That word again, thought Randall. He recalled that, under the Federal Rules of Evidence, section 804(b)(2), a statement made by a declarant, while believing that his death was imminent, concerning the cause or circumstances of what he believed to be his impending death is not excluded by the hearsay rule. In other words, thought Randall, if, just before he died, or just before he *thought* he was going to die, he said, "This brain tumor is killing me," that statement could be admissible evidence in a court of law, even though the declarant, Randall Killigan, was dead.

But so what!? he realized, suddenly verging on tears. *Who cares?* He'd be dead! All of his knowledge would molder into gray pudding, six feet under in a bowl at the back of his grinning skull. Forty years of reading. Twenty-five years of billable hours. Gone! Twenty-five times three hundred and sixty-five times twelve, minus a few weeks off. At least 100,000 hours. Gone!

Randall swallowed hard to keep the emotion out of his voice. "Father," he said, "I'm ready to pray now."

The smell of cedar and musty velvet. The light again on his own foreign hand. Silence. A susurrus. Breathing. Air passing through a stricture.

"Father?" said Randall, hearing only the faint sound of another suspiration. *The wind blows where it will,* he suddenly remembered. *You hear the sound it makes but you do not know where it comes from, or where it goes. So it is with everyone begotten of the Spirit.*

"Father?"

The old man's vocal cords groaned softly in a delicate snore on the other side of the purple curtain.

Randall shuddered, alone in the velvet darkness. What if it happened now? He would never know how close he had come to making his confession, because the last person he had turned to for help, his confessor, had nodded off! What if death was coming now? And Randall, the penitent manqué, was a seed or an encapsulated soul lodged in a dark pneumatic tube. There would be a sucking of air, and he would be drawn down, and flushed into the bowels of eternal night, far, far below, where his body would be resurrected and plunged into the void. His hands and fingers, his muscles and nerves would lose all sense of themselves and melt in the liquid blackness. His eyes would be clotted with night, they would swell and burst in bootless attempts to see.

Maybe, at first, he would be happy to discover that his mind seemed to have survived. But what about its legendary cravings for knowledge and information? The darkness visible contained no reading material. His Code, his *Wall Street Journal,* his *New York Times,* his *Forbes*—all the pages were gone! Only the ink had survived, had somehow drained off the pages of history and pooled into an infinite blackness. His intellect became disembodied appetite, foraging for food, sifting the depths of sunless oceans through the fine mesh of reason, desperate for something—anything!—to devour. Never mind his Code then, anything to give him some small pleasure. How about a flyer advertising a sale at a grocery store in another century, or maybe the back of a Chinese cereal box? And a candle to read it by?

Instead, he would find only himself, and his awareness of himself, floating, and straining the still seas of nothingness. In a final act of desperation, his imagination would turn itself inside out and create a chamber for him to think in, a single room walled in blackness, furnished only with memories from the split second that had been his earthly life. Alone in the desolation of absolute solitude, his memories would disintegrate, one by one, from being handled too often by his intellectual powers, and the particles would slip through the mesh . . .

The priest snored softly on the other side of the screen. Randall stared contemptuously, listening.

Catholic superstitions! Phantom circuits, paleopsychic eruptions! Buck up! What if somebody had him on film? The best bankruptcy lawyer in the Seventh Circuit? Wringing his hands and sniveling in a cedar closet? This was all caused by some organic dysfunction. Had to be! But OK, then. Take it like a man! If death was coming, he would meet it on his feet, with his boots on, in bankruptcy court. Let them tell stories about how three months after they had told him he had three months to live, he had shown up in bankruptcy court with a battle-ax, cleaved the skull of his opponent, and poured despoiled brains into his briefcase! In death, they would say, he was even more fearsome!

The legend would live on!

(**13**)

Jenisa lay abed, grinding her teeth in fear and listening to the sound of wings slashing the night and wind whistling in the teeth of Luba, who had transformed herself into a fruit bat and was swooping through the village looking for children to eat. Luba and the other witches in her coven fluttered in the eaves of the compounds and made the loud *crawk-aw-aw-awk* of witch birds, announcing their hunger for fresh infant blood. She heard Luba and her coven of scavenging night creatures; she *knew* Luba was a witch, but she fled in terror from the thought. As everyone knew, if Luba was a witch, she would instantly sense any suspicion harbored by others—even total strangers—and would kill any potential accusers before they could reveal her true nature.

Instead, Jenisa desperately tried to think only of the clothes she would have to brook tomorrow, about how Yotta, the big wife, was fat, ugly, and smelled like a bush cow, about the palm oil she would sell tomorrow along the highway, about her mother, who was sick with fever and needed her help, or even, if she had to, about how her husband, the section chief, had not sent for her to share his bed for many weeks, about how he was probably angry, because the Sande women had said that adultery, and maybe even witchcraft, had caused her to lose two children, about two baby girls whom she could have taken out on the morning of the third day after their births, and announced, "Resemble me in all my ways and deeds, being named after me," and whom she would have taught so well to love and suffer without complaining of pain or hardship, about her *poo-mui* love man who was lost somewhere in the bush. She thought of anything and everything she could, to keep from thinking the one thought that pursued all the others like a leopard chasing prey in the bush at night.

Maybe Luba the witch had already sensed the danger lurking in the half-formed hunches racing to catch Jenisa's thoughts. Maybe that was why Luba was fluttering outside in the eaves. Maybe Luba knew what Jenisa had felt just this morning while she was drawing a bucket of water from the well. The sickness coming in waves to her belly, the flush of heat in the cool morning air. She was at once ecstatic that she might at last bring a son or daughter to her wife man, and terrified that Luba would learn of her condition and eat the child before it could be born.

Just yesterday, Jenisa had argued with Luba over some palm-oil soap that had been left at the washing place. It was Jenisa's soap, but Luba tried to claim it as her own.

As other women had gathered to watch the argument, Luba—dressed as usual in rags, with mud smeared onto her shaved head—had thrown the soap on the ground and had said, "Take it, then. I don't want it," and walked away.

"It wasn't yours to want," Jenisa had shouted after her, and instantly regretted her boldness.

Luba turned and marched back to the soap, now wedged in the sand. She stared into Jenisa's eyes and a wicked smile spread across her face.

"I think we should give your soap to the washing and probing man who prepares the dead for burial."

This shocked everyone. What could such talk mean? She was not only evil but insane as well.

"I don't need soap," she said, holding out her filthy arms, bedraggled with the tatters of a country cloth dress.

"You," she said with a grin, "need soap!" Then she jerked and scared the gathering crowd, laughing at them when they gasped and drew back. "Some night soon," she said, staring off over the treetops of the surrounding bush, where the rest of her coven was probably roaming in the shape of animals, "I will dream about the woman whose soap belongs to the washing man."

Jenisa went straight to her hut in the *mawe*. She made sure that the witch nets were properly hung over the doors; she made sure the bamboo witch guns were in place. Then she sank onto her mattress in despair. For now, maybe the witch gun or her prayers would keep Luba at bay, but soon Luba would assume the shape of whatever animal would carry her into Jenisa's hut, so she could settle her witch weight on the young girl's face, and suffocate her, or eat another one of her children before it could be born.

Jenisa's only hope was the medicine. She had given the white stranger's gift to the juju man, just as the looking-around man had instructed. The juju man had placed the small canister of mosquito medicine into his pouch, then had asked her many questions about what kind of medicine she wished to let loose in the world. Was she seeking only to protect herself from Luba's malignant powers or was she seeking to harm or destroy the author of her sorrows? Destroy or defend?

"Destroy," Jenisa had said through clenched teeth. "She ate my children, then she wiped her lips and laughed."

"The medicine I will make for you is illegal," said the juju man. "I would never make such a medicine or let such a swear loose on anyone, no matter what they did to me. But this person has torn your heart to shreds, has dashed your dreams, and has destroyed your children. Who is qualified to sit in judgment of this monster that has eaten your children? Who can know the agonies you have suffered waking each morning and knowing that two beautiful children would be frolicking at your feet, living and loving you, but for the wickedness of Luba? You alone are able to decide all that must be done. You have paid me money and purchased my confidence and my skill. I will make the medicine and give it to you, but I do not want to know what you do with this evil thing. You alone will know. You must not tell anyone. You will answer before your ancestors and before *Ngewo*."

Some days later, the juju man met her in the bush at night and gave her a small black bundle with the *poo-mui* medicine sticking out of it like a spout at the top. He did not want to know whether or when she intended to use it, but if she wished to destroy an enemy with the medicine, she should obtain something from her enemy's house—an article of clothing, a lock of hair—and then bury it, together with the medicine, near her enemy's house. If your enemy is a witch, the next time the witch's shade leaves on a night journey, the medicine will fly into the bush after it, catch it, and kill it. When the shade does not return, the human form will slip into a coma and die.

So many feared that all the deaths in the village were caused by witches, but none dared speak of it. Jenisa did not even discuss it with Amida, her mate and her closest friend, for fear of retribution. Jenisa knew it was Luba, Amida knew it was Luba, everyone knew that Luba the witch was eating all the children in the village, but no one dared accuse her, even in private, for fear that Luba would come for them at night, settle on their faces, and suffocate them.

The night before Pa Gigba was shot by the hunter, Mama Saso's twins died during childbirth. Their birth had been foretold in a dream, in which Mama Saso went down to brook clothes at the river and saw two snakes twining around the washing rock. For months, sacrifices of rice and fowl had been left at altars made from termite mounds, where twins are worshipped. An older twin from another village was summoned to pray at the altars. The twin told Jenisa that *Ngewo* made two kinds of people: twins and the rest of the human race. Twins have the power to foretell the future, to cure diseases, to protect entire villages from witchcraft, and to make farms bear rice.

But Mama Saso's twins would never enjoy such powers, or use them to bring health and prosperity to their parents. They were dead. One week ago, Jenisa's cousin, Fatmata, who lived in the *mawe* near the dyeing yard, suddenly lost an infant. A week before that, another child had died. Jenisa's children had died. Amida had lost a child. Mariamu, who had borne three strong sons and two daughters, also, inexplicably, lost her little Borboh. Now Pa Gigba was dead.

The women went to their men, the men went to the old pas, and the old pas went to Pa Ansumana and the chief. Pa Ansumana and the chief went to Kabba Lundo, the Paramount Chief, who carried a staff topped with a brass ornament bearing the British coat of arms and ruled his province from a wooden throne given to his father by the British in 1961.

The Paramount Chief and Pa Ansumana had both lived long lives. They knew that witches thrived in villages poisoned by suspicion, fear, and despair. It was meaningless to ask if the witches caused death and disaster or if death and disaster terrorized human hearts and allowed witches to exercise their powers over their victims. Somehow the cycle had to be broken before more plans were laid and more afflictions hatched. Once the hysteria engendered by several tragedies got its grip on the village, mothers all but gave up caring for their children. Why bother? Why care for a sick child? If the witches were eating it from the inside out, no medicine or nourishment would do any good. But Pa Ansumana and Kabba Lundo had seen witchcraft take hold every decade or so, and once a village fell under its thrall, nothing would free the people except the powers of a witchfinder.

•

Luba could see across the courtyard and straight into a *mawe* filled with children she would love to eat. The mother, Mama Amida, had witch nets and witch guns hanging everywhere inside the hut and kept the curtain drawn because she was afraid of Luba. Luba laughed and then giggled hysterically at the pathetic attempts of these solid citizens to protect themselves from powers so awesome their imaginations could not contain them.

She watched them huddle together in their *mawes*. "We are families," they said. "We have each other. This surely must be the highest good." Luba had no family. She lived alone; her neighbors considered this a state so depraved and unnatural that only a warped and evil creature could endure it without dying. "We are happy," said her neighbors. "We love each other. We live with our families. We don't live alone in the dark like . . ." They made her sick with their petty conceits, the paltry rewards of their labors, the miserable glee they took in the accomplishments of their children. They were all so smug in the bosoms of their families, blessed with children to love and parents to honor.

But being happy was not enough for them. They needed Luba to hate. They selected her because she lived alone and had no one to protect her. Those with no families, those who were old or infirm or lived alone, with no one to take their part—these were the hateable ones, those without others. They must be warped and strange indeed, for who would sit alone in a hut with no one? Only a deviant, only someone who must harbor an intense hatred against happy families.

They had all turned against her, shunned her, and had given her a shed on the side of her husband's house, and rags to wear. And after they had driven her into herself, after her many hours of solitude and fear, she had turned inward for the first time and discovered an entire world, a universe, of which she had known nothing. She found she could control her dreams, she could fly at night, she could change herself into shapes and go out into the bush. She discovered that at night, in the bush, *anything* was possible, *anything and everything.* There were no rules for her. She could eat infants as she pleased, she could sex their fathers, she could suffocate their mothers. The light of day was such a humdrum affair. Once night came, she closed her eyes and roamed free.

She drew designs on herself with a sharp stick. She never washed, so she could savor all of her wonderful odors. She discovered her smells one by one, rich bouquets that grew more pungent and varietal as each day passed, and she reveled in them. What is the difference between an odor and a fragrance, between a weed and a flower, between a diamond and any other rock? Only that others tell you one is valuable and the other worthless. But Luba had learned that they are all exactly the same; nothing was better than anything else, unless thinking made it so. She baked and sweated in her shed, and soon she discovered that her own smells were far more interesting to her than the company of others had ever been. What were people but engines in search of fuel, whether food to feed their bellies or the admiration of others to feed their self-absorbed cravings for belonging? What did she have to say to them except to laugh hysterically at their own pitiful vanities? Why did they hate her? Because she could see their thoughts; they knew their hearts were open to her.

If people in the village wanted nothing to do with her, then she would live with animals in the bush. When she laughed, bats swarmed out of her mouth and flew into the bush, where they took up her laughter, spreading it far and wide, until the night echoed with the cackles of Luba the witch. When she was angry, her wrath grew teeth and claws and leapt out of her in the shape of a powerful leopard who bounded through the bush on the limbs of trees, scanning the path below for humans to eat.

Luba sat in her shed with her head in her knees. She giggled deliriously into her kneecaps. She had heard about several infant deaths in the village of Jormu, and she searched her dreams, wondering if it was there her magic shell had taken her. She burped contentedly, and the bellyful of infant blood she had siphoned during her night travels made her sleepy. It was her turn to laugh. She, who wore rags and slept in a shed, now had the power to terrorize entire villages. She made them all pay for their sins against her. The most powerful chiefs and medicine men were helpless against her!

She closed her eyes and smiled, recalling the exhilaration of her

night flights. She collected all the hatred and evil her neighbors
had showered on her; she saved it in a big witch pot, and then she
poured it back on their heads at night. She was a deep and dark
reservoir of their malice and hatred, made in their image and like-
ness, and when they saw themselves reflected in that dark pool, it
made them hate her even more! The infant deaths, the suffocations,
the paralysis, the poisons she put in the wells at night, the crops
she destroyed, the blood she drank, all this they had brought upon
themselves. They had chosen her to punish them for their own evil
deeds. She was their conscience! Did the poor childless mothers
have something to say to her? Did Luba pity them as they clawed
the dirt in their anguish over the loss of their infant sons and daughters? They killed their children as surely as if they had done it with
a knife. Their fathers, brothers, sons, sisters, wives, and mothers
had shunned her. They all but sent her flying into the skies at night.
Let them blame themselves!

She felt the wings growing from the sides of her throat, opening
like the gills of a fish that swims in the night. She soared into the
moonlit bush and watched rodents scattering in terror beneath her.
If she were wearing her human shape, she would laugh; instead
she filled her lungs with the humid night air and screamed at them,
paralyzing them with her *craw-aww-awwk!* Luba the witch done
come, you pathetic little creatures. Which one shall I eat? Which
one wants to die tonight?

The unborn children were her favorite dish, so tender and moist
and unsullied by human hands. She could puncture them with her
teeth and suck them like yolk from an egg. Sweet and succulent,
the flesh and blood of innocence. And having tasted such delights,
she could no longer live without wanting more and more, and the
more she ate, the more powerful she became. The pitiful charms
and amulets worn by the women were useless against her!

Sooner or later she would no doubt be killed by a witch gun, or
caught and starved in a witch net. But what choice did she have?
She could sit in her shed and rot to death, alone, or she could roam
at night and enjoy power over the entire world, if only for a time.

She had revenge on her enemies and made men love her who
would never have looked twice at her in the light of day. Men are
the weakest creatures! If she touched them just so, they sexed her,
no matter what the cost or penalty. They submitted to her, even
though they suspected her of witchcraft and feared that she might

capture their souls at the moment of orgasm. And after she sexed them, she ate their children for dinner.

She went out of her way to make herself as ugly as possible. She did not bathe. She covered herself in mud. And despite her filth, she could make men sex her. This was her proudest achievement. She touched them just so, or let them do things to her that a Mende wife would never allow, and the men succumbed. When it was over, she laughed at them, as they pulled up their pants and sheepishly sneaked back into the village. But on the path back to their families, the men had to listen to the bush ring with the taunts and laughter of Luba the witch: *"You did not want me enough to put a big gift in my funeral basket, but you sneak out here in the bush at night and sex me by the light of the moon! You spill your human seed on the land that feeds your family! Someday I will see you in the place of everlasting hunger, where we can gnaw on each other's knees!"*

(**14**)

A troop of monkeys in a stand of mango trees shrieked at Boone as he ascended the path back to Nymuhun, where he intended to collect his belongings and travel to Killigan's village. Dusk seeped into the rank hells of green on either side of the path, but aloft in the riggings of vines and plaited palms, he could see his biological ancestors crawling on all fours across the limbs and screaming down at him, throwing sticks and mangoes at him, probably warning each other that a white devil on hind legs was traversing their territory, maybe wondering if they all fell on him together, could they take him?

There but for the grace of some fortuitous prehistoric genetic mutation go I, thought Boone. If his ancestors had been born in the bush, instead of the village, he would be up there on all fours, baring his teeth and screaming at his rivals, anguishing over the more coveted females, and plotting his career as an alpha male. Instead of growing up in a mango tree, he had been to college, and he had his job as an insurance claims adjuster waiting for him back in Indianapolis, where he would end up walking on two legs in a nice little office, baring his teeth and screaming at his rivals, anguishing over the more coveted females, and plotting his career as an alpha male.

While climbing the path to the village, he reviewed his options. He had been to see the police in Bo, where he had learned that Section Chief Moiwo had thoughtfully taken Moussa Kamara's body back to the boy's family in Ndevehun. He could journey the next morning to Killigan's village, where, he had been given to understand by the Volunteers in Bo, he would be welcomed as Michael

Killigan's brother, and where he could perhaps seek an audience with the Paramount Chief, Kabba Lundo, who was Killigan's African father. Or he could wait in Sisay's village for Lewis, who had offered to pick him up in three days and companion him on the journey to find Moiwo and ask after Killigan. Boone was impatient to do his own investigating, but he had the barest understanding of Krio, and was able to pick out only the obvious English words, and then only when it was spoken slowly by a villager who had had some schooling.

When he arrived at his temporary home, the cooking fires were already smoking in the village *mawes* and courtyards. The harvest rice was laid out everywhere on mats, and there was singing and dancing, men and women shuffling in place in the Mende fashion and shaking seed-pod rattles and bangles. The children streamed in and out of the courtyards, thrilled at the prospect of another late night of games and songs, because the moon was out.

"Evening-O, Mistah Gutawa," the villagers shouted. "How de body?"

"I tell God tank ya," said Boone.

He turned down an invitation to join a game of *warri*, which was under way in the baffa of Sisay's courtyard.

"Mistah Aruna get febah," said one peekin, pointing at Sisay's compound.

Boone should have known something was up, because the boom box was playing African music—Johnny Clegg and Savouka—instead of Sisay's precious Grateful Dead.

"Kong, kong."

Boone found his host prostrate on the cot in his quarters, shirtless, and chewing on a wet rag. A sheen of sweat shone in the light of the hurricane lamp. A woman in a headwrap tended him, handing him oranges and daubing him with damp cloths.

"Febah done hold me," Sisay said weakly.

Boone, who had come prepared to rage at his host for providing him with misinformation and possibly withholding important knowledge about Poro and powerful medicines, was at a loss for words. Sisay's face was a pallid grimace splotched with fever rashes, and he squirmed, panting shallowly, and soaking the sheets of his cot with sweat.

"Oh sha," Boone finally managed, recalling the Krio expression of condolence and commiseration. "Can I get a . . . doctor for you. Is there one in Bo, or . . ."

Sisay turned his sweaty head and grinned. "Yeah," he said between pants, "I think I need a blood transfusion, and maybe a CAT scan." He laughed bitterly and shivered in a chill. "I take the chloroquine," he said. "Other than keeping your fluids up, that's all you can do."

He sucked an orange and curled up on his side. "Your time will come. It's the common cold of West Africa, but *poo-muis* seem to have a much harder time of it than Africans. Take a good look, this is mild compared to what a white man gets the first time."

"You told me Moussa Kamara was dead," Boone said.

"And he wasn't," Sisay said, his fevering eyes looking up into Boone's. "I'm sorry. Our esteemed chief, Bockarie Koroma, told me that he had received word from Section Chief Moiwo that Moussa Kamara had been found dead outside his village, hanging from a tree, as I told you. After you left, I learned this was not true. I heard about the tiefman business in Bo."

Sisay put the rag back into his mouth. He turned on his side and shook with the rigors of fever. The woman wrung the cooling cloths into a bucket and touched them to him.

"Tell me more about this Moiwo character," said Boone. "His wife brought me food as a gift from him. He lives here?"

"He's got farms, houses, and wives in several villages, and apartments in Bo and Freetown. He went to an American University and studied somewhere in England. Then he came back here and made a 'gift of himself,' as he puts it, to the people of Sierra Leone. That's why he came back out to the bush, so he could reestablish his tribal roots, even though he was the son of a minister and raised in Freetown. He needs tribal roots because he's taking the long view: President Moiwo. When he talks to the Temne, he's a Temne man, because his mother was a Temne woman and his father was nearly half Temne. When he talks to the Mende, he's a Mende man, because his father was a Mende man and his mother was nearly half Mende. First he'll make a run at being an elected Paramount Chief, then he'll shoot for a vice presidency, then . . . who knows? Maybe he'll make *Time* magazine.

"He knows your friend is missing. He's probably doing everything possible to find him, because it would only add to his popularity at election time."

"It was one of Moiwo's men that started the tiefman beating in Bo," said Boone, stopping short of telling his host about the note.

"Some of the people in the street said that Moussa Kamara was not a tiefman, and that Moiwo had falsely accused him of stealing, then stood by while the mob did its work."

Sisay groaned and shook his head into the pillow. "Election business," he said. "Why did the white man bring elections to West Africa? It was so much easier when the chief with the most strong war boys was the headman. Now we put on a skit for the West every five years called 'democracy,' which means we have six months of secret society intrigue, witchcraft, bad medicine, riots, and ritual murders, followed by something called an election. If Moiwo is mixed up in this, then it's politics, it's control of smuggling and the mines, it's development money, and it's bad medicine."

"I'm going to go talk to Moiwo," said Boone. "I went to the police in Bo and found out he had left to take Moussa Kamara's body back to Killigan's village."

"At least consult the looking-around man here," said Sisay, "where I can translate for you. I've also asked Pa Ansumana to come and talk with us. Sam-King Kebbie, the looking-around man I told you about from Kenema, is here. Maybe tomorrow we should consult with him, and then hang heads with Pa Ansumana."

"I also saw Lewis in Bo," Boone ventured. "He didn't think much of the idea of a looking-around man. He thought we should hire someone to threaten Killigan's village with thunder medicine."

Sisay shook his head. "Lewis is so white," he said ruefully. "Just another *poo-mui* gangster come to plunder the dark continent."

He sucked an orange and sipped water from a ladle the woman held to his lips.

"The people in Killigan's village love him like a son. His disappearance has already caused them untold anguish and shame. They've combed the bush and the surrounding villages. Thunder medicine would only draw even more attention to their failure to find their favorite white stranger."

"But Lewis keeps talking about illegal medicines, pouches or bundles of stuff we could use to terrorize Killigan's enemies, if he has any, and maybe force them to turn him over."

Sisay shook his head again. "Well," he said weakly, "the first problem you will have using illegal medicine is that it is *illegal*. The jails here are a lot like hell, only the humidity is worse."

"He told me about a medicine called *bofima* that is fed with human fat . . ."

Sisay pointed a finger at Boone. "*Bofima* is *the* most illegal medicine in the country. You can swing from the gallows in Freetown
for even talking about it. It is illegal, antisocial, and evil. To make
the medicine, men dressed as leopards or baboons capture victims
and silence them by breaking their jaws with metal claws. Then
the victim's body parts are used to prepare or replenish the medicine.
New members, or hapless travelers who stumble upon the meetings
in the bush, are forced to join in the ritual cannibalism, then they
are required to provide the next victim, usually a member of the
initiate's own family. As I said, I would not even use the word,
unless you're looking to get arrested and deported or executed."

"His suggestion was that you perhaps had used illegal medicine,
and that you might know something more about it than you were
saying."

"If I were ever going to use illegal medicine, I think my first
victim would be Sam Lewis," he said weakly, closing his eyes in
disgust.

"He also said you were high up in this Poro Society," Boone said,
and paused.

"Well, then I'm sure he also told you that once a man is initiated
into Poro, he is forbidden to speak about Poro matters to those who
aren't members."

"He did," said Boone.

Sisay irritably cast an orange aside.

"Don't forget that you are a 'strangah,' " he said, emphasizing the
Krio pronunciation. "It translates not so much as stranger but as
'guest.' A guest living temporarily with men who are almost all
members of the men's society and women who are almost all members of the women's society. Both sworn to secrecy about their
respective activities. Death or miscarriage will befall any woman
who dares peek in the Poro bush. Elephantiasis and hernias the
size of watermelons are what happens to the Mende man who dares
peek into the Sande bush to observe the women's initiation rituals
or Sande business. I'm not sure I know what would happen to a
white man who went snooping into the Poro bush, but I can ask
around."

"And are you forbidden to speak about Poro matters?"

"Of course," said Sisay.

"Because you are a member," said Boone.

"I am," said Sisay, without hesitation. "So is your African grandfather and most of the adult males in the village. But you are *not* a Poro member, and this fact is never far from your neighbors' thoughts."

"I respect their secrets," said Boone, "and I am grateful for their hospitality, but if Poro business has anything to do with Michael Killigan's disappearance, then I don't have much choice but to ask about it, do I?"

Sisay allowed a long silence to intrude, while Boone waited, not caring if his host ordered him to leave the village or berated him for his investigatory methods.

"As long as we're on the subject of manners," he said at last. "There's another question of etiquette that needs discussing. You've been a guest in this village now for almost ten days. The people have welcomed you into their community, but they aren't sure if you are happy or comfortable here."

Boone studied his host's sweaty face in the firelight.

"My best friend is missing," said Boone. "I'm in a foreign country where I don't speak the language. The climate is fetid. I have sores, dysentery, no leads so far. Yes, I'm uncomfortable."

"That's true," said Sisay, "your best friend is missing. I have a fever, and I left my American family long ago. I may never see them again. God gives every person his burdens to carry. But that doesn't mean that we turn away from the rest of the village, just because we are asked to bear a serious misfortune."

"Now, I'm not bearing my misfortunes correctly," Boone said, "is that it?"

"I'm saying there was much discussion of village business while you were in Bo. The elders, including your African grandfather, hung heads in the court *barri* for many hours, discussing the death of Pa Gigba and the deaths of children in the village, the election turmoil, your search for your American brother, and you were . . . discussed. Your name was mentioned several times, and I tell you this, not to impugn you or your ways in the least, but just to tell you that your behavior affects the village. Some even suggested that you had brought misfortune with you, though this was disputed by others, most notably your grandfather."

"What are you saying?" Boone asked. The guy seemed to be insinuating something and reassuring him at the same time.

"The Mende are very sensitive to a person's *social* personality. Let me regress to anthropology for an explanation. Where you come from, individual personalities happen to have relationships with others. Here, in Mendeland, and in most African villages, your relationship with others *is* your personality. People are never alone. People who enjoy spending time alone are suspect, because they seem to be developing some kind of marginal, extrasocial personality."

"What does all this have to do with me?" asked Boone.

"Your neighbors sense that you are the kind of person who enjoys spending time alone," said Sisay. "And they take it personally."

"Alone?" said Boone. He was suddenly angry. After he had gone out of his way to accommodate their insatiable curiosity about the contents of his backpack, their nagging questions about how things worked in the land of *Poo*, their insistent desire to see just how he did everything, from taking a crap to reading a book, from sneezing to picking wax out of his ears, now he was being criticized for spending too much time alone. He had patiently allowed them almost constant access to his company, allowed their children to squeal *poo-mui* at him the livelong day, let them touch the yellow hair on his arms, let them touch his boots, and marvel over his fingernail clippers. Now this? He was being accused of selfishness and ingratitude. He should spend *more* time with them. He should behave like his host, who rose at dawn, began talking Mende, continued talking Mende as the sun journeyed across the sky, paused just enough to gorge himself at dinner, and then resumed yacketing until the wee hours.

"You can't get two seconds alone in this hothouse of humanity," Boone protested. "The veranda is crammed with villagers all day, and if I go to my room at night, the *National Geographic* crew comes in to talk. Don't get me wrong, I *like* these people. But I'm a private person."

"That's the problem," said Sisay levelly. "Private people in Africa are . . . unusual. Most houses and huts have one large room, which sleeps ten or more. So the only way to spend time alone is to spend time in the bush. Hunters, travelers, farmers with farms deep in the bush, all of them spend time alone in the bush. They are marginal people. The villagers may admire them, but they also suspect them, because they move too easily and comfortably about in the bush, and because they enjoy being alone, something no villager understands."

"They think I'm antisocial?"

"All Americans are antisocial compared to Africans," said Sisay. He waved him away irritably. "You're making a bigger deal of it than I intended. It's just something you should be aware of. It was mentioned. I reported the mention. End of story."

End of stay, thought Boone.

"Tomorrow we will consult the looking-around man. Then we will ask our father about these things."

"I have to warn you," said Boone, "I don't believe in fortune telling."

"It's not fortune telling," said Sisay. "Think of it as protection. It's like insurance. Didn't you say your family was in the insurance business? Insurance is looking around out in the future for the most likely risks. Your insurance man identifies the most likely risks, then protects you from them. In exchange for his protection, you pay money. It's exactly the same here. Insurance men get their power at college; over here, the looking-around men receive their powers in their dreams, usually after being visited by one of their ancestors.

"You should do a good job of hiding one of your personal belongings, so you can test the looking-around man by making him find it for you."

"I have a better idea," said Boone. "I'll tell him I hid my buddy in the bush and please go find him."

Sisay shuddered and chewed into his rag.

"Are you sure there's nothing I can do?" Boone asked.

"Mix me up some rehydration salts," he said weakly. "Then I'll try to sleep. If I start hollering and seeing things during the night, come in and tie me down. I don't know if it's the chloroquine or the fevers or both, but white men with malaria can get the screaming meemies. Voices, shapes, delusions . . . One time I watched *Butch Cassidy and the Sundance Kid* from start to finish. No VCR, no movie, nothing. Just a high fever and a loading dose of chloroquine. The Volunteers claim it's the chloroquine. You take only one tablet a week as a prophylactic, and, as you may have noticed, even that lends a certain vividness to your dreams. If you wake up at night, it takes longer to decide whether you are awake or dreaming. Once you actually come down with malaria, you take two tablets for a loading dose and one every twelve hours after that. If the fevers don't make you see things, the loading dose of chloroquine will."

"If I hear you howling," said Boone, "I'll come in and bark at you."

He mixed the salts for Sisay and returned to his room, only to feel the familiar tug in his small intestine.

.

While he waited for sleep, night fell, and the moon rose like a glowing orange in the palms, casting huge shadows in the court-yards. Boone wearily clambered out of bed and into his plastic thongs to revisit his hut with the hole in the ground. It was a homecoming of sorts, noting that his old friend the spider had been productive in his absence; there were several captured cockroaches bound and wriggling like bandaged mummies, kept alive so they would be fresh at mealtime. He lit the hurricane lamp and hid his Swiss Army knife in a chink above the spider's web, then plugged the hole with a clod of dirt.

The dark hole in the wooden platform again seemed to emanate some infrasound from the underworld. Maybe the shock of Third World travel had endowed him with a certain clairaudient perception of spirits. When he lifted the lid and shined his flashlight into the hole, he half expected to find a scene from a Hieronymus Bosch painting.

It occurred to Boone that, unlike American toilet bowls, which are protected by pure and diaphanous beings, the outhouses and latrines of the Third World are probably inhabited by creatures with darker intentions—slithering around somewhere down there, clap-ping their warty hands with glee whenever a traveler from the First World staggers in to drop another payload of gastric acids. If he dared peer again into the black hole, he could probably see them, gnarled, ratlike apparitions, about the size and shape of a mongoose or a subterranean gargoyle, rooting around in the dark pit, feeding like duck-billed platypuses, sifting microorganisms with the mem-branes in their snouts. Little turd urchins, he suddenly thought. If they existed, they would probably wear fetid leather jerkins and britches, stained by fecal spume that splashed up under the latrine boards. They would have bulging brown eyes, weepy with thick mucus to protect their eyes during their burrowings, and they could curse in a dozen Third World languages. They would come and go between the visible and the invisible world as easily as Boone covered himself with a sheet. They would manage to stay one step outside the periphery of human sight, even though they were a tad clubfooted and not nearly as agile as the fairies and pixies of European folklore. At times, they popped up out of their shit swamps and went to work with wood-burning tools on afflicted assholes of travelers, snickering as they etched hexagrams, pentagrams, and other magic or satanic figures on swollen rosebuds.

Maybe the turd urchins would not fancy American bathrooms, because their food supply would be repeatedly wiped out by antiseptic blue fluids and abrasive cleansers. Maybe the turd urchins of America would evolve into little well-dressed maids and butlers in starched white morning dress, with whisk brooms, basin-tub-and-tile cleaners, and puffed silk wipe-ettes for daubing the pampered assholes of the First World, five or six times, until the sixth wipe-ette comes back snowy white. And the delicate, wholesome First World asshole would be given a light mist of perfume from an atomizer.

"That should do it, master," the conscientious First World maid would say. "You're ready for another day of eating as much as you want."

Boone settled wearily onto his heels and dropped another cataract of shit water aft. *God is very big*, he prayed. *Bigger*, he thought, than the wicked little mole creatures hissing from the shadows below; bigger than the carnivorous flies circling and waiting to lay their eggs under his skin.

He picked up a stray section from what once was a hardback book and discovered he held the preface to something called *Human Leopards: An Account of the Trials of Human Leopards Before the Special Commission Court*. Somebody—Sisay?—had made a slash in the margin, next to a passage describing the bush:

I have been in many forests, but in none which seemed to me to be so uncanny as the Sierra Leone bush. In Mende-land the bush is not high, as a rule it is little more than scrub, nor is the vegetation exceptionally rank, but there is something about the Sierra Leone bush, and about the bush villages as well, which makes one's flesh creep. It may be the low hills with enclosed swampy valleys, or the associations of the slave trade, or the knowledge that the country is alive with Human Leopards; but to my mind the chief factor in the uncanniness is the presence of numerous half-human chimpanzees with their maniacal shrieks and cries.

The bush seemed to me pervaded with something supernatural, a spirit which was striving to bridge the animal and the human. Some of the weird spirit of their surroundings has, I think, entered into the people, and accounts for their weird customs. The people are by no means a low, savage race. I found many of them highly intelligent, shrewd, with more than the average sense of humour, and with the most marvelous faculty for keeping hidden what they did not wish to be known—the result probably of secret societies for countless generations. But beyond such reasoning powers as are required for their daily necessities their whole mental energies are absorbed in fetish, witchcraft, "medicine" such as the Bofima and the like. What they need is a substitute for their bottomless wells of secret societies, for their playing at being leopards or alligators and acting the part with such realism that they not only kill their quarry but even devour it. In my opinion the only way to extirpate these objectionable societies is the introduction of the four R's—the fourth, Religion, being specially needed to supply the place of the native crude beliefs. No doubt the energetic action of the Government, and in a lesser degree the labours of the Special Commission Court, will have a good effect; but, I fear, only a temporary effect. The remedy must go deeper than mere punishment: the Human Leopard Society must be superseded by Education and Religion.

W. Brandford Griffith
2 Essex Court, Temple, September 1915

In the midst of his fanciful reading, he heard a sudden rustle of leaves, then a whisper, coming from somewhere behind him and outside the latrine. Again the whisper, and a horripilating chill swept through him.

"Will you feed the medicine?" a voice hissed at his back.

He whirled on the balls of his feet and almost dropped a leg into the hole. He searched behind him, the lamp's flame bobbing and making the mud walls dance with shadows. He peered at several chinks and thought he saw black skin move behind a crevice. A cheek? A woman's forearm?

"Will you feed the medicine?" the whisper asked, the sex of the speaker masked in sibilance.

Boone hitched up his drawers, grabbed the lamp, and went outside, realizing at once that he would have been better off with only the light of the nitid moon, for the lantern bathed the ambits of the latrine in a nearsighted glare and turned the bush into an army of warring shadows. From the village at his back, he heard the songs of dancing children, and more African music on the boom box.

He dialed down the wick and waited for his pupils to swell in the moonlight. Ahead of him, at a distance impossible to estimate, two orange pinpricks of light, as fixed as the bush itself, stared eyelike in the night, like distant bifocals reflecting the light of a fire.

"Scat," he said, instinctively hissing at the thing, thinking that if it was the eyeshine of a bush cat, he could startle it into movement.

"Scat," he said again, and hissed.

He took one step forward and promptly realized that to reach the lights, he would have to leave the path and make his way through overgrown bush.

Then it whispered, and he froze again.

"Will you feed the medicine?" it hissed.

"Who are you?" Boone whispered hoarsely.

"Will you feed the medicine?"

"Yes," said Boone, trying to raise a different response from whatever was hissing at him.

"If you keep me secret, I will teach you how to feed the medicine."

"Tell me your name," Boone said, scanning thc bush shadows for a shape he could seize with his eyes.

This time the thing adopted Boone's intonation and hissed, "Scat." The orange eyes moved soundlessly away from him, appearing to recede into the bush without rustling the surrounding vegetation.

Boone returned to the latrine for his flashlight and tore out the marked page he had read. He took it back to Sisay, and found him still burning up, his sweat glistening in the light of a hurricane lamp.

"Is that your mark next to this description of the Sierra Leone bush?"

Sisay studied the page and smiled, then chuckled sentimentally. "It is. I read that passage before I came here, when I was still a graduate student. At the time, I thought it was a good description of the Sierra Leone bush, but I didn't mark it then. After I had lived here a few years, I found it again, and I marked it, because I thought it was a good example of a white man setting out to describe West Africa and winding up describing his own unconscious instead."

•

Boone rose at dawn to the tune of "Allah akbar" and found mold in his boots. The shirt he had hung up to dry the night before had simply absorbed more humidity. His tropical sores ached, his hair was sticky with sweat, and he realized for the tenth time that he was living in a climate where nothing ever dried: wounds, damp clothes, hair, navels, armpits, and underwear (if one was silly enough to wear it).

He found Sisay propped in bed and skipping morning prayers.

"I'm much better this morning," said Sisay, lifting himself onto one elbow. "But that doesn't mean anything. The fevers come in cycles, depending on which strain of malaria has been injected by the mosquito, and sometimes you're lucky enough to have more than one strain."

"Oh sha," said Boone.

As if to illustrate his anthropology lecture of the night before, Sisay hailed a corps of well-wishers, who were assembled on the veranda, and asked them into his rooms to cheer him up during the respite of his fever.

Boone grinned as conspicuously as possible and resisted the urge to go to his room.

After breakfast and the best wishes of half the village—including Pa Usman, who appeared with his *nomoloi* and served it a cola— the looking-around man arrived with his assistant and the paraphernalia needed for the ritual. Sam-King Kebbie and his assistant introduced themselves and engaged in the usual verbal waltz of greetings and inquiries after one another's wives, families, farms, and livestock, tales of recent journeys undertaken, the state of the economy, the upcoming elections—during which time Boone stared vacantly at the paraphernalia the looking-around man had brought with him: a bundle of sticks, a mat, a bag of pebbles, and kindling and herbs for building a small fire.

The assistant wore the usual leggings, sandals, and cotton shirt, topped off with a clay pipe and a skullcap. Sam-King Kebbie sported a shirt of country cloth studded with Koranic amulets and inked with symbols. Whenever he caught Boone looking at him, Sam-King promptly stared off into space, his eyes glazing in the throes of some psychic revelation.

After introductions, the looking-around man, who spoke only Mende, asked Sisay what Boone had hidden for him to find, and Boone described the Swiss Army knife. Then Boone was interviewed about the purpose of his visit to Sierra Leone and his stay in the village, which he reported was a happy one, except for runny belly, tropical sores, and the lack of cold beer. He was asked about steps he had taken to find his brother and about his journey to Bo.

Then Sam-King and his assistant rose, thanked the white men, and said they would return shortly with the Swiss Army knife.

After they had gone, Boone asked his big brother, "Do these guys go to school and get a degree in the looking-around sciences, or what?"

"Usually a looking-around man receives his powers in a dream, but he may also serve an apprenticeship to another looking-around man. Sam-King's grandfather was a very powerful looking-around man and later became one of the famed Tongo Players, who once traveled the country exposing and exterminating cannibals. His grandfather was able to detect them by having suspects in every village pick up a stone and hold it. Then he took the stones to a cotton tree and prayed over them until he was able to tell which of the stones had been handled by a cannibal.

"When Sam-King Kebbie was still a boy, and after his grandfather had died, a female genie came to him in a dream and began bargaining with him. His grandfather had taught him all about genies, so Sam-King knew he was involved in perilous negotiations. Either one acts boldly and assumes control over the genie or the genie takes control and makes a slave of the person, demanding exorbitant sacrifices, sexual favors, and constant attention. Sam-King bested the genie and was shown seven ranks of river pebbles spread on a mat. The genie also showed him the leaves of a plant and told him that the leaves and the pebbles were gifts from his grandfather, the Tongo Player.

"Next day, Sam-King picked pebbles from the river and scattered them in seven ranks on the mat. Then he went into the bush and obtained the leaves of the plant the genie had shown him in the dream. Sam-King washed his eyes in a lotion made from the leaves, and ever since he has been able to read the stones. People consult him when they are anxious or confused, sick, or about to undertake a journey or a project of importance. Sam-King then reads the stones and recommends a sacrifice, which will either protect his client from evil or help a favorable prediction come true."

"For a fee," Boone inserted, and made a face.

"Valuable services are seldom provided free of charge," said Sisay, "especially where you come from."

"And I'll bet he's never wrong about his predictions," said Boone sarcastically.

"Errors of cure and prognosis occur in every profession," said Sisay. "What if a devil or a witch or an angry ancestor interferes with the divination process for its own purposes, maybe to mislead the client with a false message? What if a swear or a curse from another source affects the diviner's prediction without his knowledge? What if the prescribed sacrifice fails to ward off evil because those participating in the offering are guilty of adultery or of other failings in their duties to their ancestors?"

"How convenient," said Boone acidly. "So it's never the looking-around man who's at fault, there's always another explanation."

"There's no malpractice insurance in these parts," Sisay said with a smile.

"Will he be able to tell me who is responsible for Michael Killigan's disappearance and whether bad medicine is the cause of it?"

"Possibly," said Sisay. "Names are almost never used. The looking-around man typically describes individuals whom one eventually recognizes, or who later reveal themselves."

"And if it's bad medicine, as your bosom buddy Lewis suspects, will he give me a counter-swear, or some kind of remedy, or what?"

"It would depend on what kind of illegal medicine is involved," said Sisay. "If it's witchcraft, Sam-King would send you to the *kondobla*, the antidote people. If it's bad medicine rather than witchcraft, he may very discreetly send you to a *hale nyamubla*, a bad medicine man or juju man. But, as I said, this would be illegal medicine. If it's simply ancestral displeasure, he would handle it himself by prescribing a suitable sacrifice. Think of Sam-King as a general practitioner, or a family physician, who would refer you to various specialists if your problem warranted such attentions."

Think of Sam-King as a mountebank or a palm reader, thought Boone. *Money inspires him with visions into the future.*

"Kong, kong," said a voice at the door, and the looking-around man's assistant entered alone, without speaking to Boone or Sisay.

"Where's my pocketknife?" said Boone.

Sisay put his finger to his lips and frowned.

The assistant built a small fire and spread a woven mat on the floor. On the mat, he placed the bundle of sticks and the bag of pebbles.

Sisay deferentially whispered a question in Mende, and the assistant gave a curt nod.

Sam-King appeared at the door and seated himself at the stick fire, placing herbs on the coals, closing his eyes and inhaling the smoke slowly and deeply. After a few minutes, one of his feet began twitching. Soon after, a hand did the same, and the tremblings spread to his limbs, torso, and head, mild at first, but gaining in intensity, until Sam-King's entire body was in convulsions, which appeared to be involuntary. The assistant solicitously prevented Sam-King from hurting himself on the furniture or extending his feet into the fire.

The convulsions gradually subsided, and the looking-around man opened his eyes in a blank stare. He reached down and picked up the short bundle of sticks and stared into it, squinting one eye, as if peering into a telescope of sticks. Then he set the bundle aside, burned more herbs, breathed more smoke, went into even more violent convulsions, and peered again into the stick bundle, this time with the astonished expression of an astronomer discovering a new planet.

He lowered the stick bundle and cried, "*Koli-bla!*"

Sisay stared aghast at Sam-King, then slowly moved his eyes to Boone.

"What'd he say?"

Sisay glanced again at the looking-around man, who was staring off in an amazed altered state.

"Baboon People," he said.

Sam-King chanted and turned toward the mat and the bag of stones. He selected seven pebbles and held them out toward Boone in his cupped hand and said something in Mende.

"Hold the pebbles in your right hand," said Sisay, "and think about what you want to know."

Boone did as instructed and returned the pebbles.

Sam-King placed the pebbles in ranks on the mat, murmuring and chanting as he worked. Boone looked at Sisay for translation, but he only shook his head.

Sam-King studied the stones for at least a quarter of an hour, occasionally speaking to them, singing or chanting. Then he closed his eyes, and again the convulsions set in. After they subsided, he opened his eyes and stared at the wall in a trance and began speaking in a monotone with an unblinking, expressionless face.

"Your brother is in the bush," said Sisay, "hiding from bad men. Your brother used very bad medicine against his enemies, and now the men who keep the medicine say it needs to be fed. Your brother must feed the medicine, or they will turn it against him."

Sam-King stopped talking and stared again, off in another transported vision.

"What does that mean?" Boone shouted in exasperation. "What kind of medicine? How's he supposed to feed it? Where *is* he? And how can I *find* him? That's what I'm paying twenty bucks for. Make sure he understands that!"

Sam-King collected all the stones and placed them in his hands, chanting again and gently tapping the back of his hands against the floor, like a dice thrower tapping the table for good luck. Again the stones were placed and studied. Again the convulsions, and the subsequent trance, monologue, and translation.

"A big man is going to ask you to offer a sacrifice. One of this big man's wives will take you to a holy place where the sacrifice will be offered. You must go with her to the holy place. If the sacrifice is offered according to instructions, your brother will return safely."

At the conclusion of this pronouncement, Sam-King curled up on the floor and appeared to sleep, except that he whispered and hummed, and occasionally gestured or sighed without opening his eyes. After a few minutes, he rose slowly, as if awakening from a deep sleep, uncertain of his whereabouts and of how he had arrived in Sisay's house.

"Ask him where I can find my brother now!" Boone said.

"It's not like that," said Sisay. "Once he's out of the trance, he has no memory of what was said, or what the stones said."

"Really!" yelled Boone. "I have no memory of my twenty bucks either! It's gone!"

Sam-King rubbed his eyes and looked genuinely confused, until his assistant apparently gave him a report of what had transpired. After more conversation, the two men rose to leave.

"Hey," called Boone. "What about my pocketknife?"

Sam-King paused on the threshold and smiled back at Boone. He patted the pocket of his pants, then pointed at Boone's pants and left.

Boone felt a smooth lump in his pocket. He refused to believe his fingers and brought the Swiss Army knife out where his eyes could do the job. He looked askance at Sisay and received only a wry smile.

Somehow these two con artists had found his knife and slipped it back into his pocket during the ceremony. Then left with his money.

"Where did you hide it?" asked Sisay.

"In the latrine," said Boone. "Above the spider's nest. I put it in a hole and plugged it with a dirt clod."

"Kong, kong," called Pa Ansumana, poking his head in the door and bestowing greetings on his sons with the gusto of a fraternity brother.

Sisay promptly described the session with the looking-around man, provoking the old man first to laughter, then to grave concern, then to laughter again when the narrative apparently concluded with the pocketknife.

Pa Ansumana chuckled loudly, rocked back onto his heels, and then erupted in outright laughter.

"What's so funny?" asked Boone.

Sisay covered his mouth, then explained. "He says a white man hiding something in the latrine is like a woman hiding something in her kitchen, or a peekin hiding something under its pillow. Where else do white men spend their time in Africa except in latrines? Next time you test a looking-around man, he says you should pick a better hiding place than the latrine you've been sitting in for ten days."

He seemed not the least troubled by the tragic death of Gigba, the disappearance of Killigan, Sisay's illness, the rumors of witchcraft in the village, or the unrest attending the elections. He placed a hand on Sisay's brow and pretended to burn himself, blowing on his fingers and shaking them, while merrily winking at Boone. Finally he flexed his arm and made a fist, the same "Be strong" signal he had made for Boone.

He settled on the floor and tended his pipe, remarking, according to Sisay, on the frail constitutions of white people and their almost continuous infirmities.

"I will explain all of this business to him," said Sisay. "The false news of Moussa Kamara's death, the beating in Bo, the report Pa Gigba gave us before he changed himself into a leopard and was killed in the bush, Sam-King's looking around."

Sisay spoke Mende, pausing now and again for deep feeble breaths, careful not to show his father pain or weakness. Pa Ansumana listened quietly, deliberatively sucking on the pipe Boone had given him as a gift on his naming day; occasionally his father interrupted Sisay with a brief question or a chuckle.

"He says Pa Gigba was not a sorcerer," said Sisay. "The leopard ear the hunter showed him was at least two days old. Pa Gigba was killed while traveling in the bush in his human shape."

"I've been hearing about all kinds of weird shit for the past two weeks," said Boone. "But nobody is going to convince me that a man can change himself into an animal."

As soon as the translation cleared Sisay's lips, Pa Ansumana gave a merry "so what?" shrug, and waited patiently for something more entertaining to talk about.

"I came here to find my brother," said Boone, "who is lost in the bush and may be in serious danger."

Sisay cleared his throat and translated. Boone twiddled his thumbs. Pa Ansumana tamped his pipe, using a shiny new *poo-mui* pipe nail, which also had been given to him by his new son, and which he used like a new broom.

"He says you will find your brother if God wants him to be found. In the meantime, he thinks you should learn to talk about something else. You talk only about your own misfortunes. And you never ask about the misfortunes of others."

"Ask him to tell me what he knows about Moiwo," said Boone. "Please," he added in the interest of being mannerly.

"He says Moiwo is a powerful man with a lot of land, many wives, and the ability to read *poo-mui* books. He has seen men like Moiwo only once or twice in his life, so powerful they are almost sorcerers, or forces from God. But he says Moiwo is a force that is trying to decide whether it should be good or bad. Like many powerful men, Moiwo asks himself whether it would be really wrong to do something bad on the way to doing something good. I have a son who is sometimes like that," which caused Sisay to blush afterward, almost as if he had translated it without understanding.

"Ask him if he thinks Moiwo had anything to do with Michael Killigan's disappearance."

"He says the Americans and the other *poo-mui* countries are giving Moiwo money because he gives them access to the diamonds and the minerals. So Moiwo has more money and men than the current Paramount Chief, Kabba Lundo, who sits on a wooden throne given to him by the British to commemorate Sierra Leone's independence. Kabba Lundo carries an elephant-tail fan, given to him by a Koranko chief, and he carries a staff topped with brass given to his ancestors by the British, and wears a tunic made of woven country cloth, which has been boiled in medicines, stamped with motifs that have secret meanings, and then adorned with Koranic amulets, called *sebeh*—all of which protect the chief from evil forces. He can barely move he is wrapped in so much power. Pa has seen bullets bounce off the garment."

Pa Ansumana paused and stuffed more tobacco in on top of the ashes in his pipe.

"But Kabba Lundo is getting old," Sisay said, resuming when Pa did. "Some say he is getting weak. Some say he is backing the wrong men in Freetown. Now Moiwo wants to be a Paramount Chief, and maybe it is his time, but sometimes old men do not give up power easily. They sometimes hold themselves in office by trickery instead of force, for old men can be extremely clever. Because they have lived longer, they know more tricks," he said, tamping his pipe and smiling smugly.

"Your brother was a particular favorite of Kabba Lundo, who was forever trying to get him to forget the American secret societies and join up with him as a Mende man. If your brother was openly supporting Kabba Lundo in the elections, that could make Moiwo angry. But not angry enough to humbug a *poo-mui*, that would take something much more serious. But just yesterday I have heard that when the *poo-muis* learned of your brother's disappearance, they contacted Section Chief Moiwo for assistance, not Kabba Lundo, who knew nothing of the disappearance until only recently. This was an insult to the Paramount Chief, and a tribute from the *poo-muis* to Moiwo, who lets them take the stones and metals from the mines without paying taxes on them. Kabba Lundo makes them pay the taxes.

"He went to see Kabba Lundo himself a short time ago, because of all the infant deaths in the village and all the talk of witchcraft. He and Kabba Lundo have their own plans for finding your brother and finding out if Moiwo had anything to do with your brother disappearing. You will see how two old men can outsmart a more powerful young one."

Pa giggled and appeared to be turning his and Kabba Lundo's plan over in his mind, savoring its ingenuity.

"Maybe Moiwo has been to see the Baboon Men," Sisay translated. "He can't say, but he would not be surprised. Who knows why people change themselves into animals and put their faith in bad medicines? Moiwo is probably changing himself into a baboon right now . . . a fat one, he suspects."

"Ask him if he *personally* has ever witnessed a person change into an animal, or an animal change into a human," asked Boone derisively.

When Sisay translated this question, Pa Ansumana snorted and spouted ash from his pipe, which swung dangerously off-beam, until his ragged molars reasserted themselves. He spoke in Mende, with the expression of a Brooklyn subway attendant telling somebody from Nebraska where to deposit the token.

"Sorcerers only change into animals when they are alone," translated Sisay, "so it is impossible for someone to see them change. Even if someone saw a person changing into an elephant or a baboon, they would never speak about it, or even admit it, because the witch or the shape-shifter would instantly kill the witness before the secret could be revealed."

"How convenient," said Boone.

Pa Ansumana interrupted Sisay before the latter could finish the answer, and the two of them spoke in Mende, Sisay gesturing periodically at Boone, while apparently explaining his skepticism.

"He says you don't believe people can change into animals because you come from the land of *Poo*. He has been told that in *poo-mui* land, the villages are no longer surrounded by bush, so the people there have no need of changing into animals. The *poo-mui* villages grew so big that they swallowed up all the bush, so in the land of *Poo* it is the animals who must learn shape-shifting, so they can assume human form and live in villages that cover the entire country."

Pa Ansumana tugged on the pipe Boone had given him and chuckled mischievously, then continued.

"He says white men have magic boxes with windows that contain stories, and if they see a story in the box, then they believe it, but if someone tells them what they saw with their own eyes, they don't believe it.

"He says I should ask you if you believe that *poo-muis* really walked around up on the moon, and if so, did you actually see them do it? Personally, he does not believe that *poo-muis* walked on the moon. He believes it was just a story *poo-muis* saw in the window of their magic box. When all the people in Sierra Leone were talking about how *poo-muis* were supposedly up walking on the moon, there was an outbreak of eye infections." Sisay stopped. "What you would call 'pinkeye.' And to this day, the people in Sierra Leone call pink-eye, or conjunctivitis, 'Apollo,' because they believe that when the *poo-muis* were up walking around on the moon, they shook so much moon dust loose that it irritated the eyes of people all over Sierra Leone. He himself does not believe this, because he has lived long enough to know that there was an even worse outbreak of pinkeye long ago, before people were claiming that *poo-muis* could walk on the moon."

"Tell him it's made of cheese," interrupted Boone. "And if he turns himself into a cow, he can grab a bite on the way over."

Sisay glowered at Boone and nodded for Pa to continue.

"All over Sierra Leone, hunters quickly cut the ears off the animals they kill for just this reason. If they kill a witch or a sorcerer traveling in the shape of an animal, the animal will change back into its human form, and they will be accused of murder. Do you think every hunter in Sierra Leone would cut the ears off their prey if they did not know as sure as we are sitting here that they may have killed a human in the shape of an animal?"

"That's like saying Sun Myung Moon must be God because there are so many Moonies," snapped Boone.

"When he was a young man," Sisay continued, "his first big wife was suspected of witchcraft because she had dreamed about a woman and caused the death of the woman's son. One morning when he went out to his farm, he found the big wife had been caught and killed in one of the traps they had made together on the farm. Do you think that if she was wearing her human shape she would be stupid enough to walk into a bush pig trap that she herself had helped build? No, she had obviously been traveling on the farm in the shape of a bush pig and had been caught and killed, which of course had changed her back to her human shape."

Boone took his weary head in his hands and shook it, groaning, "Ask him—please!—does he have *any* idea what happened to my brother?" said Boone.

Pa Ansumana made a comment, then laughed through his clenched teeth.

"What?" said Boone.

"He said maybe another white man has gone and killed himself."

Boone looked at his grandfather's face, which was a map of laugh lines, his eyes a-twinkle with amusement. "Real funny, I guess," said Boone.

"It's an inside joke," said Sisay. "Don't be offended. As far as I can tell, the Mende don't believe in suicide."

"You mean, they discourage people from killing themselves?" said Boone. "What a sound social policy."

"No," said Sisay, "I don't think they believe that anyone has ever committed suicide. I can't explain it to them. After I'd been here a year or so, a Peace Corps Volunteer up north in Koranko country killed himself, and the whole northern province went into shock. Word spread and soon the entire country was talking about it. The Mende men in the village came to me laughing uproariously, expecting me to tell them that this was an elaborate *poo-mui* prank. What would these *poo-muis* think of next? Not even a *poo-mui* would be crazy enough to kill *himself*. I tried to tell them that it was more a question of despair or depression, not simple craziness. They laughed uproariously.

"I tried again, and they laughed even harder. To them I was just carrying on with an outlandish farce. Why would a man kill *himself*, they wanted to know, and not his enemy, mind you, who probably had caused his despair by fraud or witchcraft? This was too rich for them. They could never swallow it. They forced themselves to admire the ingenuity of the story, but it was time to come clean.

"I was up half the night in a roundtable discussion in the *barri*. No African man would think of killing himself, they said, and certainly no *poo-mui* who came from a country where there was food everywhere and everyone was attractively plump, well fed, and protected by powerful medicines. I said that in the land of *Poo* quite a few *poo-muis* considered killing themselves from time to time, and some of them actually did it; that this was something that everyone in America had heard of or had seen. I told them that I personally had a friend who had lost his child and had become so sad that he had tried to kill himself, but someone had stopped him, just in time.

"The Mende men all looked at themselves and held their breath, as if to say, 'Shall we let this king trickster get away with this monkey business or shall we call him on it?' They laughed again and refused to hear any more.

"So now, whenever we reach a point in our conversations where there seems to be no conceivable explanation for what has happened, the people in this village throw up their hands and say, 'Well, maybe another *poo-mui* has gone and killed himself.' It's a standing joke. The way you or I would say, 'Once in a blue moon . . .' "

(**15**)

"**B**at shit," said Mack over the speakerphone. "Let me see, I think the technical term is 'guano.' So says the lab analysis report, which they just faxed to us. And the black strips holding the whole mess together are strips of cured boa constrictor skins. The red spout is some kind of mineral found over there, and," he added, "something a little weird here . . . Human blood. AB negative. They said it's a very rare blood type." Mack snickered. "That's your blood type, right?"

"How did you know that?" Randall demanded.

"I didn't know it," Mack said quickly. "I didn't. It was a joke. I was kidding."

"So was I," said Randall. "Mine's type O," he lied. "Must be African blood."

"Yeah," said Mack.

"So that's it? Nothing else?"

"That's it," said Mack. "Bat shit, boa constrictor skin, a mineral, and human blood. The people at the lab said they would put it back together as best they could and mail it back to you."

"Blood, bat shit, and boa constrictor skins," Randall muttered under his breath. "Somebody sent me blood and bat shit from Africa."

"How's our search for an anthropologist who knows about . . . what tribe?"

"The Mende," said Mack. "He returns from sabbatical today. I left a detailed description of the . . . bundle with one of his graduate students, and told him you needed an expert witness or a consultant. Professor Harris Sawyer, University of Pennsylvania. And the

Comco people are waiting for you down the hall on the Beach Cove foreclosure."

Randall left his notebook computer and drifted down the hall to conference room A. He wondered momentarily how it was that he was walking on the floor. What if since birth he had seen people walking only on the ceilings? Then walking on the floor would be the odd thing to do. What if these walls were not solid at all, but laser holograms that looked exactly like wallpaper patterns?

In the conference room, Randall found two in-house flunkies from Comco flanking the bank's lead counsel, Mr. Lance Buboe, a senior VP and old friend of the name partners of Randall's firm. Buboe was known chiefly for a nine-inch flap of hair that grew out of the left side of his head, just above his ear, and was trained and pasted up and across the glowing pink convexity of his head, all the way over to his right ear. Flap, the associates called him. Flap and company were wearing ties. Randall was also wearing a tie. And he was suddenly struck by the absolute uselessness of ties. Where did they come from? Who wore the first one? Why? Are these things vestigial bibs? Are they symbolic yokes? Tethers? Ornaments? They are not worn by the kind of people who are concerned about adding a splash of color to their wardrobe. Were they meant to cover cracked shirt buttons? What kind of costume had they all dressed in that day without even stopping for a second to wonder why?

"There he is," said Buboe, rising from his chair with a warm smile. "Genghis Khan. Look at him, boys! There are a lot of young associates vying to hold this man's armor! Great work on that lift stay," said Buboe extravagantly. "Brilliant work. Chuck is very pleased also," he added, giving Randall a knowing look. "Very pleased. And he controls all the work coming out of Chicago."

"I want to suggest something," said Randall, wondering if he would be able to go through with what he had in mind. "It's about this Beach Cove deal."

"What's there to discuss?" said Buboe. "Thanks to you, the stay's lifted. We foreclose, take the property away from these assholes, and sell it."

"I just want to propose something," said Randall.

I went to church this morning, Randall could say. He could tell Buboe and his boys what had happened. *I haven't told you*, he could say, *but I may be very sick. If I have cancer, it's in my brain. It could kill me very quickly. Within months. If it's not cancer, it's something else that's . . . affecting me. So I went to church, and I was trying to pray, because I've been so . . . desperate lately. So helpless. So afraid. It changes you. I was praying. I was trying to pray, because I had no choice. I had nothing else left. I was alone, and I was afraid that I could be dead soon, or maybe that I was having some kind of breakdown. And after I started praying, it occurred to me that if God would let me go on living, I would do more good. I could at least try to do more good. Instead of looking for fights, I could bring people together and help them resolve their disputes. I was wondering if Comco would be willing to give the Beach Cove partners another chance?*

And if he actually said that, how long would he have to stare into their open mouths? News of the psychotic break would make it around the firm and out to the coastal offices within an hour. Every lawyer in the place would be behind closed doors talking about how Randall Killigan hosted a prayer breakfast and then tried to give away the store to an adverse party. *Get a straitjacket. Get some sedatives. Who knows what he'll do next?*

Instead, he regained his composure and said, "I was just making sure there was absolutely no question of a deal."

"If you suggested that we should deal with those assholes," said Buboe with a horse laugh, "I'd find a new lawyer."

"If you *wanted* to deal with them," Randall said jovially, "I'd get a new client. As it is, I'm charging Mr. Bilksteen tuition and trying to find him work in estate planning."

Once the Comco business was wrapped up, he stormed back to his office and tried to act warlike. Maybe all this tumor business was interfering with him. Maybe he was walking around thinking about dying without even realizing it. Maybe he needed a designated driver to run over people when they got in his way.

A messenger from a firm across town and a phone slip on his computer desktop program told him that someone had pulled a fast one on him over in Judge Baxter's court. The hearing he had spent two weeks preparing for had been continued, and the continuance had the potential for sending the whole case to hell's basement. He had his Code in his hands looking for a section he could pull out of his shoe like a razor blade.

He fed the messages to Benjy and swore. *See what happens if you as much as look the other way to take a pee? Wham, they fuck you!*

The speakerphone buzzed. Randall drew his broadsword as in days of yore and stabbed the blinking button.

"Indiana Jones on line three," said Mack, "back from Africa and ready to consult. Harris Sawyer, professor of anthropology, University of Pennsylvania."

As he introduced himself and was acquainted with the professor's qualifications, Randall calmly reminded himself that he was about to speak with a person who was not a bankruptcy attorney—was not even a lawyer—which meant he could not terrorize or annihilate the person, but instead had to be nice to him. Getting something out of somebody by being nice to them took at least three times as long as a simple threat to destroy their careers and seize all their tangible assets, which was why he gritted his teeth and looked at his watch whenever he was forced to be nice.

"I have a client who is a wealthy, eccentric collector, whom I shall not identify, but let's call her Colette. Colette married an entrepreneur in the import-export business. Let's call him, I don't know, Trader Vic, how's that? Trader Vic travels to West Africa a couple times a year and mails back African art, cloths, carvings, that sort of thing, to Colette. Anyway, on his last trip, Vic went to a place called Sierra Leone to buy some art from a tribe called the Mende tribe, which my associate tells me you know a lot about."

"I do," said Sawyer.

"We're, of course, prepared to pay a reasonable consultation fee, by the way," said Randall, "but on the last trip, the one to see the Mende, Vic disappeared . . . vanished! The next thing Colette knows, she gets a parcel from Freetown, Sierra Leone, and inside is a little black bundle, shaped like a big egg or a little football, and it has this red spout sticking out of it. And here's the funny part: She knows Vic didn't send it because the label on the package was not in his handwriting and whoever sent the thing misspelled her name."

Professor Sawyer cleared his throat. "A Mende person wishes to harm your client," he said, "or, more likely, someone wants to kill her. I suppose the other possibility is that they want to harm Trader Vic by harming his wife. The red spout is called *tingoi*; together with the black bundle, it's called *ndilei*, a powerful, malignant, illegal medicine, which is created by a witch or a juju man and is used to harm people."

Randall's scalp pringled and his heart jumped a notch, stalled, then sped onward.

"Why would witches or juju men want to harm my client?"

"My guess is somebody hired them to do the job," said Sawyer. "I hope you don't take umbrage at the comparison, but villagers hire bad medicine men, or *hale nyamubla*, to harm an enemy with witchcraft or bad medicine the same way an American would, say, hire a lawyer to sue somebody."

"A *medicine?*" asked Randall.

"Yes," said Sawyer, "but in the broad African sense of a charm, or a talisman. *Ndilei* is especially associated with witches and witchcraft, or 'witch business,' as the Mende call it. Once the bundle is placed in or near the victim's house, the person who planted it selects a night to dream of the victim, and on that night the medicine transforms itself into a witch spirit, takes on the shape of a bat or a boa constrictor, and attacks."

"Attacks?" said Randall hoarsely, flushing to his ears and breathing harder. "What would it do to, uh, Colette?"

"You get different opinions on the subject," said Sawyer, "depending on whether the bundle was created by a witch or a juju man. But most Mende would say that the *ndilei* assumes its animal form at the appointed hour and then sucks blood from the neck or a limb of the victim, and later the victim sickens and dies, or one of the victim's limbs withers or becomes paralyzed. What we call polio the Mende believe is caused by a boa constrictor swallowing the limbs of its sleeping victims. But more often the victim simply gets sick and slowly dies. Hemorrhage seems to be a favorite, fever followed by coma, hallucinations, seizures . . ."

"Hallucinations?" asked Randall hoarsely. "Coma?"

"Yes," said Sawyer, "but remember, these are physical symptoms, part of the physical world. In the spiritual realm, what's happening is that the witch spirit has attacked the soul, or *ngafei*, the vital force of the human victim while he or she is asleep."

"But, but . . ." said Randall, violently loosening his tie, "if, uh, Colette claims she *saw* a bat one night, but it was some time ago, and . . . Well, nothing happened to her. I mean, she doesn't have any withered limbs . . ."

"Another favorite," interrupted Sawyer, "is pulmonary tuberculosis, in which case the witches are believed to have poured hot witch water on the person's soul, *ngafei*, causing blisters and the burning sensation one feels after a spasm of violent coughing."

"Witch water?" repeated Randall, struggling for air and planting his fist on his chest.

"But any physical manifestations are almost beside the point, because, as I said, what's happening takes place in the supernatural realm. The attack is on the person's *ngafei*, or soul, which is an inseparable counterpart of the victim's human form. But in Africa the supernatural *is* the physical, so it is described in physical terms, as the witch giving the victim witch meat to eat, or the witch spirit eating the victim's belly, or the witch spirit sucking blood from a vein, or . . ."

"Blood?" said Randall. "That's significant? You said that before. I mean, Colette did say something about blood, like, I think, once she said there was blood coming out of the bundle. Does that mean anything?"

A long silence filled Randall's ear.

"When my students ask me these questions," said Sawyer, "I use the two-hat method. First I'll put on my Caucasian anthropologist hat. Some anthropologists who have studied the Mende speculate that the *ndilei* or witch bundle has bladders or small bottles of blood inside of it, so that when the witch doctor finds it and accuses its owner of witchcraft, he can prove that it has been used to harm people. Now, off with the anthropologist's hat, and on with my villager's cap. As a person who lived in a Mende village for four years, I would say that a witch bundle containing blood is one that has obviously already taken on its animal form and attacked at least one victim, from whom it had siphoned blood. As we've discussed, a villager would now expect the victim to sicken and die."

Randall tore his tie completely off and threw it on the floor.

"But if he, if she, let's say Colette," Randall said, stuttering and having difficulty breathing. "Even if she was silly enough to believe in this wacky stuff. I mean, if the witch spirit had *entered* her, she'd know about it, right?"

Sawyer chuckled in Randall's ear.

"WHAT'S SO GODDAMN MOTHERFUCKING FUNNY?" Randall screamed, hurling a glass paperweight commemorating the Marauder Reorganization at the wall and backhanding a picture of Marjorie on her horse off his desk.

In the hallway, paralegals and secretaries scurried by, giving Randall's open door a wide berth, and once safely out of range rolled their eyes with looks that said, *Steer clear! He's at it again! Somebody must have queered another deal on him.*

"I didn't mean to be flip, Mr. Killigan," Sawyer hurriedly explained. "I was just amused that our conversation was touching upon one thorny anthropological conundrum after another, and that these enigmas are almost impossible to explain in a single sentence. But even more than that," he quickly added, "I was impressed at how a man of your intellectual prowess intuitively poses the very questions that anthropologists argue over for decades without resolving."

"And?" Randall said. "So? If a witch spirit had, I don't know, *gone* into her, then maybe she wouldn't know? It would just be there, hiding, or something? Talk! TALK TO ME! Don't giggle into the phone about conundrums! Sure it's a big puzzle for you. I've got a client who wants to know if this *thing* did anything to her. She's quite superstitious. Yes, very superstitious! So I would like to explain the entire matter to her, the way the Africans think of it, so I can put her mind at ease."

"I don't think the African explanation will put her mind at ease," said Sawyer, "because it is changeable and, by definition, mysterious. It is tempting to always talk about the *honei*, or witch spirit, as traveling in the shape of a witch bird or a voracious wild animal, in short as a foreign power operating at night, *outside* of its host. But the Mende also talk of the witch spirit as an *extension* or a replica of the host.

"I always use the example of cancer," said Sawyer.

"Cancer!" shouted Randall. "Witches cause cancer!?"

"No, no," said Sawyer. "Well," he added, "maybe. But no. It's a comparison I use in class. People in our country like to describe cancer as an invader attacking a victim, even though most cancers come from a single mutation of the person's *own* cell. There is no invading virus or bacterium. Cancer *is* the person, but it is also a deviant . . . *force*, which grows until it takes over . . . and kills the person."

"But she's not dying!" Randall argued, verging on a desperate whine. "Nothing's happened to her. She hasn't coughed up any witch meat, or gone into a coma, or gotten polio. So what I want to tell her is, that if this witch *thing* attacked her, she would know about it, because she would get sick. Right?"

"If your question is, do the Mende believe that the *ndilei* will *always* kill or maim its intended victim, the answer is no."

"I would hope so," said Randall. "I mean, the whole thing is completely fucking ridiculous to begin with. But I guess I was asking my question with an eye toward reassuring her that, even if she thought there was something to this witch or juju stuff, I could tell her that it doesn't always make you sick, or paralyze you, or kill you. I could tell her that not even the Mende believe that."

"That's correct," said Sawyer. "Because sometimes the witch spirit sets out to kill its victim and discovers, instead, that the person harbors a kindred spirit, or that the victim would be more useful to the witch as a host."

"A host," Randall repeated, feeling his throat tighten. "What do you mean, a host?"

"A witch host," Sawyer said. "Instead of killing or injuring the person, the witch spirit—or *honei*, in Mende—enters the person's belly and sets up housekeeping, turning him into a witch host, or witch person—a *honei-mui*. The two then spend the rest of their lives together destroying farms, eating children . . . feeding on the spirits of others."

·

The people in Ndevehun were accustomed to seeing a vehicle arrive every month or so, with supplies for the midwife including Guinness stout, which she sold on the side, and sometimes aspirins, or if fever was rampant, perhaps some *poo-mui* fever medicine. But no one could remember the last time a real medical doctor had seen patients in the village itself. The clinic was fifteen miles down the road in Mattru, where it was not unusual, after waiting in line in the sun all day, to be turned away in the evening without getting in to see the doctor.

On this particular day, one of the missionary doctors, a Krio from Freetown who had been to medical school in England, was receiving patients inside the midwife's quarters. All the women of the village had lined up outside—alone or with their children—chatting excitedly about the prospect of *poo-mui* medicine, free and in their own village! As each woman emerged from her visit with the doctor, she was closely interrogated by the women standing in line about the symptoms she had described to the visiting physician and the treatment she had received. The first four women had received only tablets of medicine for their treatment. At last, a woman emerged who had been given an injection, which, as all the women knew, was the most powerful medicine dispensed by doctors of white medicine. The woman said she had complained of fevers and headaches at night and nausea after eating.

One after another, the women in line went into the hut and complained of fevers and headaches at night and nausea after eating. Sometimes the gambit worked, and the patient emerged, holding a cotton swab over the injection site and beaming with satisfaction, but other times they emerged downcast, with only pills or lotions to show for their pains.

While the clinic was in progress, two Land-Rovers pulled into the village, containing *poo-muis* from Freetown and several Africans, one of whom the villagers recognized as Section Chief Idrissa Moiwo, along with other African big men, who wore the epaulets and military chapeaus of various ministries in Freetown. Section Chief Moiwo's speaker stood on a bench in the court *barri* and addressed the village through a bullhorn. The doctor had been hired by Mistah Randall Killigan of America. The medicine was being provided as a gift from Mistah Randall Killigan, father of Michael Killigan, also known to the villagers as Lamin Kaikai, who recently could not be found in his village, and whose father was desperate to find him. More medicine would be provided as a gift, including injections, vaccinations, rehydration fluids, infant formula, and all the most powerful *poo-mui* medicines. In addition, a pump was to be installed at one of the village wells, courtesy of Mistah Randall Killigan, as a gift to the people of this village, who it was hoped would provide any information they might have on the whereabouts of Lamin Kaikai to their chief, or to the speaker of Section Chief Idrissa Moiwo, who, though he had been to England and America for schooling and could read *poo-mui* books, had come back to the land of his birth and made a gift of himself to the Mende people. He was a Mende man. His mother was a Mende woman. His father was part Temne, but his father's heart had been with the Mende people. He loved his people and he knew his people loved Lamin Kaikai, so he was doing everything in his power to find brother Lamin. All rumors of Lamin's whereabouts should be reported to the speaker of Section Chief Idrissa Moiwo as soon as possible.

Also, if a villager or anyone else could provide information that would lead to the discovery of Lamin Kaikai, that person or persons would receive cash in the amount of five thousand United States dollars, or the exchange equivalent in leones.

Next, Section Chief Idrissa Moiwo was introduced, a stout man with the haunches and bulbous behind of a man who did a lot of sitting and eating, bound up in safari shorts and jacket, with black sunglasses and a quasi-military beret, complete with a medallion commemorating his service as a Minister of Finance for the former President in Freetown. Section Chief Moiwo effusively paid tribute to the absent American, Mistah Randall Killigan, for his generous gifts to the village, and refrained from mentioning that he himself had received an air-conditioned Land-Rover as a gift from the American to assist him in his investigation of the disappearance of the fine young Peace Corps Volunteer, Mr. Michael Killigan, the friend and counselor to the people of the village, whose disappearance had so saddened the people of his village, and whose hearts have been filled with sorrow and anguish since his disappearance. Construction of the pump for the well would begin as soon as parts arrived from Freetown. And the doctor would remain in the village, operating out of the midwife's quarters, until the people had received all the medical care they needed or desired.

A truck would arrive shortly bearing fifty bags of rice, also a gift from the generous Mistah Randall Killigan, who was desperately seeking information about the whereabouts of his son, Michael Killigan, Lamin Kaikai.

When the rice arrived, it was emblazoned with the logo of USAID, along with the warning in big red letters, which no one could read: "THIS RICE IS A GIFT FROM THE PEOPLE OF THE UNITED STATES. IT IS NOT TO BE SOLD IN WHOLE OR IN PART." The bags of rice had been turned over to the government at the docks in Freetown, and sold in the usual fashion to various wholesalers, who then normally transported it to the outlying town markets, where it was sold again, and on down to the villages, where it was sold by the cup to other villagers. In this case, Randall Killigan had arranged from Indiana for the purchase of fifty bags of the USAID rice from the Ministry of Agriculture, before it was sold to the wholesalers. Then he arranged to have it delivered to Killigan's village. Moiwo graciously arranged for the delivery of the rice to the village, and even allowed it to be given away. But he charged the chief a healthy tariff, and permitted him to tax any resale of the rice in the markets or along the roadside.

The injection of free rice into the village economy cut the going rate for a bag of rice by half. The farmers who had worked all year to bring in rice crops were forced to compete with traders who had paid nothing for their rice.

The offer of a reward amounting to an unimaginable sum of money threw the village into a turmoil and started a bull market in black magic and divination, for everyone knew that a looking-around man or a juju man was the best way to find someone or something that was lost. Within a week, the offer of the reward drove the village insane with greed. First off, all of the medicines dispensed from the midwife's hut by the Krio doctor were collected in a pail, and the pharmacopoeia of multicolored pills was hauled off and sold to the citizens of other villages, who randomly selected pills, paid outrageous sums, and took them to remedy everything from hernias to gas to gangrene. The money from the sale of the pills was then paid to looking-around men who advised their clients on how to find the missing *poo-mui*.

Back in Ndevehun, the crime rate soared as people stole radios, tape decks, farm implements, batteries, medicines, kerosene, and anything else that wasn't nailed down to raise money to consult the best diviners and find the missing *poo-mui* before someone else did. But consulting diviners was not good enough to ensure the success of the various search teams comprised of eager young men who left their farms and mines in hopes of winning the reward. With such money at stake, they also had to hire juju men to sabotage the efforts of their neighbors and thwart the competition. Before long the village of Ndevehun was a hornet's nest of swears, counter-swears, juju, witch business, and sorcery.

Next, the first woman who had received the injection on the first day became quite ill with a terrible gastritis. When the other women who had received injections heard of her illness, they too fell sick, convinced that it was the injection that had caused their neighbor's illness and equally convinced that they were similarly afflicted. Some of the medicines being sold out of buckets aggravated the conditions of patients who took them, and the overall health of the village plummeted. After the pump was mounted on the well and cemented in place with concrete, a bolt which had been improperly secured to the plunger snapped, and no water could be pumped or drawn from the well because it was now sealed shut by the fixture.

And that was only the beginning, for rumor had it that even more money was on its way.

(16)

Following the session with the looking-around man, Sisay took to his quarters with another bout of fevers, and sent the women, children, Boone, and the other helpless, dependent relatives to eat at Pa Ansumana's house. With no translator, conversation consisted of short guttural sentences followed by exaggerated nods when Pa and Boone pretended to understand each other.

After dinner, Pa took a gnawed drumstick bone and placed it in front of Boone. Then the old man selected one for himself and bit it in half, chewing contentedly and pausing to suck marrow from the bone, until it was as hollow as a whistle.

"*Nyandengo!*" said Pa, again nudging a bone in Boone's direction.

Had Boone known this meal would have to last him three days, maybe he would have tried a chew and tasted a little bone marrow, which Sisay had told him was a delicacy in these parts. Instead, he thanked his father, but declined the bone, patting his belly repeatedly and saying, "Belly full too much."

After dinner, he went back to his room, extinguished his hurricane lamp, and sat in the moonlight streaming in through the cracks of his shutters. He threw open the shutters and peered up into the blue-jeweled vaults overhead. Was *Ngewo* up there somewhere in His cave, frolicking every now and again with the ancestors, who lived across the river in the village of white sands? Did He like to receive a chicken and a big pot of sweet upland rice? Did He call Himself Allah and demand that men face the east, bow, and pray to Him five times a day? Did He thrive on devotion, as the Catholics believed? Did He annually like to watch while a heart was cut out of a victim's chest and offered up to Him at dawn, as the Aztecs and thoracic surgeons believed? Did it really bother Him if people didn't worship on the Sabbath?

Maybe only His name changes through the ages, and every person's conception of Him is correct, as in the parable of the blind men feeling the elephant, with each blind man describing a different animal, depending upon which part of the beast they had hold of at the time. And to the Mende? *Ngewo mu gbate mahei:* God is the chief who made us. *Na leke Ngewo keni ta a lo ma:* Nothing happens, unless God agrees (to let it happen). *Ngewo lo maha le:* God, the chief, has the last word.

A chill swept through him, and nothing resembling a breeze occurred at this time in the dry season. He steadied himself, saw his friends the diamond maggots spinning again, then fell to his knees. He operated his heavy, cold limbs from afar, like a puppeteer in charge of a man-sized dummy. He could feel his blood—cold as crimson slush—coursing under his skin and flushing through his organs.

He took two of the chloroquine pills and lay down in the moonlight, waiting to see if he indeed had malaria. After the cold came heat and hot sweats. The next bout of fevers rattled his teeth and confirmed his suspicions. Borrowing Sisay's technique, he knotted a T-shirt and used it as a safety mouthpiece. Soon his lower back glowed, a rack of inflamed meninges, simmering like an order of large-end ribs on a bed of coals.

Pa Ansumana sent a woman to dab him with cool rags, but otherwise he was alone, listening to Sisay groan from time to time in the next room, hoping he would not die an ignoble death stranded in a village in West Africa. *Would they send his body home?* he suddenly wondered. Maybe the Mende would just inter him somewhere in the bush, where his flesh would keep for at least a week before microorganisms would chew him back into topsoil and loam.

He curled up in bed and waited for Missus Sickness. Soon he would be studying the ebb and flow of his fevers, charting the complex reproductive cycles of the malarial parasites, multiplying feverishly into hordes, then lysing into cellular debris at the hands of his immune system. He had read enough to know that he was now what parasitologists called an *intermediate host* for the malarial parasite, genus *Plasmodium*, a microscopic creature with the most complicated reproductive cycle in all of microbiology. The *definitive host*, the anopheles mosquito, had drunk blood from some other malaria victim, probably Sisay, containing cells that then multiplied sexually with other cells in the mosquito, until they were injected into Boone—the intermediate host—who was now providing a breeding reservoir for another batch of parasites that would infest his red blood cells and reproduce asexually. The furious reproductive cycles coincided nicely with the quartan fevers, until his blood was awash in toxins and the debris of his own exploded red blood cells.

If he had the sometimes fatal *falciparum* malaria, the parasite-infected red blood cells could choke off the supply of blood to his brain, leaving brain stew (simmer on low, until it thickens, then remove . . .).

When he wasn't shaking with chills, he warmed to his new ecological role of intermediate host. It occurred to him that perhaps humans were parasites breeding in the definitive host of the earth. While on earth, they multiplied sexually, until they were transformed by death and injected into some cosmological intermediate host, where they reproduced asexually, until they were returned to the earth again as gametocytes with a fresh urge to mate.

After the first set of high fevers, he slept until dawn and woke in a profound lethargy, at once depressing and peaceful. He heard an internal-combustion engine, which charged through his dreams like some freakish metal bush creature powered by fire and explosions. Eventually, he woke up without moving a muscle, stared out his window, and watched the world, of which he was no longer a part. If death came, he could not care; death's fevers could not be any worse than the ones he had already thrown off. And if life continued, what future terror could disturb him now, in this resting place of exhaustion and euphoria? He was spent and utterly passive, a heap of organs and bones in a sack of membranes, with limbs that moved self-consciously through space.

He spent the tropical morning sucking oranges, and after sucking them he looked at the mangled green rinds and thought about himself—empty, feeble, dehydrated, sticky, and sick to death of Africa. He would leave, if leaving were not so difficult; and if the woman at the Peace Corps information desk had been there, she could have said, "I told you so." It would be a twelve-hour trip into Freetown, another day or two lining up a plane ticket, a day or two waiting for a plane that would be scheduled and rescheduled without ever leaving. WAIT. Even then, he would first have to fly to Europe or North Africa, and make more arrangements. The first day after recuperating, he would wake up and wonder what had possessed him to leave Sierra Leone without first finding his best friend.

A servant girl tapped at his door with a fresh batch of rehydration salts and more sucking oranges. Behind her came another "Kong, kong" and the shaggy head of Sam Lewis appeared.

"Ain't it funny how white people run into each other in this country?" he said. "Oh sha about the fever business," he added. "Do you have plenty of the pills?"

Boone nodded. Lewis pulled up the lone chair.

"I got a ride here with Moiwo," he said. "After I left Bo, I had agriculture business down in that neck of the bush, so I stopped in Killigan's village to nose around for you. I ran into Moiwo and chewed the fat with him. He's in touch with Killigan's dad," Lewis explained, "and Killigan's dad is bankrolling a manhunt. As for Moussa Kamara, the guy was a thief from the get-go. His own father admitted as much to me. I talked to them after Moiwo dropped the body off. The groundnut girl was his kid sister, who always stuck up for him, even when he was caught red-handed, so I wouldn't put much stock in her version of the story. Moiwo's hot to find your buddy, though. He's got three Land-Rovers on the job, staffed with his own men, and doing a thorough job of it."

"What about the body parts and the Baboon business you were telling me he was into?" asked Boone weakly.

"That's election business," Lewis said. "Probably rumors started by his opponents. That's got nothing to do with your buddy. Though there are those in his village who say that your buddy was into illegal medicine himself and got in over his head. Again, pure gossip. *Congosa*, as they say in Freetown talk. As near as I can tell, Moiwo's got nothing against your friend. In fact, if he finds him it will bolster his reputation with the government men and *poo-mui* embassies in Freetown, and there's money. There's a five-thousand-dollar reward out for information, and Moiwo gets more on top if he gets the job done right. I think Killigan's old man has found the right guy for the job. Moiwo will find your buddy, if he can be found."

"Where's Moiwo now?" asked Boone.

"Here," said Lewis, "over in his compound, probably working over one of his young wives. He's been on the road, you know. He wants to take you back to Freetown with him, so you can meet with the embassy people."

They were interrupted by people banging pots in the courtyard. And from the direction of the *barri*, where the woman-damage cases were argued, Boone could hear an announcement being made.

"Everybody come out dae houses! Everybody listen! Everybody come out! Witchfinders done come just now! Paramount Chief Kabba Lundo he done bring witchfinders for cleansing our village. Everybody come out dae houses! Everybody listen!"

Boone's door opened, and a wan and haggard Sisay appeared. He barely acknowledged Lewis with a nod of his head, and summoned Boone out of bed.

"Is that a real witchfinder they got out there?" Lewis asked.

Sisay nodded. "So I'm told. I was also told that we all must go to the *barri*."

"I've heard about these witch cleansings," said Lewis. "Never seen one, mind you, but I've heard. They take three days, and there's no eating or sleeping allowed. If it's all the same to you boys, I'm leaving. And my advice to you," he said in Boone's direction, "is to get out of here while you still can."

"It's too late," said Sisay, weakened by fever and fatigue, and not liking Lewis any more for it. "The witchfinder has sealed off the village. No one may leave until it's over."

"We'll see about that," said Lewis. "I'm taking the first *podah-podah* into Bo town."

Lewis marched out the door first, followed by Boone and Sisay, who walked stiffly and gingerly out to the *barri* and seated themselves on a mud wall. Lewis went to Moiwo's Land-Rover and grabbed his daypack out of the back. He spoke briefly to the section chief, who was ensconced in the passenger's seat conferring with other uniformed men. Then he headed across the courtyard for the path that led from the village.

Villagers were assembling in the *barri* and gathering around a slight man in a simple powder-blue burnoose. His head was shaved or naturally bald, and the flesh of his face followed the contours of his skull, throwing huge black eyes that seemed to be all pupil and no iris into high relief. If this was the witchfinder, he did not go in for the amulets, cowrie shells, animal teeth, and medicine pouches that adorned the hunters, the looking-around man, and the chiefs. Instead, he held a wooden staff, with animal totems, figurines, and designs carved into it. The top of the staff was notched, and lashed in the notch was a wooden hand mirror. Except for the staff and the shaved head, the witchfinder looked like a typical old pa on his way to morning prayers.

Another speaker stood and announced that the witchfinder had completely surrounded the village with a white cotton thread, and that if anyone broke the thread or crossed the boundary, he or she would surely sicken and die.

Several of the villagers pointed at Lewis and shouted, alarmed at the prospect of anyone attempting to leave the village. The man in the blue burnoose rose to his feet and called out to Lewis, then set off after the *poo-mui* fool, twirling his staff and summoning two assistants to follow him. Lewis waved off the witchfinder. The crowd rose to its feet and talked excitedly among themselves.

As Lewis made for the path out of the village, the witchfinder called out to him that if he crossed the boundary marked by the white thread, he would die. As the witchfinder drew abreast of him, Lewis turned and spoke in Krio, telling his pursuer that he did not live in this village and did not intend to partake in a witch cleansing, which, he had heard, could last as long as a week. He was leaving, and the witchfinder could take his white cotton thread to hell and rot with it.

While Lewis explained himself, the witchfinder skillfully and un-obtrusively positioned his staff so that the mirror showed Lewis his own reflection as he spoke. At least twice, Lewis noted his own annoyed reflection in the glass and irritably waved it off.

Boone and Sisay and the rest of the villagers had left the *barri*, where they had been assembling, and were now gathering around the witchfinder and Lewis, anxious to see if this reckless *poo-mui* would ignore the warnings of a real witchfinder.

As Boone brought up the rear of the crowd, he saw that, indeed, a cotton thread crossed the path and had been fastened to the twigs and branches of the bush fronting the village, continuing along the perimeter until it was obscured by the huts and compounds it sur-rounded. He was relieved to see that the thread seemed to pass behind the row of pan-roofed outhouses, preserving access to the latrines.

Lewis stopped at the boundary, turned, and apologized to the witchfinder for his previous rude remarks, but again explained that he did not live in this village and that he would not be staying for the witch cleansing. Again, the witchfinder twirled the mirror just so, and annoyed Lewis with his own reflection.

The witchfinder allowed the crowd to gather. He was a frail man with innocent eyes and a tender, soothing voice. He seemed earnest, but at the same time amused, as if he knew that he made his living off the folly of the human race, but somebody had to do the job, and fate had appointed him with the best qualifications. This confrontation with a pompous *poo-mui* seemed to put a little fun into the otherwise humdrum task of purging witches from villages.

As the witchfinder spoke, Sisay weakly translated almost in monotone, clearly wanting only to go back to the *barri* and sit down, but—along with everyone else—he was engrossed in the high-wire daring of Lewis, and translated the witchfinder's words for Boone.

"The witchfinder has sealed off the village with a white cotton thread. Witches may no longer enter the village, and all the witches and bad medicines within the village will be purged when his work is done. Here is a white man who thinks he can cross the boundary set up by the witchfinder. White men have many powerful medicines, but they are nothing compared to the powers of the witchfinder."

Lewis grimaced and politely waited for the witchfinder to finish, to minimize the disrespect he was about to show in leaving.

The witchfinder summoned one of his assistants from the crowd. A young man in an embroidered African shirt came forward bearing a platter with a knife on it, the blade curved and gleaming like a small scimitar, the handle made of carved bone or ivory, with diagonal, stylized masks or faces carved into it. The witchfinder handed his staff to the assistant, took the knife from the platter, and continued his announcement.

"If this man leaves the village he will never eat food again," Sisay translated. "If he tries to eat food, he will choke on his own tongue and die."

At the conclusion of this speech, the witchfinder smiled at Lewis and opened his mouth so wide the skin stretched even tighter against his skull. Then he stuck out his tongue, unfurling it in a single sinuous gesture, like a reptile stretching and tasting the air while sunning itself on a rock. The witchfinder laughed and wagged his tongue at Lewis in a display that, under other circumstances, might have been grotesquely humorous. With a careful, elaborate gesture, and with one eye on the crowd, the witchfinder made a pincer out of his first two fingers and his thumb and seized his own tongue. He brought the knife to his mouth, inserted the blade, and with a single quick flick sliced his tongue out of his mouth and threw it on the platter, which was still patiently being held by the assistant.

The crowd gasped and gagged. Children threw themselves on the ground. Adults backed away, terror and disbelief competing for expression on their faces. Boone trembled with nausea, and a new fever roared through his veins.

Lewis stared dumbfounded at the tongue, which was covered with blood and appeared to be writhing as the assistant tilted and rotated the platter, allowing the white man every opportunity to inspect it. The witchfinder opened his mouth, which was filled with blood, and showed Lewis the stump of his tongue, covered with blood and rhythmically spurting more with each beat of the witchfinder's pulse.

Boone stared in shock, long enough to confirm that either he had just watched a man cut his own tongue out of his mouth or he had seen the best magic act of his life. Using the same elaborate pincer gesture, the witchfinder calmly picked up his tongue from the platter by its tip and reinserted it in his mouth. Another assistant appeared with a white cloth, which the witchfinder used to pat his face and wipe his mouth. Then he smiled at Lewis, opened his mouth, and again wagged his tongue at the white man, sticking the thing out as far as he could, so that all could see that the tongue was seamlessly intact and unscathed, with no trace of mayhem except for a little bloody saliva.

After this display was over, the crowd's gasps of horror and wonder had subsided. The witchfinder closed his mouth and assumed the same mild manner he had used to address them at the outset. He quietly reiterated the curse, then, according to Sisay, said, "If the witchfinder can cut out his own tongue and then put it back into his mouth, think what a simple matter it would be to make another man choke on his."

Lewis looked sheepishly at the witchfinder, then at the crowd, until his eyes fell on Sisay.

"Maybe I should stay long enough to talk this over," he said. "Maybe I could pick a better time to leave." Then walking back to join his fellow *poo-muis*, he added, "I wouldn't want you guys to worry about me after I left."

Boone had another cold shudder of fever and nausea and headed back to the *barri* with Sisay, pondering what was either some incredible breach in the laws of nature or a trick of consummate skill. Had the witchfinder concealed something in his mouth before addressing the crowd? Had he simply cheeked a bladder or plastic bag of blood, along with an animal's tongue, which he then had removed and thrown on the platter? Boone tried to replay the scene in his imagination, but the crucial details were eclipsed by the horror of the performance.

Back at the *barri* all were seated and everyone's attention was devoted to the witchfinder, who was now being introduced by the Paramount Chief, Kabba Lundo, the latter in full ceremonial dress, bearing an elephant-tail fly whisk, the staff of office, and covered in cowrie shells, amulets, and pouches. The witchfinder looked almost monklike when escorted by the chief in such regalia.

The *poo-muis* sat together in one corner and the rest of the village grouped themselves roughly according to *mawes* around the *barri*. Moiwo and his men stood outside the *barri* attending to the proceedings, but periodically conferring among themselves, as if they were deliberating about the proper protocol for a section chief confronting a witchfinder brought into the village by the elected Paramount Chief.

"Brothers and sisters," said the witchfinder, according to Sisay, who translated for Boone. "The great Kabba Lundo has asked me to cleanse all the villages in his great chiefdom. I recognize faces that were here when I came to this village many years ago. When last I saw this village, it was cleansed of witchcraft and every villager had a pure and open heart. Now I see witch business has come again. I see dark hearts and sad faces. I see hatred and scheming, distrust and selfishness. No wonder the infants are dying! No wonder men are shot as animals in the bush! I smell malice and adultery, swear and counter-swear, bad medicine and sorcery."

The witchfinder dropped his arms and lifted his head, as if sniffing the air, or listening to some distant sound. He opened his large, innocent eyes and stared.

"There is witchcraft in this village. It has been overrun with witches."

The crowd gasped and whispered frantically.

Instead of the righteous, hysterical preacher one would expect, the witchfinder seemed saddened by the discovery of witches and touched by the frailty of human nature. He opened his eyes even wider and stared over the heads of his audience.

"But now all these witches are trapped in this village, and I will find them for you. When my work is done, this village will be cleansed of witches and witch medicine, and all those witches with black hearts who walked among you every day in seeming innocence, with friendly glances and outward smiles, will be exposed. Then you will see that when these witches patted the heads of your children, they were secretly thinking about eating them; when they heard about the rice pods swelling on your farms, they went out at night to destroy them; and when they learned that your wives were in labor, they trapped the babies inside their mothers and ate them before they could be born.

"All of the pregnant women and nursing mothers will be taken to a compound that I have already purified. They will remain there until my work is done. There they will be safe when the witches come out at night. Each person in this village must pay me two thousand leones, and the money must be given to Chief Kabba Lundo before the sun goes down, or I will leave at dawn without doing my work. If the money is paid, this village will be cleansed of witchcraft. If not, I will leave you as I have found you, just as the proverb says, and I will go to the next village."

After finishing his speech, the witchfinder went to his guest quarters with Chief Kabba Lundo, and the *barri* erupted in fretful conversation. Sisay shambled unsteadily back to his compound, with Lewis and Boone tagging along, and a string of villagers anxious for Sisay's opinion of the witchfinder, and asking one another where they could possibly obtain two thousand leones before sundown.

Sisay collapsed in his bed, while at least a dozen villagers gathered and sat on the floor, still gesturing and talking excitedly, turning occasionally and asking him questions, which he answered with an irritated wave of his hand. Pa Ansumana appeared in the doorway and beamed over the bowl of his pipe at Sisay, as if to say, "Nothing like a good witchfinding to really shake things up."

Boone shut himself in his room with Lewis, and the two of them mulled over the incident of the excised tongue. Both concluded that it had been a magic trick, but neither ventured that it was completely safe to cross the white thread and leave. Lewis shared what little knowledge he had of witchfinding, and Boone told him of his conversations with Sisay and Pa Ansumana on the subject. During the silences of their conversation, anxious chatter poured in from the neighboring compounds, and it was clear that the same discussions were being had all over the village, as the villagers weighed the tantalizing prospect of finally freeing themselves of witchcraft against the almost impossible demand for two thousand leones, nearly twenty dollars, or more cash than at least half of them had on hand.

After exhausting their own limited knowledge of witch cleansings, Boone and Lewis peeked into Sisay's quarters and found that the crowds had gone, leaving only Pa Ansumana in conversation with his *poo-mui* son.

"Take a seat," said Sisay. "There are things you should know."

Lewis and Boone gathered at the foot of the bed like children waiting for a bedtime story. Pa Ansumana sucked on his pipe and continued his conversation.

"This witchfinder is the most powerful member of the witchfinding cult called *kema-bla*. He is an old friend of the Paramount Chief, Kabba Lundo, and a very wealthy and respected witchfinder. I told you Kabba Lundo would make things tricky for Moiwo and he has done so, for now Moiwo is trapped in this village and cannot leave. Even if, as Pa Ansumana suspects, Moiwo does not believe in the witchfinder's power, he cannot leave, or the entire village would suspect him of being a witch, or of having bad medicine. Word would spread that he fled to avoid detection at the hands of the witchfinder. The same would have happened to that crazy *poo-mui* if he had left."

Pa Ansumana pointed at Lewis, then showed him a wagging tongue.

"Of course, he would have had to live as a suspected witch only until his next meal. For then he would surely have choked on his own tongue and died."

"The witchfinder's a magician," said Lewis. "If we hadn't been so freaked out at the sight of some old guy cutting out his tongue with a knife, we could have caught him in his magic act and showed everybody how it was done."

When this was translated for Pa Ansumana, his pipe spouted like a miniature volcano and covered his legs with ash and hot sparks. He brushed them away and laughed at the overweening arrogance of *poo-muis*.

"Leave now, then, *poo-mui* fool!" he said with a wave toward the door.

Lewis laughed nervously. "I think, uh, that would be . . . culturally insensitive," he said, with a glance at Sisay. "Wouldn't that be disrespectful or something? Besides, I've heard about these witchfinders. He'd probably make sure something bad happened to me. Then all the villagers would attribute it to his powers."

Pa Ansumana gave a perfect imitation of a chicken clucking and laughed, showering himself again in sparks and ashes. After he regained control of his risibles, he continued his conversation.

"In Bambara Chiefdom, where this witchfinder lives, there is a famous whetstone, a *yenge-gotui*, mounted in the middle of a clearing. For decades, maybe even centuries, many powerful warriors and prosperous farmers have sharpened their cutlasses on this stone, and though its shape has changed from years of sharpening, it is still the best whetstone in that chiefdom. The stone is now a memorial to the skill and foresight of the ancestors who selected it. The stone has its own memory, and it has absorbed the spirits of all the fathers and sons who have used it; it is impregnated with the prayers and dreams of the ancestors. The stone enshrines a spirit who visits people in dreams as an old man wearing a yellow gown. For generations, many, many people have been visited by this spirit."

There was a long pause, during which Boone suppressed a poisonous sneer. *More spirits! I should have guessed!*

"As you know, twins have very special cultic powers," continued Sisay, still translating for Pa Ansumana.

"You don't say," said Boone.

When this was translated, Pa Ansumana leaned forward, concern furrowing his brow, as he intently tried to explain the world to this *poo-mui* man-child, who seemed to know next to nothing about it.

"They can protect their families from witches and can foretell the future with ease," said Pa Ansumana, by way of Sisay. "The only person more powerful than twins is *gbese*, which means 'the sibling born after twins.' If Mende parents bear twins, they feel at once blessed and fearful, for the power of twins can be unruly and can disrupt the entire *mawe*. That is why the parents pray for *gbese*, who is the only being powerful enough to control the awesome, sometimes dangerous, powers of twins and mediate their disputes. *Gbese* are born with the ability to talk to spirits and to recognize witches."

Valuable skills, thought Boone. *I bet they call themselves consultants.*

"This witchfinder is a *gbese*. When he was still very young, the old man wearing a yellow gown appeared to him in a dream and gave him a beautiful wooden hand mirror, the one now fastened to the end of his staff. When the witchfinder looked into the mirror, he saw an old widow of his village hiding *ndilei* medicine in the rafters of her house. When he awoke from his dream, this young *gbese* witchfinder went straight to the whetstone and found the mirror the spirit had shown to him in the dream. He reported his dream to the chief and showed him the mirror.

"Not only was *ndilei* found in the rafters of the old woman's house, but the witchfinder soon discovered that he was also able to find lost or hidden objects, simply by looking into his mirror. After testing him, the chief and the elders of the village declared him a witchfinder. Since then, he has become a very wealthy and well-respected man by purging villages that have been overrun and paralyzed by witches."

Pa Ansumana chewed on his pipe. Sisay looked at Boone. Boone looked at Lewis.

Lewis said, "He's a charlatan, right?"

"He's an African psychiatrist," said Sisay. "Back in America, demons inhabit the mind. Here, they inhabit the bush."

"So what will happen now?" asked Boone.

"I'm not sure," said Sisay. "The last time a witchfinder was called into this village was before my time. Older villagers say that the pregnant women and young mothers will be separated and placed in a hut of their own, where they will be protected until all of the witches have been eradicated. Then there is fasting and no sleep and ceremonies, after which the witchfinder will find all the *ndilei* medicine in the village. *Ndilei* is always found and that means hysteria, for each bundle of *ndilei* medicine is believed to be filled with the blood of infants the witch has eaten. Sometimes there are cowrie shells sewn onto the bundle; each shell represents five infants the witch has killed and eaten with the help of the medicine."

"I should have left when I had the chance," said Lewis.

"You never had the chance," said Sisay.

·

That night, the witchfinder's assistants built a fire in the *barri*. Though the cost was dear, the money was collected. Some villagers sold possessions to get it; others sold interests in crops that were not yet harvested, asked for advances against dowries, borrowed from the Fula man, or begged from their neighbors, but everyone paid the money. No price was too high if paying it would stop the infant deaths and rid the village of witches once and for all. Even the white men paid the money, though what choice did they have?

The witchfinder and Kabba Lundo summoned the entire village to the *barri*, and all gathered around the fire. Stones were laid in a circle around the coals, and a huge cauldron was set over the flames. The witchfinder stared into the pot for a long time, and then looked out into his audience, his face lit from below and his huge eyes glowing with firelight.

"Tomorrow, anyone who knows in their heart that he or she is a witch may confess and be healed. Tomorrow, everyone must bring any bad medicine in their possession to this *barri*. *Any* bad medicine," the witchfinder repeated, "must be brought to me. If you do not bring the medicine on your own tomorrow, I promise you that the witchfinder will find it, and there will be no escaping the punishment of fines, or worse! The amnesty for witches ends tomorrow when the sun sets behind the palm trees. Go back to your houses, but do not sleep. Stay awake! Everyone in the village is in danger, except the nursing and expectant mothers, who have been secluded and protected. In these last few days of their freedom, the witches will be looking for new places to hide their medicines. They will be looking for new victims, because they know they will soon be caught and forced to confess, compelled to surrender their medicines and their powers. They also will be poisoning the food and water, so I have ordered the wells sealed and a ban on all cooking fires. Your chief will see that any food you have is collected and destroyed.

"Stay awake! Look around you. The person sitting next to you may be a witch hiding inside of a human being. You do not know when a witch will come for you, whether at dusk, at midnight, when the cock crows, or at early dawn. Let no one sleep tonight! Instead ask yourselves: Do I know of any witch business to confess to the witchfinder tomorrow? Do I have a pure heart, or do I have medicines I bought or made to harm my fellow villagers? Be on guard! Do not let a witch come suddenly and catch you asleep!"

(**17**)

"**A**re we all here?" Randall said into his speakerphone.

The hiss, howl, and cackle of international static gave way to the voice of Ambassador Walsh in Freetown.

"My political officer, Mr. Nathan French, is here with me," said the Ambassador.

"Hello, Mr. Killigan," said French.

"And our section chief?" said Randall. "He's there too, right?"

"Well, actually, no," said French. "He's not back from his trip to get the Westfall kid and bring him back to the embassy here in Freetown."

"Not back?" said Randall. "Our last conversation was four days ago, and he had already left!"

"Mr. Killigan," said the Ambassador. "It's the bush . . . The roads . . . Native matters. Once you get outside Freetown, things don't go according to plan."

"You said it's a day's journey out there and a day's journey back. That's two days. And two days is what I told the kid's father, who runs an insurance business not a block away from here. What am I gonna tell him? I told him I'd call him after I talked to you guys! The chief's driving *my* Land-Rover. What happened to the other two-plus days?"

"We don't know," said French, "because we haven't heard from the section chief. We trust that if there were some problem he would contact us, somehow, probably from Bo."

"There already is a problem!" Randall hollered. "A big problem! My son, an American citizen, an employee of the United States government, has been missing for two weeks! Two weeks! Two days used to make me crazy! Now it's two *weeks!* This alleged chief is already into me for a Land-Rover, fifty bags of rice, medicine, reward money, you name it! Am I supposed to buy him a fucking cellular phone so he can call home and tell us what he's up to? What's gonna happen if I spend another twenty thousand dollars and another eighty hours on the phone and we wind up having the same conversation after two *months!*"

"Mr. Killigan," said Ambassador Walsh, "I have to tell you that these delays aren't the fault of the United States government. We're dealing with rebel activity. We're dealing with excursions by the Liberians in the south and east. We're trying to get information about secret society business, which, as you know, is almost impossible to come by. Every other American in Sierra Leone is safe, accounted for, or evacuated. Your son's problems most probably have to do with the nature of *his* activities, not *ours*. I can't tell you what has happened. But, as we've discussed, the reports suggest that Michael involved himself in secret society matters, or worse, interfered with the Sierra Leone government's administration of its aid programs. That's not our fault. We are doing absolutely everything in our power . . ."

"Talk," shouted Randall. "Words! We're *talking* again! I *hate* talking! I have a passport, and it's stamped with a visa for Sierra Leone. If I have to, I'll bring Senator Swanson with me. When I get there, I want results! This conversation is already over, and guess what? *I have learned nothing new!* When you have results, call me! Until then . . . goodbye!"

He stabbed buttons on his phone and raised his assistant.

"Tell Judy to go ahead with the Freetown reservations. Once you get the dates, clear everything off the calendar and put it somewhere else, then bring me the court dockets and any meetings that can't be moved."

Randall disconnected the line and sat heavily into his leather recliner. A messenger brought him an envelope containing his passport and visa. He stuffed paper into his bear's gullet and swore. Twenty years of developing a nationwide bankruptcy practice had acquainted him with the limitations of telephones, and he instinctively knew it was time for him to show up in Freetown and clean out the barn. The United States government was having trouble finding one white man who was "lost" among four million black

Africans in a country the size of Indiana. It was giving him chest pains!

He held his fist against his sternum and tried to calm himself enough to venture forth and use the men's room. If a heart attack was coming, he wanted it to happen in the privacy of his own office, not in the public halls of power. He'd had nightmares in which he had seen himself grabbing his chest and faltering . . . What if it happened in front of the elevator banks? He would look up and see the lobby spored with the faces of paralegals and litigation support personnel, rushing toward him, marveling that the mightiest of all could have something as embarrassing as a heart attack. His enemies would use it as proof positive that he had failed to properly manage stress. It would suggest that he lacked the self-discipline necessary for good health; that he had failed to exercise or had overindulged in animal fat.

A beep and a squawk chorused from the speakerphone. He canceled them by pushing buttons, then hit the speed dial.

"Guaranteed Reliable Investment Mutual Trust," said a female computer voice. "Maximum protection at minimum cost. If you are calling from a Touch-Tone phone, press 1 now . . ."

"Fuck me!" shouted Randall. When would he learn not to *ever*, under *any* circumstances, make his own phone calls? He disconnected the line and told his administrative assistant to get Walter Westfall on the line.

"The insurance guy," Randall told her. "Guaranteed Reliable something and something."

It was just like Walter's kid to jump into one of Michael's brainless intrigues. Like the time they ate LSD and wound up on Interstate 70 trying to make a citizen's arrest of an Indianapolis police officer, who was, in the boys' own words, "unlawfully restricting our access to certain modes of being." And, as usual, if one of them was in trouble, there were soon two fools stomping all over places where Satan's own angels wouldn't think about treading.

He drew his toy broadsword and stabbed his keyboard, summoning his appointment calendar onto his computer screen.

"Walter Westfall, Guaranteed, Reliable," said his assistant.

"Randall?" said Walter over the speakerphone. "Is this business or pleasure?"

"It depends," said Randall. "Who's billing whom?"

"I take it this means you don't have any news for me," interrupted Walter.

"Nothing," said Randall. "Chief Send-Me-Bucks is still out there rounding up your boy and trying to find mine."

"Nothing on this end either," said Walter. "Nothing after the telegram from Paris. No phone calls, probably because he knows we would tell him to get his ass home, or at least keep it out of Africa."

"I'm going over there," said Randall. "Day after tomorrow."

"To Africa?" asked Walter.

"No, to Liechtenstein," said Randall. "I thought I'd look there first."

"If you're going to Africa," Walter said. "I'm adding endorsements to your policies. For you . . . and for Marjorie."

"What kind of endorsements?"

"Health," said Westfall, "life, travel, accident, disability. Anything could happen over there. I won't sleep unless I know you're protected. Your present policies probably exclude most of what goes on over there. For instance, I've never seen an endorsement for damage resulting from black magic or witchcraft."

"I'm covered healthwise, aren't I?"

"You will be when I'm through," said Westfall. "Your preexisting conditions are covered under the conversion option of your firm's old plan. That's a five hundred deductible preferred provider flex plan with 70 percent coverage to five thousand dollars, 80 percent coverage to ten thousand, and a cap of two-fifty. For non-preexisting conditions, you're covered under the firm's new flex plan, which is a one thousand deductible, nonpreferred provider with 80 percent coverage to five thousand, and a million-dollar cap. Of course, during the probationary period, the deductibles are separate and noncumulative, and the exclusionary provisions may overlap, creating a gap we can cover with a supplementary rider and an ancillary, preferred-subscriber premium, which will cover subordinate exclusions and limitations caused by a conflict between the two plans."

"What are you," said Randall, "a fucking lawyer?"

"No," said Walter. "I paid you guys to draft this shit up for me. It costs a fortune to create something this impenetrable. No jury in North America could possibly pretend to understand this stuff. And there's more. Let me see if I can simplify this for you. The long and short of it is, you'll be covered under one plan or the other for accidents and diseases incurred while traveling in the Third World, so long as any treatment you receive is preauthorized by Guaranteed Reliable Investment Mutual Trust Insurance Company, who will also have the sole discretion to determine if your care is obsolete, custodial, caused by a preexisting condition, rendered by a licensed health-care professional, medically necessary, experimental or investigational, or is inconsistent with the diagnosis and treatment of your condition. What do you think?"

"I have to be preauthorized?" asked Randall. "From West Africa?"

"Bring your calling card," said Walter, "that's my advice. No telling what will happen, I don't have a crystal ball on my desk. On the life end, I know you wanted the death benefit of your whole life kicked up. I can do that for you, but the underwriter wants blood, urine, vital signs, medical records, and another two-fifty a month in premiums. I sent you the paperwork. As soon as we get the forms, they'll send a nurse out to your house to collect the specimens."

"Blood?" asked Randall.

"It's not us," said Westfall, "it's the underwriter. You can imagine how careful they have to be with the AIDS thing and all."

"Pound of flesh," muttered Randall.

"Flesh?" said Walter. "They didn't send you a biopsy form, did they? That ain't right. They're not supposed to send you a biopsy form unless something looks funny in your lab work and they need more information. If they sent you a biopsy form, they made a mistake, or maybe they have cannibals working for them over there, I don't know. I'm just trying to jump you through the hoops so your boy and Marjorie will be taken care of if anything happens to you over there."

"Yeah," said Randall. "How much?"

"How much?" said Walter. "Don't ask me that. It gives me nightmares. It reminds me of Larry Banacek. Remember him? That's what he asked me. How much? And it was too much. He canceled his policy. I see his wife in church every Sunday with those four kids. They're in a condo now, and the kids are in public schools. I blame myself," he added. "I shouldn't have let him do it. I should've picked up the extra premiums myself."

Buzz went the intercom.

"Walter, I'll send the forms," said Randall. "I'll give them the blood and the urine, and I'll let you pick up the extra premiums."

"Yeah," said Walter, "and I'll send you a statement of services using your hourly rate."

One button banished Walter Westfall, another admitted Mack.

"Boss," said Mack over the speaker.

"What?" shouted Randall.

"No loaded weapons handy, I hope."

"None," said Randall. "Why? What happened?"

"Beach Cove," said Mack. "They're filing a lender liability suit against us. They're saying we forced them to adopt unsound management practices before we would qualify them for our loans."

Randall felt a cramp forming deep in his chest. At times like these, he could believe what his cardiologist had told him, that the heart is a muscle: it flexes, it cramps, it gets stronger . . . or weaker.

"Charlie," Randall said curtly, and smote the desk with his fist.

"What?" said Mack. "Who's Charlie?"

"Charles de Blois," said Randall, a thunderhead boiling just above his brow. "The Hundred Years' War. He was an ascetic warrior who sought spirituality by mortifying his flesh with knotted cords, wearing coarse garments crawling with lice, and making pilgrimages barefoot in the snow. He loved God, but he also knew how to take a town. One of the few useful things I learned before law school. It's time for the Charlie technique."

"We mortify our flesh?" asked Mack uncertainly.

"Negative," said Randall. "First we capture twenty or thirty prisoners and decapitate them. We roll our siege engines up just below the walls of Beach Cove, then we hurl the heads into the town. That's how Charles de Blois announced his intentions to take the city of Nantes. Nothing short of divine inspiration."

"I'll call Office Services and check on the siege engines," said Mack.

"We're going to countersue the Beach Cove officers individually, personally, for fraud," said Randall, gnashing his teeth and clutching his chest. "Call those financial investigators we have on retainer. I want individual assets—assets bought with Comco money borrowed from our client and paid out in salaries to enemy officers! I want that money back! I want family members. I want trust funds. Children's assets. Everything within a bloodline's reach. I want heady murder, spoil, and villainy! Tell them to watch the blind and bloody soldier with foul hand defile the locks of their shrill-shrieking daughters! With conscience wide as hell, mowing like grass their fresh fair virgins and flowering infants! Their fathers taken by the silver beards, and their most reverend heads dashed to the walls! Naked infants spitted on pikes!"

"Boss," said Mack. "Are you OK?"

(**18**)

Boone squirmed on his tick mattress, panting in the moonlit darkness, soaking his sleeping bag, and making love to Missus Sickness, wondering what would happen if he failed to satisfy her. He longed for an air-conditioned bedroom and a refrigerator filled with cold soda. If he could only rise and throw his legs over the side of a firm mattress, sink his toes into plush carpeting, totter into the bathroom, and draw crystal-clear water from a brass tap into a clean glass— water that had already been purified by filters and engineers in white lab coats—pure, sparkling, potable, treated water, with nothing but trace amounts of PCBs, insecticides, heavy metals, and radioactive substances—all monitored by government agencies and well below federally mandated levels, as measured in parts per million, billion, or trillion. For a glass of such water, he would do such things . . . He could drink as much as he wanted, until his belly was full of cold, clean, chlorinated, fluorinated water. And it would not make him sick, at least not right away.

Back in America, newspapers were coming out every day, and he was not there to read them. Food was being thrown into garbage disposals, and he had nothing but rice and pepper sauce to eat. Billions of megabytes of information were being transmitted by way of modems, fax machines, telephones, and computer screens, and not a single byte came his way. Back in America, his peers were sitting in graduate school classrooms, listening to lectures that would provide them with information and skills they could use to make more money. They were setting and achieving long-range goals. They were acquiring the computer equipment, the sound systems, and the home entertainment modules necessary for co-cooning. And Boone Westfall was absent without pay.

Instead of a one-bedroom apartment with access to a communal pool and tennis courts, he was occupying a cot on a mud floor in West Africa, trapped in a circle of white thread, waiting for an old man in a bathrobe to tell him what to do. He had nothing to eat or drink, and microbial parasites battened on his red blood cells. The never-ending journeys to the latrine had become a long march back and forth from the underworld. He pined for a clean linoleum floor, ceramic tiles, and a porcelain toilet he could fling his arms around, embrace, and be obliviously sick in.

About two in the morning, long after the witchfinder had gone to bed, a fruit bat or some other creature trying to take a mango back to its nest must have dropped its cargo onto one of the pan roofs, and the thunderclap of zinc sent Boone's heart clambering into his throat. The adjacent dwellings disgorged anxious villagers, who seemed convinced that witches were thronging just outside the periphery of human sight, waiting to suck a meal of salty blood from anyone who dropped off, even for an instant. Then a young girl actually saw a witch in the shape of an old woman with the eyes of a leopard, fresh blood dripping from her teeth. A bush spirit hissed at some children on their way back from the latrines. Grandma Dembe reported seeing a Baboon Man stalking the perimeter of the village, its pelt glistening with human fat, its metal claws clotted with human blood.

People assembled around the fire in the *barri* and sent the chief's speaker to rouse the witchfinder. They needed protection *now*. Tomorrow would be too late! The witchfinder sent back word that the villagers had no one but themselves to blame, for it was their own wickedness that had allowed witches to take over their village. Tomorrow, they would see who among them, even now, was pretending they were not witches, while secretly scheming to get at the sequestered infants and mothers.

Meanwhile, sleep was impossible, for it was said that the witches were trapped within the cylinder of cotton thread and swooping through the village, crawking in the shapes of fruit bats, unable to get out into the bush for their night rides, frantic for one last meal of human blood. Others, it was said, were slithering about in the shapes of boa constrictors, their eyes agleam with reptilian cunning, squirming in and out of the mud huts, looking to swallow and paralyze the exposed limb of a villager foolish enough to sleep.

Inside their huts, the villagers huddled around fires, keeping each other awake, and reproaching each other for having bad medicines in the house, which would have to be turned over to the witchfinder when the sun came up. Boone spent the night sweating and panting to the beat of banging pots and pans whenever hysterical villagers ran between the compounds trying to scare away the kaw-kaw witch birds with curses and loud noises. He dozed and dreamed of the African bush, where out on the farms the sky was swarming with flying creatures. A coven of witches soared overhead riding night birds and winnowing fans, suddenly spotting crops to eat, and landing as a pack of cutting grasses. Armies of them fell on the farms like locusts, devouring the rice pods and clustering under the fronded palms, sucking red palm oil from the palm nuts. He heard the savage cry of an ancestor who had never crossed the river to the village of white sands. Stone *nomoloi* sprang to life as fleshy dwarves with clubs and cutlasses, and a ferocious battle broke out over the crops. The dwarves hacked the cutting grasses, which were howling and gnawing at the ankles of their attackers. Soon the night was fraught with battles on land and air, for when the dwarves wrestled the cutting grasses to the ground, strangled them, and tore the carcasses open, out flew witch birds and fruit bats whose shapes darkened the face of the moon and whose wings thrashed the umbels of the palm trees.

Dawn found Boone anemic and weak as a wet kitten, fever still burning in his joints. The villagers guarded the doors, windows, and crevices of their homes with bamboo witch guns and nets, anxiously discussing whether their particular bad medicine was one of those covered by the witchfinder's decree.

By midmorning, the witchfinder's assistants had the fire going under the cauldron, and the villagers were staggering about in a stupor of exhaustion and anxiety. The two dozen or so innocents who had no bad medicines of any kind had assembled in the *barri* as instructed. The other two hundred or so citizens were still surreptitiously visiting respected elders, seeking opinions about whether the particular medicine in their possession would have to be turned over.

By noon, the guilty ones began coming forward. They approached the witchfinder with their medicines hidden in a paper, wrapped in

cloths, or concealed in their garments. They tried to place the parcel
on the ground next to the witchfinder's feet, or alongside the boiling
cauldron, in the fond hope that they could scurry to their seats
before being identified as the owners. But the witchfinder stopped
each person with his mirrored staff. He tapped them gently with
the meat of it, ignoring their whispered pleas for forgiveness and
anonymity, turning them this way and that, until they faced the
seated throng. Then, while the villager hung his or her head in a
yoke of shame—the witchfinder held the reprobate's medicine aloft
for all the assembly to see: bags of animal parts and bottles of
putrefied concoctions, bundles of rags soaked in grume or excre-
tions, balls of magic string, the dried claws or gizzards of fowls,
bindles of herbs and vials of animal fat, horns of animals containing
bits of ribbons, feathers, old razor blades, human hair and fingernail
clippings, or pestled cowrie shells; Arabic writings sewn into cloths,
pouches of gecko or snake heads, scrotiform bags of animal genitals,
boa constrictor skins, even, at last, a petrified human foot.

The villagers came forward with their secret medicines and hung
their heads in shame, sheepish old grandmas, once-dignified old
pas, remorseful adolescents, distraught young wives, disgraced big
wives—almost everyone had some pathetic fetish, which was held
up for all the village to see. When the witchfinder was handed a
particularly hideous talisman of bezoars, or animal offal, or a satchel
of human body parts, he accepted it with a sad shake of his head,
as if, no matter how many times he had seen such misanthropic
confections, he still could hardly bear to imagine what dark thoughts
and wicked intentions had spawned them. Affecting a wounded,
anguished look, he paraded the pathetic mess up and down, as if
to say, "See what human beings do when they are alone at night!
See what ghastly deformities they pray over in hopes of bringing
evil into the houses of their neighbors!"

Shaking the medicine in the face of its owner, the witchfinder
then cast it into the cauldron, where a mound of accumulated rub-
bish was half submerged in a slow-boiling greenish broth. Then the
witchfinder reached out with his staff and held the mirror in front
of the culprit's face. "Na who dat?" he would ask. "Who dat you
see?" The witchfinder came alongside and looked into the mirror,
assuming a sad and piteous countenance almost matching the offender's doleful expression. Then, with a flick of his wrist, the mirror
was used to show the reprobate the witchfinder's face, and, when

he had the person's reflection in the mirror, he would say, "Look me face. See your mother," and tears would well up into the witchfinder's eyes as he assumed the sad face of a bitterly disappointed mother. Or he would say, "See me face. Look your wife," and put on a stricken mien, looking for all the world like the brokenhearted spouse of an unfaithful Mende man. "Look me face. See your father," he said to another, and cast his features in a patriarchal scowl.

If the villager cast his eyes down to avoid the accusatory stare, the witchfinder simply adjusted the mirror and patiently waited until the culprit opened his eyes. "Look me face. Your small-small peekin dae."

On it went into the tropical afternoon. The witchfinder took each amulet, greasy pouch, or bottle of poison and held it aloft, denouncing its owner and the social depravity which brought the bric-a-brac into being.

By day's end, the cauldron had a mound of charms, pouches, bundles, and balls of rags and string in it. And all the villagers were assembled, properly chagrined and afraid to look at one another. As evening fell, and the huge red tropical sun went down over the palm trees, the witchfinder stirred the pot and wept into it, sobbing and crying out against the darkness of the human heart.

"Soon," he said, "the real work will begin. Not one bundle of *ndilei* medicine has been turned over. But don't worry! The witchfinder will find each and every one! And last of all, the witchfinder will find the witch pot where the bundles of witch medicine draw their nourishment and strength."

The witchfinder stirred the pot and pointed at the setting sun. "Soon it will be too late for all witches!"

Moiwo and his men, who had all assembled as instructed but had turned over nothing in the way of medicine, fell into a hushed and heated discussion. Moiwo angrily rebuked one of his underlings, a man in a white military beret, who regarded the witchfinder with terror and quaked at his every pronouncement. The man's uniformed fellows steadied him and whispered urgently into his ear, but he pushed them away.

The assistants brought a long pole of the sort the women used for pestling rice, which had a pad or a bundle fixed to one end.

"This pestle will lead us to all the *ndilei* medicine in the village," the witchfinder announced. "And anyone who has not turned over bad medicine will be punished."

The witchfinder stirred the cauldron and looked over his shoulder at the setting sun. "Soon it will be too late for anyone who has hidden bad medicines!"

The man in the beret cried out, but was led over to the Land-Rover by Moiwo's men, resisting and pleading with his handlers.

Moiwo, who no longer wore his military uniform, but instead had donned a robe of country cloth and a necklace of cowries, stayed behind and addressed the witchfinder.

"Of course, I appreciate the great and good work the witchfinder is doing for this village. And although, as the witchfinder knows, I am quite busy with election business, I am happy to stay in this village, so that I and my family can participate in the witch cleansing. But my assistant is not a Mende man. He is from the Koranko tribe. He has no bad medicine, but he is still afraid, because he holds the witchfinder's powers in such high regard."

"If he is not a witch, and he has no bad medicine," the witchfinder said, "then he has nothing to fear."

"He is afraid the witchfinder might make a mistake and falsely accuse him of witchcraft or of bad medicine," said Moiwo.

"That," said the witchfinder, "is impossible. Bad medicine is either found in the person's possession or in his quarters, or it is not found. Mistakes are impossible."

Moiwo wandered closer to the *barri*, taking in the crowd with a sweep of his arm. "But I am sure that my Mende brothers and sisters have heard of instances where someone has been falsely accused of practicing witchcraft, or of having bad medicine, or even of cases," he said, pausing meaningfully, "where the witchfinder's powers were not real, but only illusions and trickery."

Moiwo nodded at the witchfinder. "I know that you are the most powerful witchfinder in Sierra Leone. I know you have only good and honest intentions and would never use simple tricks to make us believe you had certain powers we should pay money for," he said. "But some say that it is time for us to move beyond these superstitions and enter the modern world. Part of what I will try to do as Paramount Chief is free the people from this constant fear of witch business, of swear and counter-swear. Some say that even the most powerful witchfinder may sometimes use trickery and deception," said Moiwo with a smile, "if it serves his purposes," he added with a polite bow. "But of course I hope I know you better than that."

He bowed and grinned knowingly at the witchfinder.

Without breaking his gaze, the witchfinder put out his hand. His assistant brought the tray and the dagger.

"Come closer," said the witchfinder to Moiwo. "I want you to be sure of your eyes."

Moiwo shrugged his shoulders and half laughed, half sighed as he stepped closer to the witchfinder.

"Your eyes," said the witchfinder. "They are good eyes?"

"Of course," said Moiwo, holding the stare constant and smiling, "I have good eyes. My eyes would like to examine the witchfinder's mouth before he does any . . . work with the dagger."

"Good," said the witchfinder. "I want you to see inside my mouth." A pink cave hung with teeth opened, and he turned his cheeks out with his fingers.

The witchfinder seized the dagger from the tray and engaged Moiwo's eyes.

"You say, your eyes, they're good?"

"Very good," said Moiwo confidently.

Without a trace of rancor, the witchfinder said, "Something in my belly tells me that you do not believe in the witchfinder's powers."

The witchfinder held his robe against his stomach and placed the point of his dagger just below his sternum.

"But of course I do . . ." began Moiwo.

The witchfinder opened his mouth and screamed. One violent gouge of the knife opened his robe and his belly, allowing his assistant to catch intestines as they spilled out onto the platter, loops of viscera and membranes tumbling into a mound, followed by a fold of what appeared to be the omentum or the peritoneum.

The crowd in the *barri* screamed in terror, turning their faces aside and retching. Moiwo drew a sharp breath and put his hand over his mouth. Boone and Lewis jumped to their feet trying to inspect the opening in the garment, as the assistant pulled the last loops onto the platter, then hoisted the platter like a waiter in a restaurant and showed the pile of intestines to the crowd. The villagers gagged and clutched their children to their bosoms, struck dumb with wonder and fear. The second assistant brought a towel, which was inserted into the torn burnoose and used to wipe the witchfinder's belly. Boone shook with a hot flash and sat down, swallowing the gastric acid that had welled into the back of his throat.

The witchfinder smiled at Moiwo.

"I have removed the part that told me of your disbelief," he said innocently. Then, gesturing to the man in the white beret, who had been led away, the witchfinder said, "Perhaps you or your man would like to examine the witchfinder's belly and see that no trickery has been done."

He held open his rent garment, showing Moiwo and the crowd his smooth, thin, unblemished abdomen.

He clapped his hands, and one of the assistants provided him with his mirrored staff. "Perhaps I should ask the man questions now, so we can get a head start on our work and learn if he has anything to fear."

"That won't be necessary," Moiwo demurred. "I have never doubted the witchfinder's powers. I simply was remarking that sometimes mistakes have been made," he said with a nervous smile, "by other, perhaps less experienced, witchfinders." Then he bowed to the witchfinder and to the crowd and returned to his men.

The witchfinder dipped his staff into the cauldron and stirred. Dusk fell and the *barri* was lit only by glowing coals under the cauldron. The witchfinder sent his assistants to be certain that everyone in the village was assembled in the *barri*, except the nursing and expectant mothers. No one had slept the night before, and no one had eaten all day, as if the knotted stomachs of the villagers could have tolerated food.

When it was confirmed that all were present, the witchfinder sat in a chair with his back to the fire and to the crowd. He held his staff aloft, so he could look into the mirror and direct the firelight onto the faces of the villagers.

"Witches have been eating the children of this village," said the witchfinder calmly, the flames dartling shadows in the hollows of his face. "When mothers are sleeping at night, witches crawl from under the beds and poke their fangs into the soft skulls of the peekins."

A woman in the crowd cried out, then wept aloud for her lost child.

"It is time for us to identify witches," said the witchfinder gravely. "They are here with us. Right now! Hiding inside their human shapes! Why? Because they hope to eat more children. They want to suck children out of their mothers' bellies like the yolk of eggs, and eat the souls before they can be born!

"This pestle will find all the bad medicine in the village. We will find the witches," he said, smiling into his firelit mirror. "And after we find them, we will find the head witch and the witch pot! Woe to those who have hidden medicine from the witchfinder, they will be found out tonight!"

The huge tropical sun winked and sank below the bush. The witchfinder attended his pot, stirring with his staff and peering sadly into its swirling depths, as if he stared into the pooling oversoul of the village, a sinkhole where the lust, filth, hatred, and vengeance of all had collected. He wept into the cauldron, his tears glistening on his cheeks like tinsel in the firelight. He cried out against the wickedness of the human heart.

"Oh, mothers and fathers, grandmothers, grandfathers, sons, and daughters, this is what we have brought out from under our beds, fetched from our sacks and bundles, dug from holes in the earth, and stolen from animals in the bush. Listen to this wicked soup slap the sides of my pot! Hear this vile broth whisper with our dark desires! Smell the awful confections we prayed over in the hopes of destroying our neighbors! Look! Look what fearsome gruel has oozed forth from the wounds of our hearts!"

When darkness fell, the witchfinder sat with his back toward the crowd and twirled his mirror in the firelight. Everyone tried to avoid the witchfinder's reflection in the mirror and instead talked quietly to one another, or whispered about what might happen if witches were discovered in the village.

Boone could not see the witchfinder's face, because the mirror was aimed at the other half of the assembly. After a while, the mirror was completely still and the witchfinder stared into it for some time. Distressed murmurings erupted in the vicinity of the witchfinder's aim. The witchfinder stared without moving, then slowly raised his arm and pointed into the mirror. A hushed cry went up as Pa Usman, the man in the torn stocking cap whom Boone and Sisay had found in the bush with his stone dwarf, stood, loudly protesting and shaking his head. He quaked with fear, and strenuously shouted to those around him, throwing up his arms to proclaim his innocence of any witch business.

"The witchfinder has a suspect who needs to be interviewed," he announced.

Pa Usman? the villagers seemed to be saying in anxious disbelief.

The witchfinder showed the way with his staff, and led Pa Usman away to a neighboring courtyard, where they were hidden from the view of those in the *barri*. Small groups formed to debate the outrageous possibility that Pa Usman was somehow connected with witch business. Impossible, concluded most of the villagers. They had known him all their lives, and he was an infirm, slightly touched old man, who would not harm a driver ant, let alone a child.

Twenty minutes later, the witchfinder returned with Pa Usman in tow, the latter weeping and hiding his face in his stocking cap.

"This man has confessed to taking part in witch business," declared the witchfinder, showing Pa Usman to his seat.

The villagers gasped and stared, unable to look at the monster that had been masquerading as a kind old man for years. "There must be some mistake!" some still said. "How does the witchfinder even know what the old man is saying?"

The witchfinder summoned his assistants, who picked up the pestle and were immediately propelled, seemingly against their will, from one end of the courtyard to the other. They held on to it, throwing their heads back and gritting their teeth in their desperate efforts to control the headlong flight of the pestle. After a few minutes, the padded end of the pestle stopped at the door of Pa Usman's shed of zinc pan.

"I must have two witnesses who will come and prove that the *ndilei* medicine is indeed found," cried the witchfinder.

Lewis jumped to his feet and waved. "I am a witness!" Under his breath, he said to Boone, "I'll catch this runt in one of his tricks. Just watch."

The witchfinder summoned Lewis and another villager from the crowd. Together with the assistants and Usman himself, they entered the shed. A short while later, they emerged—the witchfinder bearing a small football-shaped black bundle of tightly wrapped rags or skins with a red tube sticking out of it and two cowrie shells sewn onto it.

As soon as the thing appeared the crowd gasped in horror.

"*Ndilei!*" the witchfinder cried, holding the bundle aloft in the light of the fire. "This pa was keeping *ndilei* medicine right under your very noses! Who knows how many infants this medicine has killed? Look at the cowrie shells and count the infant dead!"

The *barri* erupted in a clamor, some few still saying that Pa Usman, a man who had been born and raised in this village, could not possibly have a witch in his belly. But others shook their heads, whispered, and clucked their tongues, as if to say, "It just goes to show you, it's always those you least suspect!" Some reminded themselves about how Usman had started speaking nonsense some years back; how he seemed to be spending too much time in the bush with his *nomoloi*; how he was always sitting alone in his shed; and how some of these behaviors were suggestive. And if he was not a witch, why would he have a bundle of *ndilei* medicine in his shed?

Lewis returned to the *barri* and reported that, indeed, the assistants had actually discovered the black bundle inside Usman's pillow. Now the *barri* was filled with the wailing of women whose infants had recently died. Other old pas shouted reproachfully and pointed at the bundle the witchfinder still held aloft.

After things died down, the witchfinder displayed the *ndilei* once more, then dramatically hurled it into the simmering cauldron. A single cry issued from the impact: a mew of a cat, or the strangled cry of an infant, cut off. The sound brought the crowd's hysteria back with a vengeance, as people hugged each other in terror and stared into the cauldron in speechless awe.

The witchfinder sat with his back to the cauldron and the crowd. He twirled his staff and mirror, burnishing the upturned faces with firelight. People whispered anxiously and hid their eyes. The staff seemed to pause occasionally as the mirror searched and moved on. Then it came to rest. Another subdued murmur erupted in that vicinity of the crowd. The witchfinder raised his arm and pointed into the mirror.

This time, a feeble and skinny old woman rose to her feet, protesting weakly and attempting to wave the mirror away. Boone recognized her as the toothless old grandma with no fingers who had asked him and Sisay for medicine on his naming day. Grandma Dembe, the leper. She wept and shook her head, then held her arms and fingerless hands out to the crowd in supplication.

The witchfinder summoned her aside for the interview and returned with her a short time later, cordially showing her to her seat, then returning to his place next to the cauldron.

"This woman has confessed to taking part in witch business," announced the witchfinder.

The villagers moved away from Grandma Dembe and shook their heads in horror and disbelief, looking to her relatives for some explanation of how a kindly old grandmother, who had been singing songs to their children and grandchildren for as long as anyone could remember, was a witch. Was the world coming to an end? Had *Ngewo* and their ancestors left the village completely defenseless against the wiles of witches? How had this depraved witch so cunningly disguised herself? She had bathed their children, given them medicines, prayed, sang, laughed, and cried with them!

The witchfinder clapped his hands, the assistants picked up their pestle and were seemingly dragged about the village, as they dug in their heels and groaned with the effort needed to keep the powerful pestle under their control. No one was surprised when the club end of the pestle stopped at the door of the compound where Grandma Dembe lived and waited there, barely able to hold itself still long enough for someone to open the door and call the witnesses.

The witchfinder escorted Grandma Dembe, so she could be present for the search. After a few minutes, the assistants emerged with a red-spouted black bundle, and the mere sight of it filled the *barri* with squeals of horror and violent accusations. Small groups of bewildered and mortified villagers pleaded frantically with themselves, wondering how this could be so, that a gentle, sickly old woman who loved to tell the children stories in the baffas at night had been hiding witch medicine in her house! Had she turned the thing loose at night as a fruit bat or a boa constrictor to eat their unborn children!?

The witchfinder held the bundle aloft, and then, staff twirling and robe swirling, he flung it into the cauldron, whence the same stifled cry issued, sounding for all the world like the soul of an infant calling to its mother from some netherworld far out in the bush. More panic and frenzy, as the families of the witch people wept and implored their neighbors for forgiveness. "How were we to know? Would we let such a thing in our house?"

The crowd calmed itself down to a chorus of sobs and whispers reminiscent of a funeral or a deathbed vigil, and the witchfinder sat backwards and twirled his staff. This time, the blazing mirror traveled to the side of the *barri* where the *poo-muis* were sitting, and Boone was able to see the face of the witchfinder, which he had imagined would be focused in scrutiny on the faces of the crowd. He was surprised to discover that the witchfinder's expressions were quite animated, and that he seemed to change the look on his face each time he studied a different person, first sad to the point of weeping, then moving the mirror and silently laughing, then moving it, and looking askance at someone as if to ask, "Why are you looking at me?"

Then Boone realized with a shudder colder than his fever chills that he could see the witchfinder's face, because the witchfinder was staring at *him* in his mirror!

Boone quickly looked away, pretending to survey the crowd, or to watch the steam rising from the cauldron. But when he glanced back, the witchfinder was staring at him, this time wearing a look of absolute despair, as if the witchfinder were saying, "Why are you acting this way?" Boone looked up into the thatched roof of the *barri*, only to glance back and find a silent, uproarious laugh adorning the witchfinder's face. Boone pretended he had something to say to Lewis, and when he looked back into the witchfinder's flickering mirror, he found a face contorted with loathing and disgust: "How can a monster like you wear the shape of a human being?" the face seemed to be saying.

Then the witchfinder raised his arm and pointed at Boone in the mirror. Boone saw the eyes of the villagers turn on him and stare in horror.

"No," Lewis said. "You can't accuse a white man. That's impossible!"

"This is insanity!" cried Boone. He looked out over the crowd and shook his head into their reproachful stares. Heads turned together and whispered.

Sisay rose to speak, but the witchfinder silenced him with a gesture.

"The witchfinder will talk to the *poo-mui, alone*," he said in English. "The witchfinder lahrned his Engleesh," he added with a grin.

They went together to a neighboring baffa, where a solitary hurricane lamp burned on a rude table. The witchfinder sat at the table with his back to Boone and the mirror of his staff facing away from him. Boone could see blood pulsing in the vessels under the smooth scalp.

"What do you think about when you are alone?" asked the witchfinder in quite good English.

"What does that mean?" Boone retorted, staring at the back of the blue burnoose. "I think about how to find my best friend."

"Ah," said the witchfinder. "You think about your brother. If you found him, you would be happy, notoso?"

"That's why I'm here," said Boone.

"I see," said the witchfinder, twirling his staff until the mirror held a reflection of his huge eyes lit like dark pools by the hurricane lamp. "I see," he said, holding Boone's eyes in the mirror.

"You are here to find your brother," he said. "That is what you think about. If not for your brother, you would never have come to Sierra Leone. And if he cannot be found, or if he is dead, you will leave."

"I hope to find him," said Boone. "I don't like this witch interview or whatever it is," he added, with a shudder. "Those people back there think you brought me over here because . . . because I'm some kind of witch."

"Don't worry," said the witchfinder. "I did not bring you here because you are a witch. I must have words with you in private. I have a message from men who are holding your brother in the bush. If you want to see your brother alive, you must agree to feed certain powerful medicines."

The mirror swiveled slightly and the witchfinder stared at him.

"What is this *feeding* shit?" quavered Boone. "Is anybody going to tell me what it means?"

"You must bring a human victim to feed the medicine," said the witchfinder. "Then you must join the society and take the vow on the medicine. After that, both you and your brother will be allowed to return to his village, or even, if you like, return to America."

"That's nuts," said Boone, looking into the mirror, expecting to see the witchfinder's face but instead finding his own. "That's crazy. I'm supposed to give them a victim? A human being? I can't lead a human being off to be killed. Who am I supposed to give to them? You?"

"The victim has already been chosen," said the witchfinder. "You only must bring her and . . . prepare her. Others will do the feeding."

"Kill her?" asked Boone. "You want me to kill somebody?"

He could see the pupils of the witchfinder's eyes in the mirror, black contractile nodes, probing him like fingers.

"Her head will be covered," said the witchfinder. "You must only strike the blow."

"Oh," said Boone sarcastically. "Why didn't you say so! That makes it easy!"

"If you do not," said the witchfinder, "I assure you these men will kill your brother and use him to feed the medicine instead."

"I can't do it," said Boone. "Where I come from, that's called murder."

"This is Africa," said the witchfinder. "Things are different here." He chuckled. "And they are the same. Sometimes lives must be sacrificed for the good of the village. Lives are traded all the time, even in your country."

"I won't do it," said Boone.

"As you will soon learn," the witchfinder continued, "the woman Jenisa, the young wife of Section Chief Moiwo, is a witch."

He reached down beside him in the darkness, brought forth another one of the small black bundles of *ndilei* medicine, and set it on the table in the lamplight. Instead of a red spout this one appeared to have a white one, until Boone got a better look at it and saw that, sticking out of the top of the bundle, was the applicator of mosquito repellent he had given the woman named Jenisa.

"That's got nothing to do with me," Boone protested. "It's mosquito repellent."

"It *was* mosquito cream," said the witchfinder. "Now it's a very bad medicine. Now it is witch medicine."

"I gave it to her as a gift," said Boone. "Somebody else made it into this bundle. I told you, it's got nothing to do with me."

Sweat issued from his pores and fever gusted through him like a blast from a furnace.

"She had this bundle of *ndilei* medicine buried near the widow Luba's house. This woman Jenisa wants to kill the widow Luba because she is the head witch," said the witchfinder. "Neither of them would be a great loss to the village. You only must deliver the woman at the appointed place and at the appointed time. If you do not, your brother will be fed to the medicine. And then, later, when it is time for another feeding, one of the other members, or a new initiate, will deliver the woman Jenisa, and she will be killed anyway."

"This is impossible," said Boone, sweating with fever and agitation. "Even if I agreed, I barely know the woman. I can't ask her to go for a walk in the bush. She would never go."

"That is arranged," said the witchfinder. "You will be told to offer a sacrifice for your brother at a place not far from here where there is a huge cotton tree. The woman Jenisa's family offers sacrifice there to her ancestors. It will be suggested that she should lead you to the spot, and there you will feed her to the medicine."

"Murder her?" he said. "Impossible."

He ground his teeth and pondered his options. Maybe there was a way of doing this thing, he thought, desperately turning alternatives over in his mind. Maybe there was a way to play along with this, until he actually found Killigan. Then maybe they could all flee, or he could rescue the woman somehow. Maybe he should at least pretend to agree. Otherwise, it appeared, two lives would be lost instead of one.

He drew a breath to speak and looked up, only to find that the witchfinder had unobtrusively lifted his staff and was studying him in the lamplit mirror.

"Do you know that the witchfinder can see the thoughts of others?" he said with a smile. "Good, evil, humans in animal form, witches, I can see everything."

Boone stared at the witchfinder's face in the dark mirror.

"Don't worry about your conscience," the face said. "As long as you feed it, the medicine will let you believe anything you wish. It will speak to your conscience. Will you feed the medicine?"

Boone stared at the face and reconsidered.

"Sometimes you must be evil before you can be good. Notoso?"

"I am not evil," said Boone. "I'm just a visitor."

"Visitors can be very evil," said the witchfinder. "Besides, I don't care about good or evil. They are exactly the same to me. I've seen them poured into one soup after another, and they are both the same. I don't prefer one over the other. I'm paid to find witches. And do you know what? I always find them. Do you know why? My grandfathers and *Ngewo* gave me the power to see witches no matter where they are hiding."

The witchfinder flicked his mirror and spun it skillfully aloft.

"I look for witches in the bush. I look for witches in the village. And," he said, finding Boone's eyes with his mirror, "I look for witches inside other people."

The witchfinder smiled steadily into his mirror.

"I am *gbese*, the one born after twins. Nothing human or inhuman is hidden from me. I can see witches as plainly as you see me now," he said. "Can you see me?"

Boone swallowed and nodded his head.

"Witches think only of themselves. They are very easy to detect. They are so hungry for infants, especially unborn ones, that they are almost climbing out of their skins at the thought of eating infant flesh and drinking blood. They devour innocence."

The witchfinder stopped talking suddenly and flicked his mirror away, leaving Boone staring at the back of his head.

"Must I go on?"

"With what?" asked Boone.

"Are you hungry for innocence?"

"What are you talking about?"

"You are a witch," said the witchfinder. "You have three brothers. They also are witches, and your father is the head witch of the coven. There could be more brothers and sisters, but they were probably bargained away as victims for witch rituals."

"I am not a witch," said Boone, shaking suddenly and violently under the intense scrutiny of the witchfinder, because the witch-finder had somehow gotten the number of brothers right.

"I have been a witchfinder for a very long time. I must tell you that I have never heard a witch confess to witchcraft. A witch will *always* deny witchcraft," he said with a smile. "Until I force them to confess. Take you, for instance. You would probably never show yourself to the village. I would have to make you do it by telling you that unless you confess your true nature to this village, you will never see your brother alive again."

"I am not a witch," insisted Boone. "And if you want me to go back there and confess to witchcraft, I will not. And I will not take another person to be killed, not even for my best friend."

"Even white men must feed their medicines," said the witch-finder. "What about this *poo-mui* ancestor named Abraham? God's medicine was hungry. God asked Abraham to feed the medicine with the flesh of his own son. And Abraham was willing."

"That's not right," said Boone, "you're . . ."

"What about the first *poo-mui* ancestors? God told Adam and Eve they could eat all the food on earth, but not the fruit of a certain tree, because God used that fruit to feed His medicine. You see?"

"No," said Boone.

"I am told that white men build large houses with rods of powerful medicine in them. These rods make a fire that never goes out, and this fire heats the wires that make machines go. But I am also told that sometimes the medicine escapes from the rods and goes in search of people to burn and eat. I can tell you that if you would simply feed the medicine a victim from time to time, it would stop trying to feed itself.

"I am also told that *poo-mui* women feed their unborn babies to witches and white medicine men, so that medicines can be made from their bodies. And how about the medicines the white man puts on his crops to keep witches away and make them grow? Doesn't the medicine then go in search of human lives when it is hungry? Doesn't it put spells on the village wells and poison the children in the *poo-mui* villages? So what is to stop you from bringing one person who will soon be dead anyway?"

Boone almost said yes, just to see what would happen. Could he say yes, and still back out at a later time? Would he be setting something in motion that could not be stopped? Suppose he played along, telling himself he could back out of it if anything went wrong, until he got to the clearing with her and was forced to trade her for his best friend?

"Maybe I can do it," said Boone, catching a glimmer of himself in the mirror. "At least, I'll try."

The witchfinder gently rolled the staff in his fingertips and focused on Boone's reflection. He stared at Boone in the mirror, and Boone stared back. Then the witchfinder grinned so hard he showed his teeth and hissed through them, "Scat."

"It was you!" cried Boone, suddenly remembering the orange eyes in the bush behind the latrine.

"We must return," said the witchfinder. "We will talk later." .

Boone looked toward the *barri*. "When we go back there," Boone said, "what will you tell them?"

The witchfinder focused on Boone's face by way of the mirror. "Don't worry. I will tell them nothing. I will simply move on to the next suspect."

The witchfinder held Boone's stare in the mirror and grinned. "You have a very strong want," whispered the witchfinder. "You want to find your brother. This want is a witch that has laid an egg."

The witchfinder jumped to his feet.

"Come," he said. "We are returning to the *barri*."

Boone's fever roared, his knees cracked as he walked. He had to go to bed before he died on his feet.

Once back in the *barri*, he saw their eyes look away from him.

They whispered, cringed, turned from him, everyone except Lewis.

"It's OK," Boone said to him. "I'll explain later."

When he looked up, he saw that the assistants had grabbed the pestle and were being pulled about the village, in and out of courtyards, in between the compounds, back around the *barri*, until they stopped in front of Sisay's house, then followed the tug of the pestle to the door of Boone's room.

"Come!" cried the witchfinder.

"Hey," said Boone. "You said we were just going to . . . move on. What are you doing?"

Boone, Sisay, and Lewis followed the witchfinder to the door, where they were allowed to go in first. Then, as the witchfinder held the door open, the pestle led the assistants straight to Boone's bed.

"Open it," said the witchfinder, pointing at the blue nylon sleeping bag.

Boone unzipped the length of the bag and flung it open, finding a black bundle of rags with the same white spout of mosquito repellent sticking out of the top. Either there were two identical bundles or somehow the witchfinder had moved the same one from the courtyard to his sleeping bag!

"You lied to me!" Boone said, shaking with fury and indignation.

"See this spout," the witchfinder said to Lewis and Sisay. "This is the straw that allows him to drink the blood of the infants he eats!"

The assistants blocked Boone with the pestle while the witchfinder snatched up the *ndilei* and marched out of the room, triumphantly holding it aloft as he strode back to the *barri*.

Boone collapsed on the bed, panting with fever.

"What a crock of shit!" cried Lewis. "You can't let him do this to a white man!" said Lewis, touching Sisay's elbow.

Sisay shook off Lewis and looked at Boone without expression.

"They don't believe I actually had witch medicine in here," Boone yelled at Sisay, "do they?"

"During your interview, most of them were saying they would not be the least surprised," he said levelly. "Because that would explain why you always wanted to be alone with it in your room. And why you don't care about anybody or anything except finding your own precious brother!"

"Christ!" screamed Boone, covering his face with his hands. "That son of a bitch conned me! He was trying to get me to deliver a victim to a bunch of murderers! He was telling me I had to feed some fucking medicine!"

"Quiet," snapped Sisay, cocking his head. "He's talking about you. He says that you not only killed Mama Saso's twins, who died the night after you came, but that you also offered to deliver a young woman of the village to the Baboon Men."

Boone leapt out of his bed and ran out to the *barri*, shouting and cursing the witchfinder, who was still displaying the *ndilei*, describing how it had surely siphoned the blood of Mama Saso's twins the night they died.

"Infant blood, my ass! You charlatan! If anybody's a witch, it's you!"

Before Boone reached the *barri*, the witchfinder spoke to his assistant, who stooped and produced a wooden mallet. The witchfinder faced Boone with the mallet in one hand and the *ndilei* medicine in the other. He set the black bundle on a stump in front of him and gestured for Boone to come stand across from him.

"You don't believe this *ndilei* medicine contains the blood of infants who died in this village?" asked the witchfinder.

"No, I don't!" raged Boone, ready to spit in the old man's face.

But before he could, the witchfinder lifted the mallet over his head with both hands and brought it down full force on the bundle, which splattered Boone and everyone else in a ten-foot radius with blood. The crowd screamed in horror and erupted in commotion, as people fled from the *barri*.

Boone was blinded by the sticky stuff and wiped his face with his hands, only to find that they were soaked and he was daubing more of it into his eyes. He turned and staggered back toward Sisay's compound, freezing when he felt a hand take him by the upper arm.

"Lewis?" he asked hopefully.

"Mistah Gutawa," said an African voice. "We take you to your brothah now. We must leave the village now."

"Who are you?" Boone asked, resisting the hands that were escorting him. "Where are we going? Did Michael Killigan send you?"

Boone managed to clear some of the grume from his eyes, and promptly saw he was walking between two men. He daubed once more at his eyes, but before he could open them, a heavy, foul-smelling sack was thrown over his head. It had the stench of a dead animal. When he opened his mouth to scream, a ragged husk was wedged into it, which allowed him to breathe and scream, but kept him from closing his mouth to form words. He raised his arms to fight, but they were seized by strong hands and pinned.

Men were now pulling the sack over his head and torso, while others were winding ropes or lashings of some kind about his waist and chest. He tried to throw himself on the ground and roll away from them, but the same strong arms and hands held him up.

"Tie claws on his hands," he heard someone say.

He screamed, vainly trying to form words; instead he was forced to shriek wordlessly from the back of his throat, like a raging primate, through jaws that were propped open. Hands seemed to be positioning the sack on his head, and he realized, as he opened his sticky eyes, that the head cover was fitted with eyeholes of some kind, for he caught a glimpse of firelight, or a torch. He continued struggling as his hands were individually bound. It seemed that his captors had placed a handle in each of his hands, and were tying it, binding it to him.

He shrieked as loudly as he could, but "Help!" came out "He-eh-ahhhh!"

Then he was suddenly set free. He could see out of one eyehole, and he spun around, looking for his assailants. But no one was near, only a crowd of villagers coming from the *barri* and pointing at him.

When he looked through the eyeholes at his arms, he saw iron claws. He looked down at his chest and found that he had been fitted, not with a sack, but with a pelt of some kind, which was lashed so tightly to him it pinched when he gasped for air.

He looked up in time to see the mob approach. He saw them snatch up cutlasses and farming implements, staves and rocks.

"Baboon Man! Baboon Man! Baboon Man!" they screamed, pointing at him and brandishing weapons.

"Baboon Man!"

He turned and fled, taking a path out of the village, breaking the white cotton thread in his flight, and lunging headlong down a steep incline into the bush.

(**19**)

The path fell beneath his feet and lowered him into darkness and the hush of vegetation.

He tore at the animal skin with his claws and promptly blinded himself by knocking the eyeholes askew. Without breaking stride, he batted at the hood until his eyes found the apertures; then he slashed and stabbed at the lashings on his torso, wounding himself instead of the bindings with his rude iron claws.

At the next rise, he stopped and strained to hear if the villagers had followed him across the boundary, but he was deafened by the sound of his own rasping struggles for air resounding inside the hood. The moon lit the top of the bush and showed him a dark slot where the path proceeded, but he had to grope for the contours of the terrain with his charging feet. Fever roared in his chest, and sweat stung his eyes. He failed in another attempted purchase on the hood with his claws. He tore what tasted like a palm kernel or coconut shell from his mouth, and sucked air into his lungs, coughing on debris, almost tasting the dead-animal stench of the hood.

He ran down into a hollow where the path widened, and the canopy of bush parted over a clearing of trampled grass. Streaming light at once gave him back his sight and made him feel suddenly visible. He took a step back into shadows and gasped for breath.

Trunks, stalks, and branches drooped lobes and blades around him. For one irrational moment, he wondered if he could look into the shimmering leaves and study his reflection, see the baboon hood they had tied on his head. He shivered and felt like a small human animal cowering at the edge of a cage of woven bush, illuminated from above by wanton boys and girls shining torches through the eye of a dome. Maybe, as the parables say, the moon and the stars are lamps lit by the ancestors so they can see what the living do under cover of darkness, hung in the sky so that the children of the dead will know that even at night their deeds are on display.

He stopped in the clearing and seemed to feel his auditory nerves growing out of his ears, through his hood, and into the bush in search of sound, stimulation, any auditory confirmation that he was a human being with the power to move through physical space. Next he felt hair growing, not only from his head, but from his body as well—the same fine hair that covered his arms and legs, the backs of his hands, and the tops of his feet now sprouted from his skin and unfurled in the night air, forming long silken tendrils that climbed like ivy into the overgrowth, innervating the bush with fibers attached to his skin.

If something stirred afoot, instead of being able to hear it, he would feel it, disturbing the threads of the web he had spun into the night. Maybe fever had burned out the hair cells in his inner ear, and now he was profoundly deaf, submerged in a sea of palpable soundlessness, breathing liquid stillness. The trampled grass seemed almost bioluminescent, lighting his way on his journey across the floor of the ocean bush, with noctilucas bobbing around him, waving their glowing flagella at him from the depths of the night.

He held his breath and listened to silence, shivering, though he could feel the heat of fever and flight coming off of him in waves. He drew a single deep breath and stood still, straining his ears and concluding with some relief that he was the only sentient being in the bush. Until he saw a glowing human figure move in the shadows and step into the clearing with him.

A naked African man painted entirely white stopped at the edge of the clearing and stared at Boone. He held a wooden bowl in both hands and walked slowly into the cylinder of silver light, his skin glowing, as if his entire body, including his genitals and his hair, had been dipped in whitewash. The roots of his hair were pale gray and pulled straight back from his face, pasted in place with the same white glue that coated his body. Only his eyes, black and glistening, were left unpainted, and seemed to shine brighter as the figure approached. When the man spoke, a dark hole opened in the chalk whiteness of his face and a soft voice filled the silent clearing like the roar of a waterfall in a box canyon. The figure crept forward, speaking in gentle masculine tones, as if he were a hunter or a shepherd soothing an animal while approaching it.

"Boa," said Boone, using the Mende greeting.

The man was slender and shorter than Boone, completely naked and weaponless, holding only the wooden bowl, but his whiteness seemed to have an occult and malevolent purpose. He recalled that, when someone died, naked runners painted white carried news of the death to the surrounding villages.

"I'm a man," Boone stammered, tugging again at his hood and resisting the urge to run away. "You sabby Krio talk? I am a man. Somebody tied this animal skin on me."

The white figure stooped slightly as it drew near, peering into the holes of Boone's mask, searching for and finding Boone's eyes.

"I'm a man," he repeated, terrified that he had blundered into some kind of hunting ritual and was being mistaken for a baboon.

The pale figure spoke again. The words sounded nothing like Mende, but Boone was no expert, and so tried several more Mende greetings. Without uttering a single familiar word or syllable, the man pleaded, then berated him. Boone feared that he was being asked or ordered to do something, and his inability to understand was being interpreted as willful disobedience.

Boone helplessly watched sadness fill the eyes with tears. In the profound hush of the bush, the alien voice acquired the dimensions of an orchestra, filling the clearing with the sounds of human desolation and the abstract music of speech. The figure groaned and lifted the bowl, holding it up to the moon, then threw back its head, and a single groan erupted into wailing. The man's wordless despair was so contagious that Boone suddenly felt they were the last two human creatures on the planet; their families, friends, and lovers had been slaughtered by bush spirits and fed to animals. Now it was their turn to die, and this figure—chalk-white with grief—was delivering the final lamentation of the last human, through infinite space, to an empty heaven.

The figure shuddered, presented the bowl to Boone, and motioned for him to take it. Boone balanced it on his iron claws and lifted it nearer the eyeholes, tilting it until the moonlight fell on a small silvery square in the bottom of the dish and a photographic image of Michael Killigan stared up at him—a frontal head shot from a passport photo or a driver's license.

"Where is Michael Killigan?" asked Boone. "Usai Lamin Kaikai?"

he asked, seized with the fear that the photo came from the personal effects of a dead man, that the cries to heaven were part of some bush mass for the dead.

The painted man continued speaking, meaningless sounds that were at once soothing and disorienting, as if Boone and this white figure would be able to express themselves and understand each other using pure speech.

Boone handed the bowl back to the painted man, so he could point at the photo with one of his claws.

"My friend," he said. "My brother. Lamin Kaikai. Where is he?"

Without responding, the painted man gestured at Boone to follow him, or go away, he couldn't tell which. Then the figure drifted off into the bush. Boone could not find the path that had brought him into the clearing; he was able only to discern the one the white figure had taken. The first live clue of his entire visit was walking away from him in one direction, while back in the direction from which he had come, villagers carrying clubs were looking to kill him for a witch or a Baboon Man.

Another chill shook him in his sweaty pelt. He felt a tug in the still air, as if ripples were passing above him on the surface of the night, and down below the current was flowing through him. The air was so humid here, someone had once told him, that radio waves leave tracks. He crept the rest of the way through the clearing, an animal slinking through the humid night.

On the trail just outside the clearing, the path forked and the white figure veered left, nimbly scaling an embankment choked with roots.

"I may have trouble keeping up," Boone called out, as if it would do any good. "I no able for keep up," he added, in the fond hope that Krio might improve his chances of being understood. He wheezed and flushed with fever, steadying himself in a bout of giddiness. "Febah done catch me bad," he called weakly. "Food no dae inside me belly for three days. I no eat nothing. Thirsty dae 'pon me. You sabby usai foh get water foh drink?" he cried.

The white figure called back to him and passed from view over the top of the hill.

When he crested the same hill, he looked down into a shrouded clearing where paths converged, pale and barely visible in the ink of night, hanging in the shadows like vapor trails left by clay ghosts.

He barely caught sight of the whiteness moving away from him in the moonlight, down another fork in the path.

"I say, I'm weak!" called Boone. "Hold up, please!"

An explosion of vegetation overhead stopped his heart with fear, as a nest of birds or bats slashed leaves and dispersed in the canopy of bush, where he heard them perch at a safer distance from him, then felt them watching him with the pin-eyed desire of vultures.

There was probably a very good reason for all these legends, he thought, following the pale figure into yet another fork in the path. The bush had no beginning, and no end. The villages were little pockets of human civilization in a galaxy of bush. For centuries, human feet had worn the paths of least resistance. Once a year or so, one of the villagers probably took the wrong fork, or chose the wrong trail out of a clearing, and before dark, they were lost, leaving nothing but their names and a few bush devil stories for posterity. If he got lost, how long could he last out here? Without water?

At the next rise, Boone saw an orange light flickering in the gully below him, where his guide had disappeared. Then another smear of fire or torchlight, and human voices. For one terrible instant he feared he had been led in a circle, and it was the village search party assembling in the clearing. But the voices neither advanced nor receded. He heard ringing metal and the cheerless laughter of men.

He descended slowly, freezing each time a silhouetted palm or a ghostly albedo of moonlight emerged like a human shape in his path. He searched ahead for the painted figure, but only the orange lights appeared before him, resolving into streaks from the slots of shuttered windows.

A low dark structure and two huts formed a compound in a clearing, with a baffa and a porch screened in by the sort of mesh petty traders used to protect their unattended shops after market hours.

He took a narrow, overgrown trail, which broke from the path and seemed to lead to the rear of the windowed structure, where shadows moved in the firelit interior, voices muttered, and the spanging of metal hammerblows issued. A roof pipe vented smoke and filled his nostrils with the smell of cooking meat. Hunger overpowered his fear, and he crept along the wall to one of the glowing windows.

The cracks in the shutters afforded him a view of embers glowing in an open hearth under the window, and in front of it a stone table littered with tools. He held his breath, adjusted his hood, and put his eye as near as he dared to the space between the shutters and squinted.

A huge shirtless blacksmith with a pipe clamped in his teeth tended the fire and worked the handle of a canvas bellows. He pounded a piece of leather or cloth studded with metal amulets and called out in a tribal language to someone working alongside of him. Illumined by firelight from the forge, the muscles of his upper body bulged in swollen arcs, like bundles of serpents writhing under his black skin. Sweat glistened on his chest and arms and dripped off of him, sizzling on the stones around the hearth. An aproned apprentice in a skullcap appeared at the blacksmith's elbow and handed him an iron cleaver. Through one eye, the young man watched his master work, the other socket an eyeless pink scar.

The blacksmith poked a stick into the embers and used it to relight his pipe, filling the air about his head with wraiths of white smoke. Then he turned away from Boone and lurched over to another table, dragging one apparently lame leg behind him. There he lifted something and the muscles of his upper back bloomed like the hood of a huge cobra. When he turned around, he hoisted the head of a hog or a bush pig in his arms and tossed it onto the anvil with a thud and a crack of bone muffled by flesh.

He joked with the apprentice and the two laughed quietly, talking softly as they worked.

Boone angled for a different view by squinting through another crack in the shutter and saw ridgepoles strung with dozens of animal heads and masks: the raffia headdresses he had seen worn by dancing devils, the grotesque mask of Kongoli, the clowning prankster whose buffoonery sometimes turned violent, a Poro devil's mask, heads of animals fitted with collars and vests of pelts, with holes for the arms of men. Masks of bush pigs, bush cows, baboons, alligators—all suspended in the flickering shadows of the firelight, staring back at Boone with huge glass eyes, lit somehow by reflective stones or minerals set deep in their sockets.

The head on the anvil was fresh and bloody. The blacksmith rolled it sideways, and one swollen pig eye, marbled with crimson veins, stared at Boone with the innocence of a Chagall horse head. The blacksmith abruptly upended the head on the anvil and began gouging an excavation where the head had once been joined to its body, ripping muscle, cartilage, and veins from the neck with an iron claw.

The apprentice began working at his side, stitching a pelt on a table strewn with metals, gems, bones, and a carcass spilling offal onto a wooden platter.

Boone heard the hiss of footsteps in the grass behind him, but before he could turn, something hard jabbed the back of his head through the hood, and a human voice sang through his nerves.

"*Poo-mui* Baboon Man, you like bullets too much?" Boone stiffened and decided not to turn. The voice belonged to a teenager, a mere bobo from the sounds of it, and Boone was unsure whether this made matters better or worse.

"Bullets dae beaucoup inside me weapon. Her name Lady Death. You want Lady Death sing bullets foh you?"

He was pushed along the wall by a barrel in the nape of his neck.

"Try something small, Mr. Baboon. Lady Death go sing you to sleep," said the boy. "Look the door."

Inside was a room off the blacksmith's quarters, lit by a thin tongue of copper light from a hurricane lamp. The stench of something that had been dead even longer than his hood nearly suffocated him. On a whiskey stool next to the lamp sat a boy in wraparound mirror sunglasses, his legs crossed, jauntily cradling an automatic rifle. He wore a pink bandanna pirate-style, and his skinny chest was covered by a heavy necklace of cowrie shells, lashed pouches, animal claws, amulets, Duracell batteries, and what appeared to be a TV remote control attached by an eyebolt to a feathered talisman.

"Boone," said a voice he instantly recognized in the shadows to his left.

"You mean *Ba*-boon," said the pirate in sunglasses, grinning with teeth stained orange by kola nuts and training the automatic weapon in the vicinity of Boone's neck.

"Killigan . . ." Boone said, before he was pushed by the neck to a stool in the opposite corner.

He turned to see his escort through the eyeholes of the mask, a youth of no more than fifteen or sixteen, with bloodshot eyes and a mane of dreadlocks swept back and held in place by sponge-tipped headphones, wired to a small cassette player strapped to his left biceps. He too wore a yoke of amulets and juju; on closer examination, Boone saw—festooned among the shells and animal teeth —a stick applicator of Arrid Extra Dry, a rusted hemostat, and a toy magnifying glass. The boy's rifle drooped in his right hand as he sucked hard on a spliff, then passed it to his seated comrade.

"I am Double O Seven," said the seated boy in the bandanna and mirror shades, filling the room with marijuana smoke. "This is Black Master Kung Fu." He handed the spliff back to Boone's guard.

"Are you OK?" Boone asked Killigan.

His friend's upper body was cloaked in shadows; his lower half striped in black patterns thrown by moonlit mesh from a window. His clothes were dark with sweat . . . or blood.

Under the window between Boone and Michael Killigan was a table strewn with human skulls spray-painted in neon colors and adorned with sunglasses and caps.

"Everything was fine," said Killigan tonelessly, "until you came to Sierra Leone to save me."

The resignation in his voice snuffed any chance of their leaving alive.

"Blacksmith!" yelled the seated pirate.

A single blow sounded, and a heavy door slid open, grating across the dirt floor. The swollen torso of the blacksmith appeared, backlit by the glowing forge. He set a calabash and a mounded platter of rice topped with meat sauce next to the boy in the bandanna.

Double O Seven handed the huge figure a cutlass.

"Take off his head."

Boone glanced at the pile of spray-painted skulls and drew his legs under his chair, preparing for one last feckless lunge.

The blacksmith brushed the cutlass aside.

"I go able use me hands," he said, advancing on Boone, a black sternum and buckling pectorals filling the eyeholes of the mask.

Boone tried to charge out of his chair and was firmly pushed back into it by powerful arms.

"Sit, small baboon," said the blacksmith with a chuckle, prying the knots of the lashings apart with his fingers.

The blacksmith grabbed the hood, lifted Boone out of his chair, and shook him out of the pelt, then threw the headpiece over his shoulder and returned to his quarters.

Suddenly Boone was able to see the whole room with eyes that had grown accustomed to the dimness. Medicines, fetishes, weapons, body parts, and animal masks hung from the rafters and cast huge shadows on the mud walls. A third boy was prostrate on a mattress opposite under the only other window, groaning and curled in the fetal position, his eyes fever-bright and staring at Boone.

The air was close and humid, reeking of sweat, cooked meat, and decay. The top of an upended crate near Boone was painted in black and white squares, with chess pieces in place, ready for a new game, if someone would only move the .45 pistol that occupied the center of the board.

The pirate named Double O Seven poured water from the calabash into a tin cup. Boone's lips stuck together in a dry swallow. He watched the mound of rice chop steaming in the copper halo of light.

"Hungry?" asked the boy, smiling through orange teeth. "I get fine chop," he added. "Tarsty?"

"Some water," said Boone, "would be good."

"I nevah see white man begging," said Double O Seven. "This one," he said, jerking his gun at Killigan, "he no beg. *Poo-muis* get begged from, but I think say, dey no beg self. Maybe put gun dae inside dey mouth, den maybe dey go beg. I no know. Pass we find out?"

The boy with dreadlocks picked up the calabash and poured water in a prolonged, seductive trickle into a cup.

Boone watched and swallowed reflexively.

"Who are these guys?" he whispered.

"They used to be soldiers," said Killigan in the same weary tone, "who were paid six dollars and a bag of rice per month, but when the government stopped paying them, they went to work for Moiwo."

"What do they want?"

"They're holding us until Moiwo gets here," said Killigan. "Moiwo wants photographs . . . and negatives."

The boy with the dreadlocks looked at Boone with bloodshot eyes and said, "Stinken sie Deutsch?"

The bobos looked at one another and laughed.

"Stinken sie Deutsch?" repeated Double O Seven, turning his head toward Boone. The wraparound shades were opaque, holding only twin reflections of the hurricane lamp's flame.

"I'm American," said Boone.

Double O Seven laughed and adjusted his shades. "He say you smell like Jarmahn," he said with a grin, accepting the spliff from his companion. "The last *poo-mui* who been sit down dae," he said, pointing at Boone's stool, "was a Jarmahn *poo-mui* from Jarmahnay. He say you smell Jarmahn."

"I'm not German," said Boone quietly. "I'm American."

"Aftah we kill dat Jarmahn from Jarmahnay," Double O Seven said, "ihn smell too much!"

They laughed uproariously and slapped the stocks of their weapons with glee.

Finally Double O Seven touched his comrade's elbow. "Hey, Black Master Kung Fu, whatin go happen if American *poo-mui* stink past Jarmahn *poo-mui*?"

They held their noses and laughed.

"Rotten fish bonga!" said dreadlocks. "Ih rank past rank. Smell dae go 'pon person's clothes, tae ih no dae come out!"

Boone shuddered with fever and fought the urge to vomit.

When they stopped laughing, the boy in the dreadlocks held the cup of water out to Boone, and nodded for him to take it. When Boone reached for it, the boy pulled it back and drank.

"Drinken sie Deutsch?" he said, and the two of them fell to laughing again.

"Why didn't you go with Pa Gigba the first night?" whispered Killigan, under cover of their merriment.

"The old guy said he didn't know anything," said Boone.

Dreadlocks kicked the chess table a foot closer to Boone, picked up the pistol, and tucked it into the rope belt of his britches.

"You chess player?" the boy in dreadlocks asked Boone.

"Yes," said Boone, at the same instant that Killigan said, "He doesn't play."

A single click came from the weapon cradled in the pirate's lap, as he swiveled and pointed the barrel at Killigan.

"I am Black Master Kung Fu," said dreadlocks. "I take black. Your move."

"We can get some water first?" asked Boone. "Do ya, I beg," he added, sliding a dry tongue across his lower lip.

"You win, I give you water," said Black Master Kung Fu. "You lose, I kill you."

The pirate laughed so hard he rattled the shells and animal teeth of his necklace. He pointed at the table of skulls. "Those people played chess no better!"

The boy on the floor mattress groaned and panted with fever.

"I don't want to play chess," said Boone.

"Move," said the pirate, pointing the dark eye of the gun barrel at Boone's head.

"Move," said Boone's opponent. "No passant."

"What?" asked Boone.

"He doesn't like the en passant rule," said Killigan. "He doesn't allow it."

"No en passant," said Boone. "Anything else?"

"Well, sometimes he won't let you castle. And even if he lets you, it puts him in a bad mood. He doesn't like castling; I'd avoid it."

"Move!" said Boone's opponent.

"QP4," said Killigan. "I've won three times using the Queen's Gambit. I'm a little reluctant to experiment with anything else. How's your game?"

"The last time I played was with you."

"Yeah," Killigan said quietly, and cleared his throat.

"Move!" said Black Master Kung Fu, bobbing his head to tinny music from his Walkman.

The boy on the mattress went rigid and appeared to have a small seizure, his head ticking slowly in spasms. Then he swallowed and stared at Boone again.

"Febah," said the pirate, handing the boy a tin cup of water.

The sick boy drank, then watched Boone's eyes.

"That chess game we were talking about," said Killigan, "the last one we played, where I told you I sent my knight to . . . capture you . . ."

"What game?" said Boone, watching the mane of dreadlocks, while he tried to remember the sequence of the Queen's Gambit declined.

"Gigba," he whispered.

"Oh," said Boone, "that game."

"I sent my black knight to take you," said Killigan, "but you resisted. I moved him back because you would not let him take you. When I moved him out to get you again, he was—taken."

"Your knight never tried to take me," said Boone. "I gave him the chance at least three times, but he said nothing about it. He said he didn't know where you were. Only that your—castle was attacked. And you disappeared."

"The white bishop," said Killigan, "he was there too, translating?"

"He was there," said Boone, "translating. The black knight lied to you."

"No," said Killigan. "Something lost in translation, I think. Something the white bishop hopes to find in a black king, or a future Paramount Chief."

"Hey," said the pirate in sunglasses, waving his gun at Killigan. "Your mouth makes noises too much."

The pirate rested his gun in his lap and began shoveling chop into his mouth with his hand.

"These two black pawns," said Killigan. "No real threat, until the king comes. They won't take pieces on their own, unless white tries for an opening."

The boy in dreadlocks puffed on another spliff, and sang softly to music no one else could hear. He moved his bishop.

"Mr. Baboon," said Double O Seven. "Why dat white runner we done send been find you on your way here and not inside Nymuhun village? Den say dat famous *gbese* witchfinder come out Bambara Chiefdom and done close Nymuhun foh witchfinding."

"Witchfinder done close off Nymuhun," said Boone. "But someone put a hood on me. I was chased out."

"Witchfinder done find witch business and witch medicine dae inside the village?" asked the boy. "*Honei-mui* dae inside the village?"

Boone looked at Michael Killigan, and saw the dark silhouette of his friend's head slowly nod.

"Yes," said Boone. "An old man. And an old woman. Witchfinder done find witch medicine dae inside they house."

"And you come out the village before the witchfinding donedone?" asked the boy incredulously. "You carry on go with a witchfinder's swear 'pon your head?"

"I—"

"You broke the boundary?" asked Killigan.

"Yes," hissed Boone. "I had no fucking choice."

"You carry on go with a witchfinder's swear 'pon you?" asked the boy. "I done see that *gbese* witchfinder put his hand into a bucket of boiling palm oil," said the pirate. "I done see that *gbese* witchfinder kill a man dead with his fingertip," he said, touching his companion with the ball of his index finger. "Dat *gbese* witchfinder put swear on you, his swear go kill you dead past dead. No lie! Unless we kill you first."

"I don't believe in swears," said Boone.

Double O Seven laughed and slapped his friend on the back. "He no believe in swear! Whatin I done tell you, notoso? Whatin I been say? Dis *poo-mui*, he no believe in swear!"

The boy snatched his gun out of his lap and flourished it aloft, jostling bundles and implements hanging from the rafters.

"You no believe in swear?" He laughed. The mirrored shades tilted upward and he poked the barrel of his gun up into the rafters, stirring huge shadows thrown from hanging medicines and masks. Finally he pushed a birdcage into view with his gun, turned it sideways and shook it, until the cloth cover fell to the floor.

"Swear done bring you to this place!" said the boy triumphantly. "*Poo-mui* fool!"

The pinioned albino bat writhed violently in its cage, its white wings straining, its bony snout and teeth open in a pink, soundless shriek.

Double O Seven pulled off his mirrored shades, smiling through the same orange teeth Boone had seen in Bo at the Thirsty Soul. He stared at Boone with one good eye, the other swirling milky white and opalescent in the lamplight.

"Swears work best on those who don't believe in them," he boasted. "Past now you believe in swear!"

The sound of banging metal came from the blacksmith's quarters. "Runner done come! Runner done come just now," the blacksmith's voice boomed from the smithy.

The pirate kicked at the stool under Boone's opponent. Dreadlocks scowled, shook his head, shouldered his weapon, and left the room.

Outside the window, over the bed of the sick boy, the chess player's voice greeted the messenger.

"What's gonna happen to us?" whispered Boone, suddenly imagining himself a silent, throbless carcass on the floor of a clearing in West Africa. When the bullet entered his brain, the images of this squalid room and the fever-bright eyes of the boy across from him would fade from his retinas—his powers of vision evanescing like steam from his lidless, sightless eyeballs. It seemed impossible that death—as random and banal as bad weather for the villagers —was now coming for a *poo-mui* from the wholesome state of Indiana.

"We will be . . . invited to join the society," said Killigan. "We will provide and prepare a human victim to feed the medicine, or we will *be* victims and the medicine will be turned against our families."

The voices outside the window fell into whispers. Killigan straightened in his chair and leaned toward the window. The eyes of the sick boy widened. The voices seeped into the dimness, urgent, tense, fearful.

"That messenger is from your village," said Killigan. "He brings news of the witchfinding. He says the *gbese* found a bundle in your room. He says you are a—"

"*Honei!*" the sick boy screamed, his eyes widening in sudden fright, staring at Boone. "*Honei-mui!*"

The pirate jumped off his stool and trained his weapon first on Boone, then on Killigan.

"You move small-small," he said uncertainly, his hands trembling for a grip on his gun. "I go kill you dead past dead!"

The pirate jerked his head in the direction of the shuttered window over the sick boy. "I dae come!" he shouted. "I dae come!"

The door banged open and shut. The sick boy's gaze was fixed on Boone.

"*Honei-mui!*" he yelled, his eyes lit with terror.

"You're a witch!" urged Killigan. "Stare at him!" he shouted in a sudden, savage voice.

"Witch?" Boone sputtered, wondering if his friend's ordeals in the bush had pushed him over the edge. "I'm not a witch!" Killigan's face was still obscured in the shadows. Boone looked back at the sick boy.

"You're a witch!" Killigan insisted, snarling through clenched teeth, his silhouette lunging in the shadows. "He knows you're a witch. Look into his eyes," he exhorted. "Find his soul!"

The boy screamed and raised his hands, transfixed by Boone's eyes, his mouth open in an empty scream.

"Stare!" roared Killigan. "Crawl inside of him!" he cried savagely. "Down his throat! Into his belly! Kill him!"

"Eyes!" the boy screamed. "Eyes! I no able for see!" he shrieked, holding his hands in front of his face. "*Honei-mui!*"

"Kill him!" Killigan commanded, his voice blaring cruelty and bloodlust.

The door to the veranda opened slowly and the pirate reappeared with his comrade close behind. They stepped uncertainly into the room. The boy went rigid on the bed, his hands still in front of his face.

"*Honei-mui!*" The boy convulsed, his mouth stuck open in a drooling grimace.

The pirate glanced at Boone and averted his eyes.

"Stare at them," Killigan urged menacingly. "Look dae eyes!"

The boy in dreadlocks tried to ready his weapon with shaking hands, pointing it at Boone.

"No," screamed the pirate, knocking the barrel down. "You no go kill a witch! You kill ihn and ihn shade come back 'pon you and smother your face at night! You no go kill a witch! Fool!"

The sick boy went into a full-blown seizure, his mouth forming a horrible, foaming rictus, his head jerking in slow, rhythmic tics, while clonic spasms gusted through his limbs.

"Suck out their souls!" hissed Killigan. "Look dae eyes. Open holes for you to crawl inside! Down their throats!" he coaxed. "Witch done come!" he screamed.

"I dae go!" yelled the pirate, banging open the door.

The boy in dreadlocks looked wild-eyed about the room, the muzzle of his weapon following his eyes, finally settling on the chessboard, which he demolished with a burst of gunfire, filling the air with wood splinters and reeking smoke. He followed his companion out the door, where terrified voices called out to one another.

"*Honei-mui!*" someone cried from the blacksmith's quarters, followed by the sound of tools falling to the floor and another door banging open.

"*Honei-mui!*" someone screamed, banging a pot with an iron tool and cursing. "*Honei-mui!*"

"Untie me," said Killigan curtly.

The boy on the mattress covered his eyes and moaned in terror.

Boone fumbled in the dark with the twine knotted around his friend's wrists. Killigan shook the twine free, then grabbed the cutlass and the calabash of water from the table. He kicked open the door and waited.

In the courtyard, the bald earth shone with a lunar glow. The well was capped by a weathered lid draped in fetishes and protective medicines, and padlocked to a ringbolt in the concrete lip. The sound of curses and metal banging receded into the bush.

"Let's go," pressed Killigan, and they lit out, running away from the voices and banging pots, up the same trail Boone had arrived on.

Boone's chest heaved as he clambered up the path behind Killigan's bobbing silhouette. At the top of the swell, they rested, sweat dripping from their faces and hands.

"Do you know where you're going?" pleaded Boone, gasping for air.

"Yes," said Killigan.

"How far is it to the border with Guinea?" Boone asked.

"Four hours by bush path," replied Killigan, "assuming we find the way."

"Then we should just plain leave, like *now!*"

"Just like a *poo-mui,*" panted Killigan. "Come in, fuck everything up, then leave."

Boone grabbed his friend and searched his face for some semblance of sanity. "Where are we going?"

"Back to the village." Killigan pushed Boone away and turned, as if to continue on his way.

"The village!" Boone screamed on the verge of hysteria, grabbing his friend's arm. "We'll get killed! No way I'm going back to the fucking village!"

"This is Sierra Leone," said Killigan. "I've been risking my life here for three years. I'm not about to run away and let Moiwo take over because you've risked yours for two weeks."

"*You'll* die," yelled Boone. "Not me," he said, as if reassuring himself.

"No," Killigan shot back. "You'll get yourself killed, unless you go back with me and submit to the witchfinder. That I know for sure."

"The witchfinder?" Boone stopped, speechless with rage, as the import of his friend's words sank in. "Trust my life? To a bald quack in a bathrobe?"

Killigan turned and faced him down. "I can't explain Africa or witch business to you in fifteen minutes," he said bitterly. "So let's forget about witch business for a minute, OK? Let's pretend we're just *poo-muis* from Indiana," he said sarcastically.

"Good idea," said Boone.

"Now, let's reason," continued Killigan, "like good white men with good white logic! This is the bush!" he said, barely containing his rage. "There are no signs or maps! Even Africans get lost in the bush. Stoned teenage mercenaries are running around with automatic weapons. You heard them talking! The only thing they're afraid of is bad medicine and the witchfinder. I'm going to the village for protection; you're going to see the witchfinder!"

"Moiwo's in the village," said Boone.

"So's Kabba Lundo, the Paramount Chief. So's the witchfinder, who will protect us, and who apparently saw something in your nature."

Boone threw his head back and screamed in exasperation, "What the fuck are you talking about?" He studied his friend's face in breathless horror. "You believe this juju shit?"

"The African way is the only way out," insisted Killigan. "That means back through the village, not out in the bush. You'll have to take my word for it . . . or die."

Killigan turned and walked up the path without looking back.

"You too!" Boone hollered into the canopy of vegetation overhead. "I stick my fucking neck out for you! And when I finally find you . . . You're psycho too! White men go crazy here, is that it? White men go crazy?"

(**20**)

By the time the thatched huts of Nymuhun appeared on the bluffs ahead of them, dawn was oozing into the bush. Fogbows shimmered in the morning mist, and a low-rolling brume clung to the tops of the vegetation. Boone trudged along, starving and thirsty, fever glowing in his joints, and helpless rage pouring out of his mouth at his friend and his fate.

"Tell me what happened," Boone demanded between breaths.

"I told you all I can," said Killigan. "Moiwo is into bad medicine. He's smuggling. He's letting chemical companies dump all over the country. If he could sell slaves again, he would. He's got to be exposed and tried for his crimes, before he takes over the whole country and runs it even farther down the shit hole of West Africa. That's why the witchfinder is here, and why you shouldn't be."

"But why would Sisay help Moiwo?"

"Why not?" said Killigan. "It's no different here than anywhere else. Sisay's placing bets on who's going to win the election. Moiwo *lives* in Sisay's village. What do you suppose would happen if Moiwo asked him for help, Sisay said no, and then, next week, Moiwo is suddenly Paramount Chief?"

"OK, then what about this raid on your village? What was that? And why disappear into the bush? And what are these photographs?"

"I told you," said Killigan. "I went to Freetown. I had to go by bush paths, or I would have been taken. I took proof of Moiwo's doings to the proper authorities."

"To the embassy?" asked Boone.

Killigan laughed harshly. "That would be smart. Take proof of Moiwo's shit to the people he's in bed with."

"I don't understand," said Boone.

"That's right," snapped Killigan, "you don't."

"You're an American, right? You work for the United States government."

"I *used* to work for the Peace Corps," said Killigan. "Now I work for . . . other people."

"What other people?"

"No can say," said Killigan.

"Secret society mumbo jumbo, right? You can't tell me. I'm your best friend," said Boone, "I came all the way down here . . ."

"And almost got us both killed," Killigan interrupted. "My plan was perfect," he muttered. "I calculated absolutely every African variable down to the last villager. I delivered the goods on Moiwo, bought my ticket for Paris, and then I learned that a *poo-mui* greenhorn by the name of Westfall was out in the bush looking for me, just waiting to fall into the clutches of Moiwo. I forgot how effortlessly one misguided *poo-mui*—fresh off the plane—can destroy everything and anything in Africa!"

"You talk big," Boone hollered ahead. "But if I wasn't a witch, you'd be dead!"

Killigan turned to face Boone. He wiped his forehead with his bare hand, shaking sweat off of it into the bush. Then he pointed a finger into his friend's face. "I'll say this once, and then we won't discuss it again. Agreed?"

"No way," said Boone. "It depends what you say. For instance, after you're done, I might want to tell you to get fucked."

"If you had stayed in Paris," said Killigan, "and had waited according to plan, I would be there by now. I would be sipping espresso in a nice little café off the Place de la Concorde, fondly recalling the guillotine and the simple pleasures of civilized white people. Moiwo would be in jail waiting to swing from the gallows at the stadium in Freetown. My African father, Kabba Lundo, would be assured of his Paramount Chieftaincy, OK? And after our little vacation, I could come back to Sierra Leone, marry the woman I love, and settle down to a long and happy life. It's all true. Just take my word for it. But, instead, you came to Sierra Leone and threw a tenderfoot *poo-mui* into the mix."

They continued marching. Boone slogged along behind, trying to console himself with the knowledge that each step was taking him closer to a tick mattress, where he could lie down and die in peace.

After a few minutes, he decided to attempt a truce.

"Is she African?" he asked.

"No," Killigan muttered sarcastically, without turning around. "She's a headhunter's daughter from the Iban tribe of Sarawak, in Borneo, just a few thousand miles from here."

Boone cursed himself for his choice of friends, his physical weakness, the fear and exhaustion that were making him dependent on yet another abusive white man.

After a long trek uphill, they reached the village boundary, stooped under the thread, and entered unannounced. A crowd was assembled in the *barri* after what had been—from the looks of the shriven and haggard faces of the citizens—another harrowing night of witchfinding.

An old woman put a padlock back on the lid to the well and struggled to her feet, balancing a bucket of water on her head for the nursing and expectant mothers.

Water dripped from the seams of the bucket and stirred deep cravings in Boone, who considered grabbing the pail from her without so much as a by-your-leave.

She greeted Michael Killigan, and then she recognized Boone. Her eyes and mouth froze open in horror, and the bucket tumbled off of her head. She fled the clearing and ran to the *barri*, waving her hands over her head, announcing the return of the white witch.

Boone walked backward, eyeing the thread boundary and the path back out of the village.

While his friend went ahead, Boone watched the crowd rise to its feet, all but Lewis, who sat holding his head, apparently sick to death of witches and witchfinding. The witchfinder appeared, with Kabba Lundo and the elders. They met Killigan at the well and greeted him, but the exchanges seemed subdued, almost staged. Several elders glanced at Boone, but no one greeted him.

Another Land-Rover had arrived in his absence. Four soldiers in red berets sat on the roof of it, their weapons slung carelessly around their necks as props for their elbows. They were well-paid Krios from the President's special forces, and they regarded the superstitious festivities of the villagers with bemused detachment. A middle-aged African in a blue uniform and a military chapeau sat inside, hiding the kola nut he was eating from the view of the witchfinder and the villagers.

Boone watched as Killigan paid homage to the deceitful witchfinder, stooping and giving Kabba Lundo two-handed handshakes. For all the world, his best friend looked like Sisay, kissing African ass, bowing, showing respect for elders, pretending everything made perfect sense. *How nice. A witchfinding! May I bring a friend and some bad medicine along?*

The muscles in Boone's legs twitched with fatigue, his knees nearly buckled. Killigan was suddenly transformed before his eyes into a stranger. His manners, his demeanor, his posture, the way Mende rolled off his tongue, just like an African! And he was surrounded by a gathering horde of Africans in headties, burnooses, skullcaps, safari shirts, robes, and lappas. Boone felt like a deaf man in a room full of writhing dancers, and nobody had taken the trouble to explain the phenomenon called music.

"Come," beckoned the witchfinder with a smile for Boone. "Let us finish this witch business so the village will be safe again."

He had only bitter choices. Leave and go tearing through the bush until he fell over dead. Or stay here and place himself in the keeping of secret societies and jungle cults, headed up by a wacko septuagenarian with a broomstick and a mirror.

"Boone," called Killigan. "Come to the *barri*."

"Let's wind it up," begged Lewis. "The midwife has Guinness, and I am ready to eat my fucking hands I'm so hungry!"

Boone staggered forward, joining Killigan and the elders. He dragged his feet on the way across the courtyard, unwilling to trust anyone, but he had no other options.

The crowd opened and admitted them into the *barri*. Through the shifting bodies of the villagers, Boone saw a short row of chairs and a cot of some kind where a woman slept under a blanket.

"Take seat," said the witchfinder.

Killigan showed Boone one of the chairs. Boone dropped into it, only to rise to a crouch when he saw Moiwo enter, a billowing country cloth robe covering necklaces of medicines and cowrie shells.

"Brother Lamin Kaikai," Moiwo said, his face cracking open in an ugly fleer.

"Greetings," said Killigan. "My regards to the section chief," he added grimly.

Someone sat next to Boone, and the crowd began shuffling into a new formation. Instead of seating themselves in the *barri*, they remained standing, fanning out, circling.

Boone looked at the chair next to him and recognized Grandma Dembe, and next to her Pa Usman and his *nomoloi*, and, on the other side of Usman, Jenisa. He was sitting with the other accused witches. And next to them the cot, with the witchfinder's assistants on either side of a woman whose face Boone could not see. When Boone looked up to find Killigan, he found instead a ring of crowded heads staring down at him, pressing in, rank on rank, leaving just enough room for the witchfinder and those accused.

Air shuddered in and out of Boone's lungs, as he looked out at eyes which seemed to stare back at him from the bobbing appendages of a single organism, a massive hydra arrayed with human heads and hateful stares.

The witchfinder banged the cauldron with his staff and surveyed the crowd.

"I have found all the witches!" he cried.

The villagers jeered and hissed, jostling one another for better views. Boone labored for air, his chest heaving, as if he had run a great distance, only to be trapped.

"We have them all here!" shouted the witchfinder. "And, as you already know, the head witch, the creature who ate your children, the leader of the coven, and keeper of the witch pot, is dead!"

The assistants hoisted a body from the cot and held it up in the center of the crowd by its shoulders and its hair. Boone recognized the sagging, lifeless face of Luba, before it was covered with flying spittle and wounded with jabbing sticks. He gagged and covered his mouth.

The witchfinder waved his staff and spread his arms.

"The old ones here remember hearing stories of my grandfather," he said. "Kenei Lahai was one of the Tongo Players, famous for finding witches and exterminating cannibals. In those days, witches and cannibals were killed and thrown on the fire!"

The crowd cheered. Boone shook violently, looking for Killigan or Lewis, but to no avail.

"Those days are no more!" cried the witchfinder. "We no longer kill witches, we cure them, and then we fine them. This witch died only because her shade left her body while she was asleep. When it tried to escape into the bush, it was trapped in a witch net. Now she sleeps forever. But don't worry! Her shade will not return to haunt the village," he said, reaching into the folds of his robe, "because I have it here."

The witchfinder drew his hand from his loppy sleeve and held a writhing serpent over the heads of the villagers, who cried out and stumbled back in terror.

Boone tried to stand, only to be knocked back into his chair by the seething crowd.

The assistants dropped the body of the witch and covered it with a blanket, then handed the witchfinder a pouch. He poured the undulating reptile into the leather bag and tied it with a string.

"Listen to the shade die!" said the witchfinder, flinging the pouch into the cauldron and stabbing it into the mire with the butt of his staff.

A distant cry came from the bush, and the people stared in wonder, listening to the shade's death rattle, which somehow came to them from far out in the bush.

The witchfinder tended his pot, peering into the swirling morass of bad medicines and witch bundles, poison and infant blood, which had stewed for three days and now gave off the acrid scent of burning hair.

The crowd pressed in around Boone and the accused.

"Section Chief Moiwo," said the witchfinder with a nod.

"Yes, witchfinder," said Moiwo.

Boone leaned forward in his chair when he heard the chief's voice immediately behind him.

"I will now deal with the more serious charges we spoke about."

"Fortune has brought them back to us," said Moiwo. "The time is ripe."

"As I said," continued the witchfinder, "we no longer kill witches, we cure them. Sometimes we forgive them. But other very serious charges have been made. That is why Vice President Bangura has sent members of the government's special forces here. As you all know, certain bad men make very bad medicines from the bodies of human victims. These men want power so badly, they feed women and children to the medicine, and then use it to terrorize their enemies. These men are far worse than witches! They are cannibals! These we do kill. The British hanged them from the gallows in Freetown! And so shall we!"

The crowd murmured its approval.

"Now," said the witchfinder, "you will all help me find these cannibals."

Boone watched a forest of trunks and limbs crowd closer around him, stifling him with the heat of their bodies and the smell of sweat.

"Everyone close your eyes! Do not open them until I say the word."

Boone looked up at the witchfinder, who smiled down at him and winked, pulling one eyelid down with his finger and pointing at Boone. Boone tried to close his eyes, but they fluttered open and shut in nervous terror.

"Grandfather! I pray to you and *Ngewo*," cried the witchfinder, "help me teach these people to find cannibals. Teach them to see cannibals without their eyes! Teach them to see with their hands!"

Boone hunched into a ball on the chair, nauseous with terror.

"A powerful section chief tells me that certain *poo-muis* among us are cannibals in love with bad medicines. Certain *poo-muis* among us tell me that a certain section chief makes bad medicines from the bodies of young boys."

"Witchfinder," said Moiwo in a shaking voice, "this is not the . . . method we discussed."

"Grandfather! Help the people see with their hands! Find the cannibals!"

Boone's heart crawled into his throat when two heavy hands fell upon his shoulders. He kept his eyes closed and sobbed helplessly into his kneecaps, waiting for other hands to fall on him and carry him off.

"You lied!" cried the voice of the section chief. "You lied to me!"

Boone looked up to see Moiwo's fat limbs held by masses of fingers and hands.

"Lying is part of my job," said the witchfinder flatly.

He raised the butt of his staff and slowly extended it under the nose of the restrained Moiwo, tapping one of the chief's shoulders, then the other. Moiwo's limbs surged against the grip of the villagers, who held him fast.

The witchfinder tapped the chief's collarbones, gently, thoughtfully, smiling and watching the fat chief's cheeks quiver with rage.

"My grandfather taught me that a cannibal almost always shows himself by accusing others of cannibalism."

Moiwo snarled, "Be careful not to exceed your powers, witchfinder."

The witchfinder poked his staff into the necklaces around Moiwo's neck, pressing the knob of it under the cords and drawing bags, shells, and pouches out from under the country cloth robe, sifting and poking with his staff, flinging shells and animal teeth aside, until he exposed seven iron hooks sewn to a heavy pouch, swollen and gleaming with blood and fat.

"*Bofima!*" screamed the villagers, gripping the swollen limbs so tight that blood appeared around their fingernails.

"*Bofima!*" shrieked the women and children, gathering weapons and sticks in a frenzy.

An old woman with a big spoon stepped between the witchfinder and Moiwo. "Eyes!" she screamed. "Let me take them!"

"Monkey works!" someone cried. "Baboon eats!"

Cutlasses, pestles, and sticks rained blows on the section chief's head and shoulders.

The witchfinder hooked the cords of the bloody charm with his staff, lifted it from the neck of the chief, and hoisted it aloft, over the heads of the villagers.

"Stop!" cried the witchfinder, twirling the gruesome bladder overhead, its hooks spinning shadows on the ground. The fringes of the crowd fell back, cowering under the whirling medicine.

"The good people of this village don't bloody their hands killing Baboon Men!" called the witchfinder. "This one goes to the gallows in Freetown!"

The mob swarmed around Moiwo. The witchfinder flung the *bofima* into the cauldron with a splash and a swirl of his sleeves.

"Come!" he cried, marching across the courtyard toward the Land-Rovers.

The crowd surged out of the *barri*, pushing and pulling the section chief with them, sucking their teeth and cursing him.

"Witnesses!" cried the witchfinder, summoning the soldiers and the official from the government vehicle.

At the rear of Moiwo's Land-Rover, the witchfinder hooked his staff under a tarpaulin and pushed it back. Shrieks of terror rang in Boone's ears when the villagers saw the bloody cargo in Moiwo's Land-Rover: a mound of baboon pelts and masks, iron claws clotted with blood, and jars of human fat. Flies rose from lidless cardboard boxes of bones and skulls.

"Stop!" cried the witchfinder, parting the crowd with a wave of his staff.

Bloodied, covered with spittle and streaked with tears of rage, the chief fell forward, weaving and reeling in his torn robes.

"Section Chief Moiwo," said the man in the blue uniform, placing a hand under the chief's arm and turning him over to the guards.

"Monkey works!" someone shouted.

"Baboon hangs from gallows!" yelled another.

The crowd sang with infernal glee, joyfully cursing Moiwo and his men.

Kabba Lundo and the soldiers escorted Moiwo to the waiting vehicle. The African elders hung heads with the witchfinder, conferring about how to wind up the proceedings and restore the peace of the village.

Boone felt more fever radiate through him and saw the familiar fur crowd his vision. He heard the government vehicle pulling out of the village. Maybe next, the mob would come for him, but he was suddenly so numb he did not care. Death seemed about as ominous as a summer storm brewing. If Charon himself showed up to ferry him off to the underworld, Boone would have jumped aboard, convinced that he was going to a better life.

He plodded back to the *barri* in search of his chair. There he found Jenisa, her back to him, bowing over Luba's shrouded body.

"Was it a bad sickness?" she whispered. "Meestah Sickness done come for you. I hope you take him with you to the bad place." She stooped and put her mouth close to Luba's ear. "I found you in my dream."

Boone took his seat, and startled her.

"She done die," Jenisa said with a smile.

"Because she was a witch?" Boone asked.

She averted her eyes. "I no know. She fell sick." She shrugged.

"Because of witch medicine?" he asked.

"I no know," she said. "I am only a mother with small peekin dae inside. I do what I must to keep it safe," she added, looking down at her waist. "Kill, if I must."

The witchfinder banged his staff on a pot and one of his assistants cried, "Everybody listen! Everybody listen! Bad medicine done-done! All bad medicine dae inside the witchfinder's pot!"

"At last," said Boone, rising from his chair. "This fucking bullshit is over." He trudged wearily away from the *barri*, hoping to put one foot in front of the other until his head found his sleeping bag.

"The village is almost rid of witch business!" cried the witchfinder.

"As soon as the *poo-mui* witch confesses, the village will be cleansed! Come to the *barri* and rejoice!"

Boone continued stumbling toward Sisay's quarters.

"Boone," hollered Killigan. "Where are you going? Moiwo's gone. We're safe."

"Hey," said Sisay. "Get back here, or you'll be showing disrespect to the witchfinder."

Boone stopped in his tracks and shook with rage. Then he walked to Sisay's house, into his room, closed the door, and fell forward onto his mattress, hearing distant murmurings, like wasps buzzing under the eaves during a summer nap.

The door opened.

"Kong, kong," someone said.

"Wrong, wrong," Boone muttered. "Get the fuck out. I'm sick. No, wait. I'm dead. Tell them I died."

He heard African and American voices, entering his quarters, discussing him.

"It makes no difference," he heard the witchfinder say. "Yes, he is a *poo-mui*, but he is also a witch. He is a danger to the village until he confesses. Until then, all of our work is for nothing."

"Boone," said Killigan. "Listen, we have to go back out to the *barri*. You have to . . . confess."

"Fuck you," said Boone into the sleeping bag.

"He is more dangerous than all the others," said the witchfinder. "Unlike the other witches, he was allowed out on his night ride. He probably fed his medicine, and now he is waiting to use it again. Why else would he come in here alone?"

Boone covered his head with the sleeping bag.

"Boone," said Killigan. "Pa Ansumana is here. He wants you to go back to the *barri* and confess. He asks you, please, do not disgrace him after everything he has done for you."

"Someone should explain to him," said the witchfinder, "that a forced confession is very, very embarrassing and degrading for a witch. Other than being a witch in the first place, a forced confession is probably the worst thing that can happen to someone."

"Boone," said Lewis. "When in Rome, man. You know what I'm saying? Just go out there, make words with your mouth, do what they tell you, and forget about it, OK? I'm starving, and this old geezola isn't gonna let anybody eat until you confess to witch business."

Boone rolled over and sat up. "How long does it take?" he demanded, nervously running his hands through his hair.

"Not long," the witchfinder assured him. "Once we have a confession."

"OK," said Boone, without opening his eyes. "I'm a witch. I like to eat babies at night."

He turned around and flopped back onto his mattress, burrowing deeper under the sleeping bag.

"Very good," said the witchfinder. "At least now he admits it. But the confession must be made in public, before the entire village."

Boone ground his teeth and swallowed a curse, a creative one that would have insulted the witchfinder, his ancestors, and his offspring, and withered the family tree in both directions.

"Boone?" said Killigan. "Come on, man."

Boone sat up again. Lewis and Killigan stood on either side of him and helped him to his feet.

"Five minutes?" asked Boone. "Will it take longer than five minutes?"

"Probably less," said the witchfinder. "Let us go now."

In the *barri*, the villagers whispered and taunted him as he took his seat. Boone scowled and watched as the witchfinder picked up his staff, summoned his assistants, and stirred his pot. He spread his arms and embraced the community.

"I stir a wicked broth of bile and venom, of bitterness and tears, of malice and jealousy," he said, weeping again and dribbling tears into the pot. "My ears are deafened by the cries of our ancestors, who want to know how and why their children have wished these terrible things upon each other! What possessed us to turn these hideous curses loose on the world? What dark and selfish desires prompted us to visit misfortunes on our brothers and sisters? How can our eyes behold each other's faces after tonight?

"Like brings out like," he said solemnly. "We plant hate, and hate we will harvest. Now the last witch has come forward. A white witch, who came here to eat your unborn children!"

The *barri* erupted in a clamor of rage. The parents of dead children cried out for vengeance.

"Last night," said the witchfinder, "when this *poo-mui* witch was out on his night ride, we found the witch pot where he feeds his medicines. You saw with your own eyes the remains of the infant dead. Their limbs were scattered all around like the bones of slaughtered chickens! We saw infant skulls that this witch had eaten while praying over his witch medicine in his room!"

Cries of horror and condemnation assaulted Boone's ears. He spit on the ground between his feet, and gnashed his teeth.

"Now this witch has come forward and will confess his crimes. You will hear from his own lips how he ate your children and smothered the unborn babies while their mothers slept, so he could crack their skulls and suck out their brains! Now you will hear his confession!"

Boone stood unsteadily amid the insults and cries for revenge. He faced the ranting crowd, staring down every pair of eyes that dared meet his. He had already given himself up for dead. Malaria or the volatile passions of the community would probably kill him before dawn. A quirk of fate had fetched him up in this dusty thumbprint called a village, and another quirk would soon finish him. These were his last words, a deathbed speech to a ragtag assortment of human beings, who happened to be standing in the same clearing with him when God reached out of the sky and touched him.

He stared at his best friend, at Sisay, at Pa Ansumana, then walked down the file of his fellow witches. Funny, how they all looked the same. Funny, how a single blow properly administered, a stray bullet, a random virus, a bite from the right mosquito, a bucket from the wrong well, a snake slumbering in the path, a rabid dog, a swear, an enraged ancestor, or a witch's bad dream could snuff the life out of him, or any one of them.

He bowed to Kabba Lundo, and lastly fixed his gaze on the witchfinder, who smiled broadly at the prospect of finishing his work once and for all.

Boone turned to the villagers.

"I have something to say," he began, then choked, swallowed, and fell silent. He shuddered with emotion and found his tongue. "OK, listen. I have tried to be—sensitive. I'm a white man in Africa. I'm a stranger in a foreign country. I tried to be—polite. I thought I was open-minded. But now, I don't know what kind of village you people are running here. I don't know if this is folie à deux, folie à trois, folly de village, African follies, or JUST A FUCKING TROPICAL INSANE ASYLUM!"

He filled his lungs with rage and screamed into the sky, slinging spit and curses over the heads of his audience, as they recoiled from his raging hands and face.

"YOU PEOPLE ARE ALL INSANE!" he screamed. "You're human beings, I guess, but YOU'RE ALL FUCKING INSANE! ESPECIALLY THE WHITE ONES! THEY SHOULD KNOW BETTER! White, black, *poo-mui*, Mende, you're all lost in some fantastic, contwisted delusional system! Your lives are run by witches, bush devils, Baboon Men, ancestors, leprechauns, fucking genies, Leopard People, shape-shifters, mermaids, juju witch shit, bush devils, and I don't know what the fuck else!"

He marched in front of the crowd, shaking his fist in their faces. "You look like human beings!" he hollered. "I'm a human being too! Look at me! Flesh and fucking blood, just like you! But guess what? Once I got here, I had to forget *everything* I thought I knew about human beings! I forgot! Now all I know is one thing. One fucking thing!"

He strode over to where his best friend and the other *poo-muis* had collected.

"West Africa has obliterated everything I know, except for one thing! Do you know what that one thing is?" he shouted into Sisay's face. "The only thing I know," he said, drawing a huge breath and flailing the air with his arms, "is that I AM NOT A FUCKING WITCH! Does everyone understand that!? One more time: I AM NOT A FUCKING WITCH!

"Where's the bald carnival barker in the bathrobe?" cried Boone. "I want to make sure he hears this!"

The witchfinder appeared next to the cauldron wearing the expression of a homeowner who just found a household pest after an exterminator's visit.

"I am not a witch," said Boone. "I am not a Baboon Man. I am not a colt pixie, a wood nymph, a hippogriff, or a hamadryad! I am not a tooth fucking fairy! Nor am I one of Santa's elves. I'm not a worricow, a urisk, a salamander, or a goddamn bush devil! I'M A FUCKING HUMAN BEING!"

The witchfinder sheepishly crept forward and bowed his head, hoping to end the spectacle as quickly and as politely as possible.

"You say you are not a witch," said the witchfinder quietly.

"NO!" shouted Boone, so loudly that the villagers winced and covered their ears. "That's not what I said! I didn't just *say* I'm not

a witch. That doesn't seem to do any good around here! I am describing a FACT! Rational people believe in something called objective reality, OK? Objective reality contains empirical data, which
rational people call FACTS!"

The eyes of the villagers glazed over. Pa Usman yawned and
patted his *nomoloi*.

"FACT!" screamed Boone. "I am talking about a FACT! A ver-
ifiable, incontrovertible, accurate, completely valid FACT, namely,
THAT I AM NOT A FUCKING WITCH! UNDERSTAND?"

The witchfinder shook his head and sighed, dreading the thought
of the extra work this lunatic *poo-mui* was creating for him.

"May I speak now?" asked the witchfinder.

"Yes," said Boone, "but please confine yourself to discussing
FACTS."

"Facts," said the witchfinder with a nod. "I will try, but facts are
very boring. Let me say that I have been finding witches in Sierra
Leone since before you were one small peekin," said the witchfinder
wearily. "One fact is that I've never found a *poo-mui* witch before.
But I should have known that a *poo-mui* witch would be full of
disrespect and too proud to confess."

"I'm not listening," said Boone, covering his ears.

"Very well," said the witchfinder. "Pa Ansumana, you are responsible for this *poo-mui* witch?"

Pa shrugged his shoulders and shook his head.

"Mistah Lamin Kaikai," the witchfinder said to Killigan. "This
witch is your stranger? Your small American brother? He doesn't
have better manners?"

Killigan grimaced sheepishly and looked at his feet.

"Mistah Aruna Sisay?"

Sisay did a mime of washing his hands.

"Well then," said the witchfinder, looking innocently around him,
as if he had been insulted and wounded by this offensive challenge
to his powers. He clapped his hands, and his assistants brought
forth another platter, this one with two small balls of dough in the
center.

"Oh no!" shouted Boone. "No more sideshow mutilations. I don't
care if you cut your own fucking head off and put it back on again.
That doesn't mean I'm a witch. I AM NOT A FUCKING
WITCH!"

"You said you could prove to us that you are not a witch," said the witchfinder gently. "Here is your chance. This is witch poison," explained the witchfinder. "If a person eats it, no harm will come to him. If a witch eats it . . ." he said. "Well, we will see soon enough what happens when a witch eats it. That is, if you are still willing to prove that you are not a witch."

"I have a better idea," said Boone, with a malicious grin. "Let's see what happens when a non-witch eats it first."

"As you wish," said the witchfinder. He picked one ball from the plate and opened his mouth.

"Stop!" yelled Boone.

The witchfinder held the ball of dough in front of his open lips.

"I'll take that one," said Boone, holding his hand under the witch-finder's fingers.

The witchfinder shrugged and pursed his lips, then dropped the dough into Boone's palm. It was the size of a marble or a grape. Boone flattened the dough with his thumbs, inspected it for foreign objects, and sniffed it. It was as pale as bread dough, but firmer and greasier, like putty. He held it between his lips, while he seized the other ball and examined it in the same way, satisfying himself that they at least appeared to be identical. Then he rolled the second one back into a ball and placed it on the witchfinder's platter.

The witchfinder plucked the dough from the platter and popped it into his mouth, opening his teeth, and showing Boone that it indeed sat on his tongue. Then he closed his mouth and swallowed.

Boone rolled his dough back into a ball and looked at it.

"Please, wait," said the witchfinder, handing the empty platter to his assistant, and walking toward Boone. "I want you to understand what is about to happen to you."

The witchfinder held up his arms and pulled back the baggy sleeves of his robe, twisting and curling his arms, then spreading his fingers and turning his hands over for Boone to examine.

"See anything?" he asked. "Here," he said, standing close to Boone. "Under my robe," he said, guiding Boone's hands over the contours of his chest, waist, and back. "Feel anything?"

Boone reluctantly shook his head.

"Please," said the witchfinder to the crowd. "Everyone stand back from this witch, for there is no telling what effect the poison will have!"

The villagers, *poo-muis* included, stepped well away from the witchfinder and Boone.

"Please," shouted the witchfinder. "I want this witch to under-stand that no one and nothing was near him when he ate the witch poison. Please!" he said, summoning his assistants to help move the crowd back.

A circle with a radius of at least twenty feet opened around Boone and the witchfinder.

The witchfinder opened his mouth and turned out his cheeks. "The witch poison is gone," he said. "I ate it. Now it's your turn."

Boone resolutely threw the dough into the back of his throat, wetted it with spit, and swallowed. He felt it clear his throat and lodge somewhere under his sternum. He swallowed again, expect-ing to push it on through to his stomach. Instead, it stuck again and slowly erupted in a searing internal explosion, as if someone had lit a book of matches at the juncture of his esophagus and his stomach. He fell helplessly to his knees and gagged, then retched again and went down on all fours, feeling as if he had vomited, but the contents had lodged somewhere between his stomach and his throat. He heaved, and the foreign object worked its way into the back of his throat.

The witchfinder knelt down next to him and held him by the back of the neck.

"It's coming!" cried the witchfinder. "It's coming out!"

Boone gagged and saw a black hand pass under his eyes. He retched, and felt the witchfinder stick his hand into his mouth, then felt the fingers squirm and wriggle, clawing at his tongue and the back of his throat, as if the fingers were the limbs of a small animal desperately searching for a foothold inside his mouth. He heaved, one gag reflex triggering another.

"I have it!" cried the witchfinder. "I have hold of it now. I'm bringing it out!"

Boone violently retched and cleared his airway, vomiting around the witchfinder's hand and soaking the ground in front of his knees.

With the scrabbling fingers of his right hand still inside Boone's mouth, the witchfinder said, "Are your eyes open? Open your eyes," he said patiently. "I want your eyes to be open before I pull it out."

Boone wept and trembled, unable to tear the hand out of his mouth. He opened his eyes, and watched the witchfinder's hand emerge with something dark and wriggling. He blinked once and stared at the darting head and waving forelegs of a gecko, wriggling in the grip of the witchfinder, and clawing for purchase on his fingers. The witchfinder made a circlet of his thumb and forefinger, collaring the lizard and closing his hand around it. One black eye set in a streak of orange peered from the side of the head, and a red tongue flicked the air.

One of the assistants produced a small leather pouch. The witchfinder slipped the lizard inside and bound the bag with a cord.

Boone hung his head and coughed. When he stopped for a breath of air, he felt the witchfinder's lips touch his ear.

"Witchman," the voice whispered, "I have captured your shade."

(**21**)

Randall Killigan took his seat in Ambassador class on a wide-body out of Paris bound for Freetown, Sierra Leone. He pulled a shaving kit out of his carry-on bag and inventoried his medicines for the fourth time since leaving New York. Dramamine, Zantac, Lomotil, Advil, and Tylenol in one compartment. Antimalarials, antibiotics, and antihistamines, in another. Procainamide, quinidine, digoxin, beta blockers, calcium blockers, and assorted cardiac antiarrhythmics in yet another. He also had a printout from his computer detailing dosages and contraindications, along with boldface warnings about which ones should not be taken with certain others. Tricky business, because he kept cardiologists the way other men kept mistresses, and he had to make sure they didn't find out about each other. This assured him that second and third opinions were reliable and independent, but it also exposed him to dangerous synergisms whenever he took two separately prescribed heart medications that didn't belong together in his bloodstream.

After checking his medicines, he went to work connecting his notebook computer to the plane's cellular phone system, hoping to get stock quotes in real time. He had a stop loss order set to go off on his Merck if it fell more than 8 percent, but his newest fear was that it might sink just enough to trigger the sell order, then rebound to new highs.

When the hookup failed, he had words with the flight attendant, then stared out the window, grimly and stoically preparing himself for this adventure into the primitive world. What if he was making a mistake? Rushing off like this to a place where basic necessities, like patching a modem to a cellular phone network, were major ordeals?

At Lungi airport in Freetown, Randall was met by a host of special travel assistants, cheerful and knowledgeable fellows who expedited his passage through the immigration office for less than twenty dollars. For another twenty, they protected his luggage from sticky-fingered customs agents, and stoutly defended his rights to bring currency and medications into Sierra Leone. For forty dollars, they processed his papers, changed money for him, and solicited bids for transportation into Freetown. The normal price of $150.00 for a taxi and a ferry ride was halved by a robust and skillfully conducted auction. He tipped them all and took his seat in a private car, a contented white man, grateful for the attentions of the special travel assistants.

The taxi and ferry crossing took him to Freetown proper, where his car was promptly engulfed in a mass of black, half-naked human beings spilling out of shacks and open-sided markets with trays and parcels on their heads. He nearly gagged on the smell of rotten produce and drying fish. A press of naked children thrust a bouquet of flowering hands and open palms into his face. When he tried to roll up his window, the handle came off in his hand.

"White mahn, let we have ten cents. Do ya, I beg."

The crowd was loud, volatile, dressed in rags, covered with dust from unpaved streets, and streaked with mud made from their own sweat. Mouths laughed and shouted at one another, cursed and prayed. In the tangle of writhing bodies, his eyes seized upon crippled and withered limbs, raw patches of skin disease, missing digits, wounds crawling with flies, eyes clotted with ghostly white growths, unrepaired birth defects that had ripened into adult facial deformities.

"Keep you money inside you pocket," his driver warned him. "Tiefmahn dae beaucoup."

"I beg your pardon?" asked Randall.

The driver sucked his teeth and patiently urged his vehicle forward through the crush of flesh, gently nudging human beings aside with his front bumper.

In a wave of nausea and revulsion, Randall realized he had come too far; he had crossed a forbidden threshold into another dimension, had rashly charged into a realm of human chaos, where his life was suddenly as cheap as those of the beggars and urchins swarming around him.

He heaved a sigh when the crowded market slums gave out onto a main boulevard, which his driver explained would take them past a famous landmark, a five-hundred-year-old cotton tree in the center of town, in the same roundabout occupied by the American Embassy.

And what a spectacle! The tree itself was the biggest living thing he had ever seen, with massive limbs dwarfing the surrounding structures and soaring into the sky above the traffic roundabout. But even from a distance, he could see that the people of Freetown had adorned the tree with the most beautiful garments imaginable!

Spectacular capes hung from every limb and shone in the sun like pelts made of rainbows. And as he drew nearer, he could see that the capes changed colors in the breeze, like the skins of huge hooded chameleons. He had never seen such radiance in a garment, and promptly supposed that these tie-dyed wonders were probably even more beautiful than the coat of many colors worn by Joseph in the Bible.

He decided at once that he had to have one and made a mental note to ask the people at the embassy how he could arrange to buy such a beautiful cape and take it home.

By midmorning he was in conference, having his eyes peeled open with stories about his son's doings in Sierra Leone. Michael had turned up, but the explanations did not seem to fit the episodes.

"These are the kind of people your son is working to keep in power," said Ambassador Walsh, pushing a stack of photographs across the table to Killigan.

The lights flickered and the air conditioners recycled, as the power failed and the generator kicked in.

Randall looked up at the lights.

"Don't worry," said the Ambassador. "The power goes out three or four times a day. But we have our own generators, and plenty of fuel."

Randall grimaced as he studied the photographs. "They're wearing animal skins. One's a white man. You're not telling me that's my son, I hope."

"We don't know," said Walsh, with a glance at his political officer, Nathan French. "There are two other photos where one of the

African participants has his mask off, but the light and the resolution are so poor that identification is impossible."

"Are those headdresses or what?" asked Randall, all but holding his nose. "Are they killing someone? This is a human being, with holes cut into him. Are they skinning him?"

"Ritual cannibalism," said French. "They make medicines and charms out of human body parts."

"Disgusting," muttered Randall, flicking the photographs away with his finger.

"Probably the same people who sent you your package," added Mr. Moiwo with a shake of his head.

"You see the kind of benighted superstition we are dealing with, Mr. Killigan," said Walsh. "These chiefs are keeping the villages in the dark ages, so they can control the people with witchcraft and swears. They resist every attempt at rural and industrial development, because they have vested interests in the status quo. Land cannot be developed or put to commercial use because the chiefs insist the ancestors own it all, meaning that no one can buy it. Imagine trying to convince a mining or timber company to invest millions of dollars developing land they can't own."

"Under the current Paramount Chiefs," said Moiwo, "the land will be devoted only to subsistence-level farming."

"But after the election," said Randall, "you'll be in a position to change things, at least in your part of the country. Isn't that what you said?"

The other men drew breaths and looked at one another.

"There was a problem with the election," said Walsh. "It had to be postponed until we could be certain of a fair result. This Paramount Chief, Kabba Lundo, who has the devotion of your son, is devious and resilient. Somehow he has managed, through demagoguery, trickery, and intimidation, to convince the people that Section Chief Moiwo is involved in these secret, illegal societies. The symbols and activities of these cults have so infected their thinking that even presumably rational people, like your son, now accuse Chief Moiwo of certain unspeakable human sacrifices and cannibalistic rituals that have been outlawed since the turn of the century."

"It's an old trick," added French. "When the British made this kind of thing illegal, it did nothing to discourage the cannibalism, but it did allow practitioners to have their ghastly medicines and frame their opponents at the same time."

Ambassador Walsh filled a water glass from a canister at center table.

"Kabba Lundo is quite jealous of our relationship with Section Chief Moiwo, who has been a loyal friend to U.S. interests. It is no secret in the bush that we feel Moiwo is the most qualified man for the office of Paramount Chief. Our evidence suggests that Kabba Lundo—clearly from the old black magic school of African leaders—committed a so-called Baboon murder and then tried to eliminate Mr. Moiwo, his rival, by framing him with the crime. Your son, Michael, gullibly succumbed to the circumstantial evidence carefully arranged by Kabba Lundo, and was goaded into joining ranks with the old guard."

"When you do hook up with your son," said French, "don't be surprised at the vividness of his delusions. You cannot imagine the stress and privations of these initiations in the bush. All of these secret bush societies use brainwashing techniques to indoctrinate their members. After one of these sessions, your boy traveled by bush path all the way to Freetown and delivered these photographs to Vice President Joseph Bangura of the Sierra Leonean government, who himself has recently been tried and found guilty of high treason. Your son tried to tell Bangura that these photographs were pictures of Section Chief Moiwo's men."

Moiwo smiled and shook his head in disbelief. Walsh rolled his eyes, and French snorted at the absurdity of the idea.

"As you can see for yourself," said French, "identification is absolutely out of the question, and we have reason to believe that all of this was staged by Kabba Lundo and his men."

"The Peace Corps will not tolerate political activity," said Walsh. "We have reports that your son is leaving Sierra Leone and is headed up to Mali on holiday with his American friend. If you would like to go out to his village and see for yourself if he's left yet, we can provide you with a vehicle, a driver, and a translator. It's about a day's journey into the bush."

"You're offering to send me out to where those photographs came from?" Randall asked hoarsely, making an ugly face at the photos. He recalled the reckless filthy humans he had seen in the markets and realized that they were probably exemplary citizens of the country's comparatively civilized capital city. He could just imagine what kind of desperate brutes were waiting to greet him out in the bush!

"Gentlemen, I'm a lawyer from Indiana. My kid has some metabolic disorder of the brain that makes him want to go live in mud huts with superstitious Africans. He was crazy enough to go out to this jurisdiction you all call the bush, but his dementia is neither genetic nor contagious. What I want is for you to get him out of there and send him home."

The import of his own words startled him. He tried to imagine a normal, healthy college graduate from Indiana wanting to live in this cesspool of human deprivation and despair. Impossible. Next he imagined what kind of insane, ostensibly civilized person would not only venture out to the bush but live there, for three, four years! Maybe his kid was seeing bats at night. Maybe his kid had a bright object in his deep white matter. What if he went out to the bush looking for his son and found a psychotic white man sitting around a fire chanting with a bunch of secret-society juju men?

The generator stalled and the lights went off, shrouding the conversation in a full second of darkness.

"OK," someone called from another room, and the clatter resumed in a flicker of lights.

More likely, it was a case of too much privilege. And if Dad risked his neck following the kid into no-man's-land and paid his way out, what then? Treat an overdose of privilege with a bolus of protection? No, he had already done enough.

"If we find him," said the Ambassador, ignoring the lights, while Randall stared irritably at the flickering bulbs overhead, "he will be discharged from his service and forced to leave Sierra Leone. If he has already left the country, he will not be allowed to return. We can promise you that. Whether he will return to the United States is not for us to decide," said Walsh. "Maybe not even for you to decide," he added.

Randall stabbed the table top with his index finger. "You just make sure he gets out of Sierra Leone safely," he said, "and don't give him a job anywhere else. When he runs out of money, he'll come home."

"Gentlemen," said Moiwo, putting his hands on the table. "It's been my experience that difficult matters are more easily digested when accompanied by a meal. The hour is here, and I have a fine place in mind."

"If you'll excuse us for a moment," said the Ambassador as the men rose from the table, "while we advise our personnel of our plans."

After the Americans had left, Randall shook Moiwo's hand. "I can't thank you enough for your help," Randall said. "I'm sure things could have turned out much worse."

"Please," said Moiwo. "After all your country has done for us, it's the least I can do."

Randall strolled to the windows for a view of Freetown through the bars of the embassy windows. A haze of harmattan dust settled on the city. Again, he saw the magnificent capes of the cotton tree shining in the setting sun. Then he was startled to see them breaking away from the tree in pairs, and flying, flocking. Swarming around the tree. They were birds! Spectacular, beautiful birds!

"I thought those were capes of some kind," said Randall uncertainly, turning to his African host. "I thought they were beautiful garments when I saw them from the taxi. The colors were so vivid. Extraordinary!"

His heart squirmed in a momentary panic. What if this was just another vision? What if he was seeing things again? Before he left home, he had scheduled another MRI with Bean, then changed his mind and decided he would have the MRI done at the University of Chicago.

"Ah, the cotton tree capes," said Moiwo, with a wink and a laugh. "Aren't they lovely? I must warn you not to mention them to your American friends, or to anyone for that matter. The superstitions and taboos associated with them are a very painful subject locally."

"Why am I not surprised?" said Randall, sighing with relief. "Still, they are absolutely beautiful."

"The tourists who appreciate fine garments often want to buy them, when they see them in the daylight. But as you can see, it's impossible. They are not for sale."

"I'll admit that buying one was my first thought," said Randall, "and I thought to myself they must be very valuable," he added with a laugh, "until I saw them flying. What kind of bird are they?"

"The citizens call them witch birds," said Moiwo, "but if you check with your zoologists over at USAID, you will find that they are fruit bats. Giant fruit bats that have been nesting in that tree since the land was sold to the British."

Randall stared at the swarming forms, now dark in the setting sun, and settling on the limbs of the tree, their silhouettes filing slowly across the limbs like hooded figures filling pews. He heard loud sounds, like a huge percussion orchestra of boards and blocks of wood striking other pieces of wood.

"Shall I arrange for you to have one?" asked Moiwo with another wink. "But," he added with a facetious grin, "I will only get it for you if you will keep it absolutely secret. The legend says that once you own one, it is fatal to tell anyone about it, or to give it away."

"Fruit bats," said Randall dully. "Witch birds."

"And I won't accept a penny for it," said Moiwo with a chuckle. "It is a gift from me. After all your country has done for me, it's the least I can do."

(22)

Well-fed poets may dream of finding the world within a grain of sand, but a starving man can find the entire universe and all the ecstasies of eternity in a mouthful of groundnut stew and a tin cup of well water. Boone and Killigan sat in a circle with their extended African families in the single huge room of Pa Ansumana's house. A candle cast a blood-colored aureole over a mounded platter of food. Pa apportioned beef to the men, then gave the signal, and the scrimmage was on. Dark arms, hands, and fingers reached from the shadows and scooped up gobbets of chop. Boone gouged softball-sized wads of rice from the tray with his right hand and stuffed them into his mouth, licking orange palm oil from his fingers, and finally mastering the art of the chewless swallow.

Nyandengo!

Soft laughter, grunts of pleasure. He had come down off another roaring fever and landed in the familiar post-febrile euphoria. Cold cups of well water soothed burning nerves at the back of his throat. There was no rust on God, no rust on the human beings who sat with him in the dark, feeding themselves, as if the food all went to a communal tongue, gullet, and belly, aglow with the elemental pleasure of nourishment.

Yesterday they would have crushed his skull at a word from the witchfinder, today they were praising God and feeding the ancestors in his name. Once the *honei* had been removed from the *mui*, it seemed he was again a harmless figure of fun. To the immense delight of his brothers and sisters, the after-dinner conversation consisted of resurrected latrine jokes and puns about a white belly running back and forth from the outhouse at night. He was told for the first time that his name, Gutawa, meant "great ass." Gales of laughter greeted each rendition of the line: "I am not a fucking witch." He was the same white-skinned doofus who had stumbled into their village two weeks ago not knowing enough to cover his head in the midday sun, lacking even a peekin's knowledge about how to protect himself from witchcraft, vulnerable to the mildest fluctuations of diet and climate, prey to the most obvious wiles of God, men, and witches. Now it seemed his helplessness had endeared him to them. He was their feeble-minded charge, who, for some reason known only to God and the ancestors, had been born in a white skin, grew up in a cave with heaps of money, treasures, food, disposable pipe cleaners, and medicines, went to *poo-mui* schools for twenty-some years, and came out a middle-aged, white bobo, barely able to feed himself.

After dinner, Killigan and Boone retired to Boone's shed next to Sisay's house and stood each other go-downs of palm wine.

"Here's to my small *poo-mui* brother," said Killigan, giving his friend a long, tender look and clinking his tin mug against Boone's. "I tell God tank ya."

Boone looked into a face he had first seen twenty-three years ago in kindergarten. The lineaments and expressions were still there, but now they were stubbled with a beard that looked as if it had been trimmed with a blunt cutlass. The eyes flashed with the same slightly deranged intelligence that had once shown his kindergarten classmates how to occlude a drinking straw full of chocolate milk and carry it over to the aquarium, but now those eyes were flanked by pale tribal scars on his temples. The cheerful disregard for the opinions of others and the expectations of his father that had gotten Michael Killigan in trouble as a teenager had brought him to West Africa and had seen him through the privations of the bush as well as the treachery of his political enemies.

"I'm bigger than you," said Boone. "I'm older than you, and I'm smarter than you. If we have to be brothers I'll be the big brother."

"But you came to Africa after I did," chided Killigan. "Any Mende man would call you my small brother. I am your host. You came here to visit me. I am responsible for you."

"I didn't come here to visit," said Boone. "I came here to find your ass. Instead, I ended up being had by some African mountebank."

"In the words of a *poo-mui* proverb no African would subscribe to," said Killigan, "it's the thought that counts. You took big risks to come here and endanger my life. I owe you." He smiled. "But you should have stayed in Paris and thought about coming."

"All I want to know is how the old guy did it," said Boone, scowling and refilling his cup from another Esso oil jug, which apparently was the preferred method for storing palm wine.

"You mean how he captured your shade?" asked Killigan.

Boone spat and clenched his teeth.

"You mean, how he knew you were a witch?" Killigan asked. "Simple. He is a *gbese*, the one born after twins, and the most respected witchfinder in Sierra Leone. He can see everything. Who else would suspect a witch spirit of hiding inside of a *poo-mui*?"

Boone waited for a smile, but none was forthcoming. His best friend stared implacably into his eyes as if he were discussing Boone's recent recuperation from a nasty case of poison ivy.

Boone made a mental note to settle this thing with fisticuffs once they got back to civilization. For the moment, he ignored the superstitious misfit seated next to him, and instead talked aloud to himself. "His robe probably has more pockets than a fishing vest. He told everybody to move back, and that's when he pulled the gecko out of his robe, or had one of his assistants hand it to him."

"Still trying to find your way around Sierra Leone with a map of Indiana?" asked Killigan.

"Look," said Boone irritably, "why don't you and Sisay go off somewhere and start a village for culturally sensitive white people. You could spend the rest of your lives pretending you believe in witchcraft and native medicine." He stamped his spittle into the floor with the sole of his boot. "Hey, speaking of Sisay, where is old Machiavelli anyway?"

"They don't call them woodsheds over here," said Killigan, "but I suspect that's where he is, with Pa Ansumana and Kabba Lundo."

"And Lewis? Where'd he go?"

"To do me a favor," said Killigan. "He took Jenisa to Freetown. To immigration. Do you mind?"

"Mind what?"

"If she comes with us?" said Killigan. "I can't take the chance of leaving her here. Moiwo might get loose. Or what if they won't let me back into the country after our travel?"

"I take it this means you like her more than Mary Lou Cratville?"

"Small brother," said Killigan. "This woman is fine-O. Size one.

Woman past woman. And," he added with a taut smile, "one small peekin is on its way."

Boone's momentary considerations of cultural barriers and practical difficulties were eclipsed by the force field emanating from his best friend's passion.

"Will the government let her leave the country?" he asked.

"Mas-mas," said Killigan, rubbing imaginary bills between his fingertips. "The 'sweet of office.' I gave Lewis the money. She'll get the papers."

"Well then," said Boone, "bring her along. The two of us can start another coven. Maybe paralyze one of your limbs one night while you're sleeping. I won't say which one. And where are we going?"

"Mali," said Killigan. "The Dogon country, beautiful villages built into the Bandiagara cliffs. After that, Timbuktu. There's a flight every other day from Freetown to Bamako, Mali. Air Mali," he added, "also known as Air Maybe. After that to Niger by bush taxi, across the Sahara on trucks to Tunisia, and then a ferry to Sicily. For the next few months, we'll be four world travelers in search of a place to raise one small peekin."

"Kong, kong," said a voice at the door.

"Here they come," sighed Boone. "What have they been doing with themselves all night?" He poured Killigan another slug of palm wine. "We've been in here alone for at least fifteen minutes."

Pa Ansumana came first, pipe stoked and spewing smoke. Next came one of the witchfinder's assistants, with a live white chicken swaddled in his arms.

Pa and Killigan spoke Mende.

"I don't mean to interrupt," said Boone, "but why is there a chicken in my bedroom?"

"I was hoping to talk to you about it before they got here," said Killigan. "You are leaving on a long journey. Your grandfather wants to be sure that all is 'right' between you and your ancestors, and that you will reach your destination safely."

"OK," said Boone.

"So," continued Killigan, glancing at the assistant and the chicken, "it's kind of like a diagnostic procedure. You're nothing but a passive participant. It's painless, I promise. Your grandfather has pulled *sara* for you, meaning he has offered sacrifices for you, to make sure that none of his ancestors are angry about you and your witch business, and that your many transgressions against them have been forgiven."

"This is something I have to do, right?" murmured Boone, looking up and seeing his grandfather's face frowning down at him from a cloud of smoke.

"I'm afraid so," said Killigan. "The assistant will prepare you and then put grains on your palms and your tongue. If the chicken eats the grains, then the ancestors are happy, they have accepted Pa's gifts, and they will watch over you on your journey."

"What happens if the chicken doesn't eat the grain?" asked Boone.

"Then we turn you into a chicken," said Killigan. "Just kidding. It means Pa will have to offer more sacrifices and spend more money on looking-around men until the ancestors are satisfied."

"OK," said Boone. "What do I do?" he asked, regarding the assistant with a wary eye.

"Take off your boots and sit up with your bare feet in front of you."

The assistant handed the chicken to Pa and approached Boone with a ball of cotton thread. He spoke Mende to Killigan.

"Turn out your palms," said Killigan.

Boone sat on the floor and opened his hands.

The assistant unraveled a length of white thread, wrapping one end of it around his left big toe, then stringing it up to his left thumb, where it was wrapped again, then to his left ear and wrapped, behind his head, over to his right ear, down to his right thumb, then to his right big toe.

"I'm Gulliver, right?" said Boone, relaxing his hands slightly.

"Palms up," said Killigan. "And stick out your tongue."

"Can't we just do the palms?" said Boone. "I'm not sure I want to be pecked in the tongue by a chicken."

Pa muttered gravely, as if he had all but written off this *poo-mui* son of his but was giving him one last chance to redeem himself.

Boone stuck out his tongue.

The assistant drew a pouch from his shirt and sprinkled grains onto each of Boone's hands, then placed grains on Boone's extended tongue.

Pa handed the chicken to the assistant, nodded, and spoke Mende to Killigan.

The assistant cradled the hen and approached, holding it between Boone's supine palms.

The head tilted and one beady eye glinted with orange lamplight. The hen pecked the grains out of his right hand, then his left.

The feathered head cocked an eye for a gander at the food on Boone's tongue. Its head tilted and the other eye probed furiously, sparkling with hunger.

"Fathers and grandfathers," said Killigan, translating for Pa, "please accept our gifts and look with favor on our son."

Boone stared into the firelit eye and saw himself sitting on a dirt floor in West Africa, sweating, slightly addled by palm wine, covered with tropical sores, woozy from malaria—a human being, an organism breathing, eating, and aging in the bush. The chicken's eye blinked open like a small tear in the material world fitted with a tiny, convex monocle. When Boone peered inside, he saw a fire burning in a huge dark room on the other side of the lens. Thronged around the hearth were his ancestors—hordes of them silhouetted and staring out at him, thousands of eyes on bobbing heads, watching his every gesture, hearing his every word. They were telling each other stories about how he had lived his life. When the ancestors saw him hurt their living relatives or take advantage of them, they shook their heads and disowned him, an adopted *poo-mui* with no training, a spoiled and selfish son raised by greedy people in the land of *Poo*. When the ancestors saw him help their relatives on earth, they were proud of him and boasted about how much he resembled them, how their strength of character had been successfully passed from one generation to the next, and had even managed to find its way into an adopted *poo-mui*.

The head darted, stopped, and cocked.

Boone seemed to hear his audience draw breaths and hold them.

The hen pecked the grain from his tongue.

(**23**)

"**N**othing," said Bean, walking out of the radiology booth and tucking a ballpoint pen into the vest pocket of his lab coat.

Randall sat up on the scanning table.

"You're clean," said Bean. "No unidentified bright object in the deep white matter. No tumor. No arteriovenous malformation. No cyst. Nothing. You're cured. More likely, you were never sick. False positive."

"Nothing," repeated Randall, sitting on a stool next to the MRI machine. "If something was there, you could see it?"

"We could see it," said Bean clapping him on the back. "You get the best pictures in the universe out of these things. You can see everything. There's nothing there. The UBO was a false positive. And you saved yourself a trip to Chicago."

"Yeah," said Randall, putting his tie back on and looking around for his suit coat.

"Well?" said Bean. "You're happy, right?"

"I'm . . . happy," said Randall vaguely, avoiding his buddy's stare. "But . . ."

"But what?" Bean demanded.

"But . . . now there's no . . . explanation. I just saw a huge, ugly West African bat flying over my bed at three in the morning, and—"

"You are *impossible* to please," said Bean, throwing up his hands. "Never mind! Forget what I just said! I was *hiding* things from you again!"

"You were?" asked Randall, in a single instant of panic.

"Yes," howled Bean. "I was trying to *deceive* you. That's my job!

I'm a doctor! I'm a master of deception! I didn't want you to know that the MRI shows a malignant brain tumor the size of a grapefruit! That's right! And that's why you saw the bat, OK? There! *Now are you happy?*"

Randall hung his head.

"You've got six weeks to live," shouted Bean, throwing the MRI films into a rack. "But don't worry, we'll get you in downstairs! We'll cut that massive brain tumor right out of there!" he hollered. "And the next time you're in the decathlon, you can use it in the fucking shot put!"

•

He drove back downtown, trying to develop an appreciation for the newly discovered purity of his deep white matter. He was healed. He was an American citizen. He was well into the top 1 percent in terms of disposable income. Life had laid out a banquet for him. He was not huddled in some mud hut in a backwater Third World country, where he would have to think about drinking water and food every day.

Maybe the bat was just a freak illusion. But what about the bloody bundle? Was *that* real? And what about the capes? What about this peculiar . . . aura around everything, almost as if objects—reality —*radiated* light, instead of just reflecting the sun's? Even in the middle of the morning, everything seemed to glow with swamp gas, or St. Elmo's fire, or the phosphorescence of the sea at night . . .

He rode up the elevator with two junior partners who were talking golf and going nowhere as lawyers. Just *having* the huge chunk of time available for a golf game was indicative of a floundering career, and these profligates had wasted it twice by playing with each other, instead of with clients.

At his floor, Randall got out, and firm personnel streamed through the lobby, greeting him by name, asking him how was his trip to Africa, telling him how glad they were that his son had turned up OK.

He suddenly realized that these people knew everything about him, even though he didn't even know their first names! Until today, this had always seemed normal. With a hundred and twenty partners and eighty-some associates, it was enough to keep track of the lawyers' names. And he had far too much on his plate to be chatting about people's families or how they had spent their weekends. Now he realized that he had walked past these people twenty times a day for years, decades! And he didn't know their names!

At the reception area, he received swatches of pink message slips stacked according to days. He turned to walk from the marble floor of the reception area onto the carpeted hallway that led to his office, and almost paused. The chocolate-colored carpeting looked firm and plush. He had never once noticed the color, or thought of it as having anything but a solid floor underneath it. Now he wondered. What if it was actually . . . insubstantial? What if he stepped onto it and sank up to his knees in some frosting-like substance? Or worse, found himself swimming in institutional-colored quicksand?

He hurried to the familiar surroundings of his desk and work-tables, switched on his computer, and stabbed the intercom.

"Commander," said Mack with a giggle.

"I'm back," said Randall.

"First, good news," said Mack. "Remember that motion to dismiss the Beach Cove lender liability suit that Spontoon drafted up for us? Judge Hamilton granted it. Case dismissed."

"That's great," said Randall. "Did you tell Comco?"

"I sent Flap a copy of the judge's order, with a note over your signature. He's thrilled. I think he left a tribute to your awesome powers on your voice mail."

"What's the bad news?" asked Randall, flipping through faxes stamped URGENT.

"Real weird," said Mack tonelessly. "Our friend Mr. Bilksteen argued the Beach Cove motion before Judge Hamilton. Spontoon demolished him; the judge reamed him a new asshole and dismissed the case. Then Bilksteen went back to his office and had some kind of . . . coronary event."

"A what?" said Randall, throwing the faxes aside.

"They said it was a . . . coronary event," said Mack. "He's in intensive care over at St. Dymphna's Medical Center. Not doing real well, from the sound of it."

"Bilksteen had a heart attack after he argued the Beach Cove motion?" asked Randall, looking around his office, wondering if the walls and ceiling were collapsible, or maybe porous, or inflatable, or maybe . . . they were breathing, or billowing softly, like swamps of viscous paint somehow defying gravity . . .

"Well," said Mack uncomfortably, "they didn't *call* it a heart attack."

"That's weird," said Randall. "Uh, I'll get back to you on some other stuff, after I . . . take care of some . . . matters . . ."

"Yes, boss," said Mack.

"But wait a second," said Randall. "I need something, kind of right away."

"Yeah," said Mack eagerly.

"I need that anthropologist. The Mende expert. His name . . ."

"Harris Sawyer," said Mack. "University of Pennsylvania."

"Yeah," said Randall. "Get him for me again. Tell him it's important."

"Righto," said Mack.

Randall started feeding pink slips and faxes to his bear. He saw a messenger come in and add another hateful piece of paper to the miasm engulfing his desk, his life, his ability to . . . think clearly.

When he turned back to begin clearing the stuff, he found a mound of crawling white membranes scored with ancient writings and cryptograms. The pages multiplied like cells under his fingers, spilled around him like white leaves encrypted with occult symbols, cuneiform script and insignias in ogham, alchemical equations and ancient Hebrew from the Dead Sea Scrolls. The pile heaved under his hands like a white-skinned animal shedding reams of papyrus scored with runes and hieroglyphics. Paper! Words! Symbols!

Out of the swimming print, he spotted a fax bearing today's date and the style of the Beach Cove lender liability suit. Under the style of the case, in bold caption, it said: NOTIFICATION OF CHANGE OF COUNSEL, followed by two sentences advising all attorneys of record and all named parties that Attorney Thomas R. Bilksteen, of McGrath, Becker & Warren, was deceased, and that representation of the debtor would be assumed by the surviving partners of the firm.

Beep went the intercom.

"Line one," said Mack. "*Dr. Harris Sawyer, University of Pennsylvania.*"

"Dr. Sawyer," said Randall, clearing his throat and setting papers aside, "I appreciate your promptness. I'm just back from . . . being out of the office. My . . . client . . . What was it we called her? Colette? Yes, Colette's having problems again. Serious ones, I think."

"I'm sorry to hear that," said Sawyer. "I hope I can be of some help."

"Yeah, well, as I told you, she's very superstitious," said Randall. "Yes, very superstitious. And now she believes this bundle thing may have . . . I don't know . . . *done* something to her. Things actually *look* different to her. Things are happening to her which she cannot explain. Certain unusual perceptual phenomena . . ."

"How unfortunate," said Sawyer.

"Yeah," said Randall. "I guess, well, let me share with you what I'd like to do. I really need to tell her that if this bundle turned into a witch spirit and, I don't know, *entered* her, or *bit* her, or *infected* her, or whatever it's supposed to do, she would *know* about it, wouldn't she? I mean, even the Mende would say that if she was a . . . Whaddaya call it? Witch host? Or witch person? Then she would *know* she was a witch host. Right? I mean, let's face it," said Randall with a hoarse laugh, "this is all superstitious shit! It's not real! I can tell her that! I can tell her it's not real. I can tell her that even if she believed in this kind of *silly shit*, the juju or whatever, then something would have happened to her by now. Do you follow me? I mean, even one of these African tribesmen would say that if she's not dead, or, or sick . . . then the thing didn't work, if you know what I'm trying to say. Blood or no blood! *It didn't do anything!*"

"I trust you recall the two-hat method," said Sawyer. "And I think you know that the Caucasian anthropologist might suggest that Colette avail herself of some counseling, or maybe psychological help, but that's not why you called me."

"No," said Randall quickly. "See, it's as I said before, she's so superstitious she likes to have these things explained to her from the African point of view, so she can be absolutely sure she understands the entire phenomenon, from every perspective . . . You follow me?"

"Of course," said Sawyer. "The issue, then, is whether a witch person, or witch host would always know he or she had a witch spirit. The Mende disagree on this point, and so do the anthropologists. Some say that when a witch enters a village, it is like a powerful sound in a room filled with tuning forks. Or let's use a Mende proverb: *Hinda a wa hinda.* 'Something brings something,' or, even better, 'Like brings out like.' In the Midwest, they might say, 'If you plant corn, you get corn,' something like that. Anyway, some forks respond to the frequency, others don't, and those responding can 'feel' the frequency—they *know* they are witches, even though they will always deny it. But that's not Colette's case, I take it," said Sawyer.

"No," said Randall with a dismissive laugh, "she doesn't know. At least she's not telling me," he quickly added.

"But others say," Sawyer continued, "that often a witch host sees only malice, chaos, destruction, and evil all around him. As time goes on, he senses that the evil seems always to be linked to him. Then, perhaps, he has a dream, or is skillfully questioned by a looking-around man or a witchfinder. And then," said Sawyer, pausing.

"Then what?" Randall urged.

"Then suddenly," he said, warming to his role as a Mende villager. "Suddenly the witch host realizes that the darkness he always so quickly saw in others is really only his own dark powers reflected in the looking glasses of their innocent hearts. He discovers that the evil he had always ascribed to human nature is really the fruit of his own wicked labors. He planted seeds, and now the harvest has come in. His life is filled with evil people, because they are his converts, members of his coven. In one horrible instant, he sees that he is the *cause* of much of the despair, destruction, and evil in his life. He may have convinced himself that he was only using bad medicine to protect himself—so-called defensive medicines, or counter-swears—but before long, he discovers that he has a witch spirit, and the witch spirit has gradually . . . taken over."

The line fell silent.

"Mr. Killigan," said Sawyer. "Mr. Killigan, are you there?"

ACKNOWLEDGMENTS

In the early 1980s, I lived in villages and towns in Sierra Leone for approximately seven months. The Mende people of Sierra Leone generously shared their homes, their food, their conversation, and their way of life with me. Most often, my hosts were very poor villagers who refused to accept any compensation for their hospitality.

White Man's Grave is a work of fiction. Although it purports to describe the rituals of several secret societies, legal and illegal, these descriptions were not provided by any member of a secret society, nor did any member of any secret society, legal or illegal, ever reveal any society secrets to me.

I returned from Sierra Leone and invented the story *White Man's Grave* after studying several books on the Mende and Sierra Leone, including the following texts.

The mysteries of the Mende culture are set forth with poetic grace and scholarly clarity in two books: W. T. Harris and Harry Sawyerr, *The Springs of Mende Belief and Conduct* (Freetown Sierra Leone University Press, 1968). Kenneth Little, *The Mende of Sierra Leone* (Routledge & Kegan Paul, 1967).

The character of the witchfinder was inspired, in part, by the captivating eyewitness accounts contained in Anthony J. Gittins's *Mende Religion* (Steyler Verlag—Wort und Werk Nettetal, 1987).

Michael Jackson's *Paths Toward a Clearing* (Indiana University Press, 1989) is denominated as "anthropology," but is actually poetry, philosophy, literature, psychology, and anthropology all set forth in one excellent book about human nature and the Koranko tribe of Sierra Leone.

Sierra Leonean Krio is a very beautiful spoken language containing more wit, proverbs, and human wisdom than all of Shakespeare. However, its various written manifestations are almost impossible to decipher unless one already knows the language. I have attempted to invent a printed Krio, which I hope "sounds" like Krio but is also quickly apprehended by the English-speaking reader.

I am grateful to Michael Becker, Gregory Willard, and Dr. John Adair for their advice and technical expertise.

Finally, the *Grave* was shallower and a lot narrower until Jean Naggar placed the manuscript and its lazy author in the keeping of editor John Glusman.